Storm Constantine is the author of the highly acclaimed WRAETHTHU novels. She lives in Stafford.

Also from Orbit by Storm Constantine:

THE ENCHANTMENTS OF FLESH AND SPIRIT:
The First Book of Wraeththu

THE BEWITCHMENTS OF LOVE AND HATE:
The Second Book of Wraeththu

THE FULFILMENTS OF FATE AND DESIRE:
The Third Book of Wraeththu

THE

MONSTROUS

REGIMENT

Storm Constantine

Orbit

ISBN 0 7088 8326 5

Printed and bound in Great Britain by
The Guernsey Press Co. Ltd, Guernsey, Channel Islands

Futura Publications
A Division of
Macdonald & Co. (Publishers) Ltd
Orbit House
1 New Fetter Lane
LONDON EC4A 1AR

A member of Maxwell Macmillan Pergamon Publishing Corporation

For my father, John, whose misogynistic view of female writers I hope to have changed somewhat . . . And with thanks to John Jarrold, editor extraordinaire, for his invaluable insight and experience which nibbled off the corners, the Grey Lady for her care and corrections, and Jayle Summers, the Angel Technician, for Realtime.

'And therefore let such as assist her, take heed what they do. For assuredly the empire and reign is a wall without foundation . . . It hath been underpropped this blind time that is past, with the foolishness of people . . . But the fire . . . is already laid to those rotten props and presently they burn, albeit we espy not the flame: when they are consumed (as shortly they will be, for stubble and dry timber cannot long endure the fire) that rotten wall, the usurped and unjust empire of women shall fall by itself in despite of all man, to the destruction of so many, as shall labour to uphold it. And therefore let all man be advertised, for the trumpet hath once blown . . .

John Knox

From: *'The First Blast of the Trumpet Against The Monstrous Regiment of Women.' 1553*

CHAPTER ONE

IT WAS TWO hours before noon and even in the less than reputable Denderberry sector, the city was a hive of activity. Freda Street, a lane so named for one of the settlement's founders, lay virtually in the centre of Denderberry. Overcast at one end by a black, disused factory, a sanctuary for vagrants and less desirable rodents, it opened out at the southern end onto a small, cobbled square. No doubt the residents were thankful that there was a singular, in fact remarkable, lack of cages and gibbets in this square. Such features were, if not decorative, at least common in Denderberry. Perhaps their absence was merely an oversight on the part of those who inhabited Palace Mount, and possibly soon to be rectified. Then again, perhaps not. Hardly any high-ranking families remained in Denderberry; the days when it could have been known as fashionable were long past, but on Freda Street the last daughter of the last respected family to be found outside Palace Mount remained defiantly in possession of her ancestral home. The family name was Garmelding and it must be said that their respectability was failing fast. Very soon, no-one on the Mount would care if the view from the Garmelding house gave offence. Gibbets were on the way; it was only a matter of time.

Two hours before noon, Tarasday, the fourth day of the month of Helen in the year 307 post settlement. On Freda Street, sunlight was falling in hazy, dusty bars through the high narrow windows of Milady Garmelding's high, narrow house. As opposed to the city, activity in the house was confined at this time to the imagination and hence

7

more subdued. Rosanel Garmelding, daughter of Evelyn (now dead these past two years), paced an empty gallery on the first floor; windows to one side of her, dark panelled walls to the other, creaking, dull boards beneath her feet. Sometimes she would pause, wipe her face with an agitated hand. Both her face and hands were white. She was dressed in a robe of deepest indigo, her feet silent in black, felt slippers. If Rosanel spent as much time at court as she should, she would be celebrated as a great beauty. However the women of the court not only bored, but offended her. Rosanel looked elsewhere for companionship and entertainment. Soon this was destined to change her life. Time progressed, minute by painful minute. To Rosanel Garmelding, waiting and afraid as she was, it seemed both too fast and too slow. Could she ever be prepared? At five minutes past the hour, the door at the end of the gallery was opened. The lady stopped pacing. She stood in a ray of light, hands clasped, betraying a nervousness she sought to hide from her face.

'Yes, Collin?' A grey-haired servant stood in the doorway. He bowed.

'The General is here, milady.'

Rosanel Garmelding nodded. 'Very well. Show her to my parlour.'

'I have already done so, milady.'

'Good. Have someone bring us the ebony port.'

'That too is already done, milady.'

Rosanel smiled nervously, nodded. 'Then be about your business Collin . . . or pray. Whatever seems best to you.' The servant bowed.

'We all have faith in you, milady.'

'Faith in me has nothing to do with it. I have no control over this situation, Collin. Don't expect miracles from me.'

The servant did not answer. Rosanel knew that, of course, he did expect miracles from her. They all would. Wasn't she Evelyn's daughter? The door to the gallery closed behind her and, as demurely composed as she could be, Rosanel walked slowly downstairs.

General Carmenya Oralien waited in milady's parlour.

8

General Oralien, a tall, lithe creature whose femininity was concealed in black leather, brooded in milady's favourite chair, close to the fire. It was late summer; already the mornings were dawning cold. Carmenya's first words were, 'You should have your people draw the drapes back from the windows more Rosanel. You will only grow whiter brooding in the dark.'

Rosanel closed the heavy door behind her, leaned upon it, conscious of the inquisitive ear of her servant pressed against the other side.

'This is not a warm country, General. I prefer darkness to dankness.'

'So frail?'

'Perhaps I do not share your constitution, General.'

'Perhaps not.'

'Would you care for a measure of ebony port?' Rosanel had her hands upon the decanter. Damn! Why did they have to shake so much? This woman knew nothing, could prove nothing. Not for the first time, Milady Garmelding, questioned her worthiness for the role that she had somehow fallen into. This bitch must smell my fear, she thought.

'Port may well come later, milady,' Carmenya said with infuriating silkiness. Rosanel knew what would come next. 'First, I regret, I must ask if my people may search your premises.'

'Search here? But what for?' Rosanel could not look up. She counted every bead of moisture upon the decanter's slim, fragile neck.

Carmenya laughed. It was a man's laugh. Stolen laughter, Rosanel decided. 'Goddess, I'm too old for this. Let it be over. Let me be safe.'

'I think you know what we're looking for,' Carmenya said, a faint, ironic humour trickling through these easy words. Rosanel could not speak. Anger, just as much as fear, kept her silent. 'Well, milady, do I have your permission?'

'Do you need it?' Perhaps an unwise remark. Carmenya did not answer. Rosanel looked at her. 'I'm sorry. Of course, please go ahead.'

'Thank you. We will.'

Rosanel thought, 'Of course you will! My words mean nothing.' She was perfectly aware that if she refused, they'd cart her off to the Confinery. And they'd still find Elvon L'Belder; it would all have been for nothing. One of Rosanel Garmelding's ambitions was never to die within the Confinery's walls. She did not look upon this as unreasonable, even though she was walking dangerously close to discovery. Carmenya strode past her; she could not help but flinch.

'If we find L'Belder here, milady, you realise what an awkward position I'd be in? You're most inconsiderate.'

'Who's L'Belder?'

Carmenya shook her head, smiled. 'Obviously, you're under the delusion your motives for this unwise behaviour are noble. You're misled, my dear. He must have fed you a plate of lies. History should tell you that. You're being very foolish. Not even your mother's reputation will save you if you're caught. You do realise that, don't you?'

'I've no idea what you think I'm guilty of,' Rosanel said.

'Rosanel, Rosanel, the Dominatrix has ears and eyes in every corner, more so in this less than salubrious place you choose you remain in. L'Belder is a fugitive. He is a trouble-maker, a religious fanatic, a murderer. What he preaches is a foolishness women fled an entire world to eradicate. We can't let it take control here. Have you no sense at all?'

'I don't know who this L'Belder is, I've told you. I don't know anything!'

General Carmenya sighed. 'I wish I could believe you, Rosanel. For your mother's sake, I'll give you this advice. Make yourself visible at court again; you can't have been there more than twice since your mother's death. Take part in community activities. Your absence is noted – and commented upon. You have a responsibility to your family name. Hiding here in the dark leaves you open to dark suppositions which may, or may not, be rooted in fact. Put an end to it, milady. Come back to the court. It may save your life.' Rosanel poured ebony port into a metal goblet. She drank, gulping.

'Search my house, General. There is nothing here I'm ashamed of.'

It took them several hours to complete the search. Rosanel Garmelding stood drinking measure after measure of ebony port in her parlour, listening to the devastation being committed in the rooms above her head. She heard her servants cry out. Over and over, she breathed, Goddess, forgive me, Goddess forgive me. The deity she prayed to was not Carmenya's goddess.

They found nothing. Rosanel's servants were tortured; Carmenya's bullies learned nothing. Rosanel's companion, Inezia, an outlander from the north, was beaten senseless. They suspected her too, because L'Belder came from the north. He had allies there. But still they found nothing. Rosanel herself was only exempt from harsh treatment because of the flimsy protection of her family name. She knew this. She also knew that Carmenya would treat her people more cruelly because of that. There was no other way for them to touch her. In the late afternoon, Carmenya admitted defeat and called her thugs off. She marched into the parlour once more. Rosanel's body was aching and stiff; she had barely moved since Carmenya had left her. 'Did you find what you were looking for, General?' she asked.

Carmenya waved a stiff finger under Rosanel's nose. 'He was here, milady. I know he was here!'

'Did you find anything to corroborate that, General?' Out of the corner of her eye, Rosanel could see Carmenya's hands flexing at her sides. Go on, strike *me*! Rosanel thought, knowing full well the General would not do that. She'd found nothing.

'My sources are infallible, milady. If they say L'Belder was here, then he was here. But he won't get far, I promise you.' She smiled, took Rosanel's goblet from her white, cold hand and drained the contents. 'Clean up your house, milady. Such untidiness does your mother's memory a discredit! We shall expect you at morning court come Savanday. Good day to you, Rosanel.'

'Good day General. I wish you success with your search.'

Carmenya curled her lip in disdain and marched out, calling for her people to follow her. Rosanel sighed; a deep, shuddering sigh. Still shaking, she poured herself more ebony port, using another goblet because she could not stand drinking from the one Carmenya had touched. She could not face her people yet, not before she'd had another drink. She could almost feel the house, hear it, groaning around her in pain. It had stood unmolested for three hundred years. Rosanel had read the history books, no matter what Carmenya said. She knew all about the home world; it had been drummed into her since birth. Blood seeped into the boards of her house. The resonance of fear would linger in it like a foul smoke for many days. Rosanel sank to her knees, forehead against the table and let herself weep at last. She would never be the same again; hardness and resolve would follow this outrage. The sound of her sadness echoed through the wooden corridors, reaching the ears of her people, filling them with despair because she was their only rock in a sea of unease. Something huge and dark was sweeping its way towards them all. What had begun three hundred years ago had finally found its form, and it was very different from the way those first settlers had envisaged it. Rosanel had read the history books, even the forbidden ones. Now she said, 'We have come home,' and in her mind, a different moon rose in the sky.

CHAPTER TWO

LATE SUMMER. THE nights were cold, unwelcoming. Three days hike northwest of the city, marshes covered the land. Elvon L'Belder headed that way. He was a young man, but unused to living rough; the journey had been hard and he knew it would get worse. His wounds were old, but they ached. A different kind of ache filled his heart because of what might have befallen his friends back in the city, Rosanel Garmelding in particular, whom he loved. He knew Carmenya Oralien would come after him. He did not know how much time he had. The Cause he'd espoused seemed a dim, fruitless thing now. How could anyone ever be free? There was too much complacency. People didn't seem to realise that even though the Dominatrix's new laws might not affect them now, the consequences of them could be disastrous. Eventually everyone would be affected, and he still believed that those who religiously embraced the Dominatrix's plans were in a minority, albeit a powerful, strongly voiced one. People would not listen; he was a man, therefore his words were not to be trusted. Neither would it have made a difference if he'd been female; the people did not want to hear what he had to say; they would not want to believe it. Fools! Now, all his plans had been destroyed. It was too dangerous to stay in the city of Silven Crescent and where else in this world was it possible to push for reform? The thought of doing nothing frightened him; he was beyond rage. That had been exhausted a long time ago, but he didn't know what to do next, other than survive. The marshes were vast, full of dangers for the inexperienced traveller. He prayed that the families who lived there

13

would be less rigid, less conventional, than the city people. He had to find sanctuary somewhere, if only to recover his strength. How? He had no contacts, little knowledge of the terrain, no money, hardly any supplies. Even his clothes, which he'd supposed to be hard-wearing, were clearly unsuitable for marsh travel. At night he would sleep in cluts of dapplegrass and dream of freedom. At nights, the shadows would purr like the engines of Carmenya's marsh-skippers, but he'd keep on going, and if his cause was as worthy as he believed it to be, he would not die. Yet.

CHAPTER THREE

SAVANDAYS WERE NEVER good days for vanyips. This was mainly because the east wind always drove away the moist clouds on Danasday evenings, and by morning the ground was too dry, even here in the marshes. Corinna Trotgarden swung her basket (nearly empty but for a pale cap or two in the bottom) and marched through the squidgy tufts and puddles. Some distance in front of her, her younger brother Orblin poked at likely tussocks with a black stick, searching for fungus. Corinna dreamed along behind him, ignoring his chatter and backward flung remarks. Because she was angeldt, and because of the visitors expected back at the farm later in the day, Corinna's mother had forced her to wear skirts that morning. Corinna had not been pleased but argument had proved fruitless. Useless garments, Corinna thought, all right for ladies at the court in Silven Crescent but so pointless out here! By the time she got home, her sandals would be soaked and filthy with swamp-dirt. When they dried the leather would crack. Normally, Corinna wore waterproof leggings and boots, but today she had to play her part of angeldt to the letter. Dannel Trotgarden would be upset if her daughter should be seen in public with soiled skirts so Corinna had tucked the full, linen pleats up into her waistband to keep the material dry. An upset Mother meant the particularly exquisite pain of persistent silences or persistent nagging.

A vague cloud scuttled across the wide blue above her. Corinna tilted back her head and breathed deeply, taking in the late summer scent of the marsh. Orblin came splashing back to her, his hands full, but with treasures other than vanyips. 'Look, C'rin, look,' he said reverently, holding up his find to her. Blue blossoms like animal tongues spilled between his fingers. They exuded a sharp, bitter perfume that stung Corinna's eyes. 'Shall we take them for the table, C'rin? Will the General like them?' Corinna smiled, imagining everybody trying to eat with streaming eyes and noses.

'Don't think so, Orble, my little roof-rat. General Oralien doesn't strike me as a flowery type. Let's throw them to the cranes, o.k.?'

Orblin ran out into a silver spear shallow and tossed the flowers high into the air. Corinna smiled, a twinge of sentiment making her uneasy. There was a shrill, whittled voice in her ears saying, 'hurry up, don't be late. Hurry up!' Her mother's voice. 'Orb!' she called. 'Come on now!'

Earlier they had been told that General Carmenya Oralien, an old friend of their mother, would be arriving that evening. 'She'll be here for a few days,' Dannel had said. 'I think we should have vanyips for dessert at Breadlemen tonight, Corinna. Off you go. Take Orblin with you and see if the pair of you can bring home a basketful.' The General was especially partial to the odd succulent, purple-fleshed vanyip. Dannel made sure all her family and staff were acquainted with Carmenya's likes and dislikes, for she made at least two trips a year to visit the Trotgardens. Corinna's protests about the unavailability of vanyips on Savandays were met with a steely gaze. 'At least, *try*,' Dannel had said.

Corinna wrinkled her nose towards the horizon, wondering whether the General had arrived at Vangery yet; pale, thin arms holding the basket in front of her, skirt trailing down at the back. The smaller sun, Guimo, was almost setting; the first of his pale, moon wives, his cold, unyielding keepers, sailing up into the sky as if dancing to be free of his light. When the second sun, Shamberel, set, it would be dark. Already the light was vague and purple; haunt-light, as Orblin called it. They had only two hours to get home and had wandered far that afternoon. Squinting up, she decided that Shamberel looked worn

out, fit to fall. Time to head back, vanyips or no vanyips.
'Orblin! What are you doing! Come on, or it'll be you the
General eats for dessert!' All around them, the marsh
stretched out its watery, creepery, treacherous tussocks.
Occasionally, gnarled, stooping spinneys would stand like
a group of gossiping witches, ankle deep in water,
outrageous twig hair standing up all over. Corinna
suspected that, in truth, witches were not like that at all,
but her childhood story-books denied her pictures of
beauty and power, offering only humped and wizened
beldames, so imagination was all she had to go on. Oh, to
have power, *real* power, where destiny was held by both
ends in either hand, and nobody's voice could be louder
than yours! Corinna sighed. She was seventeen, and
chafing at her chain a little.

'Here, C'rin, I've found some!' Orblin's shape was
already indistinct. Corinna splashed towards him and
helped him tear the meagre clutch of vanyips from their
tussock.
'Not enough to feed a wervel, never mind a general!'
Corinna sighed. 'Ah, never mind. At least she'll know
we've bothered.' She covered their harvest with hag-moss
to keep them moist. 'Home, roof-rat, home! I'll race you
to the next tussock!' They charged through the silver
shallows, sending up spray that caught the light like gems.
On the marsh, white villa-farms claimed islands of lawn
and threadwood. They were miles apart, but the land was
so flat the Trotgardens could see several from their upper
windows, pale against the darker, more distant mass of the
floating forests of Ire and Penitence. Corinna and Orblin
ran past Yashchel Tendaughter's place, a large, ramblng
estate, lilac-roofed in the sunset. They had two piers there;
quiet affluence was the emblem of the Tendaughters. It
had been supposed for years that Yaschel's anaemic son
Sander would one day be mated to Corinna, but the girl
had known for several months that her mother had
become slightly more ambitious for her since the original,
albeit tenuous, arrangements had been made with the
Tendaughters. If the rumour that had fallen Corinna's

17

way was to be believed, then none other than General Oralien herself had taken an interest in her. It could be true, despite the fact that it had originated from Gabriel the head cook at Vangery; a beautiful yet charmingly malicious creature for whom Dannel had paid a fortune. Corinna had always felt rather prickly round the edges whenever the General had come to call. That woman's eyes were like bullets. Corinna had mixed feelings about the whole business. In this world there were two types of women and one type of man. The first type of woman was the Flamist, a creature of action, wielder of intellect and tongue, and in many cases, even weapons. The second was angeldt, as Corinna herself was, not a lesser breed by any means, but a creature of grace, intuition, the organiser behind the Flamist. Men were the lesser breed; slaves, breeding machines, beasts of burden, decorative dandies or dumb brutes whose mistress was the rod, the whip, the curse. It had always been this way, at least on Artemis. Before that, well, it was only legends now and life has to be lived and the seasons wait for no woman. Best not think about it. After all, Dannel was a fair mistress of her household. She never spoke out about the worthlessness of men. Orblin, for example, enjoyed as much freedom and privileges as Corinna herself. Everyone knew how in Silven Crescent, males young and old were often treated most cruelly. No man could ever hold a position of responsibility there. The marsh people were not so stringent. How could they be when the hardships of wrenching a living from the marsh meant that everyone had to work together or let their crops perish? Women carried the family name, true, and the family responsibility. Men had no power and some of them were indeed slaves, but there was no outright cruelty. Men were relatively safe on the marsh. Except for one person perhaps, namely the man whom Carmenya was out here looking for.

Advance word had come to the marsh families to look out for a criminal named Elvon L'Belder; his crimes were unspecified. Corinna wondered why Carmenya was chasing a criminal this far. What had he done? Surely it was

18

impossible for a man to escape the city unless he had the help of a woman? That didn't add up. No woman would ever help a killer or rapist and those reasons were the only ones Corinna could think of that were serious enough to justify pursuing him this far. The whole thing gave her an uncomfortable feeling. They don't tell us everything, she thought. There was something about the city women's attitude toward life that she didn't like — and that wasn't just their feelings towards men. Now there was the possibility that she would have to go to Silven Crescent herself. Corinna had been taught, along with how to glide correctly in pleats and folds, to trust her intuition. She knew for a fact that once in Carmenya's clutches she might as well look on freedom as a pleasant memory. She didn't dislike the woman, exactly. After all, she was powerful, loved, handsome, indeed almost horribly wonderful, respected by every woman in the land. Being taken under the wing of Carmenya's entourage was a privilege too ineffable even to speak of in tones louder than a whisper, but once part of it, the strictures of a life at court, of being truly angeldt, would become the main focus of her existence. Corinna didn't like the thought of that. She was unsure what she wanted from life herself yet, but was unconvinced that it was anything like what Carmenya and her people wanted. Of course, it would be impractical to stay on at Vangery, because, one day, her elder sister Bolivia would inherit it, and she could be a sharp creature. Corinna had never got on very well with Bolivia and had no desire to be under her control. If she mated with Sander, they would be expected to live with the Trotgar-dens, always subservient to Vangery's matriarch. It seemed the city was the only alternative left to her.

Corinna had lagged behind her brother again, thinking rather glumly about her future as she slopped along. 'Maybe,' she thought, daring for a moment to lift the damp corners of her unease and examine what lay beneath, 'maybe, I don't want to go to the city because I'm afraid of being alone, away from my own kind. Neither do

I want to leave the marsh.' She was also aware that it was likely she would be expected to mate with a male even less savoury than Sander. As angeldt, it would be considered her duty to rear children one day. There was talk that city women never slept with men nowadays, conceiving their young by artificial means. Corinna was not convinced of that. It seemed too unlikely. She shuddered, automatically increasing her pace with discomfort. Second by second, Shamberel, slipped towards the horizon ahead of her. Alarmed by Orblin's splashing progress, a great flock of honking ditch-cranes lifted as one from the flat, silver surface of a nearby spear-shallow, moving the air around Corinna's head, setting the kale-rushes all into a wicked panic of motion. 'Leave here? Never!' she cried aloud, and the cranes rattled round her head, dipping, swaying, their transparent wing-feathers ruddy at the tips with sunset light. Leave here, leave here, leave here, their pinions seemed to whisper. Corinna stood still, up to her knees in cold water. She closed her eyes at the sky, head back, filled with a strange, sad, powerful emotion. It had happened before. She knew this feeling well. It was a feeling of presentiment that was as exciting as it was terrifying. Soon, something would happen. Corinna only hoped she had some say in what that would be. Orblin's worried voice broke into her thoughts. 'C'rin, are you all right?' She opened her eyes. The world looked the same. She smiled, and with a deep sigh, took Orblin's hand in her own, kicking the soft, water-logged turf as they made their way home.

Vangery, their mother's ranch, had a large, viridian isle all of its own. The outbuildings and the house itself stood on thick, wooden stilts; protection against seasonal floods. At the back of the farm was a respectable stand of skin-pines, plaisel and aromatic ground shrubs, hiding in their leafy skirts the remains of fortifications, left over from the days when bitter altercations between the marsh families had been a physical rather than verbal custom. Corinna knew, that in those times, another building would have stood there. Now, only the foundations and part of a wall remained. Everything else had been taken by the floods years ago. The Trotgardens had been living in Vangery for three generations now, and, except for the ruins concealed among the trees, had systematically removed all remaining signs of the previous occupants of the grass isle. Once, Corinna had heard her mother's husband, Meonel, hint at how the Trotgardens had forcibly taken Vangery from another family, how much blood had been spilt upon the grass. Meonel, Corinna was sure, had no love whatever for any of the Trotgardens. He had come to Vangery at a very young age, bought by Dannel, Corinna's mother, from a passing slave-fair. It had happened a year or so after Corinna's father had been overcome by an incurable scourge which Dannel maintained he'd picked up from a marsh animal. He had died before Corinna's sixth birthday; she could barely remember him. Dannel, though not a great beauty herself, was fond of filling Vangery with beautiful men. Meonel was no exception, although he always looked so sour it was hard to see beauty in him now. He'd always fascinated Corinna. Ever since her childhood, she had enjoyed his company, no matter how abrasive his mood had been. Sometimes, his frustration was like a glowing colour round his head, which she could not help to heal. Meonel was twenty-six years old and kept on a short leash. Everyone knew that because of the fate of her first husband, Dannel feared 'something happening' to Meonel, which was why she rarely let him out alone. Corinna felt sorry for him. Meonel was aware of this which, she knew, annoyed him intensely. Bolivia made no secret of the fact that she loathed Meonel, which sometimes caused bitter arguments among the family. Bolivia, even though her only experience of the city was second hand through Carmenya and her people, was a staunch supporter of the Silven Crescent way of treating men. Corinna suspected it would be a miserable day for everyone when Bolivia took the reins of control from Dannel's hands.

The banks of Vangery's isle were slippery under Corinna's sandalled feet. Orblin had nimbly raced ahead of her, brandishing the basket of fungus. 'Take them to

21

the kitchen, Orb,' she said. 'I have to go to the stables. I'll be in shortly.' All around them the quality of the light was swiftly changing, casting shadows, stick-beast shadows, of the stunted threadwoods dipping their toes in the spear-shallows. Now the water was blood-purple, not silver. Scampering, shuffling creatures were stretching and yawning in their nests of feather-grasses and rushes. Glow-backs were crawling from the water to speckle the marsh with vague lights, pulsing as they breathed, squeaking and wheezing their celebration of the returning night, and also the approach of any insects blind enough to fall prey to their grasping, flicking tongues. The singular smell of the marsh at dusk rose popping and hissing from mud and water. A wet smell of fertility and death and life; the planet's breath. Shadows moved over the marsh as Shamberel swiftly completed his descent. Everywhere the chorus of nocturnal animals, the winking of their lights in the gloom; chirrup, burp, squee, flicker, flicker. Corinna, always a little unnerved by the secret life of the dark, scrambled faster up the bank. She could see that the landing light had already been lit beside the low water of Vangery outlet, illuminating the summer-time causeway farther up the island. Two leaning skippers were beached on the low slope, their vanes drooping, skeletal against the sky. That meant visitors; visitors who were rich enough for more than animal transport. General Carmenya Oralien was here already. Corinna hoped they were not too late. It was not beyond Dannel to upbraid her in public if agitated enough. She thought about what might be cooking for dinner, whether they'd brought home enough of the dessert-fungus to satisfy their honoured guest. Dannel would say to Carmenya, 'My daughter, Corinna, gathered these for you herself', with no mention of her son of course, and then Corinna would have to blush coyly. Not a pleasant prospect.

The low shed where the Trotgardens moored their sole, inferior skipper and two narrow boats was in darkness. The boats weren't used much until the harvest. Fuel for the skipper was expensive so Dannel discouraged its use except for emergencies and for the monthly supplies-purchasing visit to Stilt Vashti, a large settlement some twenty miles to the south. All the families that the Trotgardens were on speaking terms with lived either within walking or dank-beast riding distance. Corinna could now hear the excited moan of her own dank-beast; he must have caught her scent, knowing she would call in with a tit-bit for him on her way up to the house. As she passed the low boat-shed, a movement beyond the furry windows made Corinna jump. What was that? She stopped, tilting her head. There was a scuffling sound, then silence, then another scuffle coming from the boat-house. It sounded like an animal. The servants must have opened the shed up some time today and locked a creature inside. Wervels, a breed of curious, intelligent rodent, would often come up from the marsh, brazenly approaching any humans they could find to demand food in high, peremptory squeakings. Delightful as they were roguish, three or four families of wervels had decided to adopt the Trotgardens as their benefactors and had charmed their way into the hearts and kitchens of Vangery's staff. Doubtless there was now one locked in the shed. Corinna ran over to the side door. Yes, the lock was off. Someone had been in there today. She could hear her dank-beast still calling. Lights from the house were clearly visible; she could see figures moving beyond the windows. Corinna opened the door to the boat-house and ducked inside. She made a clucking sound and said, 'Come on, come on, let's have you out.' It was not a wervel she found inside . . .

CHAPTER FOUR

MEONEL WAS BORED again. Even the marsh, a place he had grown to love despite everything, held no splendour for him that evening. As on most days, he'd been mulling over his dissatisfaction with life and the fact that he couldn't break the ice with the new attendent his wife had provided for him. It was pleasant to lie here on the back porch being fanned and fussed over, but conversation with the silent youth would have been far more gratifying. Meonel watched the sunset. Guimo appeared beneath the high eaves of the house and slid to his nightly rest, his nightly respite from the world of women. What a shame we can't do the same, Meonel thought. As he lay there, a glass of iced, tart cordial clasped (warming) to his half-covered chest, he turned his attention to Dannel, his wife. This was another of Meonel's common daydreams. He liked to swear at her in his head, where the hatred he felt for her was deep and satisfying and, for the most part, unjustified. Meonel was one of those men who did not realise when he was well off. To him, the fair-minded if a little over-protective Dannel was just an obscene colossus he had been forced to marry. Naturally he had heard the same rumours about Silven Crescent that Corinna had, but was incapable of relating them to himself. The bonds he professed to chafe against were those of luxury, laziness and security. It was Dannel's fault, of course; she had created her own monster in trying to protect him.

He knew that at this very moment Dannel was creeping round the insufferable, posturing, mangak, Carmenya. All men referred to flamist woman as mangaks when there were no females around to hear them. The sound of

24

Dannel's wheedling, favour-currying was audible even out on the veranda. Meonel closed his eyes as a brief, cat-lick of pain touched his soul. Dannel had mentioned the Carmenya bitch had an interest in Corinna; disgusting! Blind in her sycophancy, the old sow didn't realise what she'd be selling her precious daughter into. Oh yes, and it was *selling*; there was no doubt of that. What would Dannel get in return? Oh, plenty! A new skipper maybe, extra beasts, tools for harvesting the shemble-frack . . . maybe even a couple of man-slaves. Meonel had heard nothing about the L'Belder business yet. He was usually the last person in the house to hear gossip. Turning his head a little, Meonel sneaked a quick glance at the youth operating the fan behind his head. Well-bred, that one, come down from the north, all pale skin and dark eyes. Unaware of Meonel's scrutiny, he stared blankly at the sky. Oh, this one had been a bad boy once upon a time. Meonel knew. He could see the vague tracings of old scars down the youth's chest, visible even through his flimsy shirt. Those scars meant trouble, trouble long gone because the scars were old, but Meonel was well aware of what they meant. He knew for a fact that the youth was gelded.

'Shyya.' The boy jumped at the sound of his name.

'Yes, sir.'

'A little to the left if you please. Pleasant evening isn't it?'

'Yes, sir.'

Meonel drank some cordial. Why the hell do I bother? he wondered. What kind of marsh-muck am I coming out with? Who cares? The boy thinks I'm a lap-dog! He wanted to say. 'How well you've adapted, Shyya. No-one ever sees pain or fury in your eyes, yet I'm sure you're full of it. You must show me the trick', but the words remained unspoken. Meonel had no allies in this house. Never had done, since the day he'd lost his name to her. Ridiculous name! All fat and cosy, hiding the stinking rot inside. Like her! Meonel trusted nobody, perceiving scorn in every-body's eyes whether it was there or not. Granted, the majority of the staff thought he was a fool. They envied his position and many were frustrated and stung by the rebuffs he'd given their friendly advances. It was a

25

standing joke that everyone tried to become Meonel's lover when they first arrived in Vangery, so far without success. He was an attractive man and apparently celibate. Corinna was the nearest he had to a confidante, and she was female.

Meonel put down his glass on the warm wood of the verandah floor, swung his legs over the side of the hammock, sat up. Shyya stopped fanning. Meonel narrowed his eyes at the sinking sun, taking in the familiar night sounds; the honking of ditch-cranes, the sharp bark of squill. Ember moths were beginning to circle the house to congregate, chittering, under the eaves. Meonel heard the excited squeal of a dank-beast. It sounded like Corinna's. Meonel strolled through the first of the screen doors. Shrill and carping of voice was his step-daughter's dank-beast; a Dannel of animals. He smiled to himself. Shyya, followed at a distance, bent to retrieve items that Meonel had dropped (or hurled?) onto the floor during the afternoon.

Climbing the wooden stairs to the living-floor of the tall-house, Meonel could hear Dannel's voice coming from the facewater salon. The bitter reek of Carmenya's dark green cigarettes could be detected. The General's voice was low, a musical contrast to Dannel Trotgarden's excited chatter. Meonel attempted to sneak past the door to the salon, which, naturally, was open wide. Dannel spotted him and shrieked his name. He allowed himself the luxury of a brief, insulting freeze before responding. General Carmenya was sitting on the window seat, legs curled under her, deceptively girlish. She turned her head gracefully towards the door as Meonel entered the room. Her presence smacked him straight in the gut, as it always did. Too severe, too gaunt to be termed beautiful, Carmenya was simply striking to behold. Long, chestnut hair, most of it braided round her head, wisped over her neck and shoulders, artfully careless. She wore leather, fingerless gauntlets, shirt and trousers of thin, green suede. If she had been male, Meonel would have loved her passionately, privately. When she smiled, he was always relieved to see

26

she had a tooth missing on the left side of her upper jaw. He often wondered how she'd lost it. Somehow, common decay seemed a concept alien to this vibrant, powerful creature. Surely, it would have to have been torn or knocked, bleeding, from its socket during some heated combat. Meonel attempted to resist the disturbing mind-chant: as she killed a man. Killed him. Killed him. He felt as if Carmenya could see to the core of men's souls. Dannel too was sitting on the window-seat, but straight-backed, demure. A certain anxiety was confessed only by the kneading of hands in her lap. Why Carmenya should be on such intimate terms with his fat, brainless wife remained a mystery to Meonel. They were not even the same age; Carmenya being some five years the junior. Meonel didn't even know, couldn't even guess, how they had met. Carmenya was a star; held in high esteem by the Dominatrix herself. Why did she still make this depressing journey out over the marsh to visit such provincial bumpkins as the Trotgardens? It was beyond him. He was unconvinced it was simply Carmenya's interest in Corinna that was the reason this time. Carmenya would never be that obsessive. Perhaps it was just proof that women were, ultimately, incomprehensible to him; he could not know his enemy.

'Meonel,' Dannel said, more imperiously than was necessary, or usual. 'Have you seen Corinna about? Gabriel is waiting to finish the dinner and the wretched girl hasn't come back in yet.'

Meonel shrugged. He was sure Carmenya thought it unlikely that Dannel's daughter would spend any time in his company. Let her think what she liked! He was happy to see the General raise an affronted eyebrow at his disrespectful shrug.

'I wonder where she is?' Dannel continued, oblivious of such undercurrents. 'Shyya!' Meonel's attendent had been lurking in the doorway, unsure of whether to remain with his master or sneak off to the kitchens. 'Shyya, will you go to the landing and see if she's about. We can't wait here all night.' She turned to Carmenya. 'I'm sorry about this, Cam. She went out to pick vanyips for you . . .' Her voice tailed off.

27

'How thoughtful of her,' Carmenya replied with polite warmth.

'Meonel, come in properly! Sit down! Don't stand there so awkwardly!'

Die in your own blood, sag-tit, Meonel thought as he obeyed his wife's command. There were some moments of uncomfortable silence, Carmenya smiling to herself, doubtlessly enjoying them.

'So, how is life in the city?' Meonel asked her, painfully aware of Dannel's relief as he broke the silence.

The General lifted one hand, pulled a face. 'As it always is, hectic.'

'The marsh must be a welcome relief for you then.'

She did not laugh. 'Different, maybe.' She briefly touched Dannel's frantically knitting fingers. 'Nice to see old friends. I've always liked Vangery. It is peaceful and, indeed, very beautiful.'

'Where's Corinna?' Dannel asked, perplexed. The marsh, even after a lifetime, still seemed a place of hostile dangers to her.

'Oh, don't worry,' Meonel said. 'She knows how to take care of herself. She knows the marsh inside-out.'

'I have business with the marsh,' Carmenya announced.

Look out marsh, Meonel thought.

'Yes, we'd heard that,' Dannel said, tearing her eyes away from the window.

'And what business is that?' Meonel asked. 'Thinking of starting your own shemble-frack farm, General?'

Carmenya grimaced. 'Hardly! Haven't you heard? A lunatic from the city is running about out there somewhere. We have to take him back; he's dangerous. Wouldn't want any of the marsh families having trouble, would we!'

'What's he done?' Meonel asked, fairly sure the answer would be evasive or a downright lie. It must be killing Carmenya having to answer a man's questions for the sake of politeness.

'I told you; he's mad.'

'A murderer?' Dannel squeaked, a hand fluttering to her mouth.

28

'Not directly,' Carmenya answered carefully, 'but his actions have caused deaths, yes.'

'Ah, a rebel then,' Meonel said. Carmenya became visibly agitated, as if longing to bark an order to silence him.

'That's not a word I'd use. Troublemaker is enough. We have a secure society here on Artemis and don't need anyone trying to change it for their own ends. Oh, people can moan, Meonel, but I can assure you that conditions on other worlds would appall them into silence. Personally, I would advocate the dispersal of criminals to the outer moons of Jamboree where I am told that people may only survive by consuming each other. There is no plant-life, no animals and I don't believe rock and silt to be a particularly sustaining diet!'

'Then why does anyone live there at all?' Meonel asked. He didn't believe Carmenya's fairy-tales.

She didn't answer his question with her reply. 'The fugitive, Elvon L'Belder has been out there for nearly two weeks now.'

'Then he's probably dead,' Dannel decided simply, with some relief.

'Not necessarily. He may have friends on the marsh.'

'Oh, I doubt that!' Meonel said. 'You should know, General, how traditional the marsh families are. Can you really see any of them risking the Dominatrix's displeasure by harbouring a criminal?'

'No need to make that sound so despicable,' Carmenya said equably. 'We are aware of the marsh families' loyalty, but L'Belder is something of a charmer. It is not beyond him to wheedle his way into someone's house, make them take pity on him. Violence is not his way, but that does not make him any less dangerous. He is a liar, a cheat, an opportunist who will use anyone to further himself, regardless of what effect that may have on his supporters.'

'Such as the hospitality of the Confinery, I suppose.'

Carmenya smiled, a dead-eyed squill's grin. 'You could say that some of L'Belder's friends are being entertained within the Confinery's walls, yes.'

'You don't think *we'd* have anything to do with this

person, do you?!' Dannel cried, in some alarm. It had taken her a while to come to this conclusion.

Carmenya laughed. 'Of course not, my dear. I trust *you* implicitly.' Then she looked hard at Meonel and she was no longer laughing.

CHAPTER FIVE

SHYYA STOOD AT the water's edge, gazing at the marsh. Like all things of beauty, he knew it to be a dangerous thing. Because of this, he had an urge to run madly into its midst and let its wild, hidden, sentient life claim him once and for all. He often thought romantically about self-destruction and romance it was, for despite whatever life had thrown his way, he loved it helplessly, passionately. Standing there, feeling the power of the world beneath his feet could only fill him with a weird and secret joy. The land was beyond the rule of women and of men. It existed, it tolerated the fleeting presence of humanity, slowly turning towards a time when they would be just a memory, and perhaps not even that. Tonight, his scars itched and fretted. Tonight, he felt full of energy. He could not find Corinna. Unlike Meonel, who hated all females on principle, Shyya did not feel particularly antipathic towards women. He felt they were caught upon a path just as stony and twisting as any the men followed. As for Corinna, he empathised with her thwarted desire for autonomy, admired her reckless nature. Nobody in Vangery knew he felt this way. Shyya never opened his heart to a living soul. He had learnt, hard, at a young age that silence was the most precious thing a man could own. He did not pull at his woman-made bonds, straining towards a freedom he could never have, being content to sit back and watch the world turn, watch how things developed. He'd not always been that way, but since the mutilation he'd had to mature spiritually or go insane. His body, though flawless in most respects, was no longer a thing for him to take pride in, but his mind was as

31

untouched and strong as the spirit of the world itself. No-one could take that from him. No-one.

'Shyya.' He heard his name spoken through the dusk and turning, saw a pale figure coming towards him, along the damp banks. Corinna. He perceived instantly that something was wrong with her. She slipped on the mud, panting as she reached him, although there was no sign of injury. He hadn't been in Vangery long, but had swiftly developed a fondness for her. She was unlike most of the women he'd known in that a person's sex appeared to mean little to her. She conversed as happily with himself and Meonel as with any of her female friends.

'Are you alright?' he asked.

'Yes. Why?'

He shrugged. 'You look a little wild around the eyes, I guess.'

'I'm out of breath!'

He smiled. 'Your mother sent me to look for you. They're waiting to eat.'

Corinna pushed back her hair, rubbing her face. Nervously? No, it wasn't that, he decided. She looked excited, but not nervous. What had she been up to out here?

'I don't want to go back yet,' she said, pulling a face.

'I think you ought to. General Carmenya is here.'

'Yes, I know.'

Shyya was aware of several other exchanges that passed between them. First that Corinna recognised his concern for her, second, that neither of them seemed particularly overjoyed about the General's presence, third, they both knew Dannel would probably make a scene. They began to walk along the bank. There was a tense silence. Something *had* happened to her. What? She was different. '*Is* there something wrong, Corinna?'

She was trudging doggedly beside him, staring at the ground. 'You seem to think so.'

'Sorry, but you don't seem yourself.'

'What do you expect. I'm the main course at breadle-men, aren't I?' The harshness in her voice was something new. She had always appeared to be a sunny, carefree

32

creature to Shyya. He knew what she was referring to, because the whole household did, but didn't know what to say. They'd only spoken to each other on a superficial level before. He didn't know yet how much he could say to her before the female defences went up and he was accused of rudeness or impropriety. No matter how liberal the woman, there was always a limit. He knew that much. She touched his arm.

'Stop a minute. Look at the sky.' She folded her arms. 'So many stars.' A sigh. Shyya was beginning to wonder whether she was suffering from some intrinsic female complaint. He cast a mournful glance at the house but Corinna hadn't finished. 'Shyya, have we ever been alone together before?'

He couldn't help a nervous turn of the head in case anyone had heard her. 'I don't believe we have, Corinna. Why?'

'Oh, no specific reason. It's just that we know so little about each other. It's the same with everybody in Vangery, I think.'

'Everyone is very busy, what with the harvest . . .'

'That's not what I mean, and you know it!' She reached out jerkily as if to touch him, her hands falling away before contact was made. 'There's more to it than that. Is it fear? Pride? Arrogance? What is *wrong*, Shyya?'

'I asked you that!' he said, unable to follow clearly the train of her thoughts.

'No!' She shook her head fiercely, eyes screwed up. 'What is *wrong*? If you stand still for long enough, you can sense it, can't you?'

'If I can, I have learned it is dangerous to say so!' he said carefully, wondering if he'd drastically misconstrued her meaning.

'Yes!' Corinna agreed fervently, and now she did touch him, grabbing both his arms. She didn't appear to notice that she had. 'That is it, precisely! We're not free at all. People came from the home world to escape slavery, didn't they?'

'That was hundreds of years ago!'

'I know that! But, can't you see, half of us are slaves,

33

perhaps more than half?'

'Corinna, have you only just realised this?'

She paused, noticed her hands on his arms, and took them away. She began to walk towards the house. 'Yes,' she said, and did not utter another word until yellow light from the windows shone upon them. Then she said, 'Will you keep this a secret?'

He smiled. 'Keep what a secret exactly?'

'Just what I said. I'm not sure what I mean . . . yet. Don't tell Meonel.' Corinna was unaware of the limited extent of the companionship between Shyya and her step-father.

'I won't tell Meonel,' he said. 'Has it upset you, Carmenya coming here? Have you been out on the marsh all alone thinking yourself into a corner?'

'I have mixed feelings about going to Silven Crescent,' she said tightly.

'Then don't go.'

'I don't think I have a choice,' she answered, and there was more in those words than it sounded.

CHAPTER SIX

WHAT WAS WRONG with that girl? Dannel watched her daughter covertly as she chewed her way through the second course of breadlemen. Could Carmenya sense that Corinna was behaving oddly? Dannel hoped not, hoped that only she could see the feverish flame fizzing in Corinna's body, making her cheeks flush, her eyes dip this way and that. Perhaps Carmenya's presence was actually causing the phenomenon. It was possible the girl had picked up gossip concerning the general's suit. Dannel sat at the head of the table in the Brinkshallow Salon of the house, which had windows overlooking the trees and the silvery puddles that came with evening when a vague tide would stir the marsh. Lights had been kindled all around the verandah, an effect that Dannel loved, because it always reminded her of festivals and childhood. Evening, fluttering lights, fluttering moths and balmy air. Not even a hint of frost yet; that would be some weeks in coming. The marsh did not have an Autumn season exactly. It changed from Summer to Winter in the space of just a few days. Summer vegetation would turn to glass beneath a cold moon before it turned yellow. That was the time to gather Ash fruit, becore the secondary frosts came, when the fruit was still a shade tart, but filled the mouth with sweetness. Later fruit would be fit only for cooking or preserving or wine-making; holding a taint of sickliness because its flesh was truly killed by cold. Now, Dannel found herself thinking, it was as if Corinna was the Ash fruit touch by the first frost. No longer hard and small and tasteless, but beginning to swell with bittersweet juice. In her daughter's blossoming, Dannel could see the shade of

35

her own mortality, her own ageing. And that led her eyes to Meonel. There he was, in a dream world as usual, pushing food around his plate. She had tried so hard throughout the years to please him, but had somehow never succeeded. It annoyed her at times. After all, it wasn't she who made the laws, nor she who tried to enforce them. Had she been free from the fear of censure, she would have admitted that she had no interest in laws whatsoever; Dannel was an emotional, rather than intellectual, creature. She'd never hidden from the fact, however, that she was physically less than splendid. She was a woman who loved her food and no amount of exercise about the farm seemed to shift the heavy, solid bags of fat from her thighs and stomach. She knew too, that Meonel was her complete opposite, being slim and intelligent, and found women totally repellent. Dannel loved men. In secret, she would be tempted to shout this aloud. She loved their bodies, their eyes, their contained wildness. Although they were repressed, Dannel felt that men still dreamed of being the mythical stag and stallion, running over the hidden places of the world. In Meonel she could see the quivering hint of these legendary beasts. Carmenya's news about the fugitive had filled Dannel's heart with dread, as if a treasured, forbidden secret of hers was about to be discovered. She often fantasised about a secret race of men who lived with the beasts and ran with the beasts and preyed with the beasts. These men would be free; they would unbind the chained God. But even though these thoughts were only fantasies, Dannel knew that Carmenya would regard them with a less than sympathetic eye if she got to know about them. Carmenya would consider them treason. If anyone on the marsh would give shelter to Elvon L'Belder, Dannel Trotgarden was that person. Her sick perversion was in danger of being brought to light, but fortunately, she was unaware that the danger even existed.

Carmenya had been looking at Corinna too. She said, 'You look hot, my dear. I hope you're not coming down with a chill.' Corinna did not appear particularly interested in her food.

'No, General, but we had to run nearly all the way home, this evening. We walked farther than we meant to this afternoon, didn't we Orb.'

'Corinna, how many times do I have to tell you not to do that!' Dannel exclaimed, trying to divert attention, but merely sounding carping. 'You should always ride the dank if you leave Vangery. What if you should step on a nest of root-leeches out there? You'd be drained of blood before you could even cry for help!'

'I know what I'm doing, Mother,' Corinna replied carefully. 'If you respect the marsh, it cannot harm you.'

Bolivia, Dannel's older daughter, made a disparaging sound at this. Dannel knew that Bolivia would now give examples of unlucky accidents that had befallen people on the marsh. Dannel did not want to hear them. She said, 'Please ride in future, all of you. I'm sure the General wouldn't like to see you harmed, Corinna.' This introduced the prickly subject of Corinna's future, prickly because Dannel herself was not sure whether she wanted her younger daughter to leave the farm. She was aware that Corinna was a quick-witted girl who would not be allowed much joy under the firm hand of Bolivia. Perhaps it would be best for Corinna to join the court in the city. Just because this life suited Dannel, did not mean it would suit Corinna. Dannel knew the whole family, including Corinna herself, suspected her of seeking favour with Carmenya and of having no other motive for handing Corinna over to her. People liked to believe that and Dannel couldn't convince them otherwise. She would never admit to anyone how much that upset her.

'Would you like to come to the city?' Carmenya asked Corinna. The girl didn't look up from her plate.

'In the Spring perhaps . . .' she said.

Dannel winced. Why couldn't Corinna just say 'yes' with the appropriate thanks. Could she really want to stay here?

'I was thinking it would be better if you came south for the mid-winter festival,' Carmenya continued, unperturbed. 'You'd enjoy that. All the streets are decorated . . . everyone dresses up.'

'That is the time when the twin Sun Gods are born,' Corinna said.

'Yes,' Carmenya added drily. She picked up her fork and began to eat once more. Dannel attempted to uncurl her toes within her slippers, without much success. Sooner or later some bright spark in the city would change the semantics of the winter festival, male orientated as they were at present.

'I think everyone is aware of the religious significance of mid-Winter,' she said.

'What do you want me to do?' Corinna asked her. 'Do you want me to leave before the Spring?'

Dannel was flummoxed. What she really wanted was to avoid offending Carmenya, so that Corinna's chances wouldn't be ruined.

'You are a bright girl, Corinna,' Carmenya said, before Dannel could answer. 'I think you'd be wasted staying here in Vangery. You've already experienced seventeen Winters on the marsh. Don't you think it's time you broadened your horizons?'

'When it's put that way, I can hardly refuse, can I!' Corinna said.

'Corinna!' Dannel cried, her face turning deep red.

'Oh, it's alright, Dannel. The girl just has spirit!' Carmenya said, waving Dannel's blustering away with a careless hand. 'She's predictably nervous of change, and it would be a big change. Isn't that so, Corinna? Are you frightened of the city?'

'I wouldn't know anybody. Mother, do you want me to go?' Now there was silence. Everyone was looking at Dannel. She would have to answer.

'I'm not trying to get rid of you,' she said, evasively.

'You think I should go?'

'Yes. I think it would be good for you.'

'Fine!' Corinna threw down her knife and fork, and flounced from the room, leaving a somewhat shocked silence into which Meonel smiled vaguely.

CHAPTER SEVEN

IN THE MORNING, General Carmenya and her six companions set off to scour the marsh for Elvon L'Belder, and to question surrounding marsh families. Corinna had heard the city women complaining because they'd been accommodated in the servants' quarters amongst the stilt-legs of the house. They considered this beneath them. She had also heard Carmenya brush their complaints away harshly. Corinna was always in two minds about what she thought of Carmenya. Sometimes the woman surprised her by being extremely liberal, even non-conformist. Sometimes she could be infuriatingly rigid and unbending in her views; she fascinated and frightened the girl. Corinna was not sure how she'd get on with Carmenya if they ever spent any time alone together. Would Carmenya consider Corinna a trouble-maker if she got to know her inner mind? There were many things Carmenya must not get to know.

Corinna stood on the verandah of the Facewater Salon and watched the city women's skippers skim gracefully away from Vangery. Carmenya was standing upright in the stern of the larger of the two craft, her hair blowing out behind her. A small herd of tussock-antelope sprang away from them, keening their displeasure. Birds circled in the morning sunlight. Corinna could see a curl of smoke rising from the heating stacks of the nearby farm belonging to Yaschel Tendaughter. The Trotgardens had not ignited their heating yet. Perhaps they did not feel the cold as much. A silver streak arrowed across the sky, straight up. A flying boat from the city, maybe, darting towards another sun, another world. Now *there* was a change Corinna would almost welcome! She had heard rumours that, in Silven Crescent, the only place on Artemis with a functioning space-craft terminal, visitors from the skies were becoming rather less regular than in the past. As far as anyone knew, a tenuous link was maintained with the other worlds within Guimo and Shamberel's system – this presumably a custom left over from the first days of colonisation when it must have been a necessity. However, nowadays, it was whispered that the people of Amflax, Wellspring and Eden, the worlds closest to Artemis, and with whom Artemis had once enjoyed healthy relations, were becoming very wary of the extremist politics becoming popular on Artemis. These were based on ideals close to the heart of the Dominatrix, Yani Gisbandrun, ideals currently burrowing their way into the heart of Artemisian culture. Off-worlders were suspicious of the hint of hysteria in this and, somehow, Corinna didn't blame them. In just a few minutes last night, her view of the world had expanded, exploding in a great rush of colour. In the settling of the sparkling, multi-hued dust had come an understanding that had always been within her but unrecognised, formless. Yesterday, she hadn't been sure whether Carmenya's offer was concrete or not. Now she knew. Yesterday, her coccoon had been split. In the boathouse.

Corinna was afraid of going back to the boathouse, although she knew she had to. Wandering into the kitchen, she gathered bread, fruit, half a cooked sausage and a stoppered pot of Ash juice. The servants, all male, appeared to be unconcerned with her actions, an appearance she did not trust. Well, let them say what they liked. If anyone asked, she was getting ready for a long ride out on the marsh. Still, she was nervous of going back to the boathouse alone. Unfortunately, the only other person she thought she could trust in Vangery was Shyya and there was no way she could ask him to go with her without arousing suspicion. If she only knew him better! Corinna had been impressed by Shyya's beauty from the day of his arrival, although the rest of the household tended to shun him because he was a eunuch. Corinna didn't care about that. She sensed depth in Shyya and it intrigued her. He played the game of shadows with studied ease, though Corinna was not deceived. He carried Meonel's belongings, ran Meonel's errands, let Meonel believe that, in some measure, he was master of the house; this demanded skill. Shyya's skills would have come in useful for what she'd taken on; a pity.

Putting off the moment when she would have to go outside, Corinna went to Meonel's private sitting-room, the Lawnview Salon. Meonel was sprawled in a high-backed leather chair next to the half shuttered window, listening to Shyya read from a book. Shyya was leaning informally against a table leg, sitting on the floor. Corinna paused in the open doorway, eavesdropping on what she supposed was the nearest these two got to intimacy. Shyya had a clear, melodious voice, not feminine, but not really masculine either. What had happened last night had somehow brought Corinna closer to Shyya. As they'd met on the banks of the marsh, a strangeness about everything had brought them into each other's light. She was pleased to be looking at him now, pleased to know that soon they would speak.

'Meonel,' she said, and Shyya immediately stopped reading and looked up.

Meonel smiled rather cruelly. 'Looking for an ally, Corinna?' he said. She ventured into the room. Shyya looked at the book on his raised knees, turning pages quickly. Corinna noticed the way his hair parted on his neck, revealing knobs of spine through a poreless, pale skin. Had Meonel ever noticed that? Meonel was not an artist. He was an exploding force kept under control in an airless vacuum, incapable, Corinna suspected, of seeing beauty in anything nowadays.

'Maybe I am ally-hunting,' she said and went to sit on the window-sill. Meonel studied her warily.

'So the great woman is to spirit you away, Corinna!'

'No need to sound so gleeful, Meonel,' she replied. 'Do you think Carmenya will find her renegade male?'

Meonel shrugged. 'I don't care.' He continued studying

41

her. 'Do you?'

'I wonder what it is he says that worries her so much? What is he advocating? Has he any power, real power?'

'Have you come here then to talk about the fugitive?'

'Perhaps I identify with him. I shall be carted off to the city too, but my bonds will be invisible.'

'Neither, I hope, will you be put to death! Corinna, you would disturb your mother with such talk!'

'Why? Why can't we speak our minds?'

'The same reason I can't own property, my dear. Would you like some wine? Shyya, wine for the daughter!'

Shyya unwound himself from the floor and poured Corinna a drink. It was early in the day for it, but Meonel always began drinking early. Shyya looked thoughtful. 'The possibility of equality among the sexes is an old idea,' he said. Corinna went cold. Had she made any mention of that, however veiled? Had she? Shyya smiled at her.

'If it's so old, how come it's never happened?' she said inadequately.

'Because men and women being human, one always has to have the upper hand,' Shyya replied. 'The majority don't want to be equal; they never have. In the old times, when women were regarded as the weaker sex, the vociferous ones that spoke out against it desired only to have masculine power. They didn't want to be equal; they wanted to be men. Here on Artemis, they have their wish.'

'I can't agree with that,' Corinna said. 'The first settlers wanted equality, that's why they came here.'

'And that, presumably, is why they subjugated men, right?'

Corinna shrugged uncomfortably.

'If women wanted equality of the sexes, they'd encourage the female side of men, not try to subdue their own.'

'I am the female side of woman,' Corinna said. 'I am angeldt.'

Shyya made a gesture. 'There you are then. Does that speak of comfortable equality? Even women are divided now.'

Meonel, though silent, was looking at Shyya sharply. Corinna could see a hundred conflicting thoughts cross his eyes. He was taken aback.

'But is there anything we can do about it?' he said, saying each word separately, as if trying them out.

Shyya shrugged, wrinkled his nose, then shook his head. 'Probably not. The women who left the home world wanted to found their own society and they have succeeded. Artemis has come a long way in only a few hundred years. It is our misfortune to be born on such a world. Our only escape, or respite, would be to leave it . . . in one way or another.'

'How?' Corinna asked.

'By travelling to Wellspring, perhaps? Or Eden, or wherever?' Meonel suggested.

Corinna shook her head. 'How would anyone get to Wellspring or Eden or wherever? Passage comes dear on a flying boat and places are few.'

'Presupposing people from those worlds would want Artemisians anyway,' Shyya added. 'Wellspring's politics revolve solely around the planet's income. I doubt whether they'd want to risk contamination from hysterical matriarchs! Similarly, the city deliberately makes it difficult for people to leave Artemis, for whatever reason.'

Meonel pulled a glum face. 'Yes, you are right, travelling is discouraged.'

'Indeed, but there is one place where, even though travelling is discouraged, it cannot be so easily prevented,' Shyya said.

'Which is?' Meonel asked rhetorically.

'Artemis herself, of course. We know only a corner of it.'

Meonel shook his head. 'The Dominatrix must have good reason in stopping people from venturing beyond the marsh. It is dangerous, perhaps inhospitable to human life.'

Shyya shrugged. 'Maybe.'

Corinna sighed. 'Well, these dreams are all very well, but in a short time I will be sent to Carmenya in the city.'

'That may not be so bad,' Meonel said. 'She's a handsome brute. If I were you, I think I'd be looking forward to it.'

'Meonel, you're disgusting!' Corinna stood up. 'Now, I

have to go to the boathouse.' She looked at Shyya who smiled back. No, she couldn't ask him. 'See you crawling males later then!' She waved and turned around.

'Corinna,' Meonel said, calling her back. She paused at the door, but did not look at him.

'What?'

'You've changed. Is this a late puberty?'

'What?'

'You do not speak as a woman should, as a good woman should.' Corinna perceived a certain challenge in his words. She turned and looked at him and he appeared so old in the bright, filtered sunlight. Life was passing him by; she could sense it, smell it, touch it. His cynicism and his beauty, which she had loved, had somehow shrunk. I am confused, she thought. I'm not sure what I think anymore. She was seeing Meonel with new eyes, that she could not trust.

'Meonel,' she began, tailing off. He raised his brows, as if he knew what she was thinking. But he didn't. He couldn't. 'Yes, I've changed,' she said. 'I had to. I can't afford the luxury of complacency like you. I'm a condemned woman!'

Meonel laughed. 'You sould like a crazy! Is this what you think about sloshing around on your own every day out there?' He paused to laugh again. 'It seems your mother and the General are right; you should leave here. Possibly before you go mad.'

She couldn't confide in him, that was sure! Shyya smiled at her in a veiled, wan way, perhaps picking up some urgent, mental message from her, and went back to studying the book. Corinna left them.

She had walked into the boathouse and he had grabbed her. Not harshly, but firmly. She had seen his wild eyes. She had gasped, but not screamed. His first words had been, 'Be still, I am at one with you', an incongruous, but somehow moving, introduction. Thus Corinna ran head-first into the fugitive Elvon L'Belder. He had not made her feel afraid. One of his gifts was the diffusion of calm wherever he found panic or chaos. It made him very good with animals, not to mention humans. In the gloom

44

behind them, boats had creaked and clicked, and water licked thickly at wood.

'Who are you? What are you doing here?' she'd asked in a whisper, an unnecessary precaution for there was no-one else around. He'd shaken his head, dropped his hands from her arm, hurried to the window to see if she had come alone. 'Who are you?' she asked, even though she knew. 'Where do you come from?'

'I need help,' he said.

'Clearly! What do you want?' She could see how filthy he was, and not just that; here was a man on the verge of collapse.

'What do I want? That's simple; silence. The greatest gift; your silence.'

'Not just that, I feel. You're the one General Carmenya's looking for, aren't you?'

He narrowed his eyes at her, unsure. 'Don't worry,' Corinna said, 'I'm not going to run screaming to her and tell her where you are.'

'Am I safe here then?'

'I wouldn't say that, no. Not in here.'

He didn't look surprised. 'Where am I?'

'Vangery.'

'Vangery? Where's that?'

'A long way from where you ought to be, Elvon L'Belder. General Carmenya is staying here.'

The man's eyes widened. 'No!' Then he laughed. 'Well, that's typical. I don't suppose Lady Fate would ever let me try to hide anywhere else!'

'What have you done, that she's so determined to take you back?' Corinna had wondered, at this point, whether she ought to feel afraid.

'Done? Nothing bad. Nothing. I haven't killed or raped, if that's what you're afraid of! Let's just say that my beliefs are somewhat at variance with those of the Dominatrix. Do you understand?'

'Yes.'

'Will you help me?' He'd turned those wild, compelling eyes on her. Why did he trust her? Because he knew the power of his eyes and trusted them completely?

'If I can,' Corinna had answered; an immediate response. There was no question about it. She'd gestured to a pile of tarpaulins at the back of the shed. 'It might be best if you got inside those. Are you hungry?'

The man smiled. 'A little. Can you bring me food?'

'Not tonight. It would be too risky. If Carmenya wasn't here, it'd be no problem. It'll have to be tomorrow now. Can you wait till then?'

'I've waited three days. One more night won't make much difference.' Three days? But on the marsh, there was shemble-frack, tweeter bud, potato thistle to eat; didn't he know that?

'I'll be as early as I can tomorrow.'

'Bless you, girl.' He'd taken her hands in his own. 'You probably know nothing about my cause, but I speak for fairness, justice and equality. Every man and woman on this world is equal in the eyes of the gods,' he said. 'Believe that, and believe it true. You shall be rewarded for your kindness, threefold. Piece by piece the picture shall come together and darkness shall be pushed back. Do you understand me?'

She nodded. 'I think so.'

'Good girl.' He'd let her go. 'Keep silent. My life is in your hands at this time.'

'Don't worry.' She'd gone to the door. 'I'll lock you in. Someone may check inside otherwise.' Already she'd no longer been able to see him.

'I thank you,' he'd said, and she had locked him in.

That had been last night. Now she sat on the wooden floor of the boathouse and watched him eat. He tore at the food, mindless, starving; the only sounds were those of his busy jaws and the clicking of wood against water.

'I don't know when Carmenya will be back,' she said. 'But I don't think you should stay here. There are any number of reasons why someone might come out here . . .'

'Are you afraid of her then?' he asked, wiping his mouth, picking up the bottle of juice. Corinna sighed.

'I was not thinking of my own safety exactly, if that's what you mean. I don't know if I'm afraid of her. I don't know her very well. I'm only aware of her position and her

46

authority.'

'Well, I'm afraid of her!' L'Belder sucked greedily on the bottle.

'Then why do things that get you in trouble?'

He looked at Corinna keenly. 'Someone has to.'

'How can it make any difference, though? One person can't change things, I'm sure.'

'You are right. But I have friends who believe as I do; both women and men.'

'In the city? Many of them?'

He laughed. 'You look alarmed. Yes, in the city. Many? How many is many. Not enough yet. Maybe a hundred.' His expression clouded. 'That is, there *were* a hundred when I escaped Silven Crescent . . .'

'Tell me about it,' Corinna said. L'Belder smiled at her earnestness, although she thought he was smiling because he didn't think she was serious or could care that much.

'I'm an egotist. I don't like being told what to do. I'm also fair-minded. I don't like seeing others being treated in a way that I hate myself.'

'Is it as bad in Silven Crescent as people say then?'

He shrugged. 'Depends on what you've heard. In my opinion, the Dominatrix is going slowly insane and as her madness progresses she invents new rules and codes for the people to live by. Your family should be concerned about this; one day it will affect you too . . . unless someone has the guts to try and do something about it.'

'You.'

He smiled. 'I really don't know. They've outwitted us so far. It's very difficult to trust people. Obviously, her spies are a problem, although our network is small. We experimented with our own power by hitting a few key targets in the city; governmental buildings, army facilities, that kind of thing. We don't kill though – ever. Some of my people disagree with that, but it's something I insist on. I don't believe in outright terrorism.'

'No? I admit I know nothing about how to run rebellions, but even so, a bloodless one can't really be effective can it?'

L'Belder gave her a hard look. Corinna shrugged. 'O.k.,

so I'm a woman. Perhaps your way is beyond me.' Her sarcasm didn't amuse him. 'So what are you going to do now?'

He twirled and twirled the juice bottle in his hands. 'Goddess, I don't know! There are tales about the marsh. Maybe I've come this way to see if they're true. If they're not, then I'll keep heading north and see what turns up.'

'You won't give up then?'

'I can't. This world is distorted by injustice. I've got to keep trying, no matter how little I achieve.'

It was becoming clear to Corinna that L'Belder's cause was pretty well hopeless at the moment. None of his ideas seemed very practical. 'So, what are these tales you hope to verify?' she asked.

'The Greylids,' he answered, but not without some discomfort.

Corinna pulled a wry face. 'Really? My mother used to tell us tales of them. I thought it was just make believe. You really think they exist?'

'Most legends have their roots in fact.'

'But no-one's ever seen a Greylid – ever.'

'How do you know that?'

Corinna shrugged; she didn't.

'Perhaps they don't want to be seen,' L'Belder said. 'Besides, in the city there are plenty of tales to be heard from travellers who think they've seen something on the fringes of the floating forests. There are too many tales not to take notice of them.'

Corinna sighed. 'But tales! Is that all you have to go on? What else makes you think they're there? You must have some reason.'

L'Belder smiled. 'You think I'm crazy now don't you! But just look around you; Artemis is an old world, very similar in many respects to the one our race originated on. How come there's no indigenous, intelligent people here?'

Corinna laughed. 'Well, there are the wervels. Do you think they classify?'

'What?'

She explained what they were. L'Belder shook his head vehemently. 'No, nothing like that; Greylids.'

'It's far-fetched, L'Belder.'

'Not really. There's another reason. Other people have turned their backs on the cities. Where did they go? I can't believe they've all been caught and disposed of over the years.'

'That does sound more feasible. What are you looking for in them, allies or sanctuary?'

L'Belder shrugged. He didn't like to say, because most of what he wanted was dreams. 'I'll just settle for finding them right now.'

Corinna smiled at him. 'You know, I can remember my mother talking about the people in the forests. Bedtime stories. It was a long time ago, but one of her favourite subjects. Sometimes, I'd dream about them after she'd gone. She always made it sound so real; there was something spooky about her voice. Perhaps she liked to scare herself! Men on the marsh who couldn't be seen properly? Not only scary but probably illegal to think about.'

'Has this marsh been properly charted?' L'Belder asked.

Corinna shook her head. 'Not all of it; it's too big. The marsh families occupy about a hundred and seventy square miles of it, but some bits inbetween the isles are unfarmed. Further east the floating forests make the land impossible to farm at all. We have enough land anyway. If more people wanted to come from the city then maybe they'd try to clear the forests and chart the marsh beyond our boundary, but as it stands, we don't bother.'

'Take what you need not what you want, eh?' He smiled at her warmly.

'That seems sensible, doesn't it. Why should we take too much?'

'L'Belder laughed. 'Say that in the city and you'll find yourself in the Confinery, I expect.'

Recollection brought a sourness to her eyes. 'I have to go to the city soon.'

'You do? She noticed his face light up and knew he was thinking of his friends, and whether he could use her.

'Yes, in Carmenya's entourage. Don't look at me like that, Elvon L'Belder. I won't join your cause in that way.

I have to find my feet first.'

'Yet you sympathise, don't you.'

'I sympathise, but that's all for now.'

'How long will our dear General be staying here?'

'I don't know. Not long. She doesn't usually. Depends on whether she finds you, doesn't it, or how long she'll pursue the search if she doesn't.' He didn't comment on this.

'Will it be safe for me to stay here until she leaves?'

'I really don't know. She has eyes like a hawk. She's bound to notice if I'm making secret trips out here carrying baskets of food.'

'I need your help.'

'I know. I'll come back this evening when I go to see my dank. I'll think about it.' He thanked her. She left.

She wanted support, advice, someone else's wisdom. What had begun as a fine morning had become grey and overcast. Angry clouds hurried across the sky, edged with brown and purple. A rain wind brought sharp perfume to the land. Soon the storms would come and there'd be no dry places in the boathouse. What the hell should she do? It crossed her mind to tell Carmenya everything. That would be the easiest way. L'Belder was coercive. She found herself agreeing to help him, when she knew she shouldn't for her own sake, and when *he* knew she shouldn't but hung on to her because she was all he had. What a situation. Did she really care what went on in Silvan Crescent? Wasn't it most likely he was exaggerating when he spoke of the Dominatrix? Could her hand really be flexing to reach out and touch the marsh people? I don't know. I don't know! she thought, and large, widely-spaced raindrops began to fall. She hurried indoors.

CHAPTER EIGHT

MEONEL SAID, 'SHUT the window, Shyya.' The wind was getting cold. When would the old bag order the heating to be started up? When the whole household had taken to their beds with chills? He watched Shyya reach up and fiddle with the catch, patient as always. Ever since Corinna had left them, Meonel's mind had been racing madly. The three of them had talked together like conspirators. For the first time, he dared to think that perhaps he was not as alone as he thought. Corinna was changing; that was obvious. He'd never thought of her as nervous or particularly highly strung before but now she seemed so restless. When had the change occurred? He couldn't remember. Coupled with a certain euphoria over their sudden, brief closeness though, Meonel experienced a twinge of dread. It was as if the house was swaying dangerously on its stilts, as if the stilts themselves were no longer safe.

Shyya sat down again. 'Would you like me to continue reading?' he asked. Meonel said yes, although he wanted desperately to talk about their earlier conversation. Now he was afraid to. It was as if Shyya were more powerful than he, as if he had to wait for Shyya to broach the subject himself. Meonel had always felt small. He'd been made to feel that way and he hated it. Not listening to Shyya's words at all, he put one hand across his eyes. His head had begun to ache. Shyya stopped reading. He looked up and all was quiet for a moment, but for the wind outside.

'Shall I fetch your woollen?' he asked. 'Are you cold, sir?' Meonel shook his head.

'I'm not cold. A headache.'

51

'May I ease it for you?'

He went to put his long fingers on Meonel's neck, seeking nerves, which hurt and also brought pictures to Meonel's eyes. The pain did not go away completely, but it did lessen.

'Is that better?' Shyya asked.

'Yes, much.'

'You are lying. Your thoughts are bursting. That's what's causing the headache.'

Meonel did not speak. Shyya sat on the floor, picked up the book. He flicked through the pages and said, 'Why don't you say what's on your mind? That way, the pain will go altogether.'

'Carry on reading. I think I know my own mind.'

Shyya flicked him a quick glance. 'As you wish.'

As he read the words, Meonel was continuing the conversation that could have taken place had he not cut it dead. He was saying, 'Shyya, I'm not happy', and Shyya was responding quietly, 'What do you want?' He could shut his eyes and still feel the youth standing behind his chair. In his head Meonel was saying, 'I want you, I want you, I want you.'

Dannel was in her private study. She examined a sheet of figures. It had been a good crop of shemble-frack this year and the antelope were prolific. The Trotgardens had meat and skins to sell as well as vegetable produce. The farm was going well. She poured herself a cup of wine and gazed out of the window. She could see the smoke rising from the Tendaughters' place and shivered. Perhaps I'd better have the heating on soon, she thought. She should be feeling contented, but she wasn't and could only suppose Carmenya had something to do with that. Their friendship went back a long way, but it had always been a strain to keep up, at least on Dannel's part. She never felt at ease with Carmenya and this business with the fugitive was ringing alarm bells in her head; she didn't know why. Carmenya always stayed at Vangery when she visited the marsh; there was nothing unusual in that. Dannel wondered why she couldn't dispel the niggling feeling that the

General *suspected* her somehow. She'd never shared fantasies with the woman. In fact, she often found herself wondering why Carmenya bothered to keep up the friendship at all. What did they have in common now? Since leaving the city after completing the education her mother had insisted on, Dannel had only grown fat and homely in the marsh. She had never shared Carmenya's zeal, her belief in the Dominatrix. Now the unspoken words stood between them like a wall. Dannel would have liked to say, 'The Dominatrix is crazy.' There had always been people who'd dared to stand up and speak out against her, and Dannel had always privately agreed with them. Unfortunately, those people were fewer and farther between nowadays and tended to disappear very quickly. The occasional move to liberate the men was only the tip of the iceberg, she felt. Thank the Goddess she lived here on the marsh, where it was safe.

Dannel sighed. She sifted her papers together, thinking about visiting the kitchen. Soon they must make their journey to Stilt Vashti; a stock-take was needed. Just as she rose, slowly, from her chair, a knock came at the door. Heavily, she sat down again. 'Come in.' There was Corinna hovering in the doorway. Dannel thought, Oh no! feeling that more argument about Corinna's move to the city was imminent. She couldn't help sounding sharp when she said, 'Yes, what is it?'

'I want to apologise for last night,' Corinna said, moving into the room, and creeping round its edge.

'It's for your own good, Corinna. You need something to fall back on.'

'I know. I realise that. It's just that Carmenya is . . . well . . . intimidating. What will she expect of me?'

Dannel didn't know. 'Just keep your mouth shut and watch how others behave,' she said.

'It's not going to be easy for me, is it?'

'Corinna, I spent some time in the city myself when I was younger, as you know. I learnt a lot.' Not the least of which was how much she appreciated life on the marsh, but she didn't mention that. Corinna leaned on the window sill behind Dannel's desk and gazed out at the marsh, as Dannel had done earlier.

'Remember when you used to tell me tales of the Greylids?' she said. Dannel's heart almost stopped. It was like another omen, another warning. To a degree she had told her fantasies to her children, under the guise of bedtime tales, forgetting that those children would grow up, and perhaps remember those tales. Agitated, Dannel shoved her papers in a drawer and slammed it shut.

'You're grown up now, Corinna,' she said.

'You know, I used to think you believed in it all,' Corinna continued, dreamily. Dannel wasn't deceived. By the Goddess, was it possible Carmenya had set her own daughter up against her? Could Corinna be checking her out for the General?

'Don't be stupid, girl!' she snapped. 'Fairytales for children! Didn't you enjoy them?'

'Very much.'

'That was why I told them.'

'Do they tell stories to their children like that in the city, I wonder?'

Dannel stared at her daughter's back. The little bitch! she thought. 'I expect you'll soon find out, Corinna!' she said. 'Excuse me, I have work to do.' She stood up and squeezed from behind her chair. Corinna looked disappointed. Good! Little Madam! 'I don't think you'll have any problem adapting to city life!' she said coldly and held the door open for Corinna to walk past her.

Corinna walked thoughtfully down to the stables. What had she done to upset her mother now? All she'd wanted was a little information, a clue as to whether those stories could have been true, handed down by generations of marsh families. Perhaps Dannel had heard them from her own mother. She'd like to be able to tell L'Belder he had something to look for. Dannel was so prickly, terrified of doing anything that wasn't 'Right'. Conformist. Corinna hissed derisively through her teeth. Her dank beast came to his stable door, whistling and honking, pushing his chest against the wood. She scratched him behind one of his huge cup ears, looking back at the house. Her mother was watching her from one of the salon windows. Corinna stood back. Could Dannel suspect something of her secret? Had she seen her go down to the boathouse that morning? Dannel moved away, into the gloom beyond. Corinna could no longer see her. She shivered. The day was damp, the wind penetrating. She wished she'd put her woollen jacket on. Part of her chores included the exercising of the dank beasts. Usually she took them all into one of the dry pastures next to the house, riding one, so that the others would follow, and galloped them round for half an hour. They loved that; it was a great treat to them, all lolloping together, hooting and bucking, pushing each other around. Today, she fancied a ride onto the marsh.

At first, Fitching, her mount, seemed edgy. It had been a long time since he'd been off the island; nearly a month. Despite Dannel's misgivings concerning safety, most of the Vangery people were happy to stroll across the marsh in summer, not least because it was a beautiful place and difficult to be afraid of. Boats and rafts were used for transporting the crops; the danks were mostly riding animals. Now they had become fat and lazy, nervous in the open space, where the breeze might sometimes smell of death. Corinna cantered Fitching steadily through a shallow stream which formed a watery road heading towards the Tendaughters' place. She kept reliving her conversations with L'Belder in her head, her conversations with Shyya and Meonel. 'What the hell am I doing?' she said aloud, wondering how this situation could ever right itself. She wished that Shyya was with her now, that she didn't feel so awkward about approaching him. She supposed she was out here looking for signs of the Greylids, even though it was unlikely such signs would exist so close to civilisation. She passed some of the Tendaughters' people out gathering the last flush of their willow fruit. Soon Yaschel would come trundling over to Vangery to trade with the Trotgardens before both families went off to market. One of the men, up to his knees in water, threw her a fruit, which she caught deftly.

'Corinna!' And there was Sander, like herself riding a dank, splashing up the waterway towards her.

'Hello, Sander. Your harvest nearly over, is it?' Corinna bit into the fruit. It was perfect; perfumed yet with a sting to freeze the tongue. She looked sideways at Sander and found herself comparing him to Shyya which was a bit unfair because Sander obviously had one big advantage over the eunuch. He was not half so nice to look at though, and did not give off anywhere near the same feeling of underground power that Shyya did. Then a picture of Elvon L'Belder flashed into her mind and she couldn't help laughing out loud at this pale, slender youth who was probably the epitome of the kind of male the Dominatrix would like to have as the only kind.

'Since when has harvesting been so funny?' Sander asked, aware of a tinge of cruelty in her laughter.

'Oh, I'm just in a laughing mood today!'

'Little to laugh about,' Sander grumbled. 'The storms will be here early this season.'

'And next summer will be glorious because of it,' Corinna added. Suddenly she was feeling ecstatically happy. Strange.

'Where are you going?' Sander asked.

'To the forests of Ire and Pentitence.'

'You can't. It would take you days.'

'I know. I was only joking. I'm just exercising old Fitching here.'

'Fat, isn't he.'

'Mmm. A trip to the forests would probably do him good.'

'You really want to go there? We could take a trip out next summer if you like. We could camp.'

'A daring idea, Sander; you know the forests are impenetrable,' Corinna answered, deciding it wouldn't be a good idea for the Tendaughters to find out she wouldn't be around here next summer yet.

'Just to the edge,' Sander replied irritably.

'To look for Greylids?'

'For what?'

'Oh, nothing.'

'Do you want to go then?'

'Alright. Next summer's a long way off yet, though.'

Sander nodded. 'I know. Still, it'll be something to look forward to.' He brightened. 'We should be up at your place sometime soon.' He was having some trouble raising his animal's head where it was buried, munching, in needle rush and wild ground cherry. 'Be sure to have hot milk-suds ready for us!'

'We will. I must be off, Sander. Good-day to you.'

He saluted her and smiled. 'Good-day, Corinna Trot-garden.'

She urged her dank into a ground-devouring lope and splashed away from him. Now the air was fresh, with just a hint of sweet storm and electric breath from the clouds above. Corinna rode through every spinney, examining the ground, the trees, tumbled stones. She didn't know what she was looking for really, but there was nothing out of the ordinary to see. Hunger woke in her belly after a while and told her to go home. She felt too cold to carry on searching anyway. Flicking his tail fronds with excite-ment, the dank took over the minute she pointed him in the direction of Vangery. Spray flew up around them both, frightening birds into the air, and once surprising a dozing spring of tussock antelope who flew up before them, screaming, scattering in all directions. Corinna laughed. She'd found no sign of hidden people, had reached no conclusion in her head over anything, but the morning had been good. She felt full of energy.

CHAPTER NINE

Elvon L'Belder sat crouched among the tarpaulins in the Trotgarden's boathouse. Every creak, every subtle lick of the water made him tremble. He could almost see the dark, stooped form of a questing Carmenya creeping towards him, a smile on her shadowed face, her hands clenched. Goddess, what horrible whim of Fate had made him choose this place to hide in, so close to his enemy? Why had the boathouse been open yesterday? But if it had been locked, his reason argued, you might still be out on the marsh, more dead than alive, and today she would have found you. He shivered, unable to get warm, still hungry. L'Belder would be the first to agree that he wasn't really suited to a life of privation out in the wilds. He was used to city dwelling. Even as he'd stumbled onwards, wanting only to put miles between himself and Silven Crescent, he realised that he should have been able to feed himself. The marsh was a rich source of food, both animal and vegetable, but he'd never killed anything in his life, and didn't know which plants were poisonous and which suitable to eat. Frustration had made him furious with himself. If he'd had any proper sense of organisation, he'd have thought long ago of flight as an eventual necessity and would have prepared himself for it. Twice he'd been bitten by a large, aggressive type of insect, whose venom had made his tongue swell and tinged his vision with red. The first time, he'd thought he might die, unaware that by simply chewing a rush-root, he'd have been able to dispel the discomfort in minutes. He'd suffered for a couple of hours, lying half in, half out of a spear shallow, until the effects of the bite seemed magically to disappear.

Then he'd carried on, heading blindly north, too tired to panic, but horribly aware of how helpless he was.

The moment Corinna had walked into the boathouse had been one of the worst of his life. He'd had to throw into their meeting all the remnants of energy he possessed; he'd had to make her 'see'. See him as he was; not a threat, but someone who needed help and was worth the trouble. Luck had been with him; it had worked. L'Belder might not be able to live off the land, or have the constitution of a warrior, but he had immense charisma, which was what made him so successful as a leader. People loved him and he loved them back; he was an honest man.

He tried to feel optimistic. The girl was trying to help him, although there wasn't much she could do for him while the 'mangak' was in residence. He knew she wouldn't betray him, yet was aware of her mixed feelings in becoming involved. He couldn't really blame her. Obviously, she would think the problems of Silven Crescent nothing to do with her, or her family. He doubted whether she could see how far the Dominatrix's ambitions were beginning to stretch. L'Belder was in possession of dangerous knowledge and it was because he knew this Carmenya was hunting him so relentlessly. The Dominatrix had to make sure he was dead; she couldn't dare risk him surviving the marsh, when she was at a critical point in her plans. Only careful, stealthy nurturing and coercion would sway the Artemisians' opinions in her favour. What she was proposing was radical, so radical that if L'Belder was given the opportunity to make public what he knew at this tender time, it was highly probable that many women (not all women being crazy like their leader) would react strongly against it. No man would agree with it, of course, but then men didn't matter. Somehow he must find enough people who did matter, who would listen to him; people with whom this secret knowledge could be shared and used; L'Belder opposed violence strongly but would gladly puree the head of any man stupid enough to let the Dominatrix have her way without a struggle.

He sighed and lay back among the tarpaulins. What use his dreams now? If he got out of the marsh alive he'd be lucky. In a way, he was beginning to wish he'd never found out what was going on. He remembered how it had all started so clearly. It hadn't been luck, just fate, that had swayed the decision of the Head Archivist in the palace. He hadn't even wanted the job particularly, but any position in the palace had to be leapt at. Information came easier that way, and though not politically active at the time, L'Belder liked to know what was going on. The Archivist's assistant had been one Semele Dante, a young, ambitious woman who was bitter before her time because the Head Archivist was only a year older than her; the job would never be Semele's and Semele craved power. Elvon L'Belder had a sympathetic face and the friendship had started because Semele needed someone to moan to. She liked to tell L'Belder how the Head Archivist was sloppy in her work, disorganised, impatient. L'Belder would nod understandingly. Eventually, further confidences had taken place. Semele also liked to gossip. She had friends who worked in the Chamber of Government on the floor above the Archives. Occasionally, Semele would tell L'Belder things that men in the street would never get to hear. She told him in confidence, which at first, was respected. When Elvon L'Belder first went to work in the Archives he could never have been termed an active dissident. Eventually, as his views strengthened, he'd managed to hand his job to a friend. Semele was just as happy to talk to her, which released L'Belder to take a more active political stance. There was no way he could have kept his job in the palace if he'd spoken out while working there, and he realised quickly that an ear beside the mouth of Semele Dante was quite an asset to any rebellious cause and the continuance of such an asset must be ensured. But it was not from Semele that the dissidents learned of the Great Plan of the Dominatrix. No, that came from higher up, from a source that, unfortunately, had now been rendered silent. The plan would affect everyone. It was far-fetched, but chilling in its detail. Yani Gisbandrun believed in her plan and would stop at nothing to implement it. Of course, because of its rather extreme nature, it might be that the implementation would need

60

physical force behind it. That too, had been worked out. The Dominatrix was ready. All she had to do now was lull the majority of her people into accepting it. There would be promises of vast benefits; many would fall for that, even those who, at the moment, might sympathise with the dissidents' cause. L'Belder also distrusted people's ability to see beyond the boundaries of their own fences, thinking that because her initial measures might not affect them directly, they could be ignored. It was terrifying to think of what might come next. Maybe women with red hair would be ostracised and bred out of the community or people who were left-handed. Unfortunately, the Dominatrix possessed the same qualities as L'Belder; great charisma and a power to convince. She also possessed the advantage of being female; more people would listen to her and the men needed the support of women. So, L'Belder had realised he'd have to risk his neck and speak out – loudly. The people must learn what was going on – before it was too late. The Dominatrix was weaning her women away from men, but she was doing it slowly. There had still been time. L'Belder realised the risk he was taking. His group of supporters numbered just about a hundred, but it was too dangerous for them all to meet at once. Large gatherings attracted unwanted eyes. So the news had to be imparted selectively and one of the selections had been wrong. Luckily, the dissidents had a contact who had a friend working for Carmenya Oralien. Through her had come a warning. 'Get L'Belder out of Silven Crescent; now! Tell your people to destroy all evidence that they ever knew him; now!' He had been ready to make his stand, but never got the chance. Now, it was up to Rosanel to carry on, if she had the stomach for it. Rosanel. He was relieved he could still conjure up an image of her face. So often the memory of a friend's face could fade with time. He'd been under no illusions about how passionately she was devoted to his cause. He knew that the passion and devotion had been for himself, that without him she might not ever have thought about the fate of men. It was possible Rosanel had turned her back on it now. He remembered her face when she'd told

61

him the news of his imminent arrest. They'd known that Carmenya Oralien would soon be at the house. They'd had so little time for goodbyes. He'd not said enough to her. He should have fuelled the fire that would keep the cause burning within her. No time. In the upstairs gallery of the house on Freda Street, he'd hidden between the boards of the wall and the bricks themselves, almost squashed flat. That night, he'd made his escape to the marsh.

L'Belder didn't know if he was really looking for the fairytale Greylids. He was certainly looking for hope and inspiration and knowledge of how to fight, but had no idea of how he could convince the Greylids to help him even if he found them. He had no real plans at all. What had happened to his friends in the city? Had they all been discovered? What of Rosanel herself? He shook his head with pain; no, he did not want to think of her. Live for the moment, he told himself. You are still alive; think of that. Rain began a furtive patter on the wooden roof of the boathouse. Wind came through cracks in the walls, finding him, finding his bones at which it gnawed with relish.

CHAPTER TEN

CORINNA WAS NOT pleased that the afternoon turned out so dreary. She'd hoped to take other danks out onto the marsh and had thought about going as far as Imo Guardwell's farm, where she had an occasionally kept up friendship with Imo's daughter Kirsten. Kirsten was a bit of a lump, but a well-meaning soul. Sometimes she could be infuriatingly stupid for the quick-brained Corinna, but she was often good fun to be with. Now the thought of getting wet during a two hour ride put Corinna off going. This annoyed Dannel because Dannel had decided she wanted to borrow the Guardwell's wide-boat to harvest the boundary pasture. That area was nearly always well under water and Dannel was anxious to gather the shemble frack there before the promised storm arrived. Corinna had no desire to take the even longer route home so she could float the wide boat back to Vangery. A brief argument ensued with Corinna storming off to the stables to clean Fitching's legs and change bedding. This left Dannel agonising over wildly imaginative speculations as to why Corinna's behaviour seemed so changed recently. Thunder squealed and scraped in the south, where the sky was dirty pink and purple. Everyone in Vangery was on edge that day.

Meonel went out to the sauna shack and had Shyya pamper him until breadlemen, but his head was still full of pain and nothing could shift it. By the time it got dark and the house was fragrant with cooking meat, Carmenya had still not returned from the marsh. The family sat down to eat without her.

'I'll give it two days,' Bolivia intoned, fastidiously cutting her meat into squares. 'Two days to the storm.'

'How long is Carmenya here for?' Corinna asked quickly, realising she had perhaps only those two days to do something with the fugitive in the boathouse.

'She hasn't told me,' Dannel said. Bolivia looked up inquisitively at her mother's sharp tone. 'Meonel, you're not eating. What's the matter? Are you unwell?'

'A headache, Dannel, that's all. Probably caused by the approaching storm.' He put down his knife and fork, now he no longer had to pretend he had an appetite. 'Would you all excuse me if I went to my room now?'

'Yes, yes,' Dannel said impatiently, waving her fork at him. Corinna caught his eye and smiled, but he didn't smile back.

'What's the matter with everybody?' Bolivia asked, once Meonel had gone.

'I'm alright,' Orblin said, which everyone ignored.

'What do you mean, Bolivia?' Dannel asked.

'Well, there isn't an even temper in the house, is there? Do you know, Gabriel had the affrontery to answer me back this morning! It's even affecting the servants you see.'

'I expect it's because of Carmenya being here,' Corinna said. 'You can't blame the men for being wary of her.'

'And it's not just the men that seem affected by her presence,' Dannel said meaningfully. Corinna went scarlet, which confirmed some of Dannel's suspicions.

'Is she coming back tonight?' Corinna asked. Dannel had noticed how the girl had been glancing out of the window throughout the meal. Was she that obsessed with Carmenya? What had been going on between those two? Carmenya had no right to initiate anything without Dannel's permission.

'Why are you so concerned, Corinna?'

'I'm not. I just wondered.'

'Perhaps she found her fugitive,' Orblin said, with relish. 'Perhaps we'll get to see the body, if there's anything left of it.'

'Don't be disgusting, Orblin,' Dannel said. 'This is a family mealtime. If you have to be gruesome, please wait

64

until we've finished eating.'

'There's nothing gruesome about that, mother,' Bolivia said. 'It's what we should all be hoping for.'

Dannel caught Corinna's eye. The girl looked ready to jump out of her skin. What *was* she up to?

'Do you think anyone on the marsh *would* help him?' Bolivia wondered. 'Would anyone be so foolish?'

'I don't think it's anything to do with us,' Corinna said.

'You look green, Corinna. Has Kirsten or Sander told you something?'

'No! Shut up, Bolivia! Who do you think you are to make snide suggestions like that?!'

'Alright, alright, that's enough!' Dannel growled. 'I expect Carmenya will go back to the city before the storm comes. Then perhaps we can get on with our lives as normal. We'll have to work hard. It's a good crop this year and we don't want to lose any of it.'

'Well, if our dear Corinna spent less time flapping about on the marsh, it might help!' Bolivia spat.

'Bolivia, be quiet! Finish your meals. You can all help the men with some sorting of stock later.' Dannel couldn't help wondering how on earth such a reedy, sour creature as Bolivia could have come from her own body. The girls' father hadn't had an evil bone in him either. Sometimes, when she's got one of her moods on her, I'd hate her, if she wasn't my daughter, Dannel thought. In some respects, Dannel would far have preferred to leave Vangery to Corinna, who though whimsical because of her age, would mature into a shrewd and hard-working woman. But the law decreed that the first-born daughter should inherit, so unless Bolivia should meet with an unforeseen accident, the farm would one day be hers. Sometimes Dannel felt that she'd rather burn the place and all the staff with it, than let them fall into Bolivia's cold hands. Even as a baby, Bolivia had been thin and spiteful. Dannel's own mother had told her, 'there's trouble in that one, Danny. A dark soul if ever I saw one.' At the time, Dannel had protested against such a pronouncement fiercely, being full of maternal love for her first born. In fact, only during the last year or so had she admitted to·

herself that Bolivia's softer side, if it existed, had never manifested itself to her at all. It was all self, self, self with that one. Now Corinna seemed to be going peculiar as well. Goddess, will I be glad when Carmenya leaves here! Dannel thought furiously.

After the meal, Corinna was itching to visit Elvon L'Belder again. She had thought about taking him some warm blankets and hot food this time. It must be miserable out there in the boathouse for him all alone, wondering whether Carmenya was going to burst in on him at any moment. She was still toying with the idea of telling Shyya about it, but it was difficult to get Shyya alone, and she wondered whether it would be really fair of her to involve him anyway. Managing to sneak away from Orblin and Bolivia, she went down to the kitchens and examined the contents of the pots on the huge stove. Meat was simmering in gravy for the servants' evening meal. 'Can I have some of this?' Corinna asked the cook.

'If you want to,' Gabriel replied, though he was wondering why she wanted more food after such a big meal.

'Could you put some in a carrying pot for me? I'll take it down to the stables. I still have some work to do in there.'

'Alright.'

'And could I have a flask of hot milk-suds and bitters?'

Gabriel laughed. 'Corinna, I've never known you to have such an appetite!'

'Oh, Bolivia was on form during dinner and it put me off eating. Know what I mean?'

Gabriel gave her a dry smile, but did not comment. He was another of Dannel's handsome young finds, who habitually got his underlings to do most of his work so that he could preen and look beautiful in case anyone interesting came in. Meonel was probably the most interesting person in Vangery and he wouldn't notice if someone had their head on backwards, so it was largely a waste of time on Gabriel's part.

Corinna thanked him and crept off down the back steps of the house. It was still raining outside, but not as hard.

Vangery isle was clothed in mist. The landing lights were on and so were the stable lights. Corinna hurried past them. She ran down the steps into the rock garden, looking back over her shoulder at the house. She could see no-one. In the shrubbery, it was dark, and comforting because of that, but Corinna kept one ear open for the hum of skippers approaching. She hurried through the darkness, sometimes sliding on the damp stone, trying to keep the pot of stew upright. The boathouse loomed up ahead of her, and there was greyness all across the marsh; the ghost grey of fog.

Dannel had sat for some moments alone after her family left the dinner table. Only two low lights burned upon the walls, peaceful, orange light that made the room beautiful. Even the remains of food upon the plates had a mournful, nostalgic quality. She felt restless, uneasy. Corinna's earlier questions had disturbed her more than she could admit to herself. The Greylids. What were they? Had they ever been real? Marsh-gazing was one of Dannel's favourite pastimes. She liked to sit at night, trying to penetrate the secrets of her beloved homeland, letting its force wash over her, through the windows of her house. She knew the land was old, the planet ancient. In her youth, at the College in the city, the history of Artemis before colonisation was barely touched upon. It seemed almost a taboo subject. Dannel was far from stupid. As a girl, she had realised that three hundred years ago, somebody must have surveyed this world to ensure that it was habitable for human life. It was a Paradise, so why had there been no superior, intelligent race living upon it then? It really made no sense when you thought about it. And what made even less sense, to Dannel, was that none of the Artemisians ever *did* think about it. Human beings occupied such a small area of Artemis. She knew they had all they needed here, but why had no-one ever wanted to investigate further? On the other side of the world might there not be native Artemisians living unaware of the colony? It was possible, wasn't it? There *were* ruins on the marsh, but it was always said that these were of buildings that the first Artemesians had built, that had been destroyed during conflict in the past. And there was another puzzle. If the colonists had fled another world to found a peaceful society, why had there been conflict anyway? There were so many questions unanswered and nobody seemed to care about that. People were ridiculously short-sighted, almost dangerously so. Dannel had also learned that it was frowned upon to ask those questions. In College she'd once aproached one of the tutors and enquired, 'Was Artemis once populated by intelligent beings, before we came?' The tutor had stared at her hard. She replied, 'Dannel, our ancestors came here to build a new society. We went back to the land because our own land had been murdered. Artemis has no past to us; it cannot affect us. We love this world and nurture it. Lessons have been learned about greed and ambition. If there were people here before us, they wiped themselves out, so we could only contaminate ourselves by learning about them. Do you understand?'

'Is that why we never go beyond the Four Cities and the marsh?'

'Dannel! Such inquisitiveness about the past is fruitless. Think about the future; your future. We have no need to extend our boundaries; to even think of it is greedy. We have all that we require to live and grow within the boundaries we know. The area is vast. It is doubtful whether you could explore it all within your own lifetime. Why should we want more?'

'Curiosity,' Dannel persisted. 'Not to acquire but to *see*.'

'Precisely,' her tutor replied, feeling Dannel's words had illustrated emphatically what she'd been trying to point out. Dannel never learned anything more than that. Now she contented herself with solitary wondering, pensively staring at the marsh at night. Sometimes, it seemed to stare back.

She pushed her chair away from the table and got heavily to her feet. Moving slowly, she doused both the lights and the room was in darkness. She felt her way to the window, somehow more graceful in the dark. Outside fog moved steadily from west to east. If you stared hard enough until your eyes went out of focus, it looked like a cloud of restless spirits. Dannel could almost see forms within it, open mouths, eyes turned upwards. Where was Carmenya? Had she found her fugitive? Did she suspect Dannel of traitorous thoughts? It was even possible that Carmenya had become lost in the fog. Even as she denied it, that thought gave Dannel a brief thrill of relief. Then Dannel saw movement and the quality of that movement spoke of furtiveness, secrecy. She squinted through the glass, half wrapped in a curtain, concealed. She saw her daughter Corinna scurrying past the stables. She saw the girl pause and glance guiltily at the house, before hurrying on, down the steps to the rockery, towards the landing. Dannel's heart almost stopped. Immediately the thought that Corinna was going to meet Carmenya shot into her mind with such force that it was undeniable. To Dannel, it was positive proof. Filled by an uncharacteristic rage, she virtually ran across the room and threw herself into the corridor beyond, where peace reigned in a glow of mellow light. The little bitch! Dannel was thinking. She paused only to grab a shawl as protection against the stinging fog before she left the house. She followed Corinna.

CHAPTER ELEVEN

AGAIN, L'BELDER ATE the food Corinna had brought him like a famished dog. Corinna sat on the damp boards and watched him in silence. She waited until he had finished, which wasn't long, before she said, 'There is not much time. Within two days, the storm will come and this building will be mostly underwater.' She pointed at the ceiling some twenty feet above them. 'You see those beams up there. That will be the only dry place. You can't stay here. The boathouse must be cleared of tools. I'll do that myself, which will give you more time, but you can't stay here.'

L'Belder stared at her almost stupidly. 'Then what can I do?'

Corinna shrugged. 'I don't know. There are places on the marsh you could hide in, but there is no way of telling which will be flooded.'

L'Belder looked at the boats. 'What about in one of those?' Corinna laughed, she couldn't help it. 'It will be very difficult for me to bring food out for you; I'd probably have to swim for a week. You'd be so cold, you'd die of exposure.'

'It's the only chance I have though, isn't it?'

'L'Belder, what *are* you going to do? You can't stay here forever!' She knew as well as he did that there was little he could do. Corinna had a vague idea that she'd have to equip him as best she could, give him a dank and send him off northwards. She'd have to let all the danks loose to disguise his taking one. It was possible they'd lose all of them. That was too big a sacrifice to make for this bedraggled renegade, but she knew she couldn't send him

70

off on foot, not in the winter. She had no idea what the marsh families were like farther north. Perhaps one of them would help him.

'Tonight, I wish I was dead,' he said and his face was in his hands. Corinna put her hand on his arm. The flesh was freezing through damp cloth.

'I only wish I could help you more,' she said.

'You're risking enough as it is,' he answered and put his cold hand over hers.

'Carmenya is looking hard,' she said. 'They've not come back yet.' They huddled together in silence, the only sounds being the drip of moisture from the eaves of the boathouse, the slap of water on wood. L'Belder shuddered. Corinna realised he was weeping. Her limbs ached; she wanted to move, but dared not. An idea was taking shape in her mind. In some ways, it was too awful to think about, but perhaps the only option available to either of them.

'L'Belder,' she said. 'There is only one thing we can do. It is the only way for you to escape safely and quickly. I shall have to lead you. I shall have to come with you.'

He pulled away from her then. 'No,' he said, but his eyes were full of life and hope.

'I shall have to. You'd never manage on your own; you haven't a clue how to survive. That way, we'll only lose two danks as well.'

'What do you mean?'

She shook her head. 'Don't worry about it. My only choice for the future is Carmenya and the city anyway. Maybe this is a chance I'll have to take. I may change my mind in the morning. I don't know.'

He put his arms around her. 'Corinna, you are an angel.'

'I don't know what I am, but I don't think it's that,' she said, leaning stiffly away from him. 'I love this land. I don't want to leave it. I know I could live out there. We could go towards the forests, escape the floods . . .' After a moment's hesitation, she hugged him back, fiercely. 'L'Belder, I, too, could escape!'

Corinna felt a great, haunting weight slink away from

71

her shoulders. Already she was free. She had made the decision. It would be hard, but she knew she could do it.

The door to the boathouse banged open.

Corinna and L'Belder froze. There were no lights, only a shadow in the doorway, which seemed to fill it. L'Belder said, 'Goddess!' and the shadow said, in a voice barely recognisable, so confused it was by the rage and shock.

'Corinna, what the hell are you doing?!'

'Mother!'

'Get over here! Now!'

There was a moment's silence. 'Corinna . . .' Dannel advanced into the boathouse. In the dim light she could see her daughter huddled against a gaunt, bearded man dressed in filthy rags. She'd heard little of their conversation, but enough. This man could be none other than Carmenya's fugitive. Corinna had surprised her in every conceivable way, and when the shock wore off, Dannel would realise that the surprise was not exactly unpleasant. 'Before you try to deny anything, I'll warn you, I heard what you were saying. Corinna, you should have heard yourself! Are you mad? It would be suicide!'

'Mother, I have to go,' Corinna said.

'Corinna, you can't. Your future . . . I won't let you.'

'You'll have to tell Carmenya then!'

Dannel looked at them both. They were backed into a corner, but she could tell they were prepared to fight. Corinna looked as if she thought the end of the world had come. It was no coincidence that man had found his way here, no, not at all. It was justice, and justice that had a wry sense of black humour alright.

'Corinna, get back to the house. Now! We shall have to talk before Carmenya's brought into this.' (If she ever is, a sly voice whispered in Dannel's brain.)

'No!' Corinna cried. She had not, of course, heard the sly voice herself.

'Corinna . . .'

'Hush!' This was L'Belder. Suddenly alert and swift, he shot over to the window. Now he was prey, and fleet because of it. 'Look,' he said, 'Listen.' Yellow light glowed in the distance. A hum could be heard.

'Skippers!' Corinna cried. 'Carmenya!' She looked at her mother, wretched. Dannel took her arm.

'Come on,' she ordered. 'Quick!'

'Too late,' Corinna said. 'They'll see us coming out of here. There's no cover!'

'Shut up!' Dannel said.

'She means to betray me,' L'Belder growled and for the first time he looked menacing.

'You shut up as well! Get into the tarpaulins. Corinna, to the back of the shed. Now!' Dannel pushed her daughter ahead of her, waddling quickly behind.

'What, mother, what?' Corinna said in a low, urgent voice, staring at the back wall, half obscured by ropes and cans and tarpaulins. Dannel pushed past her and tore at the junk, rabidly, throwing things up behind her. She turned a grimed face towards her daughter. In the yellow light of the beaching skippers, Corinna could see a wild expression on that face, an exaltation.

'Here!' Dannel hissed, beckoning. Corinna hovered, uncertain. Beyond Dannel, the junk, the tarpaulins, another door had been revealed. It was heavily barred. 'Help me!' Dannel insisted, before beginning to rip at the planks nailed across the door. Corinna picked her way over the rubbish and curled her fingers round the plank. Woods shrieked, nails spat. It seemed to take an eternity. Corinna felt slivers of wood slide into her skin, one right down the side of a fingernail, but she did not stop. Dannel panted and groaned behind her. In the distance, Corinna could hear Carmenya's voice shouting orders. It was too late! Then, with a final heave, the door was open. Mother and daughter spilled out, gasping, into the chilly fog, through the briars of a thick plaisel shrub. Dannel yanked Corinna out by her arm, almost dislocating her shoulder. 'The stables' she said. 'Hurry. Round the back.' Almost double Corinna scuttled forward. She could still hear Carmenya's voice coming from the landing. She could hear her laughing. There was one hideous moment when she had to shoot across a couple of feet of open space, unshrouded by shrubs to gain access to the back of the

73

stables. Dannel was behind her and Corinna let her mother guide her. They ran towards the sauna shack. Dannel threw Corinna inside. 'Take off your clothes! Hurry!' she ordered. Already Dannel was fumbling to ignite the charcoal beneath the stones. Corinna turned on the light and crouched, shaking and grimed, on the topmost bench. Dannel clambered up beside her and sat blinking. Corinna laughed.

'This is ridiculous!'

'Is it?'

'They must have heard us bursting out of the boat-house!'

'No, I don't think so, the skippers were still running.'

'Are you sure?'

'As sure as I can be.' Already heat was invading the wooden room. Dannel hauled a metal tub of water from under the bench and began to wash her face and hands. Corinna stared at her for a moment as the reality of the situation began to sink in.

'Mother, why are you doing this?' she asked. 'You know who that man is, don't you?'

'Of course.'

'Then why?'

'Why were you in there, offering help?'

'Because I . . .' She shook her head. 'I think Carmenya is wrong to hunt him.'

Dannel turned and stared at her daughter. 'That's the trouble with young people,' she said. 'They think they're the only ones that know anything. I have to think. I can't give you a proper answer yet; I have to think.'

What had really happened was that from the moment she'd seen Corinna and the fugitive together, the inner Dannel had scrambled from darkness to light. A strong protective urge had blossomed, some great triumph screamed in release. It was never in doubt that Dannel would have acted the way she did. Never.

CHAPTER TWELVE

WHEN DANNEL THOUGHT the coast was clear, the two women wrapped themselves in towels and climbed the steps to the rear entrance of the house. They could hear loud, city voices coming from the kitchens. One of them was ribbing a member of Dannel's staff. Mother looked at daughter in silence; an empathy warmed between them. 'Go to your room,' Dannel said.

'Mother . . .'

'Tomorrow, rise early and begin clearing the boathouse before the storm comes. I will see you later.' Corinna looked worried. Dannel smiled. 'Go to bed now. Don't worry. You can leave it all to me.' Corinna nodded.

The morning dawned, lit by brave, weak sunlight fighting through cracks in the heavy cloud. Corinna had hardly slept. She rose at daybreak, dressed in her scruffiest workclothes and took some breakfast down to the boathouse. Walking down the path towards the rockery, it felt as if a hundred eyes were boring into her back. She tried to whistle light-heartedly and failed. L'Belder looked as manic as a cornered smoom when she went in. She almost had to coax him out to eat.

'Has your mother said anything?' he asked.

'She won't,' Corinna said, hoping she was right. 'When you've finished eating, get back in hiding. I have work to do.' She looked at the back of the shed. Apparently, L'Belder had risked trying to patch up her escape route, probably to keep the cold out. Most of the stuff had been fixed to the wall, rubbish that had rotted there for seasons. She hadn't known about the door. She began to carry empty fuel cans outside. How could so much junk accumulate in just one summer? Then came the ropes, empty boxes. She heaped them next to the landing. After an hour or so, Carmenya and her women came stomping down to their skippers. Carmenya paused to speak with Corinna.

'Well, another long day ahead of us!' she said. 'It surprises me. I thought we'd find the feeble fool by now.'

'Perhaps he's dead,' Corinna said. 'Some of the marsh animals may have eaten him. There have been carnivores sighted in this region occasionally.'

'Maybe,' Carmenya agreed reluctantly. She clearly wanted to take proof of L'Belder's demise back to the Dominatrix. 'We'll have to give up soon, in any case. No good searching in the storm. If he's still out there, he'll be dead after that anyway. The only thing left for us to do is search the outbuildings of the farms. We started yesterday in the north. Shouldn't take long, but I have to be sure.'

'Yes,' Corinna said, 'I suppose you do.'

'We must speak together soon, Corinna,' Carmenya said in a new voice, 'about your coming to the city. Obviously your mother needs you to help with the harvest right now, but perhaps in a few weeks, between the storms, you could come south. I'll have a house ready for you, if you prefer not to live at court at first.'

'Very well, we'll speak about it.'

'You don't seem very keen, Corinna. Perhaps you'd better tell me why not. Are you afraid of me?'

That must be the usual reason, Corinna thought sharply. She shrugged. 'No, it's not that.'

'Well, we'll talk about it later. o.k.?'

Corinna nodded. 'Yes, o.k.'

The General turned away and leapt onto the nearest skipper, lean and as nimble as a smoom. Corinna went back to her work, heart pounding. What was going to happen? What was going to happen? Her mind whirled.

Dannel made it known that Corinna was clearing the boathouse. She organised the household so that everyone would keep away from there, a spark of inspiration advising her to send Bolivia over to the Guardwell's to ask

for the wide-boat. Bolivia was not pleased, especially as
Dannel told her to take Orblin with her, but could produce
no reasonable excuse to get out of it. Dannel felt safer with
Bolivia out of the way. She had made up her mind to do
everything she could to prevent Elvon L'Belder from
falling into General Oralien's hands. It was as if her
fantasies had become real. It was going to be difficult
hiding him until Carmenya left, but Dannel had an idea.

Just as she was putting on her workboots and coat to go
down to the boathouse a knock came on her study door.
Hissing with irritation, she said, 'Come!' It was her
husband's attendent, Shyya. Dannel liked Shyya. She'd
thought his strange, mystical quality would have been
good for Meonel, but there'd been no visible proof of this
yet.

'What is it, Shyya? I'm very busy today.'

'I have to speak with you, Madam.'

'Can't it wait until later?'

'It could, but it won't take much of your time. I think
you should know.' Dannel sat down, heavy with presentiment.

'Well?'

'It is your husband . . . He is not well, Madam.'

'Not well? What do you mean, not well?' She didn't
mean to sound so sharp, or so cold. 'He looks alright to
me! Is he in pain? What symptoms are there?'

'You misunderstand me, madam. It is not that kind of
sickness.'

'What are you talking about, Shyya. I have no time for
riddles. Speak your mind if you feel you have to!'

'He is melancholy. He is fading.'

'What! Oh for the Goddess's sake!' She threw up her
hands. 'Meonel has always been *melancholy*, Shyya, for
years before you came here. It is in his nature. He enjoys
it. Don't let it bother you. He won't notice if it does.'

'Perhaps he notices more than you think.' There was a
lack of servility in his tone that made Dannel sit up. She
stared narrowly at him. He was an impressive creature,
like a tussock antelope with the heart and claws of a
smoom. She felt it would be a great pleasure to touch his

77

skin, if not his soul. She'd known for a long time Meonel had no interest in her. They'd had sex but had never made love. It had always been a trial for Meonel, no matter how hard she tried to please him. Her body revolted him; she was not blind to that, and because she was female he would not let himself see her mind. It had been an act of utter selflessness on her part to buy him Shyya. She loved Meonel and wanted him, but had only made him lonely and sad. She'd thought, in buying Shyya, to provide him with a lover, to make him live a little, but apparently this had not come to be.

'Shyya, what the hell do you expect me to do about this? Will you tell me that?'

He looked taken aback. 'Do? Nothing. I just thought you should know.'

She stood up. 'Do you know why I bought you? To bring that skulking, proud husband of mine back to life! That's why. Don't ever presume I don't know what's going on around here. Do what I bought you for. Get through to him!'

'Perhaps if he had more freedom . . .'

Dannel sighed, deeply. 'Shyya, Meonel has all the freedom he wants. He barely works, he has everything. I don't like any member of my family going out alone because of the simple reason that it is dangerous. Meonel is not hardened; he doesn't know the dangers, wouldn't recognise them. But if he wants the freedom of the marsh, then take him out there. Just make sure you bring him back! If he thinks he's imprisoned, he's put himself there. I haven't. Now, I've been very forbearing with you, haven't I? Be a good boy and get back to work!'

Shyya hesitated a moment and then nodded. 'I'm sorry. I didn't mean to insult you.'

'Oh in a way I'm to blame. Perhaps I should have told you this from the beginning. I was too busy.'

'I didn't understand, Madam. I will do as you suggest.'

He's a strange one, Dannel thought as she locked her study door. It had surprised her, him coming to see her. Shyya didn't normally appear to take much interest in what went on in Vangery, exhibiting an aloof kind of tolerance which annoyed the rest of the men. They were all frightened of him because of his mutilation, she knew. It was a superstitious fear, as if they got too close it could affect them too. Men were unpredictable creatures, she thought.

Meonel did not greet Shyya's suggestion of a ride on the marsh with any visible degree of enthusiasm. He looked suspicious and withdrawn. Shyya decided not to mention he'd spoken with Dannel about it.

'I have a headache,' Meonel said. Shyya relentlessly held out his coat.

'Then fresh air will clear it, sir.'

'I'm not allowed on the marsh.'

'Not alone, no, but I will be with you.'

'And what protection would you be?' Meonel asked meanly. Shyya ignored the question.

'We needn't go far; just an hour's ride.'

Meonel could tell his attendant was not going to give up on this. With a sigh, he snatched his coat and put it on.

It had been a long time since Meonel had ridden a dank. He felt uneasy, unsafe, so high from the ground. The animal, sensing this unease, was tense beneath his thighs, large ears back, head up. Shyya was leading the way, trotting his dank across the water-logged causeway.

'Where are we going?' Meonel asked in a grumpy voice.

'Don't know,' Shyya answered. He urged his mount into a lope and Meonel's jerkily followed suit. They circled widely round the boathouse to the right, the animals knee-deep in water now, their splayed feet sucking at mud and ooze. A gang of wervels followed them for a while, proclaiming in high voices. Meonel found that he was quite enjoying himself. Shyya was right, the air did feel good in his lungs, sweeping lethargy from his head and eyes. He considered why Shyya had suddenly decided to take such an interest in his welfare. Had it simply been sparked off by Corinna? Perhaps, if he'd dared to make the first move, mouth the first sentence, before, he and Shyya could have been friends these last few months. They could have explored the marsh in summer together. Meonel regretted he'd been so cynical and cowardly. They headed north.

79

After an hour neither of them had suggested heading back to Vangery. 'There is so much to see,' Shyya said, and for once, Meonel agreed. He'd forgotten how wild and lovely the landscape was, even though the last time he'd seen it in any depth had been whilst fettered to the slave wagons, heading south to Stilt Vashti and the cities. He reflected, for the first time ever, that in many ways he'd been lucky that Dannel had bought him. Because of his looks, a home in the city would probably have meant slavery of the most degrading and perverse nature. Perhaps, like Shyya, he would have been gelded to preserve his youth. 'You should have come out here before,' Shyya said, breaking his reverie. Meonel shrugged.

'I told you; Dannel wouldn't allow it.'

'You make it sound like she keeps you in chains. She doesn't.'

'Chains are not always visible,' Meonel replied defensively. 'Anyway, Dannel's first husband was virtually killed by the marsh. That's why she was afraid to let me out. It's been years. Perhaps she's losing interest now. Perhaps it would serve her purpose to have me die out here, so she can buy a new husband, who may even like her.' Shyya laughed out loud. Meonel was stung.

'I think you enjoy being miserable.'

'Oh, do you! As a slave's slave you have no right to make such observations. Be quiet.'

Shyya didn't laugh again, but kept smiling. Meonel urged his dank ahead.

They came upon a belt of lofty mossbarks, lifted high on their roots so they appeared to be standing on tip toe in the water. Lichened hillocks protruded like the backs of huge swimming animals among them. The danks clambered up the nearest one, seemingly thankful to be on dry ground again, shaking their feet and heads. At the top, Shyya dismounted and started to investigate the trees. Meonel rode to the farthest side of the hillock, where the mossbarks shrank back from the water. To the north a cable of hillocks, rock-tables and gnarled amber oaks wound into a misty distance. The marsh was alive with animal life. Herds of antelope and giant, barred oxen browsed together through natural fields of wild rice and shemble frack and ground cherry. Flocks of birds lifted and swooped like wind-tossed billows of fabric, hanging motionless in the air before descending once more with eerie cries. A couple of well-fed smooms stalked stiffly by the edge of the herds, ignoring such easy prey with whiskered disdain. Meonel's dank sneezed and nibbled the horny claws on its front feet. He dismounted. This must be an enchanted place, he thought. The colours were incredible. Behind him, he could see Shyya, pale amongst the piercing green and velvet crimson of mossy tree trunks. He was carrying a large tree fungus. How can he be so happy, Meonel wondered. He has been destroyed. What lives on is barely human . . . surely. Shyya seemed oblivious of such considerations. He was unselfconsciously enjoying himself, poking around in the moss and pebbles, finding treasures. Meonel had never seen him like that before. I must bore him rigid, he thought, and sighed, turning once more to gaze out at the marsh. Shyya joined him.

'What's going on over there?' he asked, pointing. Meonel narrowed his eyes. Some miles northwest, the birds circled in worried spirals, as if reluctant to land. This phenomenon was above a rock-table but, apart from that, there was nothing unusual to see.

'Let's go and have a look,' Shyya said, leaping onto his dank's back. Out in the open, away from Vangery, he appeared to have forgotten who was master. His vitality was overflowing but perhaps too private to infect his companion.

'What for? There's nothing. The birds are just spooked,' Meonel answered, thinking it was a good half hour's ride at a fast lope.

'No, something's going on.'

'How can you tell?'

'I just know. Come on.'

'It may be dangerous.'

Shyya rolled his eyes and started his dank skidding down the hillock bank. Meonel didn't want to be left there alone, but neither did he want to appear petty by issuing an order for Shyya to stop. He scrambled into his saddle and followed.

CHAPTER THIRTEEN

As a child, Dannel had found a secret place on the marsh, which she had made uniquely her own. She hadn't thought about it for years; her life no longer included solitary wanderings, except in her head. Some miles northeast of Vangery was a large, weathered rock-table, skirted by thick plaisel and youthful amber-oak scrub. Seed lichens shook and shivered like liquid, a veil before the entrance to a small, dry cave, halfway up the table. The entrance was invisible from the marsh and it had been quite by accident that Dannel had discovered it. When she was younger, Dannel often used to live out her fantasies in the people-free but teeming tussocks and spinneys around the rock table. In her imagination, here lived the goat-footed ones, the Free Spirits, neither angeldt or flamist, perhaps neither male or female in the accepted sense. Dannel believed that if she concentrated hard enough she would eventually get to see these creatures with her living eyes, but unfortunately, adolescence brought with it a swift wave that swept her dreams away. Reality intruded as her mother delegated more responsibility for the farm to her eldest daughter. Her visits to the rock table became less regular and the spirit of the place seemed to draw away from her. Eventually, she stopped going there altogether, because it no longer brought her happiness, but grief for what she had lost or perhaps had never even quite found. However, it was the ideal place for Elvon L'Belder to hide in until General Carmenya returned to Silven Crescent. With all her people occupied and Bolivia away from home, Dannel took three saddled danks down to the boathouse and within minutes had

Corinna and L'Belder following her northeast. L'Belder looked at the end of his strength; Dannel hoped he would be warm enough in the cave. Perhaps they could block the entrance with plaisel to keep out the wind. At least he would be safe from the floods there. Dannel only prayed that smooms or dog-bear hadn't decided to make the place their lair. That would cause problems. If L'Belder looked grey and weary, Corinna looked white, her face drawn. She was deep in thought. Dannel wondered what was causing her daughter such anxiety. Was it simply fear of Carmenya finding out what they were doing?

Two hours later, their danks were negotiating a narrow, treacherous path that wound around the flank of the rock-table. A colony of birds nesting on the flat summit, circled round them, squealing in alarm. Dannel pointed out a rarely-seen lizard-bird, who regarded them with placid topaz eyes from a hole in the rock. Neither L'Belder nor Corinna seemed particularly interested in the surroundings.

As Dannel had imagined, the cave was full of marsh rubbish. Smooms had nested here once, it was clear, but their smell was faint and the lichen bedding scattered. Perhaps two years ago, some smoom-she had raised her cubs there. Corinna wrinkled her nose at the piles of droppings and dried bones that littered the floor. It was not a large cave. L'Belder was brushing the roof of it with the top of his head, but it appeared draught-free and wasn't damp. There was a stone ledge that ran around the walls like a bench and to the right was a low hole just large enough to sleep in. Once packed with clean lichen fronds, it would be comfortable and warm. L'Belder sat down on the floor looking dejected. Dannel unpacked the bag of provisions she'd given him. 'You'll have to go out at night to get water,' she said, holding out a large flask. 'Use this; it should hold enough to last for a couple of days at a time.'

'Are you alright?' Corinna asked him. The man smiled.

'Yes, just worn out. I think it'll be frightening when I'm cut off by the floods. How long will that last?'

'Only a few days,' Corinna answered. 'The water level drops very rapidly between storms.'

'Hopefully, Carmenya will be gone soon,' Dannel said.

'Then what?' Corinna voiced the question L'Belder himself had been pondering.

'Well, we must bring him back to Vangery.' Corinna rolled her eyes. 'How? Won't that be dangerous?' She was thinking of Bolivia.

'There are ways. I'll be needing extra help once you go south, Corinna. As far as the household are concerned, L'Belder will be someone I bought in Stilt Vashti. The details can be sorted out later.'

'It seems you've thought of everything,' Corinna said, in a strange tone.

And that surprises you, Dannel thought. She was rather surprised herself. Whatever precautions were taken, it was still going to be a huge risk having L'Belder at the farm. Many niggling details would have to be worked out to make a convincing story should anyone query his presence there. 'Come on, let's get this place sorted out before we leave,' she said. 'Our friend here looks incapable of doing anything.' She started to gather the old lichen fronds.

'I appreciate you don't have to do this,' L'Belder said. 'If it wasn't for your help, I'd be dead.'

Dannel sniffed, embarrassed. 'Eat something. You need strength,' she said. 'Corinna, go out and fill the flask. Bring back as much lichen as you can carry.' L'Belder followed the girl to the mouth of the cave. Well, Dannel thought, well. My place of dreams. It looks smaller. She could almost see herself as a child, sitting on the stone ledge, communing with whatever she'd imagined inhabited that place. Now the cave was silent; not dead, but still withdrawn. She doubted whether she could ever recapture those strange, almost erotic, feelings of her childhood, when tantalising presences had seemed to hover at the edge of her vision. She wondered whether L'Belder would feel anything there. He was leaning against the rock, outlined against the white sky. What was going on in his head? Would he have to stay in Vangery for the rest of his life? Would that be safe? What about his ideals, his cause? Had he given it all up now? He was not how Dannel had ever imagined a rebel to be; he seemed weak, directionless,

85

almost pathetic. Just a dreamer, perhaps. Poor creature. She wanted to say, 'Freedom is out there if you reach for it hard enough', but the Dannel she'd become didn't know how to frame the words. The real Dannel couldn't get past the censor in her brain. The woman within was beautiful, slim and brave; Dannel knew her intimately but never considered her to be real. Reality was bulk and harshness. She worked more furiously to dispel such thoughts, throwing dried lichen and bones angrily out of the cave. L'Belder had to duck aside.

Corinna pushed past the danks and scrambled back down to the marsh. The birds were making a dreadful racket, swooping close to her head. What did they think she'd do to them for the Goddess's sake! She trudged through brackish shallows searching for a pool containing water-fur, a plant whose presence meant the water was drink-able. Now the birds were calling in harmony, describing a spiral in the air above her. It was making her ears hum. There! She recognised the waving fronds of a tussock of water-fur and splashed towards it. Why was her mother getting involved with L'Belder like this? It was not the first time she'd thought it. The moment Dannel had burst into the boathouse, Corinna had felt like she was facing death. Dannel's sympathy was the last thing she'd expected. Things are changing, she thought, and they're changing fast. She dunked the flask into the clear water.

'Corinna! What are you doing here?' The girl nearly fell backwards into the pool. Because of the birds, she hadn't heard danks approaching.

'Meonel?' she said, weakly. It had been tempting fate, thinking about Dannel's uncharacteristic behaviour.

'What are you doing here?'

'Doing? Nothing. Just wandering.'

'Have you *walked* this far?'

'Yes . . .'

'No. There are danks up there, Meonel, look.' Shyya pointed up at the rock table.

'What's going on?' Meonel dismounted. He sensed intrigue. Corinna thought he looked almost animated.

'Mother and I rode out here, that's all. It's none of your business, Meonel. Get back to the farm.' She'd never tried to use that authority with him before; she'd never tried to use it with any man. Meonel wavered. Instinctively, he wanted to back off. Shyya was staring at her, a smile on his face.

'Get back to the farm; both of you!' Corinna said, panic making her voice hard. She dared not look at Shyya. Meonel remounted his dank, his face pinched with repressed pique. It was a familiar expression with him.

'Come on, Shyya. We must leave the women to their mysteries,' he said, stiffly.

'And if anyone asks, we haven't seen you. Right?' Shyya laughed, running one hand through his stripy hair, looking wonderful. Corinna was furious that he was laughing at her, particularly as she preferred to impress him. She watched them turn their beasts around and ride away. 'Damn!' she said, aloud. Would they gossip with the other men now? How had Shyya managed to make her feel such a fool? Damn, damn, damn. She gathered as much lichen as she could carry and stomped back up the narrow path to the cave, snarling and swearing at the birds as they shot in front of her face. Halfway up, she came across L'Belder crouching behind a plaisel.

'Who were they?' he asked.

'Oh don't worry. It was only Meonel, my mother's husband and his attendant. I got rid of them.'

'Had they followed us?'

Corinna paused. 'I . . . don't know,' she said, wondering. 'No, they couldn't have!' She was thinking about how she'd never known Meonel to leave the farm before. Coincidence? She shuddered. 'Come on, let me through. I'd better tell mother.' L'Belder shrank against the rock as she passed, still peering over the plaisels in the direction Meonel had taken home. 'Don't worry,' Corinna called over her shoulder. Now, she was worried sick.

Dannel was like stone when Corinna told her. She carried on with what she was doing, without comment.

'Do you think they did follow us?' Corinna asked.

'Shyya asked to take Meonel out on the marsh,' her

mother replied. 'It's just coincidence they came this way, I'm sure.' It would have made Corinna feel better if Dannel had shown she was worried.

'I don't like it.'

'They're just men, Corinna. Even if they did suspect something of what was going on, I doubt they'd want to tell Carmenya, don't you?' Corinna shrugged. 'That isn't what worries me. They might tell the other men, let something slip . . . into the wrong ears.'

'Hmm, maybe. Just ignore it, Corinna. Letting them see we're being secretive will only whet their curiosity. Best to make out we were doing nothing out of the ordinary. Understand?'

Corinna nodded. 'Yes. I hope you're right.' Suddenly all that they were doing seemed too dangerous. Perhaps it would be better if they never came back here. They'd done all they could. Once the storm had passed, it might be more sensible to let L'Belder fend for himself.

CHAPTER FOURTEEN

MEONEL WAS SITTING on the window-seat in his room. He'd sent Shyya to make him a hot drink because now he'd got home, he felt exhausted. Perhaps it would do him good to go out riding more often. He wondered what his wife and her daughter had been up to at the rock table, although he was aware that there were many things the women did which the men had no part of. This was probably one of them. Shyya had been almost insolent today as well. This made Meonel feel uneasy. If he had no control over a eunuch slave, he had no control at all. Such fears caused him to give Shyya a hard glance when he brought the milk-suds in. 'Sweetened with wasp honey and spice, the way you like it,' Shyya said brightly. He handed Meonel a steaming mug.

'Not having one yourself?' Meonel asked. Shyya ignored this.

'I'm still wondering what those women were up to,' he said.

'It's none of our business, Shyya. Why should we care anyway?'

'Because, it may well be our business,' he said quietly.

'What the hell are you talking about? Don't be insubordinate!'

Shyya ignored the reprimand. 'I mean Corinna; something happened to her the other night.'

'Shyya, this is nothing to do with you. I am your master; the women lead their own lives. I am nothing to them; you are less than nothing.'

'Something happened to her,' Shyya persisted. He leaned forward and lifted aside the flimsy shade at the window. Meonel could smell his clean skin.

'Corinna and Dannel just went for a ride on the marsh this afternoon. That's what Corinna said. Why should we question it, even if it wasn't the truth? I've told you, it's nothing to do with us.'

'Went for a ride together did they? How innocent. Then why are they leading back a third dank, a dank which is wearing a saddle?'

Meonel followed Shyya's gaze. From here the corner of the stable block was clearly visible. Sure enough, Dannel and Corinna were returning from the marsh, leading the third dank.

'Could be any reason for that,' Meonel said, uncertain. Shyya shrugged.

'Could be. But I feel it's more than you think.'

'I don't care.'

Shyya let the shade drop back into place. It shook for a while, creaking into the silence. 'I'm wasting my breath, aren't I?' Shyya said.

Minutes before the Trotgardens sat down to their evening meal, the storm broke. Carmenya and her minions just missed being caught in it. 'I can take a soaking,' one of them had said.

'Soaking doesn't come into it,' Carmenya had replied. 'The force of the rain can beat a person to death out here.' It was true. Winds arose as if from nowhere; furious, tearing winds. Sometimes the house felt like it was waving from side to side on its stilts; it probably was. Before midnight, the gardens were flooded and water was licking at the ramps leading to the stables. Meonel went to bed early with another headache, leaving Shyya alone to stare out at the storm. He stayed in the salon after the meal; servants cleared away behind him, talking about the weather. Once they'd gone, Shyya turned out the lights, and curled up on the window-seat. The cries of the maddened elements outside were hypnotic, almost summoning. Shyya felt the pull; half of him wanted to open the window and let the storm take him. He sat there, visualising Meonel being tossed like a rag between the raging currents of wind and water. He knew it was uncharitable of him to let Meonel exasperate him the way he did. Meonel could not help being what he was. It was just so frustrating, seeing the light at the end of Meonel's tunnel, whilst the man himself just steadfastly stood with his back to it. Shyya didn't think it was weakness exactly; he could see Meonel's reasons for feeling defeated and chained, but whilst Shyya had looked within himself and discovered true freedom, Meonel was a stranger to himself. Dannel had implied that an earthier kind of relationship might be the tonic that Meonel needed. Shyya was not prudish but neither was he keen on initiating anything with so cold a person. Meonel was fond of making veiled and disparaging remarks about Shyya's mutilation. Shyya wasn't sure whether he could open himself up enough to someone whom, basically, he did not trust.

'No moons tonight, are there, Shyya?' Corinna entered the room, wearing a long, black dress and her hair all loose. Shyya knew she had been looking for him.

'No, no moons,' he said. The girl sat down beside him, feet on the floor, looking demure.

'Can you hear voices in the storm?' she asked.

'I've heard things that might be voices.'

'It used to scare me. I was scared that one day I'd hear them say my name.'

'A romantic, if doomed, fancy.'

They both laughed.

'You're very jumpy, Corinna. Is it because of Carmenya being here?'

'In a way,' she answered. 'I'm not sure about going to the city with her.'

'Understandable, but you will learn from it.'

'Learn what?'

'Circumspection, how to hide that you have secrets.'

Corinna looked away. 'You know, don't you?' she said.

Shyya was curious enough not to let this opportunity slip. 'You're like a cornered smoom at the moment. Anyone can see it. Lucky for you Carmenya is here; most people will put it down to that . . . '

'I had no choice, Shyya. No choice.'

'No . . . ?'

'Wouldn't you have done the same? I know you're male, but . . . '

'I'm not you, Corinna. How can I say?'

The girl pressed her face against the cold window. 'I hope he's alright out there. He'll be frightened . . . I wouldn't like to be alone out there.'

Shyya considered this statement. He had an idea of what she was talking about, but it seemed too incredible to be true. A careful response was called for.

'At least the storm will keep Carmenya at bay.'

'Yes, she was hoping to leave before it began. She'll not find him now. Somehow, I know that. I'm glad. He can't harm them. Why should they want to kill him? It's horrible. I don't want to be part of a life like that.'

Some kind of surprise must have been expressed on Shyya's face. Corinna looked at him and frowned.

'Do you think I'm wrong?' she asked, thinking censure was the reason for his expression. Shyya shook his head.

'Of course not. Brave of you to get involved, Corinna. Your mother too?'

Corinna nodded. 'Apparently. I don't know why. She won't tell me. Perhaps it's because we both feel strongly about what goes on in the city, even though we don't get to hear that much.'

'Do you think Bolivia will share your views?'

Corinna wrinkled her nose. 'I doubt it. Mother's working a story out to placate her. Nobody knows what L'Belder looks like. We should be fairly safe.'

'Until the next time Carmenya pays a surprise visit?'

'We can only take things one day at a time. I don't want to see him killed. Not because I care about him as a person particularly, but because of what he stands for.'

'Which is?'

'Freedom of course.'

'But don't you women have your freedom?'

'I used to think so. Now I'm not sure. In the city I'll find out, I expect.'

'You know why the women subjugated the men, don't

you, Corinna?'

She nodded. 'Of course I do. Isn't it just that it's gone too far now?'

'Perhaps it will always be one way or the other. Even if L'Belder achieved his dream for equality, eventually the pendulum might swing and it would be women who'd be the second class citizens again. I'm not convinced humanity is advanced enough to make equality work. Perhaps it's a waste of time, what L'Belder's trying to do. I'm not sure anyone would learn the right lessons from it.'

'I wouldn't have expected to hear you say something like that, Shyya. You always seem so positive, in a secretive kind of way.'

'What makes you think what I've just said isn't being positive?'

'I don't think it is, that's all. Why can't people exist together without this big power struggle thing?'

'It's complicated, Corinna, I know that.'

'You sound as if you know it all.'

'Woman is the male of this world.'

'What do you mean?'

'It's o.k. That could work. It is sort of balanced, I suppose.'

'You're talking in riddles!' she said, starting to smile. He took her hand and he felt the tremor creep right up her arm, which she had the composure to ignore.

'We're not that different,' he said.

'In your case, maybe not,' she couldn't resist adding. Shyya smiled tightly and squeezed her hand.

'Maybe you will learn,' he said.

'You sure? Don't you enjoy mystifying me?'

'Let's just watch the storm,' he said.

They sat together for hours, sometimes talking, sometimes silent. Corinna felt warmed from the core out. Here she was sitting hand in hand with this beautiful, mysterious youth whom she'd admired from afar for so long. He was a slave and virtually sexless. Because of this, she felt their relationship would soar like a bird. She felt happy. Deep in the house, Meonel groaned and tossed on

93

his bed, hands over his closed eyes and the storm cried out in those strange voices that only a sensitive few can her.

The storm raged for two days. In Vangery, Carmenya stalked the house from end to end, complaining about how she wanted to be back at Silven Crescent. Her women were restless, and tormented Dannel's staff mercilessly. Corinna, half her daily chores void because of the weather, spent most of her time with Meonel and Shyya. They invented games and had quite a pleasant time, even though wicked draughts would creep round the bones of the house and find their way inside. Dannel watched her family from the sidelines, mostly lost (and contented) in a world of her own. It was comforting to be able to catch Corinna's eye now and share their secret in unspoken compliance. Although she and Corinna had hardly spoken since taking L'Belder to the marsh, she felt a great deal closer to her daughter than ever before.

Out on the marsh, huddled in the rock table cave, L'Belder shivered and considered his good fortune which, at that particular time, was not feeling particularly good. On one occasion, he tried to build a fire, but it just filled the cave with smoke without giving off any heat. The cave was draught-free though. As Dannel had suggested, he blocked the entrance with bushy plaisel-branches. The women had left him fur blankets and extra clothes. If only he wasn't so soft, so used to city life, where even the lowest of citizens could keep warm. He did not look forward to having to spend the rest of his life on the marsh, working on a farm like Vangery. He was a speaker, an actor, a politician; not a labourer. No use feeling bitter though. Life as a farm-worker must be considered a better fate than death. Mustn't it? 'But you won't see Milady Garmelding, ever again,' a mean, little voice whispered in his brain. 'Don't think of that!' he told himself. Outside, the haunted wind seemed to speak his name.

CHAPTER FIFTEEN

PEOPLE COMMENTED THAT this was the worst storm the southern marsh had suffered for years. An entire skinpine was uprooted on Coneberry Isle and stabbed crownfirst through the wooden stairs leading to Eleanor Shavesock's front door. Two of the Tendaughters' danks were swept clean away because their stables were on a lower level than the others. For two days, the sky boiled; a cauldron of hot, angry colours where the clouds looked like smoke from some vast pyre. Strange storm-smells insinuated themselves through floorboards and around windows; bitter, smoky, electric. On Vangery Isle, General Carmenya became most twitchy. She'd never seen weather conditions like it, and remarked to Dannel that it made her realise how flimsy human beings really were. The storm raged like a giant fist, menacingly threatening them all from the sky. The Trotgardens remained calm. Their animals were safe; the bulk of their harvest gathered. It was unlikely they would suffer any great loss.

On the third morning, the sky was white, clouded but peaceful. The marsh dwellers tentatively began to open their shutters once more and glance nervously at the sky. Dampened fingers were held to the winds. Neighbours galloped danks between the farms to check if their friends were safe and well. Midmorning, a flurry of ice-spears fell from the sky, several of them landing point first in the muddied sward outside Dannel's house. 'Winter is truly on its way now,' Bolivia remarked with ghoulish glee. Meonel groaned, feeling the ice in his bones already, whilst Corinna couldn't keep her nose from the window-glass, staring north.

Carmenya requested that Corinna join herself and Dannel for a 'talk'. Corinna complied impatiently. She was anxious to visit L'Belder, watching the water level like a bird of prey, even though she knew it would not have abated enough for her to travel for at least another day. The same was true, of course, in Carmenya's case. The three women sat in the Facewater Salon and Dannel had Gabriel serve them silvertea and bittersweet biscuits. Carmenya smoked a cheroot, sprawled on a windowseat. Dannel asked Corinna to pour the tea.

'You did not find your rebel then,' Corinna said as she handed the General a cup. Carmenya sniffed.

'He is dead now. No doubt about that.'

'Will you return to Silven Crescent now?'

'Depends on whether the skippers will make it. When do you think, Dannel? Any more storms due?'

Dannel shook her head. 'No, but I would advise you to leave as soon as possible. The weather can be unpredictable on the marsh. Once Winter gets a hold you could be stuck here for months. By tomorrow the water should have dropped enough for travel to be safe.'

'I don't know how you stick it out here!' Carmenya rubbed her arms. The storm had made her feel small, and that made her uneasy.

'Oh, it's not that bad, just what we're used to,' Corinna said. 'I expect I shall discover things in the city that will discomfort me just as much.'

Carmenya assessed her with a narrow eye. 'I still get the impression you're not that happy about the move.'

Corinna shrugged. 'I'd be a liar if I denied it, General,' she said.

'Corinna!' Dannel was sharp with embarrassment. Carmenya raised a hand.

'Oh, it's alright, Danny. Let the girl speak her mind. It's not a man-slave I'm after, is it! She will need her wits about her at court. Silencing her all the time won't help her get ready for that.' She turned fluidly to Corinna. 'Tell me what's on your mind. Perhaps I can ease it.'

'Mainly it's because I'll be amongst strangers,' Corinna began. Carmenya made an eloquent gesture with her arms.

'I'll find you friends,' she said.

'People will find me dull and inexperienced.'

'That worries you?'

'Yes.'

Carmenya assumed a comtemplative frown. Then she said, 'Dannel, would you leave us for a moment, please.' Dannel looked quite surprised; she flushed scarlet and bustled out, muttering. Carmenya smiled at Corinna.

'Now, come and sit here by me,' she said. 'Perhaps you can speak more freely now.'

Corinna's heart was beating far too fast. She realised she was quite afraid. Perhaps Carmenya would be able to read her mind. She sat gingerly on the edge of the window-seat. The General laughed. 'Goddess, do I scare you that much?'

'A little. I feel that you are playing with me.' She risked a glance at the woman, who was sprawled unselfconsciously, looking supremely confident. Corinna envied her.

'Playing with you? No. You're so innocent, Corinna, aren't you!' Corinna felt heat creep up her face from her neck.

'In your eyes, probably. What will my duties be, General?'

'To work in my offices to start with; a more elevated position than the description suggests, I assure you. I have ladies around me; angeldt. They help me with my business, run my house for me. We have men-slaves, but not many. I don't like men around the place. You're overrun with them here, aren't you! It's not like this in Silven Crescent. You'll get used to it.'

'Will you expect me to have children for you?'

Carmenya pulled a face. 'Haven't thought about it! You could, if you wanted to. But not yet. You're too young and children are time-consuming. I want you to enjoy yourself first. Have you had any love affairs, Corinna?'

'What do you mean?' Corinna blustered. 'With *men*?'

Carmenya rolled her eyes. 'Goddess, you really are like animals out here, aren't you. Don't equate love with breeding all the time, my dear. No, I meant with girls your own age, or don't you have time or wit to think about such things?'

Corinna was prepared for this, but couldn't bring herself to say that on the marsh, such liaisons were not quite as *mandatory* as they were in the city. Carmenya was right; the life could often be harsh, which sometimes left little time for idle romances, but the arranged marriages and contracts of harmony between the families never seemed to cause any heartbreak. Sometimes two women might want to set up a new farmstead of their own, occupy an empty isle. These might be girls who were not in line to inherit their family homes, and quite often, they would never marry men. In the city, Corinna knew that women could have children without having to lie with men, something to do with tubes and physicians, but out on the marsh, procreation meant just one thing. Female lovers were often reluctant to have children for that reason. They might employ other women for that in the hope of adopting female heirs for their property. However, Corinna had been due to mate with Sander Tendaughter. She had no lover, male or female. Carmenya took all this in at a glance. She appeared to be considering something. Corinna guessed the General was wondering when to let the axe drop. Would it have to be tonight? Corinna prayed frantically to the Goddess that it was not so. She must have heard.

'We must discuss this more when you come to Silven Crescent,' Carmenya said, looking at Corinna as she might look at that part of a dinner plate where the finest morsel of food lies reserved for later consumption. Corinna smiled gratefully, which Carmenya took as encouragement.

'Your innocence is beguiling,' she said. 'I shall enjoy teaching you about life. Now, go call your mother. I've said enough.'

CHAPTER SIXTEEN

CARMENYA LEFT VANGERY in a hurry, all her women glancing anxiously at the sky whilst they loaded their skippers. It had been arranged that Corinna would travel south to Silven Crescent within four weeks. Corinna was glad to see Carmenya go. Now, she could risk a visit to the fugitive L'Belder. In a way, she was nervous of going alone, so approached Dannel, feeling sure her mother would want to accompany her. Dannel was harried. She had so much to do before the next storm came. 'I've had a hamper of supplies made up,' she said, 'ostensibly for Coneberry Isle. Go visit L'Belder, give him some of the stuff, and then take the rest to Coneberry. Stay there for the afternoon, Corinna. They could probably do with some extra help.'

Dragging the hamper down to the stables, Corinna, once again, wondered whether she could risk asking Shyya to go with her. Such an idea filled her with exciting warmth. A hundred scenarios flashed through her mind, conversations they would have, unintentional contact, the language of eyes. She could tell Shyya about Carmenya and ask his advice. She wanted to desperately. Up until now, she had hardly acknowledged the attraction she felt to Shyya. Only the realisation that she could never be really close to him, that soon she might leave Vangery forever, had brought her feelings to the surface. She tried to imagine what it would be like in the city without having Shyya's beauty to brighten up her days. Perhaps there would be other males there of similar kind. Would that be enough? Could she win the trust of some bitter, wary slave, to have for herself a secret friend? Shyya, come with me to the marsh . . . What would he think of L'Belder? Would Shyya think him weak too?

Out on the marsh, Corinna's dank and pack-beast swam breast-deep through cloudy water. The place looked devastated: threadwoods leaned drunkenly towards the engorged pools, mass-rope torn from their branches to wave in the wind or float in the water like hair. Dampness seeped through Corinna's waterproof leggings, making her skin raw with cold. On hills and high tussocks, herds of animals regarded her warily. Once the water levels had dropped she knew they would begin to trek north and east towards the forests, where shelter and reliable dry ground could be claimed. By tomorrow, the threadwoods would have righted themselves in preparation for the next elemental onslaught. Wervels would be packing the entrance to their underground labyrinths to crouch in the warm, breathing dark until Spring. The rock table where L'Belder was hidden was wearing a mantle of steam, probably because warm springs welled deep in the rock, a convenient kind of central heating for a hunted man huddled in the outer cave. Corinna rode her dank right up to the entrance, even though it complained and slithered on the muddy path. Some ditch-cranes, scenting food, swooped around them, landing on the pack-beast's rump. Corinna turned in the saddle, shouting and waving her arms. The birds, wobbling anyway because of the animal's gait, flapped their wings and shouted back. Corinna laughed and the cranes copied the sound.

To L'Belder it sounded as if an army of lunatics were ascending the narrow path to the cave. He picked up the nearest weapon, an old branch, and pressed himself to the wall. Then he heard Corinna's voice, scolding the birds and their insulting, mimicking response. He sighed and dropped the branch, stepping out into the light to welcome her. Her body was shapeless in waterproofs and boots; her hair, escaping from a loose coil, more beautiful because of the contrast. L'Belder thought she looked radiant, like the sky at dawn, free from clouds. Perhaps all the marsh people reflected the mood of their environ-

100

ment, so embroiled with it they were. She greeted him and he helped her unload the pack-beast. Together they carried the hamper into the cave.

'This isn't all for you,' Corinna said. 'But help yourself.' She pulled off her thick gloves with difficulty; her hands had swollen. 'Mmm, it's quite warm in here. I thought it would be; the rock table was giving off steam. Are you comfortable here?'

'It's better than the open marsh, or indeed the boat-house. Gets quite cold at night.'

'Did you block the entrance like we told you?' Corinna picked at the plaisel L'Belder had cast aside with the dawn.

'Yes. It kept the draughts out, but little else.'

'You need it thicker then. Remember that tonight. You won't suffocate!' She squatted down on the floor. 'Tried to build a fire, did you?' The forlorn remains were still mostly unmarked by the passage of flame.

'Yes, didn't work too well.'

'The tinder's damp.'

'Yes, I know. It's hard to dry it out in weather like this.' Corinna stood up.

'There's cracks in the rock there, which should provide ventilation. You should have persevered.'

'Maybe I will. Tonight. Has the General gone yet?'

Corinna nodded vigorously. 'This morning. How about sharing that warm flask of milk-suds? It won't stay hot for much longer.'

'O.k.' L'Belder thrust the flask into her hands. Corinna drank, observing the man discreetly as she did so. He was elegant, she thought. Slim, tidy-boned. Goddess, why am I seeing Shyya in everyone nowadays?'

'Why are you smiling?' he asked.

'You remind me of someone. Tell me, are you going to carry on now?'

'Carry on what?'

'Your life, the fight for freedom . . .'

L'Belder looked at the floor. 'Survival of the self is the only thing on my mind at the moment. I still haven't forgotten about the Greylids, but maybe I need to lick my wounds at present. I'm in no shape to carry on travelling.'

'No, and you won't really be able to until the Spring anyway. You're not fit for this kind of life are you?' She'd meant it as a kind of joke and was unprepared for the grim expression that crept over L'Belder's face.

'Perhaps I lived with my head in the clouds. Didn't realise. We need both kinds of strengths.'

'Both kinds? What do you mean?'

'My strength is the ability to communicate, a clever, pretty way with words. I can see things clearly, but physically . . . well, I was unprepared for hardship and have suffered for it. Not greatly, maybe, but it was a lesson I had to learn.'

'And will continue to do so, working at Vangery through the winter.'

'Do you think that's a good idea?'

'Got a better one?'

L'Belder smiled wryly. 'No. You won't be there though, will you.' Corinna flushed. She was unsure whether she should take that as a compliment or whether she would brush it aside as being importunate.

'Believe me, I wish I was going to be,' she said stiffly.

'How come you're going to the city anyway?'

Corinna pulled a face. 'Oh, because I won't inherit the farm and mother doesn't think I'll get on with my sister Bolivia. I've got to have some goal in life. Mother thinks I should find it in the city. I hope she's right.'

'You're sceptical.'

'I suppose I am. Probably because I'm a bit of a loner. I don't like following rules, being told what to do. I think I'm going to have to suppress most of myself in the city, become an actress. I'm not really into the big Man Hate thing that Carmenya lives for. I must admit I rather like men, but so too do most women on the marsh. We lead our own separate lives in a way. It works. We work together. What more can we hope for than that? Mostly, we don't think about who's cracking the whip, because there isn't the time. Property passes down through the female, yes, but in most cases, men are just as instrumental in the running of the farms as women.'

'You have an idyll here then, Corinna, and one which

the Dominatrix will not allow to continue for long, I fear.'

'Why should she bother to change it? How can it affect her? As long as the marsh still provides the goods the cities need, surely we can be left to live our lives as we like.'

'Fear,' L'Belder said. He stood up and began to arrange the food he'd chosen on the stone bench at the side of the cave.

'Fear?'

'Yes. Most fanatical people are uncomfortable until everybody shares their views. Just in case someone proves them wrong.'

'What you say makes me dread going to Silven Crescent even more.'

'You must dread it, Corinna. It would be foolish not to. Be prepared for it. You mustn't let your feelings show. At all. Cut yourself off from what you might see.' He came to squat in front of her once more.

'I would ask a favour of you,' he said.

'Which is?'

'There is a dear friend of mind in the city. A woman named Rosanel Garmelding. If you can, I would like you to contact her. She needs friends and I think you'd like her anyway.'

'Well, I'll certainly need friends,' Corinna said cheerfully. L'Belder reached for her hands and felt her freeze.

'You're like one of those leaping goats out there,' he said.

'Antelope,' Corinna corrected.

'Why are you uncomfortable?'

'I'm not.' She pulled her hands away. 'Well, maybe I am.' L'Belder raised one eyebrow, smiling at her. 'Let's build a fire,' she said.

It took a while and the cave did fill with smoke. Corinna poked twigs through the cracks in the roof to make them a little wider. 'It's only moss,' she said.

'Won't that let the cold in?' L'Belder asked. Corinna rolled her eyes.

'You'll have a fire, stupid! Keep it stoked.'

'What if someone sees the smoke . . . ?'

Corinna sighed. 'The mist around the rock-table should

hide most of it. It'll only be a small fire and you won't be here for long.' After an hour, they'd constructed a manageable blaze and the cave began to heat up.

'The light is magical,' Corinna said. 'I'd like to stay, but I must go soon. I have to go to Coneberry Isle and deliver the rest of the supplies. They had big trouble with the storm.' She stood up and picked up her gloves.

'Don't go yet,' L'Belder said. He held out his hand and she took it, automatically, without thinking. She sat down again.

Afterwards, she would think back and wonder how on earth she came to tell him what was on her mind. What cue did he give her? Was it just part of his power, his manipulativeness, that he drew it out of her? They heated water on the fire and made weak silvertea. It was a beverage earmarked for Coneberry, but they used some of it anyway. L'Belder swore when Corinna told him about what she suspected would happen to her in Carmenya's house. 'It sickens me to think of that mangak laying a finger on you,' he said. 'She looks on angeldt with hardly less scorn than she looks on men. Carmenya is all that her kind despise in the opposite sex, traits which for the most part have been beaten out of men anyway.' Corinna told him about what Shyya had said about the pendulum and L'Belder agreed that Shyya was probably right.

'Then why fight?' Corinna asked.

L'Belder shrugged. 'I just don't want the pendulum stuck, not moving, on one side of its arc. Maybe we can never have a perfect society, but at least we should seek balance. Men loving men and women loving women and each loving the other; that's what we should aim for. Mutual respect. Freedom from inhibition and fear. But most of all, love for our race as a whole.'

'I wish it could be real.'

'We can make our own realities, no matter how small.' Then she was telling him about Shyya, how she felt about him; the pointlessness of such feelings. It was like being drunk; she could say anything.

'I want him. I want his body. I want to feel him there.

104

And it's impossible.' In some corner of her mind, a choked, outraged portion of herself that spoke with her mother's voice said, 'What the hell are you doing, Corinna? This isn't you. You're a bad, bad girl for thinking such things!' She turned her back on the voice. At the moment, she didn't care about it.

'What about Carmenya?' L'Belder prompted. It was a difficult question for him, because he was sensitive enough to predict her answer.

'I would be a liar if I said she doesn't arouse me sometimes. She's so strong and feline, yet you get the impression she'd be a good lover too. I can't sympathise with her politics, it will make me angry, I know, but physically, she is magnificent. It makes me feel weak, thinking about it, yet I'm afraid at the same time. I don't feel that when I think about Shyya. Then, it's me who's in control. They're different fantasies.'

L'Belder laughed. 'Poor Corinna. Always fantasies!'

Corinna bristled. 'Some of them will become real soon enough!'

'Too soon for you, is it?'

'No, I don't think it is. Perhaps even a little late.' She lay back on the moss that they had spread on the floor and looked at the flame-shadows leaping on the cave roof. She felt powerful in this place. Talking to L'Belder had made her future seem less of a threatening thing. Why? She glanced at him, sitting with his knees up, staring at the fire, biting his thumbnails. He was like Shyya, in many ways. Not as refined, obviously, not as graceful or mysterious, not even as lovely, but there was certainly some resemblance. Perhaps it was the conversation they'd had that made her thoughts drift this way, some pressure in her loins that talk of Shyya and Carmenya had ignited. Perhaps it was the cave itself, but Corinna didn't consider that. She thought to herself: This is real power. I can have this man. I know I can and when I go to the city, I will not be as innocent as they think me. She almost laughed aloud.

'What are you thinking about?' L'Belder asked her.

'You,' she said. 'You'.

'You've made yourself horny,' he said, but it wasn't a putdown. She'd been careful. She hadn't told him she'd never had a lover. She didn't want to tell him that for she had a feeling he wouldn't want her if he knew. There was some kind of senseless nobility in him, or maybe a fear that Carmenya would know.

'You're right,' she said. They laughed.

'Was that why you built the fire?'

She didn't answer. Let him think that if he wanted to. This was marvellous. She'd never felt so strong. With Carmenya she'd be like a child, yet here she felt like a woman, like all women, stretching back and back through time and space. If she closed her eyes she was a giantess. And then L'Belder was beside her. It was so simple. 'This is the most natural thing there is,' he said. 'and we can share it. That's one of the best things about being alive.' She believed him utterly.

They washed each other with cold water, silent as if what they were doing had an almost religious significance. Even naked and damp, Corinna felt warm. The outside world had gone, behind a shield of plaisel branches. Kissing L'Belder felt like rain on her skin; there was no other way to describe it and it surprised her that she didn't even have to think of Shyya. She lay on the moss like a star, arms and legs spread and felt like nothing but the essence of all that is female. His hand was cold upon her skin and his gently probing fingers brought pain. She hid her face in his hair. He mustn't know that. She lifted her knees. It all felt so animal; she wanted it no other way. The hot tip of his phallus was pushing against her now and the slow, tearing entry made her think, 'He is becoming part of me. This is amazing. He is *inside* me.' Until that moment, she hadn't envisaged it becoming real. He knew she hadn't had a man before but he didn't say it. Neither of them spoke at all. Sound would have spoiled the moment. This is life, she thought. He is pumping life into me. Then she did make sound, wild, joyous sounds and the cave was living rock around them. More than that, they were part of the rock themselves; something old. By some magic their orgasms were nearly simultaneous and when it happened they were both singing crazy, tuneless songs that ended in laughter. The rock was warm around them; alive. 'Corinna, you're a witch!' L'Belder said, and Corinna was happy to let him think that.

They sat by the fire and finished the cooling milk-suds. At one point, they both started saying, 'Thankyou' together which initiated more hysterical laughter.

'I feel like a star!' Corinna said.

'I feel like the sun!'

'I am the sky and all the stars that ever were!'

'I am the hottest sun at the centre of the universe!'

They fell silent.

'Soon I must go back,' Corinna said.

'L'Belder touched her face. 'Don't spoil your happy times with things that haven't happened yet.'

She smiled. 'Elvon, I'm not the only witch!'

'Then we'll pool our strengths, my dear!'

Outside the suns began to fall.

CHAPTER SEVENTEEN

THE HOUSE ON Freda Street in Silven Crescent had a deep, dark cellar. On this particular night, its stale air was masked with a thick cloud of incense smoke. In the centre of the low-ceilinged chamber, a five pointed star was marked out in chalk on the floor, a white circle drawn evenly around it to touch each point of the star. Sitting naked within it, a priestess turned her eyes to the roof, breathing hoarsely. Rosanel Garmelding was pressed against the wall of the cellar, gnawing on a single white knuckle that was pressed equally firmly against her teeth. She felt no pain. Her face was streaked with tears that may have been an effect of the pungent smoke or of grief. There was no way of telling. Candles provided the only illumination, casting eerie shadows on the walls and low columns that supported the roof. The two women had been down in the cellar for nearly an hour. One of the candles sizzled and went out and, almost as if that was a signal, the priestess shuddered out a great sigh and her head sank to her breast. Rosanel's hand fell from her mouth. She leaned away from the wall.

'Are you. . . are you alright?' she asked. The priestess looked at her expressionless.

'Wait upstairs,' was the answer. Rosanel gladly fled.

They'd had no news of L'Belder. General Carmenya had returned to the city, of course, and via their spy network, the Skyreachers (as the dissidents now called themselves) had learned of the general's lack of success in locating L'Belder. The general opinion was that he must be dead, beaten to a pulp by the storms. The Skyreachers would not believe that; they wanted evidence. So, if the truth was known, did the Dominatrix. Rosanel was not blind to the fact that Yani Gisbandrun must have conducted a similar experiment to her own. A priestess of Parthenos, sympathetic to the cause, had been called upon to determine whether L'Belder was alive or not. It required great strength of mind and prolonged concentration. The Priestess had achieved results in far less time than Rosanel had anticipated. She realised that this might be because the Dominatrix had already investigated the matter and opened up channels which the Priestess could easily follow. No matter. She had to know. Things had not been going well for Rosanel since L'Belder had left the city. The Skyreachers did not trust her because she displayed her weaknesses; overcautiousness, fear. Now too, those voices which L'Belder had managed to keep down had raised themselves again. 'We should attack the Palace Mount! Fire the barracks! The Dominatrix must understand that we'll kill to have our say. It's the only language she'll understand!' Rosanel had repeated L'Belder's views on this and been accused of cowardice. 'You are dreaming!' one man had said. 'This is not a polite parlour game. Tell the relatives of those who have disappeared you're not prepared to fight and see what they think of you!' Rosanel would not give her approval to terrorist activity so they went ahead without her. Reprisals had been strong. Perhaps more people did take the Skyreachers seriously now, but many had died in the process. The group had lost its cohesion, splinter groups without organisation committing atrocities on the fringes of the city. Establishment security had been increased. No way would any Skyreacher be able to speak in public now without being shot. Rosanel was furious. The reins had been snatched from her hands. She was helpless. Those still loyal to the original cause looked to her for leadership, begging her for answers. She didn't know any. Only L'Belder could control people. She had failed him. She needed him; desperately. Rosanel was stalling people with the promise that L'Belder would soon return. How much longer would they listen to her?

The Priestess looked weary when she came into the library. Rosanel handed her a goblet of mulled wine immediately. 'Well?' she said. The Priestess smiled cynically.

'What do you think?'

'I don't know. That's why I asked you to do this! Don't play games. Is he alive or dead?'

The Priestess indulgently ignored this outburst. 'Your friend Elvon is not dead, milady,' she said quietly and sat down on a sofa to drink the wine. Rosanel put her head against the high mantelpiece.

'Thank the Goddess,' she said. 'Do you know where he is?'

'On the marsh somewhere. I couldn't pinpoint exactly. But this is a blessing, for what I can trace so can the priestesses loyal to Yani. He is safe a while longer yet, I would think.'

'Will he come back here?' Rosanel turned around. There was a mark on her forehead where the cold slate had bitten into it.

The priestess shrugged. 'Rosanel, I did not read his mind! Only you can answer that. You know him better than anybody, don't you?'

'We can't do anything without him.'

'I thought he left you in charge.'

Rosanel laughed bitterly. 'And what use was that? You know what's happening! I'm losing control. Everything's going crazy! On top of that, I'm getting gnawed from another direction. You know I'm being watched all the time at court. Nobody who talks to me is safe.'

'Don't panic, Rosanel. There is no proof of your being connected with the Skyreachers. We have all been meticulously careful. Calm down. Just sit and wait.'

'Wait!' Rosanel punched the mantelpiece. 'And how long do you think our loyal friends will allow that before they blow themselves and the city to pieces? Wait? I have been waiting!' She sucked her knuckles which had been skinned by the slate. 'Half of me dreads that the Skyreachers are as good as dead. We can do nothing and I fear *she* knows exactly who we are, every one of us.'

110

The Priestess stood up. 'You must keep on hoping, Rosanel. You still have a lot of support. The influential people are with you. Forget the others.'

'They know names, though. They could betray us.'

'And tomorrow the suns could explode, too!' The priestess shrugged herself into a long coat. 'I'm sorry, but I have to leave now. I don't want to be seen leaving Denderberry too late in the day.'

'Oh, of course,' Rosanel said, waving a hand at her. 'Thank you for what you did.'

The priestess pulled a wry face. 'It seems I've failed to put your mind at rest.'

'Only having Elvon here at my side would do that,' Rosanel replied.

'He will send word to you as soon as he can, I'm sure,' the Priestess said, pulling on her gloves. 'Goodnight, milady. I wish you a restful evening.'

'Thankyou. Yes.' Rosanel didn't watch her leave.

CHAPTER EIGHTEEN

'So, where did you say Dannel's gone today?' Meonel said carefully. The Trotgardens had long since finished breakfast, though Corinna was still mooning around the main salon, despite Bolivia's heavy-handed hints about work to be done.

'Stilt Vashti,' Corinna answered. 'She spoke of purchasing an extra pair of hands to help around the place after I've gone.'

'Don't make it sound so final, Corinna.'

'There is every likelihood that it will be, Meonel!' Corinna sighed and flopped down on one of the window seats. The garden outside still looked brown and grey and ravaged; it would do until Spring. Corinna thought that she might never see the marsh beautiful with life again. No, don't be silly, she chided herself. I'll come back, of course I'll come back . . . sometimes.

'Before you leave,' Meonel said, 'are you going to tell me what's been on your mind these last few days?' Corinna flicked him a sharp glance. 'And what you were up to on the marsh with Dannel the other day before the storm?'

Corinna knew that it wasn't normally in Meonel's nature to be curious about any of the women or their behaviour in Vangery. This had to be Shyya talking, she reasoned, quite correctly.

'I don't think it's any of your business, Meonel,' she said, somewhat archly. Meonel just pulled a face.

'You're right, I suppose. Why should I care anyway? It's the boy, you know. I think he gets bored easily. He enjoys mysteries. Now he's got me at it.'

'Sometimes, step-father, you talk like an old man.'

Corinna stood up and began to pace the room.

'I've been old since birth,' Meonel said gloomily.

Dannel had taken Shyya with her. Corinna had told her the eunuch had guessed what they were involved in. Dannel saw no reason not to trust Shyya. There had only been one major problem really; Stilt Vashti was south and L'Belder was hidden northwest. It was a risk charging across the marsh at dawn through mud-puddles and spear shallows that were still too flooded to be traversed quickly and safely. But there was no other way. It was only Bolivia who Dannel had to worry about; or any of the Trotgardens' close neighbours, but the latter were highly unlikely. Nobody would be that far from their own farms right now, for the simple reason that clearing up after the flood wouldn't give them the time to travel. Bolivia never rose particularly early in the morning. By the time breakfast was being served in Vangery, Dannel and Shyya were galloping east; L'Belder was with them.

There was a long, fairly narrow throat of threadwood that led to Stilt Vashti. It was on high ground; a knobbly spine of rock that potruded from the marsh. Although the rocks were slippery and treacherous with slimy moss, Dannel thought it best to use the cover of trees for their journey south. She'd already worked out her story. She would say she had purchased L'Belder from a caravan of slavers just outside Stilt Vashti. She would tell her family how wretched the slavers had been made by the storm, how they were selling their stock off very cheap to enable them to purchase supplies. All slavers would head for the cities now until Spring.

L'Belder was very quiet. He'd eyed Shyya with suspicion on meeting him. Dannel tried not to feel impatient. She knew men could be impetuous, barely able to control their wild, territorial instincts. L'Belder hardly spoke until Dannel called a halt in the thickest part of the threadwood belt. 'Let's eat,' she said. 'Shyya, unpack the food.' L'Belder slunk down from his dank's back and cautiously investigated the environment. Dannel caught Shyya's eye; Shyya shrugged.

'What's he looking for, do you think?' Dannel asked.

'Answers perhaps,' Shyya replied. Dannel shook her head.

'The man's crazy, Shyya. I wonder why I'm doing this . . .'

'Because somebody had to.'

'That's too trite. No, he's got something alright. If it hadn't been us, someone else would have helped him. It's not Fate; it's talent. The man's crazy, yes, but I've a feeling he's pretty damn bright, too.'

Shyya smiled at the ground.

When the suns began to sink, Dannel thought it was safe to head home. It was a brilliant sunset; sharp, angry colours, pervasive scents on the air. Back at Vangery, the new slave was taken directly to Gabriel with the instruction that his name was Joel and that he would take over Corinna's duties eventually. 'My daughter can train him,' Dannel said. 'Just give him a place to sleep, Gabriel. Get him cleaned up and fed.'

Gabriel was only too happy to comply with this, for what Dannel considered to be obvious reasons. It was easy; the house never even blinked as L'Belder was brought into it.

CHAPTER NINETEEN

IT WAS THE sheer size of the place that took Corinna's breath away. Nothing really to do with the masses of people scurrying along the streets; the men with their heads down, wearing dowdy clothes, the women splendid and proud, stepping grandly out together. No, it was that feeling she got when she put her head back and Silven Crescent stretched up and up all around her. Birds circled the highest towers; some were even crowned with nests. Carmenya had send an escort for Corinna. The whole journey from Vangery had been conducted in silence. The women had been grim-faced, somewhat condescending. They were flamist. Corinna resolved to be just as sneering and cold and had sat with her back to them, watching the winter marsh fly by through a haze of skipper spray. She had tried not to think about what she was leaving, or who she was leaving; that would cause her too much grief. Instead, she thought about what she might be able to achieve in the city. It was best to be positive. L'Belder had told her where Rosanel Garmelding lived. She knew Carmenya would not approve of such a friendship developing because of Rosanel being suspected of embracing disestablishment politics. To Corinna, Rosanel would be like a link with home; she felt she had to get to know the woman, if only as an act of defiance, to prove she was still herself. From what L'Belder had said, she'd worked out that he and Rosanel Garmelding had been lovers at one point, so it would seem likely she'd be anxious for news about him. As far as Corinna's involvement with him went, there had been no further intimacy between them since the incident on the marsh. Opportunity was virtually nil, of course, in Vangery, but Corinna had not felt that it would be right to pursue it anyway. Once was magical; it was all she needed. She didn't want to spoil it. For all she knew, that might be the only time she'd lie with a man in her life; it was not impossible. L'Belder had captivated her, as he'd captivated Dannel and would no doubt captivate most of Vangery, but Corinna did not love him. She might not be aware of it, but it was likely she'd give her life for L'Belder now if he asked it, yet there was no doubt, however, that it was still Shyya who occupied her heart. Poor Shyya, she thought. Poor me.

L'Belder had fitted easily and subtly into Vangery's routine. He didn't speak much, but just got on with his work. Corinna showed him how to look after the danks. They'd gone down to look in the boathouse on one occasion and L'Belder had put his arm round Corinna's waist and hugged her. They hadn't said anything to each other. The boathouse looked forlorn, almost violated. Branches and weed were stuck to its roof. Several of its windows had shattered. L'Belder had shivered. Corinna didn't blame him. When she looked at the boathouse she saw Carmenya's face.

Now she was here, in Carmenya's city. The escort took her directly to a house situated on a side-street, named Lavinia Drive, which was quiet but quite close to the Dominatrix's palace, on the Palace Mount itself, in fact. On one side of the street was a widely-spaced row of large residences, on the other a tree-dotted park, where angeldt women in long furs walked their tame felids and smooms. The house itself was far too large for just one girl to feel comfortable in, but Carmenya had hired a staff of two women and three men (to make Corinna feel at home, no doubt). All five members of staff were waiting in the hall of the house when she arrived. Corinna appraised the males first, even though they were skulking in the entrance to a dark corridor at the back of the hall. She wondered whether Carmenya had purposely chosen them because they were young and attractive. It seemed unlikely. They had yellow hair braided down their backs and nervous, animal expressions. As a contrast, the women were confident and smiling, slim and elegant, angeldt like herself, with personalities that gave off soothing warmth but very little intelligence. That suited Corinna just fine, for the moment. She felt as if she was a young husband who'd been brought into a new wife's house for the first time. What would be expected of her? The house felt strange; it was not hers yet, perhaps it would never be. Her female attendants, Sheba and Endaline, told her Carmenya would come by later. It was not a meeting Corinna looked forward to with any feeling of joy. She put her few belongings away in the dark, wooden drawers of her dark, wooden bedroom, and, trying not to think of home, took a walk around the house. It was a fine place. She had to admit Carmenya had chosen well. It felt strong and sturdy, its wooden floors rugged with deep crimson and black, its pale, wooden walls varnished to a colour like honey. She had a gallery room, all to herself, where long windows were leaded into little, diamond shapes. There were even domestic felids, a pair of them, with rosetted, grey fur. The animals looked as furtive as Corinna felt; the place was new to them too. They were as high as her knees and pressed close to her legs, following her round the house on her travels. She was not really surprised that her men servants wouldn't even look at her. She went into the kitchen and all five of her staff were there. The women bobbed a curtsey, the men put their foreheads to the floor.

'Oh, get up,' Corinna said, embarrassed. Then she went on to say that from now on there was no need for anyone to bow or scrape to her. 'We all live together,' she said. 'Where I come from, nobody bows to anyone. I prefer it to be that way here too.' Nobody had responded to her little speech. The women had bitten their lips and stared fixedly at the floor. Corinna fled with what she hoped was dignity. Later, Sheba timidly approached her and explained that it might not look very good if Corinna did away with the traditions of Silven Crescent in her house.

'If you wish Endaline and myself not to bow, then we shan't,' the woman said, in a whisper. 'But you must not excuse the men from their obeisance. The Dominatrix

117

commands it at all times. Men must be reminded of their position. Carmenya will be displeased if you change anything in that way.'

Corinna thanked the woman stiffly, realising that she had acted in her new mistress's best interests. Corinna didn't like it. She went out into the garden to think, glancing askance at the tamed and bound threadwoods clinging to the walls of the house. She was affronted that Sheba should dare to question her orders, but realised with a grim, self-admonishing smile that only yesterday she had never been in the position to give orders to another woman. She leaned against the wall of the house and gazed across the winter-dowdy moss lawn. In the warmer season, would she give parties here? Would the bright laughter of celebrated women from the court resound in this place? Would she be popular? Or was she too different from the women here to ever fit in successfully? Corinna sighed. At home, in Vangery, at this moment it was likely that Gabriel would be preparing the evening meal, Shyya would be seeing to the shutters in Meonel's room, Bolivia would be barking orders in the stable block. Another sigh. Already she was homesick. By tomorrow, she would even miss Bolivia, she was sure.

Two hours after sundown, Carmenya breezed into the house, bringing with her an air of vivacity and a distinctive smell of ash-flower perfume. Corinna's people had prepared a simple but superbly cooked meal, which Corinna and Carmenya sat down to eat in the newly furnished dining-room. Carmenya asked what Corinna thought of the house.

'It's lovely,' Corinna replied.

'Good, I'm glad you like it. Get used to it. In a few days, I'll take you to court and introduce you to your duties. I hope you'll enjoy working for me. I'm not a hard task-mistress, but unfortunately you might find many aspects of the job boring. Let's hope you learn swiftly, so that I can promote you.'

'It's all so strange at the moment. Don't rush me, please.'

Carmenya smiled. 'I won't have to. I'm convinced you'll surprise yourself.'

Corinna was relieved that Carmenya made no suggestion of staying on after breadlemen. She had been dreading it through the meal. Once the General had left, Corinna went to bed early, taking the felids with her for company. Sheba knocked on the door and asked if Corinna wanted to lock the men in for the night, or did she want someone else to do it?

'Is that necessary?' Corinna called back from across the room. There was a moment's pause.

'Yes,' came the muffled reply.

Corinna sighed. 'You do it,' she said. Whatever tradition demanded, Corinna felt sure that changes were in order in this house.

In the morning, she learned that the men were confined in different rooms at night to prevent them from forming intimate relationships. Corinna thought this unnecessarily hard, and said so, but was reminded by Endaline, the quieter of her two women, that once men formed alliances amongst themselves, they became dangerous, perhaps even uncontrollable. Corinna decided not to argue. Perhaps Endaline was right. The men might well be different to the ones she'd known on the marsh. They appeared confused if she addressed them directly. By the end of the second day in Silven Crescent, Corinna had decided to communicate with them only through Sheba and Endaline, for the time being. The men listened to them. After breakfast, Sheba suggested Corinna should take a walk in the city and offered to point out sites of interest. The area in which the house was situated was residential and Sheba explained that it was far prettier than the market or industrial areas. That seemed obvious. Corinna was interested in seeing the less savoury aspects of the city. Know your enemy, she thought, but Sheba was less than enthusiastic about taking her there. Corinna had no idea that her people had been given express orders by Carmenya to keep her away from anywhere where evidence of rebel activity or rebel executions might linger.

Dressed in a long, crimson wool gown and a thick fur coat (both provided by Carmenya), Corinna stepped out of her house and into the street. Sheba carried a purse containing a few coins in case Corinna should wish to pause for refreshment or visit one of the many curio shops to be found on the skirts of Palace Mount. They didn't see one male in the streets around the palace. Sheba took Corinna to the north gate. Here, splendid flamists stood dressed in links of shining silver and pleated white silk, carrying ceremonial weapons to guard the gate. Corinna noticed that on the top of the wall other women stood to attention carrying brutal-looking guns. The flamists on the gate were merely decoration.

Most of Silven Crescent was constructed of wood, but the palace itself was grey stone, sparkling with quartz. It was immense and looked as if it had stood for far longer than the three hundrerd years of Artemesian rule. After a leisurely circuit of the palace walls, Sheba took Corinna to the High Temple of Parthenos, the Goddess of Artemis. Parthenos, in her celibate aspect, stood in the centre of the shrine. She was made of white stone, a huge block of it. Corinna was awed. The atmosphere within the temple was palpably holy. Priestesses of the Goddess wafted between the incense-clouded columns. Sheba explained that at the height of their menstrual peak, the priestesses became oracles, whom women could come to consult. A brief midday ritual was about to be enacted. Sheba suggested that she and Corinna remain in the temple to participate. Women's voices, sweet and high, rose in song. Corinna's flesh prickled. Through waving bodies, waving linen and wreaths of scented smoke, the Goddess stared impartially at the farthest door. At the end of the ritual, wanting to begin taking a part in the city life, Corinna approached the altar and asked the High Priestess of that particular service if she might light a scented cone in the Goddess's honour. She was surprised to learn that this would cost her a coin. Recognising someone who must be a stranger to Silven Crescent, the priestess took time to make friendly conversation. Corinna proudly told her of her connections with Carmenya Oralien and that she would soon be working in the general's office in the palace complex.

'It must be quite a change for you,' the priestess said. 'I hope everything goes well.'

Corinna detected a certain restraint in the priestess's manner. Perhaps it had been a mistake to boast of her friendship with Carmenya. 'I hope so too,' she replied. 'I'm finding it all rather bewildering at present.'

'Is General Oralien your only friend here in the city?'

'At present. I haven't been here long enough to meet anyone yet.'

The priestess appeared to take pity on her. She recommended a certain eating house that she and her friends used regularly. 'You would be welcome to join us one evening,' she said. 'Perhaps, that way, you could make friends in the city.'

'Thankyou. I'd like that.'

The priestess laid a hand on Corinna's arm. 'I can always be reached through the temple. My name is Carudan,' she said. 'Don't wait too long to get in touch.'

Sheba was waiting for her mistress by the door. Corinna confessed to feeling hungry; the two women headed for home. On the way, Corinna told her about the priestess's offer.

'I can see you will soon settle in here,' Sheba said, pleased with herself. She obviously felt wholly responsible for Corinna's successful morning.

In the afternoon, an angeldt friend of Carmenya's came to call. She was concerned mainly that Corinna should know where the best seamstresses were to be found, the best hairdressers. She was a large, heavily scented woman, named Lady Marta Blockling. Corinna liked her at once, mainly because she reminded her of Dannel in one of her best moods. 'Of course Carmenya will bring you to court on Savanday,' Lady Marta said confidentially. 'It is imperative that you should look stunning. Everyone will be interested in you. The court loves a new face. Have you any skills?'

'Most that are necessary to existence,' Corinna answered with a smile. 'I can cook, passably. I can build boats, passably; train danks, excellently . . .'

'No, no, no!' Lady Marta exclaimed, eyes rolling and arms flapping. 'I mean *skills*, like music or dance or poetry.'

121

'Artistic skills?' Lady Marta nodded. 'Well . . .' Corinna screwed up her face. 'I suppose I can sing a little . . .'

'*Is that all?!*'

Corinna felt she had committed some dreadful solecism. 'Well, yes. I'm afraid so.'

Lady Marta rolled her eyes once more. 'Corinna, you are *angeldt*. That means you are an elegant lady, of many talents, wit and grace. Clearly, you need teachers, and quickly! If you can, you must disguise the fact that you have so little creative skill. Bluff your way through.'

'I beg your pardon, Lady Marta, but I had no time for such things back home.'

'You are in Silven Crescent now,' boomed Lady Marta with all the meaning and importance that she could instil into the words. Corinna smiled at her lap. She didn't envy anyone the task of trying to teach her to be artistic. It just wasn't in her nature.

Sure enough, next day a lady musician arrived in the morning. There was a large piano already in the house and the lady had brought several different types of wind instrument with her; all delicate and sweetly voiced. Corinna complied dutifully with the lady's instruction and, to her credit, the woman was patient. In the afternoon, a painting teacher arrived. Corinna was beginning to enjoy herself. She didn't feel she'd ever make a good artist or musician or poetess, but the lessons were interesting and made a change from manual labour. The next day, two more teachers arrived; one in language, armed with a bagful of essential reading, the other a dancing mistress. Corinna wondered when she'd have any time to do the job that Carmenya had earmarked for her.

On Danasday evening, Carmenya called in for five minutes to tell Corinna what time to be ready the next day. 'I shall send someone for you early,' the General said. 'I must say, you look very nice, Corinna.'

Corinna smoothed the skirt of the dress that Lady Marta had sent her; one of several. She felt a little embarrassed.

'Oh, your friend, Lady Marta seems to have taken me under her wing,' she said. Carmenya smiled.

'Listen to her Corinna, she's a wise old bird. See you tomorrow!'

Corinna retired into her parlour with a sweet, spicy wine that Endaline had mulled for her in the kitchen. She sat down and began to read one of the books her teacher had brought her. After a moment, she sighed, put down the book and stretched back into the deep, plush chair. 'Goddess, I'm happy!' she said aloud. Never had she imagined her new life would be so pleasant. All her fears about being brought to a grey, sombre place filled with grey-faced sufferers had been unfounded. To Corinna, Silven Crescent had shown itself as a city of light and activity, its people cultured. L'Belder's words seemed very hollow now. How could any of the intelligent women Corinna had met possibly condone the barbaric behaviour he'd mentioned, never mind participate in it. No, L'Belder was wrong, perhaps exaggerating his woes. She could see that men had a harder time of it here than in the marsh, but had so far not witnessed any deliberate physical cruelty. Overwhelmed by all the new experiences she had enjoyed, Corinna's thoughts had been far from the marsh or what she had learned there. In just a few days, she had made friends and was already acquiring the skills that would make her a perfect angeldt. Back home, she'd never been that bothered about her appearance, but by looking in the mirror, she could see that Lady Marta's advice was paying off. No more did she look like a farm girl. With her coiffed hair, painted eyes and arching brows, she looked like a complete stranger. Surely, not even Dannel would recognise her now.

Gloomy or unfomfortable subjects had been neatly pushed into a dark space at the back of her mind. Even from the second day Corinna had found that by keeping away from the kitchens, she did not have to face her male slaves very often. She did not do this consciously and would have argued vehemently if anybody had suggested it. She was so busy, she had no time to think about them. Of course she still intended to improve their conditions! The days passed, and it had become more important than she could have imagined for her to fit into the court society. The city seduced her easily and she offered no resistance. She wanted Carmenya to feel proud of her when she was introduced to her friends.

CHAPTER TWENTY

CORINNA WAS READY in the morning, way before Carmenya's woman came to collect her. Sheba and Endaline twittered round her, commenting on her beauty and presence. During the past few days, she'd hardly thought about life in Vangery. Shyya and L'Belder had become shadowy figures; now she lived in a world of women, where flamists took the place of men and angeldt were honoured for their refinement and grace. By the time she was working fully for Carmenya, it would already seem natural to Corinna that the men in her household be treated like dumb animals; fed, groomed and caged at night in return for their labour. Everyone else did it. She wouldn't even notice them as she glided through the halls of her house. All thoughts of reform would lose their importance. Silven Crescent would claim her completely. She had her own property. She had position and respect. Authority could not touch her because she was authority. She was a new woman. The old Corinna would have been appalled.

They entered the palace through the East Gate where stone female warriors brandished antique weapons and snarled at those who passed. Carmenya came hurrying up as Corinna was being led through courtyard after courtyard, mouth agape.

'I can see you're impressed,' the General said, taking her arm and dismissing her woman with a brisk wave, 'but try not to let it *show* so much, my dear.'

Corinna laughed delightedly. 'I want to thank you, General. I had no idea life in the city would be like this.'

'What were you expecting?'

Corinna shrugged. 'I don't know. Misery, bloodshed, and a kind of imprisonment for me, I suppose.'

Carmenya stopped her, one hand on each of Corinna's shoulders. 'Corinna, you are a woman! Get rid of ideas you learned on the marsh. Above all, never say, or even think, that any woman is a prisoner in Silven Crescent.'

Corinna was momentarily flustered. She hadn't meant any of it that seriously. 'I'm sorry,' she said.

'It's alright. Just be careful who you say those kind of things to. Best not to say them to anyone.'

'It was only an opinion I had before. A bit of a joke really.'

'Doesn't matter. Forget about it.' Some of Corinna's euphoria had evaporated. She had an uneasy feeling now. Carmenya sensed it and tried to lighten the atmosphere.

'Come on, I'll take you onto the gallery before we go down to the main hall. You can have a preview of what's to come.'

They climbed a tower and emerged onto a wide, red-carpeted gallery, where couches were arranged around low tables and women were sitting, conversing in subdued voices, drinking beverages. Carmenya led Corinna to the balustraded edge. 'Look,' she said. 'The cream of Silven Crescent society.'

Corinna had never seen so many beautiful people, so many luxurious clothes or splendid jewels. It was like a fairytale. 'We're too high up here to pick out faces,' Carmenya said, 'but introductions can come later anyway. What do you think?'

'Wonderful!'

'My reaction entirely the first time I saw it. I must warn you though, my dear, you'll have to watch out for a few of those people. It's not unlikely some will be jealous of you at first.'

'Why?'

Carmenya brushed Corinna's cheek with the back of her hand. 'Mainly because you are young and beautiful, but also because you'll be with me.'

'I see.'

'No need to sound so cold. I don't have that much of a

high opinion of myself. It's just a fact. Most of the angeldt here are terrible social climbers and vie for the attentions of high-ranking personages.'

'I see. Presumably they'll think that's what I'm doing.'

Carmenya laughed. 'True, I regret to say! A lot of the angeldt are here because they are famous beauties; decorations for the court. But don't be deceived. Many have sharp, clever minds which they conceal behind fluttering lashes and heavy scent. Look out also for those not so well favoured by the Goddess. They are famous for something other than looks and will make easy meat of the inexperienced.'

'Mmm'. Corinna thought of Lady Marta Blockling. Sheba had related some interesting gossip concerning that lady's protégés.

They descended a wide stair-case to the hall. Everyone appeared to be milling about, waiting for something. The light was very strange in the hall, muted, filtered, because it came from so high above. Dark drapery was held back by gold rope from arched doorways. Glossy pillars soared towards the ceiling, veined with sparkling ores. Several flamist women sauntered over to speak to Carmenya. 'Will you present your new friend today?' one of them asked. Carmenya looked at Corinna.

'I don't think so. Not yet. Corinna is very new to all this. I'm sure she'll want to settle into her new house and job first.'

'What did she mean? Presented how?' Corinna asked after the woman had left them.

'To the Dominatrix. It is customary for all new arrivals at the court to be presented to her. I think it would be best for you to find your feet first. To be frank, I would recommend waiting a couple of months at least before meeting her.'

'That awesome, is she?'

Carmenya smiled carefully. 'I'm only thinking of you, my dear. If you want to be presented today, that's up to you . . .'

'No, I think I'll wait.'

As they strolled around the hall, Carmenya pointing out

127

various people of interest, whose names Corinna forgot almost immediately, it became apparent that Corinna was creating rather a stir, as had been predicted. She caught a glimpse of one or two hostile glances and whispered conversations between angeldt, which they took no precautions to hide were about her. She didn't care. With Carmenya, she felt safe.

After only a few minutes, a blast of trumpet notes silenced the crowd. Everyone shuffled into the centre of the hall, forming perfect rows before a raised dais of several levels, at the farthest end. Corinna saw a grand throne, spread with metallic cloth, standing upon a plush indigo carpet strewn with antelope skins. The throne was surrounded by less dignified chairs which were arranged upon the lower levels of the dais. Once everybody had settled into position, a horn was sounded and a heavy crimson curtain behind the throne began to peel backwards and upwards. This must have been a signal. Every woman in the hall sank to her knees. For a moment Corinna was staring, non-plussed, at rows and rows of bent backs and heads until Carmenya hissed an order and pulled Corinna down beside her. 'What is this?' Corinna whispered.

'Sshh!' Carmenya replied. 'Our beloved leader.' Corinna stifled a laugh. Was Carmenya being sarcastic? Everybody was looking at the floor, but Corinna couldn't resist a quick upward glance. She strained her eyes to the side and saw the back of Carmenya's bent head where the chestnut hair was coiled neatly and held with pins. She looked at all the bent backs, lines of them, ahead of her, and at the raised dais. A small figure had come to stand before the throne, arranging her long robes around her feet. Corinna ducked her head down again. Someone banged what sounded like a staff upon the floor three times. As one, the women rose. And, behold, there stood the Dominatrix, revealed for all to see. She was not beautiful as Corinna had imagined, but not ugly either. Her hair was of medium length, curled around her shoulders, her figure neither slender nor plump. She smiled benignly at her

128

people and raised her arms. 'Before any business, let us worship together,' she said, and there followed a short prayer to Parthenos, thanking her for all that she provided for the women of Artemis. Then the Dominatrix sat down upon the throne and her immediate council took their places on the lower seats. One of them handed the Dominatrix a sheaf of papers. All the women in the hall sat down upon the floor, crosslegged, like children awaiting the words of a teacher.

The Dominatrix scanned the papers for a moment, nodding, stroked her lips and then cleared her throat. 'Good morning, my people,' she said. 'First of all, I would like to take this opportunity to stifle rumours concerning off-world trade. We, the government of Artemis, do not want to hear mention again of sordid tales about arms commerce. As you know, because of the unrest spreading among the so-called civilised worlds in this system, we have gradually been breaking all communication with them. The only travellers welcome on Artemis now are members of the Sisterhood of Amflax, our sisters of the Goddess. This planet is self-sufficient. We have all that we need here and that inlcudes weapons!' She paused to smile and the tension was broken by a wave of subdued laughter around the hall. The Dominatrix clasped her hands in her lap. 'Now, onto more gratifying topics. You will all be pleased to know that the group of renegade males who escaped onto the southern plain following their brutal attack on Column Street temple have been overcome. I'm sure I don't need to remind any of you of the atrocities committed by these creatures. A party of Flamists, led by General Helian, followed the group and have returned all survivors to the city. Their execution is scheduled to take place next Tarasday. I would strongly recommend that all present arrange for the males of their household, should they have any, to be witness to this event. Thus, we hope to discourage further crimes of a similar type.'

It was the first time any mention of trouble had come to Corinna's ears since she'd entered the city. She listened, with increasing discomfort, as the Dominatrix spoke of other similar crimes and punishments. 'The targets are never the army, you'll notice,' the Dominatrix pointed out sourly, 'never people equipped to defend themselves. Oh no! These brutes always attack defenceless women, destroying their property if not their lives. I implore you, every one of you, to be vigilant at this time. Be aware that violent troublemakers are attempting to destroy all the hard work that generations of women have put into making our community what it is. Keep your eyes and your ears open. The Centre for Internal Offences is open around the clock and any information you can give its operatives will be greatly appreciated. Remember, we all have to work together to keep the peace, to maintain the standard of our great city!'

All the women applauded enthusiastically, scrambling to their feet and cheering. Inclining her head in appreciation, the Dominatrix beamed smiles over everyone. Corinna felt ill. Although the things she had heard did point to the brutality of the rebels, it also reminded her that there must be another side to the story. For the first time in days, the face of Elvon L'Belder came into Corinna's mind. Why the hell should I feel ashamed? she thought. It's not my fight! It's nothing to do with me. Why the hell should I be ashamed? Goddess let me forget. I want this life! This one! Get out of my head, L'Belder! Cruelly, her disobedient mind provided a string of images connected with the lovemaking she and the fugitive had enjoyed. Corinna squirmed and made a sound. 'Are you alright?' Carmenya asked her.

'Yes,' Corinna replied, breathlessly. 'Just a little hot.'

'Don't give me that,' the General replied, softly. 'It bothers you, doesn't it? Don't worry. It's natural. You won't be so squeamish after a time.' Corinna had not expected such a sympathetic attitude from Carmenya.

'It's different,' was all she could say. Carmenya took her hand, causing a flutter of whispering up and down the row they were in. She squeezed it.

'Don't worry,' she mouthed.

There was not much in the way of other business that day. One or two people were being presented to the Dominatrix, but nobody stayed in position to watch that.

Serving girls had brought trays of refreshments and were now standing on either side of the hall. Carmenya and Corinna strolled over to get a drink and something to eat. On the way, Carmenya paused to speak to a tall, pale woman with a mass of dark, shiny hair. The woman did not seem particularly pleased to see the General. She was dressed in black, her white face relieved only by a gash of scarlet lipstick and heavily kohled eyes. Corinna had never seen such a strange or striking person. She didn't catch what she and Carmenya said to each other but decided that the stranger must be one of Carmenya's lovers. If she wasn't, Carmenya must be mad.

'Who was that?' Corinna asked as Carmenya paid for two cups of wine and a plate of sandwiches.

'Huh? Oh her! Keep away, Corinna, she's dangerous.' Corinna had the feeling Carmenya had read her mind.

'In what way?'

'Not in the way you'd think. Her name is Rosanel Garmelding and there is substantial evidence to suggest she is a rebel sympathiser. Remember that for future reference. Never admit to knowing her, is my advice.' Carmenya laughed. Corinna had gone cold.

Rosanel!

'Why is she here at court then?'

'She's doing what she's been told to do; keeping her nose clean. Hopefully, she's learned her lesson. Her family are well-respected in Silven Crescent.'

Corinna decided to indulge in a little research. 'I wonder why she is a sympathiser. From what I've heard today, the rebels don't seem to have much of a case.'

Carmenya sighed. 'Corinna, Corinna, don't be curious. Look at that beautiful face and think that it can condone, or at least turn a blind eye to, the slaughter of innocent priestesses and shopkeepers. It was she helped the fugitive L'Belder escape the city, or so we believe.' Corinna couldn't control the tide of blood that washed her face and neck. She turned away from Carmenya as if scanning the crowd. Mercifully, other women came to speak with the General. Corinna's heart was engaged in a fast, hectic

131

dance. She tried to see Rosanel Garmelding in the crowd, but she'd disappeared.

At mid-day, Carmenya took Corinna to the Officer's Dining Room for lunch. Here, other angeldt sat beside high-ranking flamists in the Dominatrix's army. The room was panelled in dark, lustrous wood and carpeted thickly in red. There must have been fifty women sitting around one long table. Corinna was impressed. Everyone conversed in low voices, punctuated only by the tinkle of expensive crystal and cutlery and the occasional cultured laugh. Corinna had never eaten food like this before; everything was marinated in wine and there were odd combinations of salt and sweet vegetables, whose delicious taste surprised her. Carmenya watched her from the corner of an eye, pleased at Corinna's rapt expression. 'My office is not far from here,' she said. 'I'll take you there after we've eaten. How about starting work next week? Or would you prefer more time to settle into your house?'

'I don't mind. I'll start as soon as you like but I think Lady Marta will be displeased. She's having me trained to be a perfect little angeldt. How will I have time for all those lessons if I'm working here?'

'Oh, your hours won't be that long. I have other women working for me. I've just made their hours shorter so you can slot in.'

'Oh, and what do they think about that?'

'Very pleased. Nobody wants to work for longer than is necessary, do they? I haven't cut their pay after all.'

After lunch, Corinna took Carmenya's arm and let herself be led through a grand doorway into a network of sombre corridors, where soft-footed women hurried along with set faces, carrying sheaves of paper. Carmenya's office, a complete suite of rooms in fact, lay at the end of one of these corridors, overlooking a courtyard where people rushed to and fro carrying boxes and barrels. Corinna understood that three others worked for the General. Only one of them was on duty that day however. This was a thin, pale girl named Ember Threadhook, whose name Corinna thought to be utterly appropriate.

She smiled a smile as thin as her face at Corinna when Carmenya introduced them. 'Your main duty will be to deliver and take messages for me,' Carmenya said. 'We have far more technology here than on the marsh. You will have to learn how to use a small switchboard.'

'A what?'

Ember lifted the handset on the desk. 'This,' she drawled. Carmenya explained patiently what it was. There were many other machines in the office, all looking as if they could be easily damaged by the unwary. Corinna had severe doubts about whether she would ever get the hang of them before disaster struck. She had a feeling that, whatever Carmenya had said, Ember Threadhook at least did not appear overjoyed about her arrival. It would probably be greeted with delight only if she made a mess of something. Corinna felt more comfortable working with things that had a brain, even if they were small ones like dank brains. She took the precaution of not expressing any doubts in front of the Threadhook girl, however. Mid-afternoon, Carmenya escorted Corinna back to her house. They walked in the pale, winter sunlight.

'You did well today,' Carmenya said.

'Did I? Some of it was very confusing.

'As I said, you'll soon get used to it. Your mother did.' Corinna smiled. She could imagine Dannel flapping about the court very well. At the front door to Corinna's house, Carmenya took the girl in her arms for the first time and, very professionally, kissed her. Corinna couldn't help but compare it to the kisses she'd shared with L'Belder. In fact, there was very little difference.

'That was unexpected,' she said.

'But not unwelcome, I trust . . .'

Corinna shrugged helplessly. She knew about the part of her duties in the city that Carmenya had been sensitive enough not to mention just yet. She knew the General had been restraining herself deliberately and was grateful.

'Corinna, may I call on you this evening?' Carmenya said.

Corinna blushed; she couldn't help it. 'This evening?'

'Have you made plans already?' Carmenya was willing

133

to wait if Corinna said no.

'Of course not. Yes, come round.'

Carmenya smiled brightly and sauntered off, with a wave of her hand.

Oh Goddess! Corinna thought, once inside. Can I handle this? She hurried to the kitchen and informed Endaline that the General would be there for dinner. Endaline was delighted and rushed off to find Sheba. Both women knew what this visit meant. Corinna felt as if she was treading on needles. Half of her was welcoming it, half of her was petrified. She didn't know why. It wasn't that she found Carmenya unattractive or that she wasn't keen on sexual encounters. The time with L'Belder had been thoroughly enjoyable and although it would have to be different with a woman, the sensations couldn't vary that much. More skill would be needed, she felt, but Carmenya was expecting her to be inexperienced anyway. Corinna spent an hour in the bath. Part of her was afraid that the General would pick up some lingering trace of L'Belder on her, which common sense told her was impossible.

Sheba and Endaline excelled themselves with the meal. The dining-room was prepared to exquisite perfection; the lights just right, the flowers just strongly-scented enough without being overpowering, all the silver cutlery gleaming in the lamp-light. Corinna wore her hair loose and dressed in a flowing robe which she belted at the hips. Her attendants were beside themselves with excitement.

'This is your moment, milady,' Sheba said, eyes shining, hands clasped beneath her chin. 'The General thinks very highly of you, I can tell. She honours few angeldt with her attentions. This is a very high honour.' These words only made Corinna more nervous.

Carmenya arrived with an expensive bottle of vintage ebony port, which Sheba took from her hands with a flutter whilst Endaline took her cloak. Corinna came into the hall. 'We've prepared dinner,' she said awkwardly.

'Good, I'm starving.' Carmenya slapped Endaline on the backside and strode past Corinna into the parlour, the women giggling behind her. 'Well, you've certainly made a home of this place,' Carmenya said, flopping down in a chair. 'Corinna, you look like you're just about to be tortured to death. Sit down.'

The meal went off very well and they drank all the ebony port. Thus, when Carmenya suggested that she and Corinna should retire for the night, Corinna was past nervousness. In Corinna's bedroom, the General stripped off unselfconsciously to display her lean, almost boyish body, something she evidently took pride in. She did not seem to expect anything of Corinna, she was only concerned that Corinna herself should gain some pleasure from the experience. 'I shall enjoy teaching you,' she said. 'How does this feel?' Corinna writhed happily beneath Carmenya's attentions. It was certainly very different to what she'd done with L'Belder, not better or worse, just different. She considered for a moment that it would be bliss to experience both kinds of lovemaking whenever she wanted to, only banishing such thoughts when she realised it was perhaps a little irreverent. She was still unsure whether the General could read her mind or not. There was so much to do; Carmenya seemed proficient in every permutation of giving pleasure. 'Oh, this was worth waiting for,' Carmenya declared. Corinna felt brave enough to try and return the caresses she'd been given and gloried in an amazing sense of power as Carmenya lost control and whimpered and tossed beneath the touch of her hand and mouth. Their encounters gradually became more frenzied. Corinna screamed out, not caring who heard her, her whole body vibrating with delight. She wanted Carmenya to tear her apart. Eventually, they just lay panting on top of the bed, Corinna with her head on Carmenya's shoulder.

'It was important to me that you enjoyed yourself tonight,' Carmenya said. 'I know you've been in two minds about this.'

'Oh, I haven't; not really. You're just a bit overpowering at times.'

'You didn't want to leave Vangery though, did you?'

'Not when I was there, no. But I haven't regretted it since moving in here.'

135

Carmenya tightened her arm around Corinna's shoulder. 'Things might get rocky for a while here, C'rinna. I'd beter warn you.'

'What do you mean?'

Carmenya sighed. 'Just politics.'

'You mean the rebels, the men.'

'Yes. I suppose you must disagree with the way men are treated here in the city, but you must realise that they are a very different species to the husbands and sons of the marsh women. No Meonels in Silven Crescent, that's for sure. They're an evil lot. We can't give them the privilege of freedom even if we wanted to because they'd abuse it and cause trouble. They'd want to take control. We have to keep them down, you see, otherwise the last three hundred years will have been wasted. Don't you know what would happen.'

'They'd enslave the women.'

'Oh, not just that! They'd try to kill the planet, just like they did on the homeworld. Men have no respect for life, human or otherwise.'

Corinna couldn't help thinking of Shyya then, gentle Shyya who wouldn't hurt a soul. Surely there had to be males like that in the city. Could they really all be dangerous lunatics? And what about L'Belder . . .? No, don't think of him, not here, not now. Corinna shivered.

'Are you cold?' Carmenya asked. 'Let's get into bed.'

'What's going to happen then?' Corinna enquired as they burrowed into the blankets.

Carmenya seemed reluctant to answer at first. 'The men need to be controlled more efficiently. We don't really need them in the city. The Dominatrix thinks it best they set up their own community outside Silven Crescent, which would be policed by Flamists.'

'Isn't that rather a risk? I thought men were supposed to be kept apart.'

Again Carmenya paused. 'They will be,' she said at last.

'In a community?' How?'

'Segregation. Enforced segregation. Real cages,' Carmenya said, and that silenced both of them.

CHAPTER TWENTY-ONE

ELVON L'BELDER WAS was out on the marsh. It was one of those rare days, between storms, when one could think of Spring and actually imagine it happening one day. Watery sunlight turned the water to metal in places where the ice had been broken. L'Belder was riding Corinna's dank; now the beast was just about used to him. His longest conversations took place with the danks. In Vangery, only Dannel and the eunuch Shyya knew who and what he was, and Dannel was still nervous of speaking to him, in case someone, such as Bolivia, should work out he was any different from the other men. He still missed Corinna occasionally. Although he'd hardly had the time to get to know her properly, he wished she could have stayed in Vangery. He often wondered what was going on in Silven Crescent, not just how the people he was fond of fared, but if the situation had degenerated any further for the men. The Dominatrix could do it, if she wanted to. Men could be farmed, just like animals. Sex was no longer essential for the procreation of children. It was a horrific situation. And here am I, L'Belder thought, stuck here, not doing anything. But what the hell can I do? He squinted into the distance towards the floating forests. With each passing day, he felt less certain of his ability to find the Greylids. He knew Dannel wanted them to exist, but she could provide no proof that they did. It would be so easy to give in and live this marsh-life, hoping Silven Crescent's ways never extended this far. It had been much better when he'd still been a child. The Dominatrix's mother had been in power then, and life had been different. Of course, there had been the odd group of extremist flamists who'd spoken out against men, small privileges that had been earned over the years had gradually been eroded, the old Dominatrix's hand had been slowly forced by a small, but loud-voiced minority; but, on the whole, life hadn't been that bad. Even now, he could find very little fault with the old ways, before Yani came to power. He could see the woman's point of view in a lot of things, because he was no fool. He knew just how power hungry some men could be. Yet he was also sure there had to be a better way of coping with it than Yani's extreme measures. The answer must be so simple. Why the hell did it have to evade him? If only he could know the truth about what had happened on Artemis when the colonists had first arrived. How had it been between men and women then? In his youth, teachers had seemed very cagey about those times. His female friends had echoed this complaint. Oh, for the days when boys had still been allowed education! he thought bitterly. Was something being deliberately kept from the people of Artemis about their history?

Yet, despite his mental turmoil, physically he felt so much stronger now. The hard-working life on Vangery had toned up his muscles and given him new vitality. He'd found the other men a little strange at first. Unlike the ones he'd known in Silven Crescent, they didn't harbour any deep hatred for women. Some of the servants even had wives – an unknown circumstance in the city now. There, marriages were only allowed between women. When he'd left, men and women lived together in the suburbs, or rather women were allowed to *keep* men there, but as far as he could tell, no female attached to the court had any truck with the opposite sex. He did not feel you could count slavery as contact. Here, on the marsh, all hostilities were tempered to a half recognisable uneasiness; nothing more. Without a doubt, effort on behalf of the city could inflame that vague uneasiness into something far worse. That was what worried him most. He could be comfortable in Vangery, but for how long? He shivered and took one last look at the smudge of the forests in the distance before turning his dank for home.

Meonel knew something was going on. He was sensitive enough to pick up a weird kind of closeness between his wife and his attendant. Ridiculous images had begun to spring to mind when he lay awake at night. Could it be possible that Dannel was eliciting some kind of physical pleasure from Shyya? No. Impossible. And yet . . . he'd seen their eyes meet with obvious conspiracy, perceived the almost imperceptible nod of Dannel's head should they pass each other. At first it made him laugh, and then made him angry. What the hell was going on? Then there was the strange man Dannel and Shyya had brought into the house. He made Meonel uneasy too, always lurking about the place with a winter face as if he carried a storm cloud above his head. He'd never known Dannel to buy a man like that before. Her tastes had always veered towards the fey and languid. Talking of which, the fey and languid Gabriel had confessed certain fears about the newcomer to Meonel. 'I hate having him out of my sight, yet I feel threatened when he's in the same room; it's uncanny,' Gabriel said. Meonel could sympathise. 'It's not as if he doesn't work,' the cook continued, 'or that he seems to resent what he's doing; far from it. There's just something strange about him. The others feel it too.'

Now Meonel was sprawled in his room, feeling as if his life was somehow falling apart at the seams. He'd thought he'd been insecure before. Now it was worse. Corinna had gone; he never realised he'd miss her. Shyya was keeping something from him; something that wouldn't have bothered him at all once. And Dannel . . . Dannel was just different. She'd stopped watching him like a bird of prey, as if she'd handed over the reins that controlled him to Shyya. What was Shyya to her? He was going to her office every day now. Meonel had once listened outside the door. He had heard only the soft murmur of conversation, the chink of china; nothing more. What did they talk about? In moments of private terror late at night, Meonel dared to wonder whether they were plotting against him in some way. Perhaps Dannel wanted to get rid of him. Perhaps this Joel person was earmarked to become her new husband! Would he be out on the marsh one day with

Shyya, having been lulled into treating it as routine, only to have the eunuch dispose of him forever? This thought was made worse by the fact that Meonel had decided he was fond of Shyya and that perhaps one day his desires might be brought out of the realm of make-believe and he and Shyya might become more than friends. His dark fantasies haunted him throughout the day. He could think of no reasons, other than threatening ones, for the secret closeness between his wife and Shyya.

Meanwhile, Shyya and Dannel were conferring in the manner that Meonel had grown to suspect. They were discussing L'Belder and how the entire household seemed to be made uncomfortable by him. Over the past few weeks, especially since Corinna had left for the city, Dannel had come to enjoy the eunuch's company more and more. It was strange for her, since previously she'd been rather a lone creature, who'd never sought deep conversation with anyone. Now, she had learned to open her heart to Shyya. It had started with Shyya reporting to her every day about how L'Belder was getting on. Gradually the meetings lengthened , eventually to include the sharing of milk-suds and biscuits. Now they talked for long after the cups were drained and the plates empty.

'In the Spring, he'll continue his search,' Shyya said. 'It's not that long to wait. Everyone will just have to put up with him until then.'

'His search for what? The Greylids?' Dannel laughed, a sound choked off when she saw Shyya didn't share her amusement. 'You think they exist?'

'I'm not sure. I've only heard tales. . . '

'What were they?'

Shyya smiled, a genuine warmth that always made Dannel's heart jump. He was a lovely creature. What a pity.

'Artemis is a big world. We know so little of it.'

'I know what you're suggesting; that the Greylids are some kind of native race. That's out of the question. This world must have been thoroughly examined for life before anyone was allowed to colonise it.'

'Think about it though. How could a world this developed in flora and fauna *not* have produced an intelligent race? The animals, I'm told, are very similar to those found on the home-world. How come there are no creatures equivalent to humans?'

'You seem to know a lot about the home-world, Shyya. How? Is it just an example of the traits that women hate in men? Was that why you were . . . mutilated . . . because of curiosity about the past?' Dannel wondered whether she'd gone too far. It was the first time his emasculation had been mentioned between them. Shyya looked her straight in the eye.

'No, it was nothing like that. Do you want to know the real reason?'

Dannel knew he would tell her if she said yes. Now she hesitated. 'Only if you want to speak of it, Shyya,' she answered vaguely.

'I hope you're not squeamish, Madam Trotgarden!' It occurred to Dannel, for the first time, that Shyya might actually need to tell someone. He existed within himself quite happily, it was obvious, but perhaps sometimes, on those low ebb days, he needed a confidante and didn't have one.

'Women did this to me,' he said.

'I know. I'd guessed that much.' She tried to be soothing. Perhaps he hadn't thought about it for a long time.

'It is different further north than here,' he began, 'it's more primitive, with less use of modern technology. Perhaps it's because they're farther from the city there, but they've really retreated into the past – humanity's past. I've only realised how much since I left there. They never have visitors from the south other than the traders. The communities are different to the shemble-frack farms you have here. Admittedly, the terrain is a little different; the isles are farther apart, but larger, supporting villages, whose people only meet socially for the major religious festivals. The northerners adhere to a very old belief system, rooted in ancient human culture. It can be fierce, its rituals barbaric.' He paused.

141

Goddess, we know so little here!' Dannel exclaimed. 'You're talking about a distance of only a day's lope-leagues away and it might as well be on Eden for all we care!'

Shyya shrugged. 'How can it matter? No Artemisians can be said to work together exactly, except for the marsh families here in the south. The northerners would not welcome interest from the Lawn Isles, believe me.'

Dannel poured them both another drink. The windows of her office were steamed up, hiding the view of the winter marsh. She leaned back in comfort and Shyya told her about the north, about himself. It was quite an education for her.

Once a year, before the Mid-Summer Ritual, the priestesses of the northern isles meet together in one of the central temples. Although the common people rarely interact throughout the year, other than to trade goods, the priestesshood of the isles is very closely linked. Between them, they select from the community a young boy in the full flower of youth, who is destined to play a major part in the ritual. This is looked upon as a great honour; all the families are eager to offer their sons for the position. Shyya's family was no exception. After the Ritual itself, the chosen boy ceremonially couples with the High Priestess in the fields beyond the temple. The people believe that this act ensures the fertility of the land for the following year. If the High Priestess should become pregnant by the chosen boy, all the better, especially should the resulting child be a girl. Such children are held in high esteem and, when adult, occupy governing positions within the community. One year, the chosen boy had been Shyya.

Dannel's eyes widened at this point in the story. Her imagination was supplying a horrific end to it. Had he escaped a terrible death?

'No, it's not as you think,' Shyya said, shaking his head. 'Admittedly, after the Ritual, there has to be some kind of symbolic demise for the chosen one, but there was no frenzied tearing of my flesh by equally frenzied women.

It was nothing like that. None of the ceremonies involve actual killing, whether of animal or man, surprisingly enough.'

He told her of the evening of the ritual, how the moons were round and full above the silver fields of still water and ground cherry. He invoked a picture in Dannel's mind of the torch-lit isles, the sounds of revelry eerily small in the enormous night, where even the animals seemed to respect the sanctity of what was taking place and kept their silence. Shyya had been taken by boat to a place some leagues away from any of the islands. Left alone, he had gazed about himself, shivering in his insubstantial ceremonial robes, which were already wet about the hems and heavy round his ankles. For a while, he had stood in the shallow water, occasionally looking back over his shoulder at the nearest isle that was wreathed in a yellow halo. He waited, trembling, not quite sure what would happen to him, but fighting his fear because he understood the importance of the event. And then, between the thick stalks of a stand of kale rushes, he saw her; a white, evanescent shape, wavering ghost-like in the light of the moons. The High Priestess, newly appointed, virgin pure, a sacred maiden.

'So lovely she was,' Shyya said, even now in a voice softened by reverence, 'hardly human, naked, her long hair swirling like smoke. She beckoned me, and I followed her.'

Through the kales, the plaisel-groves, the priestess had led the boy onwards, pausing sometimes so he could keep up with her, laughing softly, cupping her breasts as an offering, tempting and luring him far away from the flickering isles. During the pursuit, Shyya felt as if his humanity dropped away from him, along with his ruined robes, as if what hastened its way through the marsh groves was not a man, but merely the essence of all that is male. He believed he had become the God. And she, the Maiden Lady, happily basking in her power that perhaps would only be with her for this one night, she let him catch her in the shadows of a threadwood spinney, and there he took her, there the young god ploughed the fertile soil of

143

Artemis, filling it with seed. It was, he said, the most magnificent moment of his life.

'Only a few hours, but in that time we loved in all its essential meaning of the word. We were responsible for the fate of the world and our sacrifice, our coupling, would ensure prosperity for all our people. Even now, I can say that what happened afterwards cannot detract from those hours. I would go through it all again if I had the choice.'

Dannel was astonished, and in the wake of that feeling, even envious. What Shyya was telling her was that for one night he had achieved godhead. Her own religion seemed such a pale imitation, devoid of mystic experiences as it was. No wonder Shyya was so subliminally alluring. It was that time, with him for all his life, shining through his skin. Dannel was awed.

'Of course, what occurred next was nowhere near so uplifting,' Shyya said drily. 'Before dawn, they came for us. We were separated, taken back to the Temple in different boats. I didn't know what they would do to me; that's one of their secrets, and ex-chosen ones are never released again into the community to tell. Gone was my beautiful girl-bride of the previous night. Back at the temple, she was one of them again, scorning men, believing women to be all that she wanted. I suppose she must have felt a little ashamed, knowing that I had seen her as she really was, what she was supposed to be. She chose my symbolic death, and it was more of a symbol for herself than for her people, I think. She ordered them to cut me; not everything, just enough to keep me beardless, I suppose. Someone told me the women ate what they cut away. I'm not sure if that's true. I was sent to the farthest isle where all the chosen ones live out their lives, in luxury or in pious retreat, whatever they want. It was not enough for me. I felt cheated, abused, ruined. Surely, as I'd been equal to the High Priestess for that one night, I could be equal forever? I saw that the women were enforcing a lie, lying to themselves, lying to their deities. I hated them. I tried to run away, headed north, to escape the marsh. The escape hadn't been planned well enough and I'd been foolish enough to confide in one of the other men. He betrayed me and I was caught and flogged. The next time I tried it, I got a little further, but still they caught me. The High Priestess sent word that she felt I'd disappointed her. There was no further punishment. They just sold me to the next slaver that passed through.'

Shyya sighed, looked at Dannel, tried a weak smile. 'So, now you know,' he said.

'I don't know what to say to you.'

Shyya shrugged. 'I don't expect you to say anything. It was some time ago. I've come to terms with it. There are worse things that can happen, I'm sure.'

Dannel nervously poured them both another hot drink. The last one had gone cold in the cups. 'So,' she said, brightly, eager to change the subject. 'You said that back home you'd heard tales of the Greylids. What were they? Anything for our friend Elvon L'Belder to go on?'

'It's hard to say, really. People always tend to exaggerate, don't they? We heard about a tribe of people living in the far forests. Some travellers claimed they had actually traded with them.'

'What did they say these people were like?'

'They called them the Veiled Ones. It was said they would sometimes appear at night when traders were huddled round their camp-fires. They would trade wondrous tales for whatever the travellers would give them. One woman said that whatever the Greylids took would be found again in the marsh some leagues further on. The isle people were sceptical. Traders are notorious for their supernatural stories, most of which we suspected were totally fictional. Some people, my mother included, thought the Greylids, if they existed, must be individuals who'd broken away from southern cities or other communities to set up on their own, perhaps men and women who lived together as equals. Another theory was they were folk who'd been evicted from the marsh isles during the time of conflict. There were many suppositions.'

'Do you think they *could* be true natives of Artemis?'

'As a child, I liked to think so. Obviously, I have no facts to back that belief up. Perhaps it's just a romantic fancy.'

Dannel drank some suds. 'Then L'Belder might have some chance after all.'

'Of finding them, certainly. But they might not want to help him. If they exist at all, they shun the marsh society and the cities. Intruders will hardly be welcome, I think. Personally, I don't believe finding this race will be the answer to L'Belder's problems. He'd be better off trying to hide among the northern isles, where as long as men behave themselves, they're free to live as they like. There *are* injustices, but on the whole a certain amount of respect between people. Our laws were those of our religion. We respected the soil, the water, the elements. If a man was prepared to go along with that, he could find himself an unoccupied grove and live there alone if he wanted to. As long as he paid his tithes and made appearances at the festivals, he'd be left alone. If L'Belder did that, he might not be able to make the changes in the south he wants to, but at least he'd be alive.'

'I'm inclined to agree with you, Shyya.' Dannel leaned back in her chair, her face wreathed in a smile, but not because of L'Belder's plight. For the first time ever, she'd been given some proof, however tenuous, that the people of her dreams really existed. Whether they'd help L'Belder or not, she'd give her eye-teeth to catch sight of them.

'I think it would be best if you started to spend a little more time with our fugitive, Shyya,' she said. 'Find out what he's planning. It would look less suspicious coming from you, less likely to attract comment than if I started paying him too much attention.'

Shyya looked at her meaningfully. Dannel experienced a brief swell of warmth because she understood what he was thinking: they'd become that close. 'Meonel,' she said, and sighed. 'Does he know anything?'

Shyya shook his head. 'No, but I get a feeling he'll start getting curious if I befriend L'Belder. He knows I've never struck up any particular friendships here. He's also suspicious about my relationship with you. . . '

Dannel couldn't help laughing, although she recognised that it was to cover a certain amount of embarrassment. 'What did he say?'

'Nothing. He doesn't have to. I'm thoroughly acquainted with Meonel's moods by now. They can be quite graphic.'

'Well, he'll just have to suspect and be moody then! There are far bigger issues here than Meonel's comfort.'

Shyya rose to leave and Dannel followed him to the door. 'Goddess, Shyya, what are we coming to?' she asked. 'What's happening to our dull little lives?'

Shyya shrugged. 'Inevitable change, I think. There's nothing we can do except take care and see what happens.'

'I don't know what I'd do without you.'

'You'd manage, madam. There'd be someone else to help you, I'm sure.'

'No-one like you though. I'll see you tomorrow. And Shyya, in this room, I'd like you to address me as Dannel. We can be friends here, can't we?'

He smiled carefully and nodded. Dannel watched him retreat down the corridor towards Meonel's rooms. Downstairs, Gabriel was singing loudly. That must mean L'Belder was out on the marsh.

Shyya could tell that Meonel was spoiling for a fight. He'd deliberately refrained from talking about the day they'd seen the women out on the marsh ever since Corinna had told him what was going on. Meonel, who made an art out of not appearing curious, was too proud to mention it himself. Yet, Shyya could tell he thought about it sometimes, and probably wondered whether it had anything to do with the way things were changing in Vangery. Shyya took many verbal beatings off Meonel without retaliating, (usually when the man had drunk himself into a temper), because he had the capacity to see past the truculence to the bewildered child inside. Sometimes Shyya felt so much older than Meonel even though Meonel must be his senior by at least eight years. Whatever Meonel said or did, and they were sometimes very hurtful things, Shyya could not hate him. He admitted to himself that the physical attraction he felt for Meonel was strong enough to cancel out any anger his moods inspired. Shyya didn't find many people attractive. He also knew that the

147

way he felt for Meonel could not possibly be a good thing and was unlikely to come to any happy conclusion. Meonel had far too many mental problems at present to be a prospective lover, so Shyya comforted himself by sticking to the idea that the attraction was purely physical rather than emotional. It was one of the absurd lies that desperate people tell themselves. Meonel did have good days, when his sense of humour took precedence over less savoury aspects of his character, but today was not one of them. He had the familiar set about his jaw that meant trouble; spitefulness, meanness, cruelty, the usual melange.

Meonel was sitting in the dark beside a shuttered window. Shyya sighed and went to open the blinds a little. Here it came.

'Shyya! Don't do that. I like the dark.' Shyya noticed the empty bottle by Meonel's feet and braced himself.

'It's stuffy in here. I should open the window too.'

'I decide when the window opens. Shut the blind.'

Shyya's hand lingered at the cord. He could see L'Belder down at the stables, shovelling reed-straw. Meonel caught him staring.

'Was it your idea to buy him?' he said, unexpectedly.

'Don't be ridiculous. Mistress Trotgarden buys the slaves. How could I influence her?'

Meonel made an explosive sound. 'Very easily, I should think. You spend enough time with her.'

'She needs someone to talk to now Corinna's gone.'

'Strange. She didn't when Corinna was still here. I doubt if they've exchanged more than a few words since Corinna was a child.' Shyya sat on the window-sill. He thought he might as well be direct, feeling safer now that he had Dannel as an ally. Meonel could not see his face.

'Do you feel threatened because I talk to your wife,' he said. 'After all, you don't talk to her yourself very often, do you?'

Meonel shot to his feet, tripping on the bottle, arms waving. 'I've had more than enough of your silky impertinence, you arrogant gelding!' Shyya thought Meonel was going to strike him. He winced and Meonel lowered his hands. 'Does it amuse you to torment me?' he continued, less vehemently. Shyya could see that Meonel's eyes were bloodshot and unfocussed.

'I don't mean to torment you,' he said. 'Perhaps you see things that aren't there.'

Leaning on furniture, Meonel went to the middle of the room, there to stand swaying, waving a finger to punctuate his words. 'I know you're up to something, you and the bloated bag. What's going on? Why all these furtive conversations? You all think I'm a fool, that I haven't noticed, don't you! What do you know, Shyya?' His tone became wheedling. 'Come on, don't we men have to stick together? Have you no sense of loyalty? Tell me!'

For a moment, Shyya considered whether it would be wise to tell Meonel the truth or not. Could he be trusted? Meonel had no love of Bolivia, and even less of women in general. Could he ever be a threat to L'Belder? Shyya doubted it, yet he didn't really want to say anything without asking Dannel's permission. Normally, he made his own decisions, but he also respected Dannel's position in this. He would speak to her about it tomorrow.

'There's nothing for you to worry about,' he said. Meonel grabbed him by the shoulders.

'Isn't there?' A silence formed, during which Meonel became aware of what he was doing. He was plainly embarassed but couldn't move. Shyya gently removed his hands, but did not step away. They were very close.

'You're bruising me, sir.'

It was a moment when Meonel might have been able to say anything. He knew this, but still he backed away. Afterwards, he would analyse this conversation a thousand times, cursing himself, regretting things, thinking of a multitude of words that always came to mind too late. Now his mind was blank and he was afraid to initiate anything. 'Get out,' he said and Shyya left him alone.

More shaken than he liked to admit, Shyya's first instinct was to get out of the house. He grabbed a coat from the bundle that always hung, for anyone's use, by the kitchen door, and went outside. The air was damp but fresh,

149

tainted by a faint resinous reek of skin-pine oil that the Trotgardens used to fire the generator. Shyya thought he might as well go and speak to L'Belder now as any other time. At least the man was alone. He wandered down to the stables and leaned on an open door. Inside, L'Belder was still shovelling straw. After a few moments, he felt he was being watched and turned round, unconsciously brandishing the fork in a threatening manner.

'Oh, it's you,' he said, and carried on working.

'How are you getting on?'

'Fine. The room's fine, the food's fine, the work's fine, I'm even growing muscles. It's a regular holiday.'

'You've fitted in well, L'Belder, sorry, it's Joel now, isn't it? Mistress Trotgarden is pleased.'

L'Belder grunted, perhaps aware that Shyya was not being entirely truthful. Shyya went into the stable. He looked back at the house and caught a glimpse of Meonel's strained, white face at the window before he ducked aside. 'What do you want?' L'Belder asked. Shyya realised the man was uncomfortable with him for the usual reason.

'Castration is not infectious,' he said. That made L'Belder look at him at least.

'Many would like it to be,' he said.

Shyya smiled. 'Are you still thinking of leaving in the Spring?'

L'Belder attacked the straw again. There was a pause before he spoke. 'I have no other option. If I don't leave, Silven Crescent will come here for me. The mangak will be back some day. I can't take the risk of staying here.'

'None of your options are particularly inviting, L'Belder. I pity you.'

The other man laughed, without humour.

'The pity of a eunuch. It seems I can fall no further.'

Shyya was used to that kind of remark. Several months of being in Meonel's service had hardened him to it. L'Belder stopped shovelling and leaned on his fork, staring at the wall.

'Goddess . . . I'm sorry. That was unforgivable.' It was the first time that anyone had been abashed enough to apologise. Shyya felt he could get used to that kind of change.

'If it's unforgivable, why ask for forgiveness? Is that a flask of wine? May I have some.'

'Of course.'

Shyya went to sit in the clean straw at the back of the stable. He drank some of the wine. 'I've heard rumours that the people you're looking for live in the northern groves of Ire and Penitence. They were only rumours, you understand, but it might be a good idea for you to head that way.'

L'Belder's face lit up. He hunkered down next to Shyya in the straw and took the wine-flask from him.

'You're joking! This is the best news I've ever had!'

'Only rumours.'

'I had less than that to go on before.' He beamed like a happy child. Shyya had half guessed something had happened between this man and Corinna. Looking at him now, he could understand why Corinna had been tempted. Shyya had always known how much Corinna had felt for him and had enjoyed it. Selfish perhaps, but it had still pricked him with jealousy when he thought of her with this man. He could feel L'Belder's power, his compassion, his zeal. If it was not written all over his face, it at least shone from his aura. This was the kind of man Dannel should have had for a husband, he thought, and Meonel's face came into his mind. Poor Meonel. A sad wraith compared with this living force.

'Tell me what you know,' L'Belder said, and Shyya recounted what little he'd heard.

'I'm not sure if it will help, or whether, if you find them, they'll be the slightest bit interested in your troubles,' he said. 'As I said to Mistress Trotgarden, if the Greylids exist at all, they clearly shun contact with the rest of us.'

'True, but I have to try. It's the only hope we've got.' He looked hard at Shyya. 'And I mean "we"; all men.'

'Have you forgotten? I'm less than a man.'

'No you're not.' L'Belder leapt to his feet and began scattering more straw. 'Thank you, Shyya. You've lifted my spirits.'

Shyya inclined his head. 'My pleasure,' he said. He knew he should return to the house, that Meonel was probably

151

watching the stables waiting for him to come out, but now that L'Belder's hopes had been revived, his fascination was beginning to exert its influence. Shyya wanted to stay and listen to him. The city man was full of fine words and fine sentiments, most of them highly impractical. Shyya felt he knew a damn sight more about human nature than L'Belder did, but kept his mouth shut. It was pleasant to suspend belief and live in L'Belder's utopia for half an hour or so. Such a refreshing change after months of Meonel's grinding pessimism. He realised it would be a waste of breath to try and convince L'Belder to settle in the north and forget his cause. Here was a man with purpose, and Shyya had revived it with rumours. For a while, he wondered whether he'd done the right thing.

CHAPTER TWENTY-TWO

Now, as well as visiting Dannel every day, Shyya would seek out L'Belder, providing the fugitive with a much needed sympathetic ear. Dannel liked to hear what the man had said; she and Shyya discussed it every morning. This induced further edginess in Meonel. In the afternoons, if he sat in his window seat he could be sure of seeing Shyya go out riding on the marsh with the new man. In the mornings, he could hear Shyya laughing with Dannel in her office. Inevitably, Shyya was spending less time than he used to with Meonel. Dannel was always giving him something to do. Meonel suffered a wretched anger, taking his frustration out on Shyya with insults and jibes. He realised that he had once been the central figure in Vangery with Dannel suppliant to his childish petulance and Shyya rushing round him to please. Now what was he? A bystander. It seemed his comfort and well-being were no longer important. The people who'd been closest to him, and had indulged his moods, were gone. Why? He would rest his forehead on the window and see Shyya galloping his dank across the causeway, L'Belder behind. Where did they go to? Were they lovers now? If he, Meonel, in his lethargy, had bothered to extend his hand, even once, towards Shyya, would this be happening now?

One day, Meonel decided to go out riding. He hadn't bothered going out at all since the weather had got so cold, but he kept telling himself he was bored and that a shrieking wind would complement his habitual headache nicely. Once, he'd have just gone to sleep or got drunk. Now, he told himself, he'd got beyond that. It was nothing to do with Shyya. He had no desire to follow Shyya and L'Belder out onto the marsh. That afternoon, he waited until they'd been gone ten minutes before creeping outdoors.

He spared a wistful thought for the time when he hadn't been able to put a toe off Vangery Isle without Dannel's voice ringing out to call him back. Now, he was a shadow. Shyya had taught him how to saddle a dank. No-one questioned him in the stables. The men just waved and greeted him and went about their work. Even Bolivia, coming back from some errand, smiled nastily at him as she handed her dank to a stable-boy. The cold air felt good on his face. He was wrapped up well in furs; there was no discomfort. He'd chosen a big, powerful beast. Its muscles surged fluidly between his thighs and the marsh flew past them as they galloped out onto the causeway, spray flying up beneath the animal's feet. Within a few minutes, he realised he'd perhaps been a little ambitious in his choice of mount. The animal strained against his hold, honking and side-stepping, leaping into the air at every bird flying up from the marsh. Unpleasant visions of being flung into the water rose uncomfortably to mind. Meonel only hoped that if such an indignity occurred, nobody should see it. Spinneys and tussocks flew past, water flew up to strike his face. Leaning forward, he gave the beast its head and prayed it might soon exhaust itself.

He didn't expect to catch up with L'Belder and Shyya so soon. One moment he was alone, the next, he'd skirted a grove of plaisels and virtually ran straight into them. They were walking their danks, each of them leading a couple of unsaddled animals behind them. Meonel's dank squealed and splashed to an excited halt, greeting its stable-mates enthusiastically. Meonel realised, warmly, that it must have looked quite impressive. 'Meonel!' Shyya said. Further gratification was granted by the fact that Shyya sounded so surprised. But now, Meonel hadn't a clue what to say and annoyed himself by being pleasant.

'I had to get out of the house today. You were right Shyya. It's stuffy in there.' Now an uncontrollable smile was on his face. Shyya's long hair was wet with spray, his forehead smeared with mud. He looked, as always, enchanting. Meonel noticed that Joel had shaved off his beard. In many ways, he looked like an older, more rugged version of Shyya. No wonder they had gravitated towards each other.

'You can take one of these if you like,' Shyya said, holding out a set of reins. 'This one's pulling away from the others.'

Meonel followed them around the marsh for over an hour. Shyya had to deliver something from Dannel to the Tendaughters, who were still being frosty because of the jilted Sander. Yaschel came to the door herself and glared at Meonel. She asked if he'd heard from Corinna. Meonel had to say he hadn't. Yaschel grunted and slammed the door. Meonel pulled a face and Shyya and the other man laughed. The suns were sinking by the time they returned to Vangery. L'Belder offered to stable Meonel's dank, which Meonel accepted. He was tired and glad to be home, even though the afternoon had been much pleasanter than he could have hoped for. Now he would go upstairs and change, and wait for Shyya to come to him.

Shyya helped L'Belder rub the danks down with clean switches of straw. He'd been surprised that Meonel had turned up that afternoon and, he had to admit, pleased too. Meonel had been quite cheerful and hadn't been rude once. To Shyya, this was almost miraculous. Forbidden thoughts dared to hover in his mind once more, which he decided not to dismiss. In a moment, he would go to Meonel's rooms with a tray of hot milk-suds. Perhaps Meonel would continue in his mellow mood. Then L'Belder brought him down to earth in an unexpected way. 'That's the Trotgarden woman's husband, isn't it?' he said. Shyya nodded. L'Belder raised his brows.

'Is what Corinna said about them true?'

'What did she say?'

'That Dannel keeps him for his pretty face and nothing more?'

Shyya felt himself bristling. 'Not exactly, no. She's very fond of Meonel. He's just rather melancholy.'

155

'Needs excitement, no doubt. Is his hair real?'

'What do you mean, real?'

'That greeny gold colour. Is it dyed?'

'Not that I know of.'

'Maybe I shall find out!' L'Belder smiled wickedly in a conspiratorial way, which caused Shyya's heart to sink. L'Belder was a whole man. He was charismatic and handsome and whole. Meonel was lonely. End of story.

'Don't look so glum,' L'Belder said, smiling. Shyya experienced a horrifying shudder as he realised his feelings were becoming so apparent. He shook his head, turning away to rearrange dank tackle that had already been tidied. L'Belder put a hand on his shoulder and he couldn't help flinching but resisted the urge to shrug him off.

'Hey, there's no need for this you know,' the man said softly.

'What do you mean?' Shyya asked, for once truly oblivious. L'Belder turned him around.

'I'm only teasing you,' he said.

'Are you?'

'But of course. Meonel's a cold fish; I'm not that interested. Really.' A slow dawning of realisation made its presence warm and known in Shyya's mind. So, perhaps his feelings weren't that obvious. He tried to take a step back which L'Belder wouldn't allow. 'Shyya, you're a proud creature. . . '

No, I'm not, Shyya's brain protested, but he kept quiet. 'I respect your reticence. Now, I want you to know. Meonel can freeze to death for all I care. He's a fool. The elixir of life is before him and he doesn't drink. . . '

'You don't know that, Elvon L'Belder.'

'Don't I?' L'Belder raised one eyebrow. 'Tell me you don't want me, enigmatic Shyya. Tell me that.'

'Excuse me. . . ' Shyya tried to wriggle away. This would take some thinking about. It was rather a surprise.

'Why run away?'

'I won't. A dignified walk should suffice.'

L'Belder laughed. Here was a man used to having people love him. It obviously hadn't occurred to him that

156

he, Shyya, had been thinking about Meonel. He'd read the situation completely wrong.

'When you walk away then, walk to my room,' L'Belder said. 'I'll be back shortly.' He turned away, confidence incarnate, whistling cheerfully, to attend to the animals. Shyya was stunned. First because of the man's audacity and second, because he knew where he himself would be in five minutes. He left the stables.

In the house, Gabriel was still singing. Like an automaton, Shyya climbed the stairs past the kitchen. 'Hello there!' Gabriel called. Shyya didn't answer. He didn't see Gabriel come to the door, wiping his hands on a cloth, staring after him. He wasn't aware of Gabriel's imagination running overtime, as usual. Meonel's door was open. Shyya didn't look in. His flesh squeezed tight as he passed it, but there was no call to bring him back, no magic to break the spell. Perhaps Meonel hadn't seen him. L'Belder had been given a room on the topmost floor, where the marsh wind moaned loudest at night and plucked at the tiles. It was not draughty, being well sealed, but it was a strangely desolate place, far removed from the rest of the house. Dannel had obviously considered it safer to have L'Belder there. Shyya didn't light the lamps. He walked slowly round the room, taking it in: boots on the floor, still muddied; clothes tossed over a chair, the bed unmade. On a table beneath the small window, some marsh canes in fluff stood in a glass jar, next to a couple of wizened ash fruit. Beside them lay a drawing pad and charcoal – a sketch half completed. This room contained the marks, the smell, the presence, of a living being. Standing there, Shyya felt he could have known L'Belder just as well even if he'd never met him. The man's spirit lived in this room; he'd made it his own. In contrast, Meonel's quarters were devoid of life, as if their owner passed through them without ever leaving a trace of his personality behind. Shyya sat on the single chair at the table. He picked up the drawing pad and stared at the sketch. A keen eye, a sensitive hand, humour, warmth; they were all there. Should I be here? Shyya wondered. He looked through the window at the marsh and visualised Corinna riding

157

towards Vangery, her face alight, her being brimming with vitality. Shyya had seen her; he knew. L'Belder may not be a warrior; it didn't matter. Perhaps he made a fool of himself with his lack of endurance, his lack of hardiness; it didn't matter. L'Belder was alive, he was overflowing with life and he liked to share it. A little arrogant, maybe. Even vain. It only added to his allure. Shyya sighed. The man was a born leader. People would flock to him like beasts to a waterhole. Then they would drink, and he was bottomless. He would never run dry. Even in the midst of trauma, that wellspring would sustain him. That was L'Belder's magic. Whatever Shyya felt for Meonel, however this action would affect those feelings, Shyya knew he had to taste the waters of that bottomless well. It would be foolish to deny it to himself. Once he would have rushed in, holding an empty cup aloft. That was before Vangery. Something was happening to him here. Perhaps it was something he had to fight. A lesson.

The door opened. L'Belder said nothing. He took Shyya's shoulders in his hands and lifted him from the chair. He covered Shyya's face and neck with kisses. It was like being drowned by a warm, relentless sea. Shyya let it happen. He took hold of the hand when it was offered that drew him up to ride the waves. In this man's hands he was pure, untainted, made whole. It was like discovering a secret grove where the magic waters imparted strength. Corinna had discovered this place too. Perhaps now, she sampled different pools, that offered different strengths. Shyya could not tell. He only knew that in those timeless hours spent in L'Belder's room that first time, he felt close to his lost friend. He could smell her, almost see her in the room. She was laughing, a wild, free marsh creature. Corinna, I could never give you this. . . L'Belder could. He'd given it to both of them. There were no ears pressed against the door. They were alone. But Gabriel had watched the staircase and it did not take a gossip to work out what drama was enacted behind that closed door.

CHAPTER TWENTY-THREE

IT MAY BE possible that Corinna dreamed of Shyya on the first night he spent with Elvon L'Belder. She certainly awoke with the flavour of the marsh in her throat and a vision of his loveliness fading before her eyes. It cast a dark shadow over her day. For weeks she'd barely thought about Vangery and it had been at Carmenya's prompting that she'd written a letter to Dannel, even though what postal service existed was far from efficient during the winter. The letter had been overflowing with Corinna's enthusiasm for her new life. She implied, in veiled terms, something of her relationship with the General and the happiness it had brought her. Even as she wrote, Corinna could imagine Dannel's frown at reading the words. Strange really, for hadn't it been Dannel who'd insisted her daughter leave home?

Corinna had slipped into her new job with the ease Carmenya had predicted. Admittedly, the tart and brittle Ember Threadhook had still not taken to her at all, but the other two girls were friendly enough, if a little distant. Corinna had imagined that Carmenya's duties revolved wholly around keeping order, but was surprised to learn that most of the time the General had merely to sit on committees, administrating the running of the city. Corinna had always thought of Carmenya as a woman of action who would at least be uncomfortable with the tedious wordplay of council if not downright impatient. Carmenya never voiced any dissatisfaction with her role in the city, but Corinna quickly appreciated that more could be learned from what Carmenya didn't say. An impatient sigh or quick gesture implied far more than an obvious complaint. As she came to know more members of the court and employees of the government, Corinna realised that Carmenya Oralien was a star in more than one way. Although she knew that a lot of the other women's behaviour was consciously posed, and hid sharpened scheming minds, a great number of them seemed shallow in comparison, their conversation frankly stupid. Now Corinna could catch her mentor's eye and smile when in the company of others. She was sure Carmenya shared her opinions of the city women, yet never a word was blatantly spoken about it. Once, in an outspoken moment, Corinna asked Carmenya what the courts of government were like in Silven Crescent's sister cities, Rain Haven and Ilius Crown on their high stilts to the south, Leda Waters long leagues to the east and smaller than the others, and Omany Gap only a single day's skipper journey to the east.

'The Dominatrix has her favourites governing those places,' Carmenya had answered, which was answer enough. Yes, it was the same.

Outside of the court, however, Corinna had begun to make friends with women she respected and wanted to know better. Carudan, the priestess of Parthenos for one. She'd made arrangements to meet Carudan one evening and had been introduced to a company of women whose enquiring minds and quick wit had set them far apart from the angeldt of the court. Sometimes Corinna feared that mixing with the court might affect her, infect her; Carudan and her friends were Corinna's solace. In their company, she had to use her mind or appear lacklustre. It was good exercise. Occasionally, Corinna heard talk of the unrest simmering below the apparent calm of the city, evidenced only by the sporadic outbursts of rebel activity that threatened the temples and merchants' stores around the ankles of Palace Mount. No rebel had dared to attack the Mount itself, but the shopkeepers and loyalist priestesses on the outskirts were easy meat. It was a subject that never really came to life as a conversation topic however; people were too afraid. Corinna quickly gathered that the Dominatrix disapproved of her people paying too much

160

attention to the matter. 'Let the military deal with it and mind your own business,' was the quiet but clear message. It didn't stop the talk altogether, although Corinna noticed that people were extremely careful not to sound the slightest bit sympathetic to the rebels' cause. One never knew who might be listening.

Carmenya had adopted the routine of visiting Corinna twice a week, when she would stay the night so they could make love. These were the times when they had their most intimate conversations. At first, Corinna had been on guard, afraid of what she might let out, but as time progressed, her memories faded in importance; it was less likely she'd blurt them out by accident. Carmenya spoke fervently of what she wanted for the future, how in most ways she was in accord with the Dominatrix's plans for the men. It appeared General Oralien never even thought the men might have more than a few female sympathisers; an oversight that struck Corinna as uncharacteristic of the canny Carmenya she'd got to know. The General was not ashamed to speak her mind, however.

'I would be a liar if I said I wasn't afraid of men,' she admitted. 'And lies are weakness because the threat of discovery makes you vulnerable. No, male unpredictability unnerves me, their hatred makes me uneasy. My first instinct is self-preservation; it has very little to do with Yani's glowing dreams of feminist Utopia. It's far nearer to the gut than that. If they could, men would rise up and enslave us. And if they had a good leader, that isn't as improbable as it sounds.'

'Such as Elvon L'Belder,' Corinna said before she could stop herself. Carmenya looked at her sharply, then smiled.

'Do you know, I haven't thought of him in ages! You certainly lifted a dank, dark rock there my dear! Elvon L'Belder. . . hmm. . . '

'What was he really like, Carmenya?' Corinna knew she was treading on dangerous ground but couldn't resist it. She had to know what the woman she had grown to love thought of the man who had touched her with fire.

Carmenya wrinkled her nose. 'What was he like?

161

Fearsome, C'rinna. fearsome. I wanted him dead to feel safe. He wasn't savage but sneaky. He had power that one, strange power. He should have been smothered at birth.'

'Now he's dead.'

'Yes. . .' In the silence, Corinna could tell Carmenya was wondering whether she dared to believe that. L'Belder had been her bête noire; perhaps he couldn't die for that reason. Perhaps he lived in the shadows, to emerge in the dead of night and invade her nightmares. Could he take control that way? Was he dead? Was he? Was he? There had been a whisper of late about the court that the Dominatrix knew something about L'Belder, that she knew he wasn't dead. The angeldt liked to exaggerate this into the rumour that L'Belder had, in fact, *risen* from the dead. Nonsense, really. It was a horror story, and there was always plenty of those doing the rounds. Carmenya shuddered, suddenly conscious of an unseen audience. 'I am not afraid of him,' she said. 'Not any more.' In the morning, Corinna awoke from a dream of Vangery to find Carmenya had left her side before dawn.

The Winter festival came and passed. Corinna had a very pleasant time feasting and celebrating in the company of Carmenya and, when Carmenya wasn't there, Carudan and her friends. One evening, Carmenya escorted Corinna to a dinner party at Lady Marta Blockling's manse further up the Mount. Lady Marta's house was far grander than the one Corinna lived in. All the servants wore smart uniforms, but were warm and friendly with the guests, anticipating their every need. There were no men in the house at all. Lady Marta's companion, a rather insipid creature named Emilia Flossy, engaged Corinna in conversation. Corinna had never received so many insults disguised as compliments. Eventually, out of boredom more than resentment, she said, 'You are right, Emilia. Life on the marsh is, indeed, far *earthier* than in the city. I bet you've never had to gut an animal with your bare hands, have you?'

Emilia blanched and shook her head, an expression of distaste pursing her lips. No, of course not, Corinna

162

thought, with delighted malice, and then went into great detail about what gutting involved. Emilia nearly disappeared into the cushions of the sofa they were occupying. 'So you see,' Corinna concluded, 'we might be atrocious dinner party hostesses on the marsh, but we certainly aren't squeamish!' Ha, ha! Emilia did not share this amusement. Later, Corinna regretted this rather blunt treatment of Lady Marta's protégé. After all, didn't Corinna want to forget now that she ever had done things such as gutting animals? Didn't she want to be dainty and reserved like Emilia herself? I must learn to curb myself, Corinna thought. Women like Emilia are just testing me. It's to be expected. I mustn't let it get to me. I must respond with dignity and poise until they realise I'm just as mannered as they are.

As might be expected the actual significance of the festival tended to be glossed over or even ignored at court. After all, it was masculine orientated, and thus, rather an embarrassment to the women of Silven Crescent. Corinna was surprised, however, that even the priestess made no mention of it. Now was the time when the days began to lengthen, when the young suns grew strong. On the shortest day, women carried lit candles through the streets and sang to the light, summoning it. Of course, the old rituals were pretty and traditional, but Corinna still felt uneasy because she alone seemed to realise the significance of what they were doing. Parthenos needed the masculine strength of the twin suns to make her planet fertile. Woman needed man. Did that thought cross even one woman's mind as they skipped through the icy streets singing about light and warmth? Corinna, stop this! Corinna's brain ordered in exasperation. Times change. Carmenya brought her a tall, yellow candle carved into the shape of a slim woman with raised arms. Corinna lit it and watched it burn, wax dripping down until it didn't look like a woman any longer. Old concepts out! Corinna chanted, under her breath, as she watched it.

Corinna still hadn't been presented to the Dominatrix. This was mainly because Yani Gisbandrun had been absent from Silven Crescent for quite some time, making a tour of the sister cities and visiting her friends there for the holiday. Corinna was grateful for that; she was far from eager to be presented. It was strange, because she felt she had fitted in so well in Silven Crescent, yet some part of her still deeply mistrusted the Dominatrix. If she was honest with herself, she'd have admitted that she actually felt repelled by the woman that everybody adored, but nowadays, it was easier for her not to examine her misgivings too closely. After all, Yani obviously cared passionately about her people; what she felt about men wasn't really any of Corinna's business. Corinna knew no men in Silven Crescent; she didn't feel in touch with their unrest. The Dominatrix told the women she ruled in love, lived by love. Love was her byword. Corinna, however, didn't believe it was a kind of love she knew herself. Neither did she want to become familiar with it. At prayers, the Dominatrix spoke of how all should seek to vanquish ego, to become one unit, extending the power of love to each other and live in humility. Corinna sardonically scanned those gathered in the court whilst these words were being delivered. No-one present appeared to have learned from this teaching. Many vain, pompous, bigoted people were gathered here believing they lived by love. Some joke. The Dominatrix herself, while declaring she was her people's servant as well as their queen, demanded respect that was withheld at one's peril and had an ego the size of a planet. Nevertheless, she was universally adored. Those who lived beyond Palace Mount knew their ruler only as a figurehead with no personality. An icon. Idealised statues of her dominated market squares and temple courtyards. Here she was represented with madonna-like smile and open arms, welcoming her people in. Corinna unconsciously curled her lip whenever she passed one of these statues. In spite of this, however, she was not unhappy with her life at court. She was not a social climber like the majority of her peers, so had little in common with them, but she had her friends in the city and that was enough. She had Carmenya's attention, if not her love, and through her tuition became efficient at her job.

The only thing that gnawed at her sometimes was the fact that she was angeldt and not flamist. Corinna liked flamist women more. They had fire and their elegance was alloyed with a harder substance that gave them an inner wildness. Corinna was a felid curled seductively by the hearth, but Carmenya was a smoom, stalking the marshes with a growl in her throat.

One morning, Carmenya breezed into her office and informed Corinna briskly that she was to be presented to the Dominatrix that afternoon. Carmenya would not meet her eye, fidgeting with papers, flitting around the room. Corinna sat behind the desk, silenced. One of her co-workers was doing an extra duty that day, Zelia Garrow. Zelia began to rave hysterically about how fortunate Corinna was, and how the same experience for Zelia had been one of untold importance and significance.

'When I looked into the Dominatrix's face, I realised she knew me utterly. I felt her power. She was so kind. She made me feel special.' Carmenya attempted to cut off this rapturous flow by thrusting a sheaf of letters into the girl's clasped hands.

'Deal with these, Zelia,' she said and rolled her eyes at Corinna as Zelia floated from the room, euphoric on memories.

'What will be expected from me?' Corinna asked. Carmenya gave a non-commital shrug.

'Just smile and be humble, C'rinna. That's what's expected. Don't worry that you'll have to prove yourself in any way. That's not necessary and would probably be looked on unfavourably if you did. Remember your place and, of course, our beloved ruler's place.'

'My servant as well as my queen?'

Carmenya smiled carefully. 'I'll forget you said that, my dear.' Corinna blushed uncomfortably, conscious of the rebuff. Perhaps Carmenya didn't share her feelings about the Dominatrix after all, or maybe she was just being careful.

Corinna was not presented in the main Hall. An hour or so after the mid-day meal, Carmenya came to collect her. 'Where are we going?' Corinna asked.

165

'To the Dominatrix's private rooms,' Carmenya answered. 'I believe a couple of other girls are to be presented today as well.'

The Dominatrix's apartments were in the centre of the palace, arranged in a circle around a central court of sculpted gardens. There was only one known entrance to these rooms, down a long corridor lined with armed flamists. Corinna was sure there must be other ways in and out, but obviously, only Yani herself knew of those. Corinna's mouth was dry with nervousness as she followed Carmenya down the stone throat to the Dominatrix's presence. Afternoon sun fell in down one side through tall, narrow windows. The guards stood like stone themselves. At the end of the corridor, a tall pair of doors, standing open, revealed a sky-lit, smooth-floored reception hall. There was a smell of wood polish. A woman sitting behind a dark wooden desk asked Carmenya and Corinna to take a seat. Someone would come for them presently. It was very quiet in the hall. Corinna was afraid to talk because she knew her voice would sound loud and uncultured. She gazed at the stone walls hung with paintings of haughty women. Carmenya fiddled with her fingernails, frowning. Eventually, a middle-aged woman with a brisk attitude came and said, 'Would you come with me please, General Oralien?' They stood up. Corinna looked behind her. The woman at the desk was looking up from her work. She caught Corinna's eye and smiled encouragingly.

That day, Yani Gisbandrun was holding court in a room which, Carmenya and Corinna were told by their guide, was the Spring Moon Salon. It caught the sun beautifully though, however it was named. The guide opened the door and ushered them in. It was a tasteful, unpretentious room, furnished in pale colours. Low sofas were arranged around a central table and here the Dominatrix reclined, basking in the admiration of a number of women sitting around her. Carmenya and Corinna were left standing, unacknowledged for several minutes. They had to wait until Yani had finished speaking before they could be announced. During this time, Corinna discreetly observed

166

the Dominatrix's behaviour. Every one of the women present was simply a mirror for her; they fed her lines, they paid her compliments. The Dominatrix responded in a disarmingly girlish manner but Corinna could see the steel beneath this apparently coltish exterior. Nobody contradicted her; every word was lapped up without question. Even the conversation seemed staged. They were discussing removing all men from the skirts of the Mount, worried that undercover rebel activists living there may have been responsible for recent troubles. Many of the women in that area kept men as concubines and servants.

'Of course,' the Dominatrix was saying. 'I have anticipated that our sisters in this area might not understand our motives for expelling their menfolk. I have no doubt they will say their people are innocent. However, if we are misunderstood, and even reviled, it is important to stand by what we know as truth.' She leaned back on her couch and someone offered her a lit cigarette. 'Believe me, ladies, I do not hate men. What I do, I do for the good of our people, all our people. Men need our guidance, our control, our common sense. No, I do not hate them. I pity them perhaps, but all the same, I extend the same love towards them as to anyone in this city. I am their servant. What I give them is freedom from themselves. No-one can see this, but I, and. . . ' she waved a careless hand ' . . .my wisest friends.' There was a silence, during which no doubt, all present inwardly congratulated themselves. Corinna suppressed a wave of irritation.

Their guide cleared her throat and the Dominatrix sat up. As soon as she saw Carmenya, a warm smile installed itself across her face. The guide said, 'General Carmenya Oralien, your mightiness!' Yani put her head on one side in a manner carefully calculated to appear disarming, and said, 'Ah, Carmenya, how good to see you! And a newcomer too!' She beckoned with one manicured white hand. 'Come here girl, I won't bite!' Corinna shuffled forward uncomfortably, conscious of the many unsympathetic eyes upon her of those who wanted this introduction over with so they could get on with the mutual ego

167

massaging. She felt raw and awkward.

'This is Corinna Trotgarden, madam,' Carmenya said smoothly. 'From the Lawn Isles.'

'Hello, Corinna.' The Dominatrix extended a hand which Corinna had to lean forward to take in her own. The hand was warm and papery. It, more than the Dominatrix's hard eyes, spoke of how Yani would probably forget all about her once this interview was over. Hundreds of girls must be introduced in this way, each one as forgettable as the last. 'Please sit down and join us,' the Dominatrix said graciously. Corinna bobbed a bow. She felt Carmenya's hand on her back and took a seat next to her on one side of the gathering. They would have to lift their voices considerably if they wanted to take part in the conversation from here. An odd maid-servant dressed all in dark red and with a veiled face brought them cups of silvertea and small cakes.

'There,' Carmenya whispered, 'that didn't hurt, did it?'

'Was that it?' Corinna whispered back. Carmenya nodded. Corinna recognised a certain relief in Carmenya's face as well. Presently, other girls, accompanied by their mentors, began to arrive for similar presentation. Corinna observed them with scorn. Two of these girls looked overcome by meeting the woman they adored, another looked petrified. The Dominatrix treated them all in the same manner. A warm smile, a gracious manner, then total ignorance. How contemptible, Corinna thought. To her, Carmenya was far more interesting than the Dominatrix, far more beautiful, far more witty and intelligent. Nobody spared a glance for Carmenya. She was only a general. Corinna felt that if Yani had decided to speak to Carmenya, everybody would suddenly become interested in her, currying favour with their beloved leader, by directing their attention where she directed her own. It was despicable, and so false. Would anyone on the marsh believe that the woman who ruled them behaved like this, craving attention far more than Meonel had ever done in his worst spasm of childishness? It was frightening. Corinna wondered how long she was expected to sit there. She was bored. She did not want to listen to the garbage these women were coming out with. If she did, she knew it would make her angry. Better to be bored than angry. Her mind wandered as she examined the heavy tapestries hanging on the walls. Stories sprang to mind. She was dreaming quite happily. Suddenly, like being brushed by a cold wind, she became conscious of everybody's attention upon her. For one dreadful moment, she feared that the Dominatrix had penetrated her fantasies. She thought there'd been one or two men in them somewhere. Coming to, back to reality, with a jerk, Corinna found herself drawn straight into the gaze of the strongest, coldest pair of eyes she'd ever seen. They belonged, of course, to Yani Gisbandrun. For further cold moments, it was as if she and Yani were the only people in the room.

'Well, my dear?' Corinna realised, with a tremor of relief, what had happened. Apparently, for whatever reason, the Dominatrix had addressed a remark to her. Corinna, of course, hadn't been listening and had ignored it. She stared at the Dominatrix, helpless. In those agonising moments, she realised how bitterly this woman disliked being ignored. It was perhaps, just as grave an offence to commit as fantasising about men.

'Oh, I think you'll find Corinna is in complete accord over this point,' Carmenya said, gallantly coming to her rescue. 'You must forgive her shyness, madam.' She turned to Corinna. 'Wouldn't you agree, my dear, that although the men on the marsh appear docile, they still harbour the seeds of violence found in city men?' Her eyes bored into Corinna's, almost pleading.

Corinna wanted to communicate the thought, 'You're wasting your time. She knows I didn't hear,' but only nodded her head, face aflame. 'Of . . . of course,' she stuttered, and then Shyya's face was superimposing itself over her vision, blotting out the handsome arrogance of Carmenya, bringing a taste of tears to the back of her throat. In a single moment, everything had changed. It was stunning. The light was harder. The room was unreal. These people were but paper dolls. Corinna felt a cold sweat creep from her pores. She felt light-headed. She wanted to stand up and scream and run from this crazy place. She wanted to go home, but in her flight, she would run past the comfortable house Carmenya had bought for her and scurry into the marsh, knee-deep in water, mud sucking at her stupid, impractical silky skirts. Then, after this crystalline moment, a hardness, clear and bright as winter sunlight settled around her. The room looked different and when she glanced into Carmenya's eyes, she realised that she too must look different. Something had happened to her and it showed. It showed in her face. 'I'm not part of this any more,' Corinna thought, and it felt like the first clear thought she'd had in ages. 'I'm free. I'll never be part of this. *I don't want to be!*' Carmenya squeezed her shoulder and smiled briefly. The smile was strained.

'Listen to my words, girl,' the Dominatrix was saying silkily (that same, silly, useless silk, tangling, restricting). 'You will learn nothing otherwise. Do you want to sink with them?'

'No, madam,' Corinna said, with lowered eyes. 'Forgive me. I am overwhelmed.' She looked up. The Dominatrix nodded in satisfaction, unaware that she'd just sliced the last thread that might have held Corinna to her. One thing came out of that afternoon that Corinna would have preferred not to. Now she had a face to Yani Gisbandrun. She would not be forgotten like the others. She knew she'd done something terribly wrong, because megalomaniacs like Yani saw threat in the pettiest of actions, no matter how innocent they might have been, but no power in the world, or indeed Corinna herself, could have changed what had happened. The Goddess chose her moments, no matter what inconvenience it caused. It was inevitable, like beginning to menstruate when far from home and unprepared. Corinna was due for that enlightenment and it could have happened anywhere; at home when she was alone, in the street, in the office. Fate had decreed it should happen in the presence of the Dominatrix herself. Not a happy circumstance.

CHAPTER TWENTY-FOUR

THAT EVENING, CORINNA thankfully went to meet Carudan for a meal. She couldn't have endured a night with Carmenya, because she feared the questions she might have been asked, questions she was too emotional to answer at the moment. Shortly after the unpleasant incident, Carmenya had excused them both from the Dominatrix's presence, speaking of pressing appointments. Yani dismissed them courteously, apparently bearing no grudge for Corinna's little solecism. Corinna was not deceived. Now, she walked slowly through the evening streets of Silven Crescent, a heavy fur coat wrapped around her, breath steaming from the cold. The moons above her were the same moons that shone above Vangery. It was still there; her home. For the first time in weeks, Corinna wondered what was going on there. Had L'Belder settled in properly by now? Did anyone else know, or had guessed, who he was? How about her mother, that woman who had surprised her more than anyone else? Dannel. . . Though she had often cursed her mother for her shrewish tongue, now Corinna saw her as a strong and honest person, bereft of fripperies and stupidity. She saw her nagging for the genuine concern it had been, not merely a contrived inconvenience. 'Tomorrow, I shall write to her again,' Corinna thought and increased her pace. Her mind, like a dissectionist probing meat, kept flicking back to what had happened that afternoon. She couldn't let it be. Walking back to the General's office, Carmenya had made no comment on Corinna's blunder, nor on the strange mood it appeared to have invoked. Carmenya was due to visit Corinna later

171

on and stay for dinner, but that hadn't been mentioned either. Corinna wouldn't bring the subject up herself and Carmenya had left her with the briefest of goodbyes. Corinna had called Carudan immediately using the office switchboard. She hadn't wanted to be alone that evening. It was beyond Corinna why a woman like Carmenya could possibly endure the flimsy sincerity, the obvious megalomania of the Dominatrix. Corinna could easily imagine Carmenya's sarcasm making mincemeat of the woman; why didn't she ever say anything? Surely she could trust Corinna now? There was no way Corinna could believe Carmenya had any faith in that sentimental claptrap about love and servility. Corinna doubted whether the Dominatrix loved anybody but herself.

Carudan was already seated in the eating-house. Corinna joined her, blindly scanning the menu a serving-girl offered her. 'The wild-rice bake is good,' Carudan said, staring at Corinna in a discomforting, peeling manner. Corinna threw down the menu.

'I'll have that then,' she said, 'And a jug of your strongest wine.' The serving-girl smiled and drifted away.

'Oh dear,' Carudan said.

'Yes, oh dear. I was presented to the Dominatrix today.'

'Harrowing?'

Corinna pulled a face. She didn't know Carudan well enough to trust her. 'I'm not an expert at all this court behaviour business. I'm a farm girl. I'm more at home with danks than courtiers.'

'You have my sympathy.' The serving-girl reappeared with the wine and poured them each a large glass.

'Thankyou,' Corinna said and nearly drained hers in one swallow.

'Clearly, you needed that,' Carudan said, smiling and sipping daintily. The woman was rather an enigma to Corinna. She couldn't decide whether Carudan was angeldt or flamist; perhaps priestesses could be either or both. It was only the second time they'd been alone together.

'I must admit I'm beginning to wonder whether I'll ever

fit in here,' Corinna confided, carefully choosing her words. 'I thought I had done until today. Now, well. . .' She tailed off hopefully, looking sideways at her companion. Carudan drank slowly.

'Corinna, be careful,' she said, in a soft voice, not looking at her.

'What do you mean? Careful about what?'

'Dissatisfaction. You're in rather an awkward position. My advice is be happy.'

'I'm still not with you, Carudan.'

'You've heard of the famous Rosanel Garmelding, no doubt?'

'Yes.'

'Well, there you are then.'

Corinna was genuinely outraged. The accusation was too dangerous to be voiced in an eating house, however carefully implied. 'Are you suggesting I'm a sympathiser with the men?' she hissed, not wanting anyone else in the place to hear her. Carudan shook her head, unruffled.

'Not at all. I'm just trying to illustrate to you what unconventional feelings can lead to. Believe me, nobody has any definite proof that Rosanel is a sympathiser. . .'

Except me, Corinna thought, lanced by a transient dart of cold.

'I see. I'm sorry. I thought. . .'

'I know, Corinna. You're fairly new here. I'll say this once. If you want a hassle-free life, you don't voice any anti-establishment feelings, even to your lovers. It's too dangerous, and not worth it. Speak to the Goddess. She alone can be trusted.'

'She's Silven Crescent's Goddess. . .' Corinna said, meaning the Dominatrix's Goddess. Carudan shook her head.

'Corinna; no. The Goddess is everybody's Goddess; men's, women's, children's and beasts'. She is impartial. Even the Dominatrix does not have the nerve to do her business in the Goddess's name. Do you understand?'

'I think so. . .'

Carudan leaned forward confidentially. 'A long time ago, men worshipped only the God,' she said. 'He was

173

without a consort; half a deity. Cruel patriarchy, that all Artemisians fear, came about because the divine being men created for themselves was utterly without femininity. It is essential that we have both otherwise things get far too out of balance and abnormal societies can emerge.'

'Then. . . isn't it virtually the same thing now, but in reverse?' Corinna was not sure whether she should have asked that question.

Carudan skirted the query. 'The God lives, Corinna,' she said quietly. 'He has no shrines, no idols, no priestesses or priests, but he lives.'

'What are you saying?'

Carudan shrugged. 'I'm a priestess; I speak in abstracts, that's all. You have your confidantes, Corinna; that's the point. They are with you always. Look to Them, let Them give you Their strength, and things that discomfort you now will soon be revealed for the trivialities they really are.'

'You speak like Shyya,' Corinna said.

'And who's Shyya?'

'A boy I loved. Back home. He was gelded.'

Carudan winced fastidiously. 'Unfortunate for you.'

At this point, Corinna felt she could have said. 'Yes, but I found solace in the arms of a man called Elvon L'Belder.' Now, she felt it would have been safe to say that, just once. But she kept it to herself.

'I have trusted you, Corinna,' Carudan said, tracing a finger round the rim of her glass.

'I can see that. I appreciate it.'

'Good. Then we won't speak this way again.'

'Why not? You said you trusted me. . . '

Carudan shook her head mournfully. 'You've seen only the surface, Corinna. You know nothing. Not the way women can disappear without trace with no questions asked; nothing. You've seen Silven Crescent's pretty face but not its rotten heart.'

'Carudan!'

'Sshh. Enough! This must stop; now!'

'You want to speak, I know you do!' Corinna whispered urgently, leaning forward. 'Please Carudan; tell me. I

174

must know!'

'No you mustn't. Not many people do. Don't even trust me, Corinna. How do you know I'm not trying to trap you?'

Corinna reached across the table clumsily, knocking over her empty glass. She took one of Carudan's hands in her own. It was icy cold. 'I know you're not,' she said. 'I know it! Carudan, I could tell you things that would change your mind about me. . .'

The priestess drew her hand away quickly. 'No. Don't. I don't want to know!' Her cool exterior was cracking; Corinna could see that. In some way she had tapped a vein in this woman she hardly knew. Had it been the Goddess herself who'd guided Corinna to speak with Carudan on that first day in the temple? Corinna believed that coincidence possessed a mysticism all of its own. Something had happened to her that afternoon; something powerful. Now she was here in this little, dim-lit eating-house and a conversation had started that was merely an extension of what had happened to her in the Dominatrix's rooms. It was no coincidence. It couldn't be.

'Carudan, you could have avoided all of this by not telling me to be careful. You could have said anything and I would have kept my mouth shut and realised not to say anything even faintly against the Dominatrix again. You spoke of the God to me. Carudan, you know what I am. And I know what you are.'

A dreadful silence fell between them. Carudan stared at the table. As if to punctuate this awkwardness, the serving-girl returned bearing a tray of food. The silence was unbearable as she slowly laid out the cutlery and dished up the wild-rice onto two plates. After she'd gone, Carudan picked up a fork listlessly and played with the food, frowning deeply. Corinna poured them more wine.

'Carudan, do you *know* Rosanel Garmelding?'

The priestess looked up at her, warily. Perhaps she was wondering whether Corinna was a spy for Carmenya who had found her out. Perhaps she was afraid. 'Why?'

'I have a message for her.'

'A message?'

175

'Yes, I want to meet her.'

The priestess sighed. 'Corinna. . . '

'Trust me. *Please*. I'd give you my blood to prove I'm true.'

'You might have to.'

'I'm prepared. I was nearly lost, Carudan, nearly part of all this. You don't know how close to it I came. Glamorised like a stupid child. Huh! A stupid angeldt. I had a mission coming here, which I'd decided not to fulfil for comfort's sake. Help me put that right.' There was another tense silence as Carudan considered what she'd heard. Perhaps she prayed to her Goddess to help her make the right decision.

'A message, you say?'

Corinna nodded.

'Who from?'

Now it was Corinna's turn for silence. She picked up her glass to drink, put it down again.

'Elvon L'Belder,' she said at last. Carudan stared at her, expressionless. 'It's true,' Corinna continued. 'I know where he is. I've spoken with him. He wanted me to seek Rosanel Garmelding out.'

'If you're lying, Corinna, I will kill you with my own hands, crime or not.'

'You know in your heart I'm not lying.'

Carudan shrugged. 'I'll consider your words. Word will be sent to you. Wait for it.' Then, with considerable effort, she seemed to give herself a shake and become once more the cynical, bright woman Corinna had got to know. 'Now, we eat this splendid meal and finish the wine. Then we ask for more. O.k.?'

Corinna nodded and smiled. They clinked their glasses together, drank, and ate.

CHAPTER TWENTY-FIVE

WINTER STORMS SWEPT across the marsh, the vanguard of a last onslaught before the Spring. Dannel had received two letters from Corinna which she'd read out to Shyya when they arrived. The first one had caused Dannel to shake her head in some kind of unspecified disappointment; she'd censored what she'd read to Shyya. The second, well, it was hard to make head or tail of it. She read it all aloud. 'What do you think?' she asked, waving it in the air. The wind outside was making such a racket, she had to raise her voice to be heard. Shyya shook his head.

'She's obviously trying to imply something to us without raising suspicion and hasn't succeeded very well. I shouldn't worry.'

'But what's all this. "I've met a woman who knows the Goddess's consort and will guide me to please you, mother"?'

'That presumably is a reference to somebody who sympathises with men. Wouldn't you agree?'

'That Garmelding woman L'Belder told you about?'

'Possibly.'

'Shyya, you tell me not to worry, yet I'm worried. What is Corinna getting mixed up in? I don't like it. It's not our concern.'

'L'Belder thinks it is.'

'We all know what L'Belder thinks, Shyya. You more than anybody,' Dannel said archly. Shyya had felt compelled to tell her all about his relationship with the fugitive. Sometimes he wished he hadn't. Dannel had a sharp tongue occasionally, and enjoyed making barbed remarks

177

when Meonel was around that only Shyya was supposed to understand. Shyya did not want Meonel to know what was going on, even though he often fantasised about telling him himself. He would have liked to get a positive reaction from Meonel, make him jealous. Dannel knew this, which delighted her. A new sport had developed; how to make Shyya squirm whilst giving him a vicarious pleasure. It was quite perverse.

Shyya needn't have worried about Meonel discovering anything from Dannel's comments. He'd known about the situation virtually from the day it began. Gabriel had taken great pleasure in telling Meonel his suppositions. Being an intuitive person, if slightly malicious, Gabriel had divined long ago the obstacle-fraught desires of Meonel and Shyya. It had given the staff of Vangery many long, cosy evenings around the kitchen fire discussing whether the master's and the eunuch's longings would ever be consummated. The new man, Joel, was a fresh character in the drama who had spiced things up considerably, much to everyone's delight. Winter could be a tedious time on the marsh, when everyone was confined to the house for days at a time. Vangery had become a highly-charged hotbed of emotion with Meonel, Shyya and Joel being the central conductors. The family themselves were unaware of the keen observation of the staff, except perhaps for Orblin, who didn't really understand what was going on anyway.

Gabriel had waited for the right moment to pounce on the hapless Meonel: the next day, after making sure, via a thorough and efficient spy network, that Shyya had, in fact, spent the night in Joel's room. Meonel had sauntered into the kitchen the following morning, rather bewildered because Shyya hadn't brought him his breakfast. Gabriel pretended not to know this, which forced Meonel to ask for something to eat.

'Hasn't Shyya been up to you yet?' Gabriel asked innocently. 'I set your tray out an hour ago. Oh, here it is! It's still here! Now, it's all cold. Oh dear, I'd better prepare you something else.'

'Have you seen Shyya today?'

178

'No. I had someone knock on his door earlier, but there was no response.'

Meonel's normally expressionless face was now registering a satisfying concern. 'Hadn't somebody better look for him then?' he said.

'Oh, I don't think that's necessary. . . '

'Why?'

Now Gabriel affected another pretence, that he didn't know Meonel's feelings for the boy. 'Oh, well I don't really like to say anything, but I suppose it's a good thing, all in all. Shyya can't get many opportunities with his. . . unfortunate disabilities.'

'What are you talking about?' Meonel demanded, his temperature falling.

'It's quite sweet,' Gabriel said, relishing each word.

'What is? Where is my attendant, Gabriel? Tell me now!'

'Well, I can only presume he's still with Joel, sir. At least, that's where he was when we all went to bed last night. He went back there after attending to you in the evening. He'd been there most of the afternoon too I believe. . . '

Thus, Gabriel let the dreadful news sink in, and watched Meonel's reaction from the corner of his eye, recording it in detail for later replay to other staff members. Meonel stood up without a word and left the room. Later, Gabriel, a little contrite, had someone take him a tray of food up, to which he had thoughtfully added a bottle of liquor.

Meonel would not say a word to Shyya about what he knew, so Shyya went on believing, quite happily, that Meonel knew nothing. He did not know that, after hearing from Gabriel the confirmation of his suspicions, Meonel went alone to his room, locked the door and wept aloud. He'd never done that before, not even as a child. He'd learned to contain his feelings, even to deny them. Now he felt he'd lost something vital, something life-saving. If only he'd said something to Shyya sooner. Now it was clearly too late.

Shyya would go to Dannel every morning with L'Belder's dawn caresses still making his flesh tingle. He felt as if he could fly, only brought down to earth by his quick,

179

furtive scuttle past Meonel's closed door. He dreamed of
Meonel. Like Corinna, Elvon L'Belder was not the person
he loved, but the person who made him come alive, who
believed in his uniqueness as a human being. Shyya would
have liked to teach all that to Meonel, but whatever
friendship they'd had over the past few months meant
nothing now. Shyya still thought Meonel was being off-
hand with him because of his conversations with Dannel.
Although Shyya had suggested to her that they should tell
Meonel the truth about L'Belder, Dannel hadn't been
keen on the idea. Shyya still went to Meonel's room after
the mid-day meal to read aloud to him, still took him his
meals (only that once had he ever neglected his duties),
bathed him, dressed him, brushed out his green-gold hair,
but it was like attending to an imbecile, someone rendered
mindless by a terrible accident or blighted from birth by
evil in the womb. There was no conversation. Shyya felt
as if a golden glow leaked from his body through gaps in
his clothes, that Meonel must never see. It was difficult.
He tried to temper his joy in Meonel's presence, a joy that
was incomprehensible really, for here was the man that
Shyya loved, a man who would not speak to him, who
would never touch him in the way that Elvon L'Belder did.
Only the warmth of L'Belder himself lessened the pain of
knowing that. And with the Spring, loneliness would come
again when L'Belder left the farm. Shyya did not divulge
these secret thoughts to Dannel, who merely thought him
infatuated by the charisma of the fugitive. She had no idea
how Shyya felt about her husband, hence the wordplay,
the little jokes. Today, before visiting Dannel, Meonel had
brushed his breakfast tray away with sudden anger and
the plates had smashed upon the floor. Shyya had felt as
if he were one of the plates, that Meonel had really wanted
to smash him. It had unnerved him considerably, and here
was Dannel wittering on about her worries for Corinna.
Shyya did not worry about Corinna, mainly because he
trusted her integrity and her innate common sense. The
first letter hadn't bothered him as it had Dannel, and
wouldn't have done even if he'd heard it all. He would
have thought it a natural reaction to the seemingly

wonderful new way of life Corinna was enjoying. Her real self would come through eventually; it was too strong not to. Now it obviously had. His only concern was that her fervour for whatever cause she was adopting wouldn't get too hectic. He made a mental note to meditate that night and send her some calm thoughts. He should have done so before.

'Shyya, are you with me today?'

Dannel's voice broke into his reverie. He smiled vaguely at her and she shook her head. 'I don't know! Here I am, beside myself with worry, and you are dreaming like a child! Shyya, I want to speak to your beloved Elvon. Will you bring him here tomorrow?'

That night, alone in their spaceless, timeless room, listening to the wind, Shyya told L'Belder that Dannel wanted to see him. Elvon made an irritated noise. 'She's an interfering old body, isn't she?' he said without any malice. 'I hope she's not going to kick me out. You think I've upset her?'

'No. She's just curious about you, that's all. It won't be that long until the Spring. I think she wants to know what you're planning to do then.'

L'Belder folded Shyya in his arms. 'It means I'll have to leave you then, doesn't it? I don't want to, my dark-eyed mystic. I want you with me.'

'I'm sure you'll survive alone.'

'I'm not. I don't even want to. What do you say?'

'Are you asking me to leave here? Go with you?'

L'Belder kissed his brow confidently. 'Why not? You're wasted here.'

'I enjoy life, Elvon. I'm not convinced I'd have much left to me if I ran away with you.'

L'Belder laughed. 'Oh, come on! Even if we don't find the Greylids, we could find somewhere to live. I can't believe this entire world isn't safe from the mangaks. Think about it. If I can't find help, I'm going to have to reassess my whole life. I'll need support for that.'

Shyya was silent. Then he said, 'Elvon, I'm not in love with you.'

181

'Of course you're not. I know that. I also know why. That's the reason I think it would be best if you left here.'

'I didn't think you were that intuitive.'

'Doesn't require much, my dear. Your face after the trial of the evening feeding session is enough to tell me that.'

'He doesn't know about us.'

'Doesn't he? Does it make you feel better to think that? How about the possibility that he does know and doesn't care?'

Shyya pulled away. 'Don't be cruel. There's no need for that!'

L'Belder's warm arms crept around him once more. His voice was soothing. 'That's not cruelty, Shyya. You know it isn't. I'm not jealous of Meonel. I just care enough about you to want what's best for you. That man is living death; he would wither you with cold, eventually. He mocks you and humiliates you, saps your strength. You should get away from it.'

'Perhaps, but Dannel wouldn't let me go with you anyway. I belong to her. Haven't you thought of that?'

'That's a minor problem. I can get round her, believe me.'

Shyya laughed weakly. 'I believe you can. I don't know though, Elvon. I don't know whether I want to go with you.'

'Don't worry. I'll ask you again. Let it rest now.'

L'Belder soon drifted into a contented sleep, leaving Shyya awake, staring into the dark, wondering what life would be like for him if he was scrubbing an existence from the marsh away from Meonel.

Dannel was in a jovial mood the next day. She appeared to be quite at ease with L'Belder, most of her uncertainties about him having been put to death by Shyya over the last few weeks. She showed L'Belder the letter from Corinna, wondering if he could translate any of it. L'Belder scanned it thoughtfully before handing it back.

'It seems she may have made contact with Rosanel,' he said.

'Is she safe?' Dannel asked. L'Belder shrugged.

'I have to be honest with you Mistress Trotgarden, I

don't know.'

'This is your fault!' Dannel said hotly. 'You got her involved in this!'

'She got herself involved,' L'Belder replied calmly. 'The chances are something like this would have happened in Silven Crescent even if she hadn't met me first.'

'He's right,' Shyya added. 'Corinna isn't like Carmenya and the others. You know that Dannel.'

Dannel made an impatient sound. 'I hope she knows what she's doing.'

With the arrival of hot milk-suds and biscuits, conversation drifted towards travel on the marsh, the best route L'Belder should take in the Spring, what equipment he should have with him. It was then that Dannel made the suggestion L'Belder wouldn't have hoped for in his wildest dreams. 'It's clear you'd be dead within a week on your own,' she said. 'Someone must go with you, at least as far as the forest. Shyya, would you do that?' All eyes turned to Shyya. He felt horribly pinned down. Now there was no alternative. 'It's alright. You can come back whenever you want to,' Dannel continued. 'You must agree our friend here is hopeless when it comes to living rough.' Shyya shrugged.

'If you want me to, Dannel. What about Meonel, though? Won't he wonder why you're sending his attendant out onto the marsh?' He dared not say, 'Won't he object?' for fear of giving L'Belder an irresistible cue.

'Shyya. I give the orders around here. If Meonel doesn't like it, he can bring his complaints to me. I can get him another attendant. In my opinion, you're more than he deserves, anyway. When you come back, I would like you to take up the position of my personal assistant. How does that suit you?' Shyya was speechless. He made a helpless gesture. 'Good, that's settled then – I'll tell Meonel. As soon as the storms clear, I'll have someone go to Stilt Vashti and buy him a new slave; then your duties towards him will be absolved.'

'No,' Shyya said, and Dannel looked up, eyebrows raised. 'I mean, will you let me tell him? Please?' L'Belder, slouched in his chair, arms folded, legs straight out, made

183

an exasperated snort. Shyya ignored it.

'Very well,' Dannel said. 'But don't take any nonsense off him.'

It was with a mixture of dread and absurd hope that Shyya went to Meonel's door before mid-day. He knocked. There was no answer. He knocked again. Nothing. The door was unlocked, the handle turned smoothly in Shyya's hand. Inside, a corrupt smell of stale liquor and stale cigarette smoke greeted him. Instinctively, he went to the window, opened the blind and threw the window open wide. Cold, lashing air pounded into the room, blowing back his hair. A groan from behind him made him turn around. Meonel was draped over the couch, hands to eyes. 'Shut that bloody window,' he said. Shyya drew it to, leaving just a small gap to let air circulate.

'You haven't eaten your breakfast,' he said.

'What are you doing here? I don't need you this morning. Get out.'

'The room's a mess. I came to tidy it.'

'I like it like this, Shyya. Out!'

'No.'

Meonel took his hands from his eyes and propped himself up on his elbows. He looked dreadful. What do I see in this person? Shyya wondered. 'I have something to tell you,' he continued.

'No you don't,' Meonel said softly. 'There's nothing I want to know from you. Slaves don't interest me. I want to be left in peace, alone, unbothered. Can't you understand that?'

'Maybe I can't. Perhaps your next slave will.'

'What?'

'Dannel is relieving me of my duties to you. I'm going to be her personal assistant.'

Meonel lay back on the couch and laughed. 'Is that so! Worked your way in well here, haven't you, and without any balls too. Quite an achievement!'

I hate you, Shyya thought. I really hate you. You are a vile personification of everything I despise. How could I ever have thought I loved you. 'In the Spring, I'm travelling north with Joel,' he said. 'Dannel will get you a

184

new attendant by then.'

'You're leaving?'

'Yes.'

'How long for?'

'I don't know. A couple of months, maybe more.'

'With Joel?'

'Yes.'

'Why?'

'Dannel has business she wants Joel and I to conduct for her.' Shyya became slowly aware of how the vitriol had evaporated from Meonel's voice. He dared to turn away from the window. Meonel looked boyish, lying there on the couch, innocent and hurt. How strange. He sat up and reached for a bottle of wine, tried to pour some into a cup, failing dismally. Shyya did it for him.

'Here.'

Meonel took the cup and stared into it. 'I'll miss you,' he said.

'You'll miss sniping at me, certainly. Perhaps you'd better ask Dannel to get you another eunuch so you can indulge in the same sport.'

'I know what I do to you, Shyya.'

'Then why do it?'

Shyya couldn't quite grasp what was going on here. He expected Meonel to make a scathing attack if he let his defences down. That was the usual procedure. Lull him into complacency, even be a little bit pleasant, then bam! let fly with all barrels. Not this time, Shyya thought. That's over. Not this time.

'This Joel, this new slave, he. . . I know about you and him, Shyya.'

'Yes. Joel thought you did.'

'You've discussed me with him?'

'I've told him about you. Do you blame me? I have to have someone to talk to when you're such a bastard.'

'You're a slave.'

'And now I'm Dannel's personal assistant.'

Meonel raised an eyebrow. 'Well, I suppose I ought to congratulate you, Shyya. Though, I must say, I can't see why Dannel is doing this. You have no practical use other than. . .'

185

'Enough!' Shyya cried, having had more than enough. 'You can't get at me anymore, Meonel! Don't you understand? I don't have to listen to it. You're a mess. Dannel's sick of you. She knows what you are. You had beauty once and now you've let that go. Goddess knows, I tried so hard to get through to you, to help you. Every overture of friendship was greeted by cruelty. You didn't care. You didn't think about me lying alone at night hearing those insults over and over again. You think I'm less than a man because of what's been done to me, well, you're wrong. I'm more human than you and I always will be. Smooms have more compassion than you, Meonel. You ought to be punished for what you did. I want you to hurt like I did. I hope you die! I hope you die in extreme pain and misery!'

Meonel drew back in surprise from this uncharacteristic verbal attack. He shrank against the cushions. Shyya couldn't believe what he'd just said. He was thinking, 'Was I speaking the truth, was I really?'

Meonel's mouth was trying to move. Shyya was incapable of seeing himself, he could not see what he looked like towering over Meonel, dangerous with anger. 'Did I hurt you that much?' Meonel said hoarsely, with great effort of both body and spirit. 'Shyya, did I? Do you really wish that on me?'

'Yes.' He hesitated. 'No. You're pathetic. I wouldn't wish that on anyone; I feel sorry for you.'

'It's not easy for me, Shyya. It's not easy.' Meonel reached for the bottle and poured more wine.

The atmosphere was regulating itself again. Shyya felt rather self-conscious, as if he'd just made a fool of himself. He hadn't. He'd just made an impression, which was long overdue. 'You make life hard for yourself,' he said, but Meonel had recovered enough to start feeling irritated again.

'Perhaps I do. You're a smug little beast, aren't you? You walk around like that man's prick is up your arse all the time.'

'You're disgusting. I can't even be bothered to be angry. You don't know about things like love and affection,

186

Meonel. They're beyond you. What you just said is all that physical contact means to you, isn't it? Wervels on the marsh know more about love than you.'

'Take back your sentiment, then. Wish me dead.'

'How can I? You already are.'

'Oh, fine words, Shyya. You always had a way with them.'

'I thought that was your forte; the parry and thrust of the right word at the right time. Pressure upon weak spots. Maybe I learned that from you.'

Meonel sighed heavily and flopped back on the sofa. A silence descended, during which Shyya began to tidy the room. His heart was beating fast. He stole a look at Meonel and found him staring right back. What's going on in his head? Shyya wondered. He's insane. I think he could kill. *He's insane.*

'There, that will have to do,' Shyya said, the room half tidy. 'I have to get back to Dannel now.' Meonel said nothing. 'I'll have Gabriel send someone with your lunch later. Any preference?' Silence. Shyya had his hand upon the doorhandle. For the briefest moment, he rested his forehead upon the cool, smooth wood of the door. No, don't give in to it. Get out of here. Leave this place. Leave. Leave. . .

'Shyya.' He stiffened. No, I don't want to hear what he'll say. No. No. Shyya turned around. Meonel was peering over the back of the couch, resting his chin on his crossed arms.

'You're wrong, you know, you pompous little fool. I know what love is. I've loved you for ages. Now go. And I'll have shemble-frack bake for lunch.'

He disappeared back into the plump cushions and Shyya heard him sigh. He walked back to Dannel's office in a daze. Gabriel, who had heard raised voices, was already concocting an amusing anecdote to tell over lunch.

CHAPTER TWENTY-SIX

FOR TWO DAYS after meeting Carudan in the eating-house, Corinna careered around, a taut bundle of nerves. It was sheer luck that she'd swapped duties with another girl and was off work for the rest of the week. Endaline and Sheba regarded her warily, conscious of her turmoil, but misinterpreting it. Carmenya had not called for several days; doubtless she and Corinna had argued. Now Corinna was in agony wondering whether they would ever make up. In fact, Carmenya was the last person Corinna could have faced at that time. Half of her was burdened with a terrible guilt about what she was involving herself in. Carmenya was right in some respects; men could be dangerous. Men did want to vanquish the women once more and would no doubt be merciless should they get the chance. What the hell am I doing? Corinna thought, and at those times, she could not trust her own mind. Emotions were driving her, that was clear. But which ones? Disgust at the sycophancy of the court; admiration of L'Belder; curiosity about Rosanel? Perhaps it went deeper than that. When she conjured a picture of the Dominatrix's face, Corinna was filled with a rage which was almost holy in its purity. With the picture came the word LIE! emblazoned in red, hundreds of feet high. Then Corinna would weaken, smoke a cigarette, curl in her favourite chair and think, I don't care. I can't possibly care. It doesn't matter. Then Carmenya would spring to mind, and Corinna would wince and try to push the thoughts away. She admired Carmenya more than any other woman. In truth, Corinna loved her. Now she was betraying her, deceiving her. She couldn't bear to think of Carmenya's face should she

188

discover that Corinna was not what she seemed. In a perfect world, Corinna thought dreamily, I could tell Carmenya everything and she would respect what I believe, talk to me about it, make me see things more clearly, help me make up my mind; but impartially. She knew Carmenya could never be impartial about this issue.

After two days, there was still no word from Carudan, and Corinna began to relax a little. Perhaps the priestess would not contact her at all. In some ways, Corinna hoped she wouldn't. It would be easier. On Savanday evening, Carmenya showed up again. The atmosphere was tense as Endaline showed her into Corinna's parlour. Corinna, acting on intuition, had taken the precaution of getting a little drunk after dinner. She'd had a feeling Carmenya might call. 'I've offended you, haven't I?' Corinna said, wanting to get to the point as soon as possible. Carmenya did not answer at first. She had her hair loose down her back and was wearing a long robe. It made her look different.

'It's not that,' she said at last. 'Corinna. . . I don't know what to say. I'm afraid for you.'

Corinna laughed falsely. 'But why?'

Carmenya wheeled around and Corinna flinched against the blaze of anger in the other woman's face. 'Don't think that angeldt are the only ones with intuition!' she shouted. 'Corinna, your expression. . . ' She raised her eyes to the ceiling and gripped the air with frustrated hands.

'My expression?'

'Yes. I saw it! It was as if you spat in the Dominatrix's face! You little fool!'

Corinna went numb. 'Did she. . . did she know?'

Carmenya made an angry noise. 'I expect so, don't you?'

'Is that why you haven't been round this week?'

'I had to think.'

'About what.'

'Whether to take you away from court.'

Corinna went cold with horror. Because of her feelings, Carmenya wanted to discard her. The cold was soon

189

replaced by indignation.

'I see! That easy is it to throw me away? What are you going to do with me? Send me home?' Even as she said those words, Corinna experienced a small flame of pleasure in her heart.

'No, don't be stupid! I promised your mother I'd find you a home and a career in Silven Crescent and that's what I'll do. Strange as it may seem to you. I'm also very fond of you, Corinna. I don't want to send you away.' Now she came to squat before Corinna's chair and took the girl's hands in her own. 'It is because I care about you that I fear for you,' she said. 'Normally, such a small thing as you did would mean nothing. But times are changing. People are suspected of conspiracy because of the slightest thing. Yani Gisbandrum is a frightened woman if the truth were known. She sees enemies in every corner. Scapegoats are needed; examples have to be made. I know your feelings about the Dominatrix, Corinna. I can't comment on them because I have more sense, but because I know what you think, I see danger for you in the court. You don't mix in well enough. Do you see what I'm getting at?'

Corinna was shocked by the urgency in Carmenya's voice and eyes. She'd never dared to hope the woman cared for her that much. 'The Dominatrix will remember your behaviour,' Carmenya murmured. 'She will remember, Corinna, and one day, when she needs one of those scapegoats, it may be you she thinks of.'

'Like Rosanel. . .' Corinna said. Carmenya squeezed her hands very hard.

'No, C'rinna, no! Don't speak that name, don't liken yourself to her!'

'Things are happening that I don't know about, aren't they?' Corinna said, drawing her hands away from Carmenya's hold. 'You wouldn't be so worried if there weren't. It's not like you. . . Carmenya, what's going on?'

Carmenya stood up. 'You must leave the court, C'rinna. I'll find you another post, or pay for your keep myself.'

'No!' Corinna sprang from her chair. 'I can't leave the court. I don't want to.'

'Why? Don't you realise how tenuous your position is?

190

Is this the talk of a rational woman?'

Corinna shook her head desperately. 'Carmenya, I have to be up there. I have to be part of it. I know the risks, but I want to be at the centre.'

Carmenya's eyes narrowed. 'Why is it so important to you?'

Corinna checked herself, calmed herself. 'Because it's history, Carmenya, that's why. Because important things are going to happen and I want to ride the wave.'

'You're unwise, young, naive. . . '

'Maybe. Tell me. . . tell me what's going to happen.' Carmenya wasn't going to answer. In desperation, Corinna went and put her arms round Carmenya's neck. Appearances are deceiving. In Carmenya's presence, Corinna often felt so small; now she realised she wasn't that much shorter than the General really. 'Can't you trust me?'

'I don't want to involve you, C'rinna.'

'I don't care about that. What are you afraid I'll do? Do you think I'm a dissident? Is that it?' Corinna forced a laugh.

'It would serve you well to start taking this matter seriously,' Carmenya replied. 'Don't laugh, Corinna. You don't know what's going on, what plans are being made.'

'Then defend me, prepare me, make me see. Just tell me.'

Carmenya took a deep breath. She removed Corinna's arms from her neck and put a distance between them. 'If I tell you, and what I say should ever go beyond this house, you're dead, my dear. I swear it. I have very little power really. Later, everyone will know Yani's plans, but not for a while. They're not complete yet.'

'What plans?'

'The first of many. At the next quarter-year, the Dominatrix will announce that it is illegal for women to have sexual relations with men.'

The news did not come as a surprise exactly. It was merely an extension of how people lived on the Mount already, and L'Belder had hinted at such a development many times. But Corinna was not blind to the implications.

'Will that extend to the marsh?'

Carmenya shrugged helplessly. 'Eventually.'

'Then how will people have children? All the same way as in the city, with tubes and physicians. . . and things.'

Carmenya nodded. 'Our population is small, C'rinna. It will need planning but she means to do it.'

'What will happen to people who disobey?'

Carmenya turned away. 'I realise this is hard for you. Your family. . . and everything.'

'There's something else, isn't there?'

Now Carmenya was genuinely agitated. That alone alarmed Corinna more than anything. She wheeled around to face her. 'I can't tell you, C'rinna. I can't.'

'Is it the *settlements* you told me about? Are they bringing those in soon, too?' Corinna's voice was nearly hysterical. She felt powerless to control it. It was like a presentiment.

'Corinna, you don't understand how you sound. Listen to what you're saying, for the Goddess's sake! It sounds like you. . . like you. . . '

'Goddess! You can't even bring yourself to say it, can you! It sounds like I care, like I sympathise, doesn't it! It sounds like I don't kiss the feet of Yani Gisbandrun, that I have the effrontery to disagree with her! Parthenos!' She threw up her hands. 'It's like being in chains!'

Carmenya looked wild and cornered. It was as if Corinna were uttering the words of a dreadful invocation that would summon ultimate evil. Corinna realised that what she was saying made Carmenya feel afraid.

'You mustn't care! You mustn't care about them C'rinna! Please!'

'Carmenya, they're *people*! Not animals, people! We can't lock them away.'

Carmenya made a strange gesture, half nodding, half shaking her head.

'What about the marsh, Carmenya? Will this affect the marsh families?'

The General's face was bleak. Whether because of a lingering sympathy for those concerned or fear that Corinna would blame her for it, the girl could not tell. She took a deep breath, turning her back once more. 'Very

192

well, very well,' she said, as if to herself, as if conducting some inner argument against an opponent who spoke with Yani Gisbandrun's voice. 'Corinna, within a year, it is envisaged that all men shall be taken from the marsh families. There are plenty of girls in the city who could work there instead, so there will be no need for them. The men shall be taken to the camps.'

'What! You can't! You can't! The people will fight you!'

'I know that!' Carmenya slammed down her fists on the table, an incongrous mixture of her masculine day-time self clothed in the flowing robes of a more feminine creature. 'We all know that, Corinna. . . '

Corinna narrowed her eyes. 'You shouldn't have told me this.'

'You've torn it from me. You know that.'

'Is that the only reason?'

Carmenya turned around and faced her. She shook her head sorrowfully. She looked grey, like somebody feeling sick to their stomach after having witnessed an appalling accident. 'C'rinna, I've shared your bed for months. I love you. I fear for you. If you need another reason, perhaps that's why I had to tell you.'

Corinna exhaled, slowly. 'So, we're going to be honest now, are we. Tell me, apart from what happened in her rooms the other day, do you want me to leave the court because I'm a marsh girl. . . perhaps contaminated by men in the Dominatrix's eyes? Is there going to come a time when marsh women aren't exactly safe in Silven Crescent because of that?'

Carmenya stood up straight. 'Give me a drink,' she said, rubbing her face. As Corinna opened a bottle on the dresser, Carmenya composed herself to reply to the last question. 'You don't need me to answer that, do you? Are your eyes open now? Do you still want to be up there at court, Corinna?'

Corinna handed her a brimming glass of ebony port. She didn't speak, but Carmenya caught her eyes. 'I'll be supporting the Dominatrix, C'rinna, you can't rely on me for help. You do realise that, don't you?'

'Yes.'

Carmenya drank, deeply. 'Perhaps it would lead you to understand if you knew the reasons behind it all,' she said.

'I can't believe there can be any reasons I'd understand.'

'Try listening. You can do that, can't you? It all goes back a long way, back to the time when people first came to colonise the planet. They were people who were seeking a simple life, scorning the technology that enabled them to travel this far, wanting soil between their fingers, fresh air in their lungs. They were led by a group of women who had their own philosophy on life, feminist, as you can imagine but fairly moderate by today's standards. With them were other women who had been attracted to the group ideals or who wanted the chance to begin life anew on another world. They were accompanied by men sympathetic to their aims, and their children.'

'It all sounds very idyllic,' Corinna said harshly. 'So what went wrong?'

Carmenya shook her head. 'I suppose it *was* idyllic for a while. Then the children that had come with them became adults, half of them male, and suddenly there were two factions on Artemis; people who wanted a matriarchal agricultural society, which they believed would keep peace, led by the initial feminist group, and those who wanted Artemis to become part of the Worlds Economic Network, who wanted others to come to the planet, farm the whole place, mine the minerals, become in essence as patriarchal as the worlds they had left behind.'

'So what happened? War, I suppose.'

Again Carmenya shook her head. 'Not exactly. Silven Crescent was just a small town then. The people discussed their disagreements and it was decided that all those whose view was at variance to those of town leaders should leave and set up their own communities on the marsh.'

'I see. The first marsh families.'

Carmenya poured herself another drink and sat down by the fire. 'Yes, that's right. It worked happily that way for quite some time. Then the Lawn Islanders, as they called themselves, wanted to use the small space terminal outside Silven Crescent, in order to interact with other

194

worlds. The original cruisers they'd used to reach the planet were still there and the marsh people wanted to utilise them. By that time, Silven Crescent had very little communication with other worlds. It was a deliberate choice. The people there had no desire to have large numbers of off-worlders flooding the planet. The marsh people asked if they could take the cruisers somewhere else and build a new terminal. The request was denied. Now, a few influential Lawn Island men started getting worked up about the attitude of the Silven Crescent women. They claimed that the town folk were only afraid they wouldn't be able to carry on their unrealistic society if other races came here. They forgot totally about the initial goal of the settlers – a world without pollution and heartless commercial enterprise. Things went from bad to worse, coming to a head when some of the town women destroyed the cruisers beyond repair. There was a rumour that the marsh people were constructing equipment that would allow them to contact other planets and enlist their aid. The whole of Artemis was at risk. The Silven Crescent people only had to look out of their windows and imagine the skyline filled with the ugly constructions of industry, pumping foulness into the air, to justify their decision. They far outnumbered the marsh people. It was not that difficult to subdue them and take control.'

Corinna was silent.

Carmenya looked agitated and tried to reinforce her remarks. 'We cannot risk anything like that happening again. Oh, I know we're far from perfect, C'rinna. I know there are glitches in the system, but if the men were given power again, Yani feels the same problem would arise. Men are greedy. We are content with what we have. If the first settlers had had more foresight, they'd have been more careful, instituted laws, perhaps even made the discontented leave the planet. We are a small world and perhaps lucky that we're so far away from the major travel routes. Nobody bothers us here. We're just a bunch of religious crazies to outsiders, I'm sure, equivalent to the Sisterhood of Amflax who so admire us.'

'Nobody tells us these things about the past,' Corinna

195

said. 'How is it you're privileged enough to know?'

'In my position I have to know everything. I couldn't function properly otherwise.'

Corinna nodded, eyes narrowed. 'So now we have the prospect of violence again,' she said, stroking the rim of her glass. 'Has it ever occurred to you Carmenya that the question of equality keeps raising its head because it's the way things are supposed to be? As you said, we have problems within our society at present, and I agree we'd still have them if men and women were equal. They'd be different problems perhaps, but I'm sure no worse than those we have now.'

'What you're speaking is treason,' Carmenya reminded her drily.

'In your eyes maybe and in the Dominatrix's. I look on it as reality, however.'

Carmenya stood up, pacing in agitation up and down the carpet. 'Wake up, Corinna! I got you away from the marsh because I feared Yani's dreams might become truth. . . Perhaps I was wrong to do that. Perhaps you'd have been safer there. Perhaps I was selfish. The dream is real. . . it soon will be.'

'Dream?' Corinna laughed harshly. 'Oh, I'll wake up to that, Carmenya. It's no dream, it's a nightmare, whatever happened in the past! One sick woman's sick nightmare!'

The General sighed. 'Whatever. We can't fight it.'

'Do you believe it's right? Do you really?'

Carmenya turned away again. 'I don't know. . . Maybe it's inevitable.'

Inevitable. Words had become a barrier. Carmenya knew that she and Corinna were on opposite sides; no amount of hauling and goading on the General's part would get Corinna over the fence. Corinna stared at her friend, seeing within her a hundred new facets; the lines of ageing, the tremor of stress, a conflicting sense of humanity that she would fight to suppress to the bitter end. Corinna would not reach out a hand to touch her. Perhaps, if she could, some common ground could be reached. At least I have her silence, Corinna thought. At least I have that. She won't betray me. She will hide me,

keep me down, as best she can. At least I have that. . .
Carmenya drank several glasses of ebony port during a
painful, unbreakable silence. Corinna could hear floorboards creaking beyond the door. Had Endaline and
Sheba heard the raised voices? She couldn't be sure of
their loyalty. This is terrifying, she thought. Terrifying. I
am not an evil person, not even an activist yet. Why should
I have to be afraid, threatened? Why? *Because the Dominatrix fears her power is so flimsy*, another part of her mind
replied; *that's why*. The smallest thing could topple her. . .
maybe. Eventually, Carmenya sighed and straightened up.
Corinna could not hate her, even though she was aware
of the fact that it might be Carmenya herself who would
go to cart Meonel and Shyya away from Vangery, to
incarcerate them in some stinking prison camp. To be kept
for breeding. A sliver of cold made her shiver. Shyya could
not breed. . . could he? Shyya had no purpose in the
Dominatrix's world. . . Shyya might die. A vision of
slaughter arose in her mind. She felt sick. She wanted
Carmenya out of the house. Time was needed for
thought; time and solitude. When she looked Carmenya
in the eye, she saw sorrow there, for something they had
lost before it had grown properly. 'Fool!' Corinna thought.
'Why support that maniac? Why?'

'Corinna, you have no rational reason for supporting
the men,' Carmenya said at last. Corinna realised how little
the woman knew about her then. 'You are romantic. You
dislike the fawning behaviour of the court and for this
reason have decided to support those that oppose it.
That's all. See this for yourself and grow out of it quickly;
you have no time to let it run its natural course. I'll be
perfectly open with you; I know how you feel about the
Dominatrix. She does think a lot of herself, but many
leaders are like that. It's part of them. Maybe we know
better, but there's no disputing our Lady does a wonderful
job. Forget your feelings about the men, think of the
positive things we've achieved over the last ten years.
Better equipment for the marsh, beautiful cities and a
respect for our world; for what it is. There're even
rumours that soon the Dominatrix will send parties of

197

explorers south beyond the Marsh Fringe to scout the country there. We've deliberately kept our communities small. Maybe that will change. . . '

Corinna opened the door to the parlour. There was a scuffle in the corridor beyond. She didn't bother to look around the door to see what caused it. 'Carmenya, I'd like you to leave,' she said, calmly, coolly. Carmenya shrugged.

'I understand,' she said. 'But think about what I've said. I'll come around tomorrow. No need for you to report to work next week.'

'You can't remove me from my job,' Corinna said. 'You have no real reason. I do it well. I say nothing anti-establishment. What harm can I do there?'

'Very simply, this: there will be plans in my office very soon, concerning the programme of events for the institutionalising of the male sex. It is not my wish to have a sympathiser privy to those plans. Does that answer your question succinctly enough?'

Corinna could not answer. 'We'll talk some more tomorrow,' Carmenya said, mildly. And left the house.

Corinna stood for some moments in her parlour and then went out into the hall. All was silent, but for a clock ticking. She felt that in her pale clothes, she must look like a ghost standing in this dim-lit place. She looked around her, up the stately sweep of the dark stairs, down the shadowed corridors that led to the kitchens, at the mouthless, closed doors that hid the drawing room, dining-room and morning salon. It was a good house and in a short space of time she'd grown to feel very at home there. Corinna, you are a fool, she thought. Forget your wild fancies. Do as Carmenya requests. Behave. Behave. Behave. She found herself walking down the corridor towards the kitchen. As she drew nearer, the metallic sound of pots banging together testified that some of the staff were still working. There were no voices. She opened the door. One of her man-slaves was hunched over the sink. In the moment before he realised he was being watched, Corinna saw a caricature of despair etched in the line of his body, the slump of his shoulders. Then he turned around. There was a quick glance behind him, the search for an escape route, perhaps the hope that one of the other women would be there so that he did not need to speak to her; this creature, bred like a show specimen, who soon would have no purpose, not even as decoration.

'Listen to me,' Corinna said. The only response was like that you'd get from an unbroken dank; swivelling eyes, a nervousness that had almost made him deaf. Perhaps he couldn't understand her at all. 'Listen to me. . . ' She could think of nothing to say. It was pointless. She backed through the door and from the shadows, where he could not see her, said, 'You will be safe. If it is within my power, then you and your fellows in this house will be safe. It's all I can do. . . ' The chances were he had no idea what she was speaking about, but it made Corinna feel better to say it. She hoped she could keep to her words.

CHAPTER TWENTY-SEVEN

IN THE MORNING, it was Endaline who served breakfast.
Corinna asked where Sheba, who normally undertook that
duty, was. Endaline was nervous of replying but eventually
Corinna ground out of her the fact that Sheba had gone
to Carmenya's office.

'For what reason?' Corinna asked.

Endaline cast her eyes floorward, a thin, sallow woman,
whom Corinna had barely taken notice of before, mainly
because Sheba was so loud and tended to eclipse her. 'She
has gone to ask for alternative employment,' Endaline
said, flushing, which turned her a strange colour because
of her yellow skin.

'I see,' Corinna answered. So perhaps it had been Sheba
creaking the floorboards outside the parlour last night.
Sheba, being such a hidebound, conventional creature had
no doubt worried all night about being aligned to a
household over which a brooding cloud was hanging. She
was obviously afraid of being tarred with the same brush
as her mistress and was taking action to avoid that
happening. Corinna did not speak of this to Endaline. She
simply asked,

'Is this a move you are thinking of making yourself?'

'No madam. I've been very happy working for you.'

A small, but encouraging, flame of loyalty. Corinna
smiled at the woman. 'Thank you, Endaline,' she said.

Just before mid-day, Sheba returned to the house. Her
face was white, her eyes red-rimmed. Corinna came across
her in the hall. Sheba cast down her eyes and hurried to
the kitchen. At lunch, Endaline was quite willing to offer
the information that Carmenya had not sympathised with

Sheba's complaint. It was Carmenya who paid Sheba's wages and Carmenya who decided where she should work. If Sheba was so discontented working for Corinna then, of course, she was free to find alternative employment, but not within Carmenya's system. Neither need she expect to receive a favourable reference for a job elsewhere. Thus, Sheba returned, chastened, to the fold. But Corinna realised, even as she shared a private smile with Endaline, that perhaps now a stupid, frightened servant had been enlarged into a bitter spy. It would have been better for Corinna if Carmenya had let Sheba go. 'My crimes are small,' Corinna thought, 'barely crimes at all. Nothing. Yet now I am poison.' It was the way of the city. She had yet much more to learn.

After lunch, Corinna went to sit in the parlour. She tried to read, but her mind was too hectic. The ebony port was too thick and sweet for her to enjoy; she wanted something fresher, lighter, perhaps more potent. Even as she was glaring at the glass of port she'd poured there came a hesitant knock at the door. Sheba, with powdered face, announced that Corinna had a visitor. Without waiting for a summons, Carudan swept past the woman, threw down her gloves on a table and said, 'My dear, I'm so sorry I haven't been in touch earlier. So busy this week. . . ' She shook her head vaguely. Sheba was staring owlishly at this august visitor.

'May we have some tea, Sheba?' Corinna said.

'Oh, no need!' Carudan interrupted, waving a hand at Sheba behind her. 'I brought this.' She produced a large bottle of wine from the bag she'd dumped on the floor by the table.

'That will be all then, Sheba,' Corinna said. Sheba closed the door towards which Carudan flicked a quick glance.

'I expect you were wondering what had happened to me,' she said, still hearty, in a loud voice.

'Rather,' Corinna responded. She took a wooden-handled corkscrew from a wall cupboard and passed it to her guest. Carudan sat down, the bottle between her legs.

'Actually, I've come here to extend an invitation,' she said, wrenching at the cork. 'A friend of mine is having a

201

small dinner-party this evening. How do you feel about being my escort?'

'I'd love to be,' Corinna said, and then, for Sheba's benefit if she was still eavesdropping. 'I'm afraid I haven't been out much this week. Carmenya and I had an argument. . . but it seems to be o.k. now.'

'Oh, I'm sure it is.' Carudan leaned forward and Corinna held out her glass, which she found surprisingly empty of ebony port. She couldn't remember having drunk it. 'I always think it best to distrust one's staff,' Carudan said in a confidential whisper.

Corinna nodded. 'You are right,' she said. 'Shall we take our drinks into the garden?'

'That'd be lovely!'

Corinna wrestled with the capricious lock to the floor length windows. Eventually, it gave in with an outraged scraping noise and the two women were able to step out onto the terrace. There was a small, paved suntrap at the other end of a sloping lawn where wooden chairs and a table were laid out. Early Spring flowers, already beginning to burst from hardy Winter pods, released a subtle perfume into the air. It wasn't really warm enough yet to sit outside, but at least there was some degree of privacy in the garden. Corinna wished she'd brought a shawl with her. The tamed threadwoods she'd once admired now looked trussed up, imprisoned, their amputated branch stumps like crippled limbs. 'I didn't think you'd come,' Corinna said.

Carudan smiled secretively. 'We have to be careful. I had you checked out.'

'Was what you learned satisfactory?'

Here Carudan frowed a little. 'Your integrity seems in order. However, we don't generally welcome recruits who might bring unwanted attention to our company.'

'You mean my relationship with General Oralien?'

'Not just that, although it caused a few heated remarks. No, it was the other thing.'

'I suppose you're referring to my little solecism with our revered Lady,' Corinna said, smiling.

Carudan did not smile. 'Perhaps you should look on the

incident as being more serious than it appears. The Dominatrix is a paranoid woman, Corinna. You were innocent of intent, but she may not view it like that. It is known that you come from a marsh family, that men and women live together, work together, there. That would not be regarded favourably. Carmenya must have done some slick propaganda in your favour to get you to court at all.'

'Well, she has now removed me from court.'

'Yes, we heard that. A wise woman would keep her head down in your position now.'

'Don't think I haven't considered that. Carmenya told me yesterday that soon all men are to be removed from the marsh. Perhaps standing up for my family's rights is a suitable cause to take risks for. I'm afraid of what might happen to me, but how could I live knowing I sat and did nothing?'

'Wanting to do something does not necessarily mean you can have any effect, you know. Remember the Dominatrix's power, the number of her followers. You may die for this cause, Corinna. It's a fact that has to be faced.'

Corinna was suddenly presented with an image of her own death; something she hadn't really examined before. It was Carmenya with a sword. Carmenya with an agonised face coming for her with a sword. Behind her, the Dominatrix said, 'Strike, General, for the good of our people, strike!' Corinna shook her head. 'I understand the risks,' she said.

'Good. I will call for you at Sundown. Dress simply. Dark colours; nothing flowing.'

Corinna wasn't sure whether tonight was the night when she would get to meet Rosanel Garmelding. Carudan hadn't mentioned any names, understandably enough. She arrived just as Shamberel bent to kiss the horizon. The evening had become bitter; Winter's last fling. As they walked downhill towards the city's centre, Corinna even saw a scattering of ice spears plunged into a lawn. Carudan spoke little; she seemed uneasy, looking to right and left

203

all the time. Corinna guessed she was also aching to keep looking over her shoulder but was repressing the urge. 'Where are we going?' Corinna asked. She herself felt surprisingly calm, filled only with a desire for knowledge.

'To Hell, my dear,' Carudan said. Outside the temple of Parthenos, Carudan hailed a carriage, drawn by shorn and blanketed danks. A woman with cropped hair leaned down from the driver's seat and asked their destination. Carudan mumbled a street name, and bid Corinna climb up into the carriage. 'We'll have to be dropped off some distance away from where we're going,' Carudan said, 'to avoid suspicion.'

'Our destination being Freda Street,' Corinna said, pleased to note Carudan's brief expression of alarm. 'It's alright. L'Belder told me that.' Carudan nodded, chewing a thumbnail thoughtfully. Corinna looked out of the window. Already the swift-moving danks had drawn them away from the residential hill into an area Corinna had never visited before. Shrouded market stalls lined the wide cobbled streets. There were few society ladies to be seen. Women in functional clothes walked along the dusky sidewalks, carrying baskets laden with cloth-covered wares, or pushed barrows down the middle of the road. Already the next day's trading was being prepared for. The carriage driver shouted cheerful obscenities at people who blocked their path, never slackening the dank-beasts' speed. Now the streets were narrower, wooden houses leaning towards each other to block out the sky. It seemed to Corinna like an area of faded opulence. The house-doors were all carved extravagantly, but in places the carvings were broken, the metal door knockers no longer shone, slogans were scrawled upon the wood. On ground floors, many windows were boarded up and what curtains were visible looked dingy. They came to a crossroads, where the driver called her animals to a halt. Carudan hopped down from the carriage and handed the woman a fistful of coins. 'Come along,' she said, drawing Corinna after her. The carriage was soon gone, as if the driver were anxious to be free of this area. 'Where are we?' Corinna asked. Carudan drew her close against the side of a house where they were hidden under the overhanging upper storeys. 'Rosanel's house is near here,' she said.

'This is the core of the old town,' Carudan explained as they walked along, avoiding rubbish on the pavement. 'The old families built their tall houses here, before anyone had even ventured out onto the marsh. Gradually, the city crept up the hill and with it the bright, palatial homes we live in now. The old town was left to decay. It is here that the secret life of Silven Crescent does its rustling. A dangerous place, make no mistake, and a place that the Dominatrix will burn to the ground in the near future, I'm sure.'

'That will be a shame,' Corinna said, looking round her. 'I like these houses. Why can't they be reclaimed and restored?'

'You don't understand,' Carudan said. 'It's not the architecture that offends our dear ruler, but what lives within it. Denderberry Sector is a labyrinth that's easy to get lost in; there's no way the Dominatrix's mangaks can police it effectively. Soon it shall be burned and if women still live here they'll burn with it. *She* won't care; those that live here aren't the kind of people she wants on Artemis anyway.'

Corinna had never heard a woman refer to one of the Dominatrix's flamist soldiers as a mangak before. She'd always presumed it to be a derogatory term used only by men. She couldn't help feeling ridiculously impressed by Carudan's careless use of the word. 'Of course, every time I come here, I'm taking a risk,' Carudan was saying. She linked her arm through Corinna's. 'It's lucky that a priestess always has the excuse that she's out to save souls.'

Corinna thought it odd that there were to be so few people about. Carudan pulled a face at her query, barely visible in the dim light. 'Main thoroughfares like these are regularly patrolled by the Dominatrix's people. Look at that.' They had come out into a small square lit by a single lamp in its centre. Within its wavering circle Corinna could see what looked like a cage on the floor. Disturbing humped shapes were lying motionless within it.

205

'What is that?' she asked, shrinking against Carudan's side.

'One of the many forms of death careless people are likely to meet around here,' Carudan replied casually.

'Men?'

'Not always. Dissidents are starved to death in things like those. Once the wind starts blowing the other way you'll be able to tell.'

'Carudan, don't!'

Corinna's companion laughed harshly. 'Haven't you the stomach for this, my little marsh flower? So faint-hearted already?' Corinna was silent, abashed. 'What you need to do is go right up and look between the bars. Look upon the hidden face of radiant Silven Crescent. Breathe deep. And remember!' Corinna couldn't move and Carudan laughed softly. 'Oh, I'm being hard on you, my dear. Come along.' They turned into a narrow alley, where as if invoked by the priestess's words, foul smells rose from an open gully that ran down its centre. Here, more lights could be seen, though very little sky. It was like being underground. Walls ran with water, or what Corinna hoped was water, and animal life skittered through the gutters. They passed a doorway where a drab woman smoking a pipe sat breast-feeding a mewing child. Carudan murmured a greeting and the woman cried, 'Bless me Mother, and a coin in the mouth of me little'un.' Carudan made the sacred sign, uttered a few poetic words that seemed totally out of place in this slum and took a chip of metal from her purse. The woman grovelled thankfully and the two women passed on. Corinna was silenced. 'Of course, I can't do that with every one,' Carudan said, 'and if I was anything but a priestess they'd probably slit my throat to get at the whole purse. Ah well. . . '

At another crossroads stood a gibbet from which depended the hanged body of a naked youth. Perhaps the birds had taken his eyes, Corinna thought. Perhaps. Her stomach was roiling by now. The stench of death and decay, of utter despair, was everywhere. Every woman they passed entreated the priestess to pray for them, most asked for money as well. Carudan dealt with them

efficiently and firmly whilst Corinna was petrified. She'd
never seen people like this in her life before, never
believed such things possible. Dirt and despair. Women
without teeth, naked children cursing them to the grave if
they passed without offering coins, sulky males who drew
back into the shadows when they recognised the perfume
of health and cleanliness that spoke of the palace hill. And
all around the evidence of neglect and poverty, where
even clean water was probably a luxury. By the time
Carudan said, 'Ah, here we are,' Corinna was virtually at
collapsing point. Gone was the good humour and curiosity
of their walk down the hill. Only willpower was keeping
the small snack she'd had before going out in her stomach.
Strangely enough, Carudan appeared to be a lot more at
ease. Eventually, they came to a street that was far better
kept than some of those they'd passed. Carudan dragged
Corinna up the worn, swept steps of the largest building
at the end of the road. A knock upon the door was
answered by a well-dressed middle-aged man, who bowed
deeply when he saw who had arrived. Carudan swept into
the hallway, Corinna following meekly. 'I'll tell milady
you're here, madam,' the man said.'

'Thank you Collin. Where do you want us?'

'Milady has had a fire built in the library. There's a
good-sized table in there. . . '

Carudan stalked across the hall and opened large
double doors. 'Many expected tonight?' she asked, over
her shoulder.

'Seven, madam.'

'Cosy. How about a hot toddy for my friend here? It's
her first time in glorious Denderberry.'

'Let me take your coat, madam,' Collin said, and
Corinna felt his papery, shaking hands against her neck.
He smiled at her and she ducked her head appreciatively.
'If you'll follow Madam Carudan, I'll bring you something
that'll have you high-kicking round the library in no time!'
he said waggishly. Corinna smiled weakly and went into
the room.

'It's a fine old house, this,' Carudan said, leaning against
the mantlepiece and lighting a cigarette. 'No wonder

Rosanel can't bear to leave it. You had a point with your fine sentiments about restoration, C'rinna. All of Denderberry could be like this, I suppose, if someone was willing to spend money on it.' She patted the stone. 'Finest red-veined horbrin slate, mined in the north. Very rare. And expensive. I expect quite a few houses round here still have the original fittings hidden under decades of grime.'

'Perhaps the dirt preserves them,' Corinna said, sitting down in an overstuffed leather chair. She was beginning to feel a little better. The servant Collin came back into the room carrying a tray. He was accompanied by a stark, pale woman Corinna immediately recognised as Milady Rosanel Garmelding. Corinna found she had leapt to her feet. Rosanel didn't even look at her. She went straight to Carudan by the hearth, and kissed her on the mouth. 'Am I glad to see you!' Rosanel said. Corinna glanced self-consciously round the room, at the shelves and shelves of books, the dark green draperies. She wished she hadn't stood up so quickly.

'This is our new recruit,' Carudan was saying, gesturing right at her. Corinna felt a slow, insidious blush creep up her neck. Rosanel inspired her with awe far more than the Dominatrix, or even Carmenya had. Rosanel danced swiftly to her side, a testament to grace and elegance. Corinna immediately thought of L'Belder and how well the two of them would go together.

'You must be mad!' Rosanel said. 'I know I am.' She rolled her eyes. 'Sit down. Collin, where are the drinks? We could all do with one, I'm sure.'

Dazzled, Corinna sat down. Rosanel brimmed with an effervescence that was almost feverish. Eventually, Carudan persuaded her to take a seat on the sofa next to Corinna's chair and then Corinna saw something of Milady's true nature. She fidgeted endlessly and Corinna could see that her fingernails, at the end of long, beautiful fingers, were bitten to the quick.

'You can save your news for later, Corinna,' she said. 'I think the others should hear it too. What did you think of Denderberry? Did it surprise you?'

'Yes,' Corinna said, aware of how inadequate that

208

sounded. 'I don't understand. How. . .?'

'How indeed!' Rosanel said, thumping the sofa arm. She leaned sideways, resting her chin on her hands. 'What do you know of our history, Corinna?' Corinna wasn't sure what she was supposed to say. She shrugged.

'Only what I've learned from. . . people in the city. . . '

'Next to nothing, then!' Rosanel interrupted. She stood up once more and paced the thick rug in front of the hearth. 'Once upon a time, this was an affluent area. That was just after the first colonists got themselves organised. They'd brought a lot of basic materials with them from the home world, even some animals. And of course, a fine selection of lissome boys who were young enough to be subordinated but old enough to breed.'

'What happened?' Corinna asked.

'Government happened,' Rosanel explained, a slightly different version to Carmenya's, 'and hierarchies happened. Think about it. Those women came here to set up a society that was fair. They hoped to raise men who weren't of the opinion that they were the superior sex. They hoped for equality. That was the dream of the majority, I'm sure, but then the extremists took control because they had the loudest voices and they took matriarchy to its farthest point; utter suppression of men. Complete role reversal. I'm convinced the moderates must have shaken their heads and said, "Have we learned nothing?" They must have done. All the things they'd scorned about men they'd become themselves; brutal, warlike, domineering. Those moderates must have eventually become what we know as angeldt today. The women who breed, the women who bend their knees, the women who open their sheets to the dominant flamists.'

'Is the Dominatrix flamist?'

'The Dominatrix is the Dominatrix,' Rosanel replied with a sour expression. 'Her mother wasn't so bad, but this woman's a lunatic. She's formed an elite that are moulded exactly as she wants all women to be. Denderberry Sector was quite an affluent place even when my mother was alive. The last few years it's gone downhill because it's been used as a dumping ground for all those poor swine the

Dominatrix thinks are undesirable, anti-social, criminal or just plain suspect in their beliefs. They wanted me to move to the hill. I wouldn't. I'd been brought up here. Then I met Elvon, and Denderberry became simply the place I belonged. I'm under no illusions; our safety here is destined to be shortlived. We have so little time.'

'Yet you still come to the court?'

'I have no choice. Carmenya likes to keep an eye on me. I suppose it's safer for me too to show my face up there occasionally. Why do you want to join us, Corinna?' Now the nervousness, the flightiness, was gone and Corinna faced an intelligent, penetrating gaze that meant she could not lie.

'I. . . I'm not sure. Probably because I think we should all be equal. I don't want my family hurt. Because it all just feels *wrong*. I find it hard to put into words. It's just a feeling.'

'Perhaps it would help if we examine this situation and take it to its logical end,' Rosanel said.

'What do you mean?'

'Well,' Rosanel gestured with one hand. 'The Dominatrix is crazy; she hates men. She wants rid of them. Fine. Say she accomplishes it and we all get flattened. She has her own way. Then what happens? Tell me, what do *you* think happens afterwards?'

Corinna shrugged helplessly, wishing Rosanel wouldn't ask her these awkward questions that she had no time to think about. 'I don't know. Will she burn Denderberry?'

'Burn it? My dear, she will burn it, and pulverise its ashes and dance on its grave! That's just the beginning. She's paranoid. Men, and the women who support them, are the enemy she thinks are trying to overthrow her and the mangaks. Once men are gone, she still won't feel safe. A madwoman couldn't. She'll find a new scapegoat, and her eccentricity and craziness will bring about the most unbelievable era of fear and destruction you can imagine. We may all be dead, so what! Now we have to fight. We have to do something, however small.' Corinna could hear L'Belder in Rosanel's words. She could imagine him telling her all this, saying, 'Rosanel, remember my words, you are my only mouthpiece in this city.' Milady Garmelding had remembered well. She virtually spoke with his accent.

'The next obsession may even be the priestesshood,' Carudan said. 'It's a well known fact that the Dominatrix wants to make religious reforms. She just hasn't had time yet.'

'You see,' Rosanel said. 'As for the so-called help she's got from off-world, I can tell you that most self-respecting worlds wouldn't touch Artemis with a boat-hook! But there are crazies, and rogues and pirates and shady businessmen (yes, men!) who'd lend her a hand if the bait was tempting enough. Imagine, camps full of people, cluttering the outskirts of Silven Crescent and the other cities. Won't that be a nuisance! We could manage with half the number and still have enough variety in our gene pool for sperm samples. Slavers roam the heavens, my dear Corinna. I should imagine they are the kind of friends our beloved ruler is cultivating. Slavers with pirated goods that Artemis could use.' This was the first Corinna had heard of such things. She wondered if Rosanel was exaggerating. She'd never caught sight of any off-worlders after all, and hadn't the Dominatrix stopped all contact with them now anyway?

'Seems logical,' Carudan added thoughtfully, as if she hadn't heard that theory before.

'So what can we do?' Corinna asked, sounding desperate even to herself. Rosanel narrowed her eyes.

'Grow strong. I've come a long way in just a few months since Elvon left here. I've had to change my views about a lot of things.' An expression crossed her face which made Corinna think that now she might ask about L'Belder, even though she'd wanted to wait until the others got there.

'We also have to fight,' Carudan put in. 'Goddess, I'd give my life to butcher the bitch on the hill. One of us will probably have to.'

'Not just her,' Rosanel said. 'But any of her followers who could seize control after her.'

Carmenya, Corinna thought. 'Violence,' she said and the word hung in the air like the accusation it was.

'Yes,' Carudan said drily. 'Corinna, it's the only way. Moderation doesn't have a political voice here. We've learnt that. The Dominatrix has complete control. The only thing we can do which will take effect is hit her where it hurts and hit her hard. Come judgment day, we'll probably all be damned for eternity, but even as a priestess, I can say I'll make that sacrifice if it guarantees Artemis a sane future.'

Corinna thought of all she had heard about the attacks on shops and temples. Was that the only way?

'We have contacts in other cities,' Rosanel said, 'although the rebel network in Rain Haven has been infiltrated and destroyed. They were careless. We're more discreet, I hope. Nevertheless, it won't be long before that happens to us too. That's why we have to act fast.'

'I'm flattered that you trusted me,' Corinna said, aware of the enormous risk these women were taking confiding in her.

'We don't,' Rosanel said. 'Not yet. When the others get here, you'll be interrogated. There are certain codes Elvon and I had worked out. You don't know them yourself, but by questioning you we can ascertain whether you really met him and what he thinks of you. Don't be alarmed, Corinna. If you're genuine, you have nothing to fear. If you're not, you don't get out of here alive.'

'I don't understand why the Dominatrix lets you live,' Corinna said, gulping. 'She must know what you're involved in. Why hasn't she crushed you before now?'

'She's watching and waiting, that's why,' Rosanel replied. 'Oh, I'm quite sure she must know quite a bit about us. She could undoubtedly destroy us completely whenever she wants to, but she's waiting for the same thing we are.'

'Which is?'

'News of Elvon L'Belder. What he's doing, what he's planning.'

'She thinks he's dead. They couldn't find him on the marsh.'

'I knew he wasn't dead. Presumably, so does she.'

'But how?' Corinna was beginning to feel distinctly edgy. Had Carmenya brought her to Silven Crescent knowing what she'd done? Was it all a trap? Rosanel smiled.

'How? The same way I did. Through the priestesses.'

'What?'

'A trained priestess would be able to divine whether someone was alive or not, especially someone with the lifeforce of Elvon L'Belder,' Carudan said. 'It was easy for me to pick him up. Unfortunately not so easy to pinpoint exactly where he was.'

'I had no idea you had so much power,' Corinna said.

'Not enough,' Carudan replied. 'The Dominatrix had her people make a cursory search, just to placate those around her who were wittering on about it. But she knew they wouldn't find him; she knows what L'Belder is, what a slippery fish he is. She also knows that his only function is to make contact with his people here again. He's nothing without us. So she lets us alone, thinking we don't know she's onto us. When she pounces, she wants us all together; L'Belder at our head. She knows that all she has to do is wait. That's why it's vital only our most trusted people are privy to what you have to tell us, Corinna. L'Belder is the one person on this world she fears. It's almost a supernatural fear. The Dominatrix must not know his plans. If she does, it may be a death sentence for all of us.'

Corinna stared at her lap. She had so little to tell them really. Perhaps it wouldn't be enough. Perhaps they'd be angry. 'I shouldn't have come,' she thought. 'I shouldn't have got involved. I shouldn't have come.'

CHAPTER TWENTY-EIGHT

SEMELE DANTE WORKED as an archivist at the Palace; Corinna didn't think much of her to begin with. She was the first of Rosanel's people to arrive, a gaunt, sour-faced creature, whose first words were a complaint about the weather, who looked Corinna up and down without a smile and sniffed. Next to arrive were a man and a woman, Gideon Chant and Petra Sammuel. They were very much together; Corinna felt it quite a novelty after so many months in the city. The last two to join the company were a man and a boy, obviously lovers, Greylie and Ittamar, who both used the surname Derland. Now Corinna felt comfortably inconspicuous. These people had clearly not met together for a while and spent quite some time catching up on gossip. Collin sped round the room, cracking terrible jokes and dispensing drinks; the atmosphere became thick with cigarette smoke. Corinna sat way back in her chair, watching the others. It was hard to believe that these were the core of the rebel network. She could easily imagine she was just at any other dinner party, where the guests swapped pleasantries before the meal. But the moment had to come when Rosanel clapped her hands and suggested everyone should take their seats at the table. A hush descended, broken only by the scrape of chairs against the floor. Carudan guided Corinna into a chair between herself and Rosanel. The atmosphere in the room palpably changed. Corinna found herself facing the Dante woman, whose mouth was drawn into a fine, disapproving line.

'Well,' Rosanel began, 'as you know, I have called this special meeting because word has come to me of Elvon and his plans.' She gestured towards Corinna. 'Friends, I'd like to introduce Corinna Trotgarden, who has recently come to the city from the marsh. She bears a message from Elvon himself.' She smiled encouragingly at Corinna. 'If you would, my dear, tell us all you can.' All eyes were now turned on Corinna. Not having spoken aloud to so many people before, her words were garbled to start with. There were several silences as she struggled with a mind that had gone nervously blank. For comfort's sake, she made the story as brief as possible.

'So just what are his plans?' Semele Dante asked coldly. 'You don't seem to be able to tell us much.'

'He wanted me to tell you he was alive.'

'We already know that,' the woman drawled, looking with amusement at her neighbours.

'Is that my fault, or even Elvon L'Belder's?' Corinna asked. She was becoming impatient with this treatment. She didn't have to come here and suffer their interrogation. 'Why the hell did I get into this?' she wondered yet again.

'It's alright, Corinna,' Rosanel said, putting a cool, dry hand on her arm. 'I know that. But is there nothing you can tell us about what he intends to do next? Is he going to attempt to get back into the city?'

Corinna felt embarrassed having to repeat L'Belder's scheme to locate the Greylids. It seemed like the dream of a madman. There was a silence after she'd finished speaking. Semele took a breath to begin speaking but was cut off by Greylie Derland.

'Is there any proof these people exist?' he asked. Corinna shrugged.

'I must admit I'd thought it only fairy-tales, but Elvon seemed very keen on the idea. . . '

'He always works on intuition,' said Rosanel grandly, and with affection. 'He must be right. So, what does he expect us to do? Wait?'

'I expect so,' Corinna answered uncertainly.

'Wait?!' It was now Petra Sammuel's turn to speak out. 'Rosanel, how much longer can we wait? The extremists who have broken away from us have effectively cut whatever time we had to a minimum. I say we form our own plans now and act! We cannot risk waiting for L'Belder to return. By the time he gets here we might all be dead!'

There was a rumble of agreement from round the table.

'Have you so little faith?' Rosanel hissed. 'Elvon founded this movement; he's its heart. He will be back soon. I know he will!'

'Yes, well this is all very well,' Greylie Derland said calmly. 'Perhaps Rosanel is right, perhaps not. I say we make moves to protect ourselves and use whatever means we have to learn the Dominatrix's plans.' Here he fixed Corinna with an unwavering stare. 'Then, maybe, we can talk about acting. We need times, dates, schedules. First of all, I think we need to check this young lady out, don't you?'

Rosanel did not looked pleased. It appeared she did not have that much influence with these people. 'Yes, of course,' she said. 'Have you any objections, Corinna?'

The request could have been nothing but a formality. Corinna could hardly refuse. She nodded. 'It's o.k. What are you going to do to me?'

'Nothing to worry about,' Carudan said. 'A light trance will be induced, that's all. This is because we would prefer it if you do not remember the questions we ask you. We have to be careful. It's a safety valve, a code, as Rosanel said.'

'Well, let's get started then,' Rosanel said, standing up.

The only thing that made Corinna feel uneasy was what else she might reveal under hypnosis. How would Rosanel feel if she learned Elvon L'Belder had made love to Corinna? And what else might they ask her? Her mixed feelings about Carmenya, for example, might not please them.

'If you would lie down on the couch,' Carudan said, gesturing. Corinna did so, closing her eyes to the ring of faces looking down on her. She felt hot and out of breath. 'They will invade my mind,' she thought and wondered whether, if she made a run for it now, she could escape.

216

All this reminded her unpleasantly of the things she disliked about the Dominatrix and her regime.

Carudan began to speak, taking Corinna through a standard relaxation exercise, so proficient in her art that the girl soon felt as if she and Carudan were the only people in the room. Her body was sinking right into the couch, even through it. 'Now, I want you to imagine you are walking through the marsh on a Spring morning,' Carudan said. She led Corinna into a peaceful visualisation, banishing all fear and restraint. The last thing Corinna could remember was the feel of water round her ankles, the smell of the marsh, the honk of the cranes. It was real to her. She was there. Then came the questions, but it sounded only like the wind through the kale-rushes. Corinna was simply taking a walk through the marsh, far from the city. When Carudan brought her back, she struggled for a moment, because the memory of the city had gone. She did not know where she was.

'Hush,' Carudan said, soothing her. 'Take a deep breath. Remember. You are in Rosanel Garmelding's house in Silven Crescent. There's nothing to be afraid of.'

'Fetch her something to drink.' That was Rosanel's voice. Corinna felt as if she'd been asleep for a week. She tried to sit up and Rosanel handed her a glass. 'Are you alright?'

Corinna nodded and drank. It was hot, non-alcoholic and sweet. Whatever codes Elvon L'Belder had instilled within her without her knowing remained secret. She never found out what they were, or even what she had said during her trance. There was no indication that any of it had caused discomfort to Rosanel and her colleagues. It was noticeable that the atmosphere in the room was lighter than it had been before.

'Do you feel up to talking?' Rosanel asked her. 'I would like to speak with you alone.'

'I'm fine.'

'Good. Would you mind coming with me to my study?'

'Not at all.' Corinna answered, thinking, Oh no, it's about L'Belder. She's learned something from me.

Rosanel took her to a small, cosy parlour very similar to

217

Corinna's own in the house on Lavinia Drive. A fire glowed in the grate, thick curtains were pulled against the night. There was a faint smell of flowers. 'I understand the difficulties of your position, Corinna,' Rosanel said, sitting down in a worn, comfortable chair next to the fire. Corinna sat on the floor next to it. She didn't answer, because she couldn't think of anything to say. Rosanel didn't expect an answer. 'Carmenya has forbidden you to return to court, hasn't she?' she continued. The tone of furious dislike was unmistakable. Corinna felt Rosanel would be far from sympathetic about any emotional dilemma she might suffer over Carmenya.

Corinna nodded. 'I believe she is concerned for me,' she said carefully. Rosanel made an irritated sound.

'Don't be deceived by her. Carmenya is concerned only for her own skin. Think how bad it would look if one of her protégés was discovered to be a dissident. You must be extremely careful now. I wouldn't advise you to come here more than absolutely necessary; Carudan can keep you in touch. Perhaps it would be best if you did not learn that much at the moment.'

'Are you afraid I'll betray you all? Is that it?'

Rosanel shook her head. 'Not intentionally, but you're young, Corinna, and comparatively new to Silven Crescent. Why take unnecessary risks? As soon as Elvon contacts us, you will be told. Maybe then you will be able to use your position to assist us.'

'But I have no position now.'

Rosanel smiled, quite cruelly. 'Haven't you? You live in a house that General Carmenya Oralien procured for you. She visits you regularly, perhaps even confides in you to a small degree. That, in my eyes, is a very strong position, Corinna. Didn't Carmenya tell you of the Dominatrix's plans? She may tell you other things.'

Corinna experienced a painful numbness that crept throughout her body. It made her uncomfortable to think about betraying Carmenya further. She did not want to be a spy, not that kind of spy, who used the bedroom to steal other people's confidences. There was something unclean about it, even though a harder part of herself knew that

218

in times like these, many unsavoury tactics became necessary. 'What do you want to know?' she found herself asking.

'Time schedules mainly. We have a fairly complete idea of what's planned, but not when. I still believe she'll hold off the more extreme parts until L'Belder is vanquished. She won't want to waste her precious flamists keeping the city secure when she invades the marsh, I'm sure of that. She'll need every warrior she can get. Do you really think the marsh women will surrender their men folk without even a mutter? I don't.'

'No, neither do I.' Corinna thought of Dannel, and also Yaschel Tendaughter, who had an obsessive regard for her children, whether male or female.

'We are Skyreachers, Corinna,' Rosanel said. 'You know our name. Are you one of us?'

Corinna looked up at the pale, lovely face that stared back at her with utter confidence. She knew this woman shared L'Belder's passion for equality. It shone from her. She shared his hatred of oppression. Rosanel would let nothing stand in the way of her beliefs. Nothing.

'Yes, I'm one of you,' Corinna said.

'Hmm.' Rosanel tapped her lips thoughtfully, staring into the fire. There was an unspoken question on her lips. She looked down at the girl. Corinna couldn't work out the expression, but there was no trace of anything negative. 'Goddess, she knows!' Corinna thought. Perhaps Rosanel did, but she was either too proud or too self-disciplined to pry. 'How was he?' she said at last.

'Quite ill at first, but recovering by the time I left Vangery.'

Rosanel shook her head. 'We were unprepared. We should have known. Tell me more. I want to know everything about him, everything he said.' Corinna complied with caution. She told Rosanel how she'd discovered L'Belder in the boathouse and how she and her mother had hidden him on the marsh. Then she skipped to the story of how Dannel had brought him into the house. It was what she'd told all of them only a short time before, but with more detail. Rosanel knew there was more, that certain things were left out, but said nothing. 'I miss him,' she said. Corinna could say nothing to that. She stared, like Rosanel, into the fire. After only a few minutes, Rosanel pulled herself together. She leaned forward and put her hand on Corinna's shoulder. 'He has a good friend in you,' she said. 'Thank you for helping him. I'm more grateful than I can ever tell. He may have died without you. I apologise that we had to interrogate you, but the habit of taking precautions is too ingrained in us to ignore. Shall we return to the others now? I expect you'd like a drink.'

Corinna followed her from the room, feeling like a leaf caught in the slipstream of some powerful, air-cleaving, machine. If she fell too far behind she would drift to earth and be stamped into the mud by careless feet. Am I strong enough for this? she thought. Am I?

CHAPTER TWENTY-NINE

SPRING CAME EARLY to the marsh that year. One day, Dannel would look back and remember, yes, the plaisel had definitely bloomed before the last storm swept across the causeway, and hadn't the furze come into fluff while a few greying ice-spears still pierced the tussocks of air grass and hagmoss? It hadn't been a particularly bad Winter, but still a memorable one for the people of Vangery. The servants would talk of how, in their opinion, Meonel Trotgarden suffered a mental breakdown, whilst the Mistress herself seemed to bloom and grow as if she'd discovered some untapped reservoir of her youth.

Every morning, Elvon L'Belder would stand at the edge of Vangery Isle and sniff the air to the east, as if straining to catch some far-off whiff of Spring. Meonel often watched him from an upstairs window, a sneer on his face. The mere sight of L'Belder's swinging, loose-limbed gait, the sound of his irritating tuneless whistle, would cause Meonel to clench his fists, and his teeth, until it hurt. Whatever effect Meonel had hoped to achieve by casually revealing his true feelings to Shyya had certainly not been realised. A distant politeness was maintained. No more did Meonel explode with rage in Shyya's presence, never did a snide comment pass his lips. Shyya was uneasy with this new, listless Meonel. He was not so complacent as to think his master's brain wasn't still churning in its multi-hued conflict of emotion. For some reason, Meonel had elected to stay quiet. If this was some kind of cue, Shyya didn't take advantage of it. He performed his duties as expediently as ever, with one eye cocked behind him; from experience he knew attack usually came when you least expected it.

Dannel, spending more time alone in her study, watched the marsh and became filled with a huge yet poignant sense of calm. She was sad, but she was at peace. One morning, Shyya brought her a vase of young furze fluffets, which, in the warmth of the room, opened up within an hour; statis fountains of fibre and thread. 'A cycle comes to a close,' Dannel thought and touched one of the fluffets tenderly. Down came away in her hand. She rubbed her fingers together until the fluff became a sticky ball. Far away, from somewhere else in the house, she could hear Bolivia's strident voice giving orders. Bolivia was a practical creature. Although she could be heartless with people, she was a shrewd businesswoman. On the whole, Dannel realised, she was not so worried the farm would become Bolivia's one day. Under her control, it would continue to thrive at least. Perhaps some arrangement could be made so that all those people who had worked for Dannel could be transferred to Yaschel Tendaughter's place when Dannel died or became to old to run the place. That way, Bolivia could buy herself new staff and no-one's life would be changed for the worse. It was worth looking into, even if such action would be criticised as over-emotional. Yaschel was still being a little frosty over Corinna, but Dannel had no doubt that she'd come round pretty soon. Everybody needed extra help in the Spring. It was the time when all the farms worked together, clearing the water fields, the paddocks, pruning the trees, sowing and planting. Boundaries were vague on the marsh; there were no fences. 'Goddess,' thought Dannel, drawing herself up in some alarm, 'why am I thinking this way? The end of my working life is years away, surely. Why am I thinking this way? Because you have no way of knowing how involving yourself with L'Belder will end, her brain replied coldly. There may be danger. . . Then why am I doing it? she wondered. Why don't I just have my people tie him up and throw him in the frack cellar until I can send for Carmenya? Why not? Well, that is simple, logic replied blandly, you believe in

222

him. Whatever discomforts, however unacknowledged, you have felt in the past were soothed when L'Belder told you his dreams. In meeting him, you came home. You found that there are others like you. That is why you won't send for Carmenya. That is why you will equip him with two of your best danks and the best your kitchen can provide in supplies for his journey. Don't fool yourself, Dannel, said the brain.

There had been no further letters from Corinna. Shyya told Dannel this was probably because of the weather. It was not always possible to predict the time between storms accurately, so travelling could be a hazardous venture. Dannel responded to Shyya's soothing as best she could, yet was still uneasy. What had Corinna been alluding to in her last letter? Was she in danger now? What if. . . what if. . .? Darker, unacknowledged thoughts would follow. There was no proof Corinna was even still alive, nobody knew what was happening in the city. When L'Belder spoke of finding the Greylids, he spoke with urgency, as if he knew something Dannel did not. She had a feeling he'd tell her if she asked. She never asked.

On that morning, in appearances and routine the same as any other, Shyya made an announcement to Meonel as he was making his bed. 'Soon I shall be leaving,' he said.

'How soon is soon?' Meonel asked, drawling.

'Maybe days.' There was a brief silence, during which Shyya folded blankets with irritating thoroughness. 'Soon Dannel will find you a new attendant,' he said.

After he'd gone, Meonel drew his blinds and sat to brood in semi-darkness. His mind was a blank. It was like standing in the middle of a crossroads with every path curtained by iron. He stood up, paced the room; sat down, gnawed his knuckles. Why was Shyya leaving? He didn't believe the sole reason was because of some task Dannel had thought up. She wouldn't normally use Shyya for that. It could be dangerous out on the marsh. Meonel knew how Dannel felt about people she valued going out there. There had to be more to this than met the eye. For weeks, Meonel had put off thinking about it. He'd regarded each meeting with Shyya as a time of testing, something to be

223

analysed afterwards, when he would search for hidden nuances in the most mundane words Shyya uttered. Tone of voice, expression, body posture would give inner thoughts away. But Meonel could make no positive deductions. Shyya, as always, was an enigma to him. He cursed the days of sarcasm, cruelty and indifference, those days of artifice. He despised the image of himself that he'd projected to Shyya, but could see no way of correcting it. Outside, regular as the sunrise, he heard L'Belder whistling as he walked to the edge of the marsh. The man was not visible from Meonel's window. And there was another mystery. The new man too had taken to sitting with Dannel every morning to take milk-suds, as Shyya did. What were those three brewing together? Since Joel had come to Vangery, things had become worse for Meonel. His wife had changed towards him, no longer solicitous or pampering. Was Joel her lover now, too? What was his power? What was he? Meonel had never met a man like Joel before; he was different from the others who worked on the farm. What was that difference? They had never spoken because Meonel avoided him. He was sure Joel would laugh at him because he had lured Shyya away from Meonel. This was, of course, a delusion, apparent to anybody except Meonel. 'I must know,' Meonel thought, 'and perhaps there's only one to find out.' The suggestion of secrets was driving him mad. A decision was made. Meonel reached for his coat where it hung on the back of his door and was hurrying down the back steps to the yard before he could think about it properly.

L'Belder was standing, hands in pockets, swaying on his heels, squinting at the causeway. The marsh was an exhausted vista of grey and yellow, in some places misted with a faint suggestion of green where shoots investigated the light. All the trees looked forlorn and haggard, remembering the devastation they had suffered through the Winter. Soon they would forget that and bloom once more. Meonel crunched down the gritted path towards the muddy banks. L'Belder did not turn around. Perhaps he thought it was Shyya coming. 'How confident he looks,'

Meonel couldn't help thinking, 'how upright.' He remembered the gaunt man who had been brought into the house by Dannel; there was little resemblance to that person now. Joel had flourished in Vangery, or replenished himself. Neither, Meonel had to admit, did Joel even carry himself like a slave. There was an air of authority about him, that he obviously made an effort to conceal. This was all the more maddening because he did so with humour. Meonel could tell that Joel's spirit could never be broken; humiliation would not touch him. It was a quality that Shyya shared. Damn them both! Meonel thought. He wondered what would happen if he should break into a run now and push the hated Joel into the marsh. That was purely a romantic fancy. The water was low at this point. Joel would just get muddy.

'Looking forward to your journey?' Meonel said as he drew close. Joel turned round, surprise on his face. He smiled vaguely.

'No, sir, I can't say I am. I'm not a traveller.'

'Neither is Shyya. I wonder what's got into my wife that she's sending both of you out together like this?'

Meonel could see a suspicious expression slipping across Joel's eyes. The man was watching him very carefully.

'It is not for me to say,' he said.

'Well, maybe I should say something then. Would you like me to? I'll be honest with you, I don't want to lose Shyya as my attendant, so I'll speak to her. Do you think it's a good idea?'

Even to Meonel, his voice sounded insincere. Joel was clearly not fooled. He narrowed his eyes and then smiled widely.

'I haven't taken Shyya from you,' he said. Meonel's first reaction was to shout. 'Don't be impertinent,' but then he thought of how foolish and peevish that would sound. This man withered him. He felt so small. Who was he? Not a slave. It didn't make sense.

'Who are you?' he said. 'What are you doing here?'

Joel laughed. 'You don't like me, Meonel Trotgarden. If there was anything to hide, do you think I'd tell you, the last person I could trust?'

225

Meonel laughed, a short, harsh bark. 'And how could I damage you even if you told me? Who could I tell in turn? I'm a man; as worthless as you are.'

'Bolivia,' Joel said. 'You could tell Bolivia.'

'And what could she do? Are you afraid of her?' Meonel took care to inject scorn into those words.

Joel wrinkled his brow. 'Scared of her? No, of course not. But she could. . . ' He shook his head, realising he was saying too much. Meonel went to stand beside him. They both looked at the marsh. 'He has a kind face,' Meonel thought. 'Is that what Shyya admires in him, kindness?'

'What can I do for you?' Joel said.

'What do you mean?' Meonel was taken aback. Perhaps the man had read his mind, as he felt Shyya could sometimes.

'Well, you've never spoken to me before and I get the distinct impression you've come here to speak to me now. What do you want?' A voice in Meonel's head said, 'Tell the truth,' but pride stood in the way, as usual.

'I'm curious about what Dannel wants you and Shyya to do, that's all.'

'Why don't you ask her?'

Meonel shook his head, lost for words.

'Then say what you came to say,' Joel said.

'You're impudent!'

'Oh, don't give me that crap. You sound like one of the mangaks! It's about Shyya, presumably. Why are you ashamed? Is it because you envy me, that you think I stole him away from you?'

'Shyya's a slave and so are you!'

'And what are you?' Joel asked quietly. 'Are you happy? Are you living your life to the full? Answer me that.'

'I doubt if anybody is,' Meonel replied. 'For myself, I doubt that I have the capacity to be happy.'

'You certainly lack the capacity to be manipulative,' Joel said. good-humouredly. 'I suppose that's admirable in a way. I know how to get what I want from people, most people. Arrogance, I suppose. I expect you love Shyya deeply, very deeply, far more than I could. All I can do is use people, but I try not to hurt them in the process.'

226

'You're being very honest,' Meonel said acidly. Joel shrugged.

'Lying about it would be a weakness. I know what I am.'

This is a strange conversation, Meonel thought. It hadn't progressed as he'd intended. 'And what is my happiness to you?' he asked.

'I like to think that everybody can have it if they try hard enough.'

'It would be nice to share your optimism, Joel,' Meonel said.

He made a move to leave and Joel put his hand on his arm.

'Have I eased your mind?'

Meonel did not answer. He pulled his arm away. 'My mind is never at ease,' he thought and marched away, towards the house.

Back in his room, he realised he was brimming with energy. He felt better. Why? Nothing positive had been said, yet perhaps all they had talked about had been Shyya, in an oblique way. He opened the blinds and poured himself a glass of wine. Today, he did not intend to get drunk. How do I spend my time? he wondered. How do the days pass? I do nothing. Time just slips past me. That must change. It must be the Spring. Shyya wasn't here last Spring. This Spring will be different.

An uneasy tension hovered over the house. People looked from windows at the sky, wondering if a last storm was drawing close. After the mid-day meal, Dannel went to her study to relax and read through some notes she'd made for the crop planning. A few bloated drops of rain smacked against the window. She had to turn on the light. Around her, the house seemed very quiet. She could hear the Vangery generator humming in its shed far below her. Yes, it was very quiet. A knock on the door made her jump nervously. 'Yes?' she said. The door opened and there stood Meonel. Dannel was aware of her jaw drooping. Meonel had never visited her here before. In fact, Meonel had never come to her at all unless summoned, and even then he dragged his feet. Within the space of a single second, she saw the youth she had married stand there and grow older into this bitter, shadowed creature. Meonel had been beautiful once. Hair like waving green-gold rushes, a wide whimsical mouth, wide dark eyes. She had bought him virgin, a child, unsuspecting and she'd hoped to make him happy. Maybe she'd handled it wrong. He'd given her Orblin but that was all and, even to Dannel, Orblin was rather a nonentity, eclipsed by Bolivia and Corinna. Trying to love Meonel had become a distasteful, embarrassing experience. She'd given it up long ago. Now he was standing here, in her study, which meant he was going to communicate. Dannel was almost frightened. 'Yes, Meonel, what is it?' she said, laying down her papers and leaning back in her chair. Meonel came to hover at the other side of the desk.

'I want to talk to you,' he said.

Dannel couldn't resist saying, 'Now, after all this time?' Meonel smiled bitterly. 'May I sit down?'

Dannel extended a hand to indicate the chair he was now leaning on and he sat. 'Well?' she said.

'It's about Shyya.'

'Shyya?'

'Yes.'

'What about Shyya?'

'I'd rather not have him replaced.'

Dannel sucked in her breath. Meonel would not look her in the eye. She wanted to say, 'You had every chance, Meonel, that's why I bought him. You had every chance and now you've lost them all. Tough luck.' 'I was under the impression you were dissatisfied with Shyya,' she said.

'Because of what he said to you?' Meonel asked hotly. Dannel put up her hands.

'Shyya is a slave, Meonel, you know that. I have to use my slaves in the best possible way. I felt that I wasn't getting the best from Shyya having him abused by you. He's intelligent and willing; rare commodities as I'm sure you'll agree. He's wasted being a whipping boy for your neuroses. Need I say more?'

'You made me like this!' They looked at each other in painful silence until they both dropped their eyes. Now

228

Meonel looked very young, hands clasped between his knees, head lowered. He looked like a boy.

'Things didn't work out the way I wanted between us, Meonel, I agree, but it's not only unfair, it's untrue, for you to accuse me of mistreating you. I never have. Once I tried hard to make you happy. It didn't work. . . ' She paused, silently amazed that these words were being spoken at last. 'I wish I could reinstate Shyya as your attendant, Meonel, but I can't. It's not just a personal thing.'

'I know. I know that. What is it, then?'

She hesitated. This man was her husband. In any normal relationship she could tell him the truth and count on his support. She wanted to tell him that, and found, to her surprise, it wasn't that difficult. She told him quite a lot. Not about L'Belder or Shyya, but just about herself, what she thought and felt. It was as if a locked door had been opened and whatever had been contained within the room beyond was pouring out, jubilant in its release. Meonel listened with an expressionless face. Dannel was telling him that he had not been a husband to her. He hadn't wanted to be, but now he was glimpsing what might have been. 'I doubt whether we could ever have been successful lovers, Meonel,' Dannel said, 'but we could have been friends. I don't know who's to blame, really, or if either of us are. When I bought you, you must have been crying out inside for a lover; that's what attracted me, but I was too blind to see that I could never satisfy you. It was in your blood to need a man, not me. Goddess. . . ' she pulled a disgusted face, 'it must have been a nightmare for you.' Self-disgust. It wasn't a thing she cared to face often, the thought of what must have been crossing Meonel's mind as she tried to please him.

'It may sound like a cliché,' he said, 'but we've wasted a lot of time. These things should have been spoken about years ago.'

'They should have been spoken about before I ever touched you,' Dannel added.

'It doesn't matter now. It didn't happen, so it doesn't matter.'

229

'No.' They both fell quiet. Dannel had a bottle of liquor in her cupboard. She asked Meonel to fetch it. As she poured them both a glass, she said, 'Meonel, you remember General Carmenya being here in Summer?'

'Who could forget?'

Dannel smiled drily. 'Quite. Well, she was looking for a man named Elvon L'Belder, the freedom fighter from the city, remember?'

'Yes. Did she find him?' Meonel was wondering what this had to do with him, or any of his questions. He suspected nothing. Dannel realised this and was quite surprised. To her, it was obvious. 'No, she didn't find him, but someone else did. Corinna.'

Meonel was silent, looking at her, waiting for her to continue. 'Meonel, the man we call Joel is, in fact, the fugitive from the city. He's leading a cause for equality. Apparently, things are getting pretty bad in Silven Crescent. . . '

'Dannel, are you mad?!' The information had just sunk in. 'Carmenya will kill us all, burn Vangery? You're insane! You can't take a risk like this! What can you possibly hope to achieve?'

'Shut up!' Dannel had to cry to calm him. 'I believe in his cause, Meonel. Oh, don't look like that! You think I enslave men, don't you? Well, you know nothing! I don't want to call Shyya a slave. I don't want to own him. I don't want to own anyone! We should be working together! Oh, maybe I can't do anything to change things, but I do believe in L'Belder and I will do all I can to help him. You want to know what he and Shyya are going onto the marsh for? It's to find a race of people whom L'Belder thinks will help him. It's his only chance.'

'Dannel, you are condeming Shyya to death, if not all of us.'

She shook her head. 'No. Someone has to do something. I've trusted you, Meonel, telling you this. Do you understand the amount of trust I've put in you?'

He thought of Joel saying, 'You could tell Bolivia.' Yes, he understood.

'I've talked to him,' Dannel said. 'He's made me see his

230

vision and it's something I empathise with. He's made me
see the city as it is, Carmenya and her kind as they are.
He's made me see.'

'Dannel, you've sent Corinna there!' Meonel's voice was
agonised. He'd just realised that fact, and a brutal, callous
fact it seemed. 'She wanted to go. She's with us, Meonel.'

Meonel laughed, shook his head, turned sideways on his
chair.

'This is madness. You're all crazy. Why stick your necks
out like this? What can you achieve? Nothing. It's all
dreams. The mangaks are too strong. It's all dreams.'

'Dreams can become reality if you believe in them
enough.' That was L'Belder talking, of course. She was
quoting him, but it didn't matter. 'The Dominatrix has
plans, Meonel. I think they will affect all of us.'

'What plans?'

'I don't know. I'm afraid to know.'

'Yet you're not afraid to harbour this criminal. That
doesn't make sense.'

Dannel smiled. 'No, it doesn't. I agree.'

'Who are these people he's looking for then?'

'The Greylids.'

'Fairytales!'

'L'Belder doesn't think so.'

'And that's enough for you to go along with him?
Dannel, what's got into you?'

'Meonel, I'm not going to argue with you about this. Just
accept what I say. You wanted to know what's going on; I
told you.'

'I can't believe you're being so stupid. I thought you
loved this place.'

'I do. Perhaps that's why I want to do something.'

Meonel shook his head. Even as the explanation terrified him, it had given him some relief too. The secret
conversations had been explained at least. Whatever his
feelings for Dannel, he'd known her to be a testament to
common sense. Was she right now? He trusted her
judgement, but it was such a risk she was taking. 'Will this
L'Belder tell me all that he's told you?' he asked.

Dannel shrugged. 'How can I say? He knows everything.

231

The things I'm too scared to be told about. He knows everything. Ask him.'

When Meonel went to the stables, he found the man who called himself Joel cleaning leather, sitting on the floor. He said, 'You are Elvon L'Belder,' and the man looked up at him. Meonel saw a face completely without fear, he saw the compelling eyes of someone towards whom people are drawn like antelope to the light in a crouching smoom's eye. L'Belder said, 'And now you are one of us, Meonel Trotgarden,' and before Meonel could protest, or laugh, or walk away, he realised that L'Belder was right. Meonel was with them. Perhaps not for the same reasons that Dannel and Shyya and Corinna had joined him, but because Meonel was standing beyond the fire, and he was cold, and it was so easy to walk towards the flame so that he could be one of the people warmed by it. He would be welcomed in, no longer an outsider, but part of something. A comrade, and comrades in secrecy are close, very close.

CHAPTER THIRTY

'ONE DAY THE women will come,' L'Belder said, 'And they will take every living man away from the marsh. They will take them to a fenced camp beyond the city of Silven Crescent where they will be confined to be milked of their seed like animals.'

How long? How long before this happened? The things that L'Belder told him made Meonel realise what Dannel had only sensed. Time was running out. It would no longer be possible for the marsh people to forget about the city, shrug their shoulders and say, 'Well, their ways are different to ours, but they're entitled to live the way they please. It's nothing to do with us.' He was given horrifying visions of the marsh farms torn apart by civil strife, the matriarchs cut down defending their sons and husbands, their friends and workers. Of all those women he knew, no matter how they patronised their menfolk, Meonel could not see one of them meekly allowing Carmenya and her mangaks to take their people away from them. What L'Belder spoke of meant war, a war that the marsh people could not win.

'It isn't the first time,' L'Belder said. Meonel was sitting in L'Belder's bedroom, sitting on the bed. They were drinking ale. Shyya was not with them. He would not come in.

'Not the first time? What do you mean?'

'Well, surely you've seen the ruins on the marsh,' L'Belder said. 'A long time ago, other families cultivated these isles. They wanted no truck with the city because they'd left it to get away from what was happening there. The ideals of the first settlers were becoming perverted,

233

so those who were true to them broke away. That wasn't appreciated. The women in the city thought it was dangerous; they wanted everybody to be like them, so the Lawn Isles were routed, the families replaced with those who espoused the city way.'

'How do you know all this?'

L'Belder shrugged. 'Contacts in the right places; in this case the palace archives in Silven Crescent. What I didn't know has been filled in for me by our friend, Shyya. It seems the northern marsh people are very different to the rest of us. Perhaps more primitive and brutal in our eyes, but they don't hide their history from anyone.'

Meonel nodded in agreement, although he had little idea of what the north was really like. He'd been brought up from the southern cities, Rain Haven to be precise. Meonel shuddered and repressed the memory. 'So, now the conflict will happen again,' he said.

'Not quite the same as before, but similar.'

'It's appalling. I can't believe it.'

'You must. Now, do you see why I must go on, even if it is clutching at straws. We need help. I believe that the Greylids are remnants of those families who were thrown off the isles. I believe that, if they know about us, they will help us.'

'You can't be sure.'

'No. I can't be sure, but it's a chance.'

'I want to go with you,' Meonel said. L'Belder laughed heartily to cover his surprise.

'Meonel, you'd travel worse than I will! Nobody really knows about the floating forests. Anything could be there.'

'You are wrong to mock me,' Meonel said. L'Belder wondered why he didn't sound offended.

'I know the real reason why you want to go,' he said. 'It's to prove yourself in certain people's eyes, isn't it?'

'That sounds very melodramatic. Have you thought that I want to go because Vangery might not be here for much longer? Somehow I'd feel safer suffering deprivation in the floating forests than continually scanning the horizon for Carmenya's skippers.'

'Always your own skin then, eh, Meonel?'

Meonel raised an eyebrow and then his glass. He smiled. L'Belder slapped his leg.

'You don't fool me,' he said.

Naturally, it was Bolivia who first questioned the purpose of L'Belder's journey, and his choice of companions. She cornered her mother even as Dannel was supervising the packing of supplies for the travellers. Dannel had previously worked out a rather flimsy excuse; that she wanted the farthest boundaries of her land examined, that she'd heard rumours a colony of sheek weed had taken root there. If that was so, it was important to gather samples now, before growth ran riot with the Spring. Potent sheek weed could be used in many ways; its leaves and flowers as a medicine, its rangy stem as a fibre, its tuberous roots as a vegetable. Bolivia said she heard no such rumours. Dannel replied that Bolivia didn't know everything.

'But why send Meonel and that eunuch, mother?' Bolivia did not intend to let go now she'd sunk her teeth in.

'It will do Meonel good. He hasn't been well this winter. As you know, Shyya has been promoted. I want him to see the land. He will need this knowledge as my assistant.'

'I've never heard of a more motley crew,' Bolivia said scathingly.

'Don't worry yourself about it,' Dannel answered.

'If anything, I should be doing the job you've given to Shyya,' Bolivia continued in a complaining tone. 'Don't I need this knowledge, too? Don't you want me to have a thorough knowledge of Vangery, so I can run it as well as you do? It seems I have to be content supervising shemble-frack harvesting and resolving the petty arguments of the staff! Aren't I worth more to you than that? You even took the eunuch with you to buy a slave! You've never taken me! What is it with him and you? He's not even a proper male. Why do you let him suck up to you so much?'

Dannel was sick of hearing Bolivia's whines.

'Shyya is a good worker,' she answered shortly. 'Other than that, I have nothing to explain to you. There's no point you knowing how I organise this place if you don't know the day-to-day running. Notice I haven't taught Shyya that. Don't be impatient, Bolivia. One day, Vangery will be yours and when it is, you will know everything. This year, I intend to widen the scope of your duties anyway.'

Bolivia seemed partly soothed by this but didn't want to show it. 'Meonel will slow them down,' she said. 'He's useless.'

Dannel didn't answer. She made a tick on the noteboard she was carrying and wandered over to another shelf. Here, dried roots were arranged in bunches. She picked a selection of medicinal ones, evidence of her lingering fear of letting people out onto the marsh. Bolivia eyed her narrowly, arms folded.

'Aren't you going to give them some of the Ash pulp?' she said, looking at the table where all the supplies were laid out. 'It's easily reconstituted and won't take up much space in the pack.'

'Good idea,' Dannel said.

'I'll find you some.' Bolivia busied herself on the other side of the room. Perhaps I misjudge her a lot, Dannel thought. Perhaps I should give her more responsibility. Is that why she's so bitter? Does she sense how I feel about her?

'Any news from Corinna yet?' Bolivia asked.

'Not yet. Pretty soon I should think. The marsh roads must be traversable now.'

'Maybe she's so engrossed in her new life, she'll forget to write. I wish I was her.'

'Really! I thought you were happy here at Vangery.'

Bolivia dumped a package on the table.

'There! Oh, I'm happy, but I'd like to see the city too.'

'Perhaps you can visit Corinna this summer, then,' Dannel said, privately sure that was undesirable, if not impossible.

'I'm not sure she'd have me,' Bolivia said. 'We've never had much in common. She'll enjoy being able to refuse me. Corinna's a devil when she has a little power, but I don't suppose you ever noticed that.'

'Don't talk that way, Livia,' Dannel said, but without

236

much conviction. 'Why don't you write to her? I expect she's grown up a lot, and grown out of childish moods. I'm sure she'll be pleased, and surprised, to hear from you.'

'I might.'

The next day dawned drizzly and cold; not the kind of morning to begin a journey. The marsh was skirted with roiling fog through which the honking of ditch cranes sounded eerie and forlorn. Looking out of his window at the weather, Meonel cursed the rather rash decision he had made to accompany L'Belder and Shyya to the forests. He put on two pairs of gloves and two coats. Upstairs, Elvon L'Belder fondly tidied his attic room for the last time. He realised he'd been quite happy in it; a time of healing. He had decided to give all his sketches to Dannel and he'd written her a short poem which expressed his gratitude unsentimentally, but would make her cry when she read it. In addition, he'd also written out all of his knowledge and suppositions about what the Dominatrix might do to the marsh and its people. He knew Dannel was afraid of knowing, but it was vital that she did. After all, he and the others might never return. It had to be faced. And Dannel had to face that soon she might be at war, with the bulk of her family and friends away from her.

This is the final step I'm taking, L'Belder thought, and shivered. Make or break. Life or death. Pain or joy. Maybe none of those. Maybe just disappointment and then the decision of what the hell to do with the rest of his life. He dreaded that more than defeat in battle with the Dominatrix. Meanwhile, Shyya was already down in the stables helping to saddle up the danks. He hadn't given any particular thought to the weather or to the outcome of the journey. He was wondering about a dream he'd had the night before of which only tantalising snippets remained in his memory. It was to do with the people he knew, but that was all he could remember. Disturbing feelings still clung to him from the dream-state; discomfort. He wished he could recall more. It had put a damper on his mood that morning. Breakfast had been consumed before sunrise. The staff were only just waking up by the time the travellers had mounted their danks and walked them, along with a pack beast, to the edge of the causeway. Dannel came down to see them off. She looked pale and ill, probably because she hadn't bothered to powder her face as she usually did but maybe because she'd been brave enough to read L'Belder's letter before they all left. She wished them luck and repeated a dozen warnings about safety and caution. They listened patiently until Dannel gave them the wave they acknowledged as their signal to leave. She stood on the muddy bank, a miserable, large figure swathed in a thick shawl. With feet frozen and fingers numb, she watched the swaying danks until the fog had wholly swallowed them.

By noon, spring sunshine had burned through the fog to reveal a bleak landscape, still half asleep from its winter rest. A family of grumpy wervels proclaimed their discontent with the cold, rubbing their forepaws together and curling back their lips. Shyya said they'd probably just woken up from hiberation. On the whole, the marsh was quite deserted to the east of Vangery. Animal herds gathered mainly in the north in the winter because of the high ground and the shelter. Naturally, smooms and other predators would tend to cluster around the same area. Soon, when the weather became warmer, the marsh would wake up fully and the animals would come south again. The travellers passed the Tendaughter farm, increasing their pace in case they met anyone who might ask questions. By late afternoon another farm was behind them; Angwells. Only two more remained to pass on their journey east; farmed land was only a minute proportion of the marsh. Perhaps the marshdwellers sensed something not quite right about the floating forests because there were so few families who'd made their homesteads in the east. West of Vangery, people were far more densely distributed. L'Belder thought, that if he had had the choice, he'd have built a home in the east. Far more peaceful and not so competitive.

The day passed without any incident of note. By nightfall they'd reached a large tussock which they'd spotted in the distance an hour before. It meant deviating from their course a little, but there was no way they could risk camping on the marsh itself. The land was too unpredictable, and even those deceptive flats of grass that didn't collapse beneath someone halfway through the night would no doubt be a roosting ground for newly spawned leeches and insect larvae with voracious appetites. Between them, the three men erected the oilskin tent. Admittedly Meonel wasn't much help, but L'Belder was patient, explaining carefully what he was doing in the hope that, after a few days, Meonel would be able to erect a tent by himself.

Meonel had never felt so cold in his life, but was too proud to say so. His fingers were too numb to help build a fire and, even once it was blazing it only warmed the front of him (too much) while his back was still solid with cold. Shyya and L'Belder cheerfully prepared a meal.

'What I'd give for my bed in Vangery, now,' Shyya said, biting into a spongy sliver of reconstituted meat.

'You should have been like Meonel and worn two of everything,' L'Belder said. 'I bet you're the only one of us not likely to freeze to death tonight, Meonel.'

They curled up inside the tent in quilted bags of feathers and vegetable fluff. Meonel could not get to sleep. The ground was hard and lumpy beneath his sleeping bag and cold air crept in from the neck. He lay listening to the eerie sounds of night birds calling out to each other. Sometimes they sounded like hysterical human voices. He imagined a horde of wild people stalking the tent, clad only in mud and hair. They carried spears and sang of drinking blood. It was not a pleasant image. Meonel tried to think of better things. Soon, it would get warmer. The marsh was like that. Cold one minute, balmy the next. The transition from Summer to Winter was just as sudden. They'd already seen signs of Spring. It would not be long. Shyya mumbled in his sleep., He sounded afraid. What was Shyya dreaming? Was it about cannibals armed with spears creeping through the marsh too? Meonel shivered and turned over so his face was close to Shyya's back. A small amount of warmth radiated from the thick sleeping-bag. 'Goddess, it's going to be a long journey,' Meonel thought miserably, but soon he was asleep.

CHAPTER THIRTY-ONE

CORINNA WAS GETTING jumpy. Perhaps it was the inactivity getting on her nerves; she'd been absent from her job for two weeks now. Her friends – such as Lady Marta – hadn't called on her, and Corinna hadn't the nerve to call on them first. Carmenya still came round about every three days, but it was tiring for both of them. Once, Carmenya would have been able to confide in Corinna; the girl knew their nights together had been balm for the General because of this. Now, for Corinna's own sake, Carmenya kept quiet. She'd stayed overnight only twice since the incident with the Dominatrix. Corinna was less happy about that than she thought she'd be. Carmenya was looking strained; there was an atmosphere in the air of Silven Crescent which spoke of important events approaching. Everyone was affected by it. Corinna was almost driven to despair. Rebel activity had been increased; sometimes shouting could be heard on the hill, carried on the night air from the lower city. Although the Dominatrix's government tried to play this down, people had now begun to whisper of how there was more than one rebel group. The Palace Mount women were becoming aware that facts were being kept from them and this caused a silent, repressed unrest.

Carudan and the other dissidents had kept their distance from the house in Lavinia Drive and Corinna had received little other communication from them. Half relieved, she wondered whether this was because she couldn't be much use to them now Carmenya had cooled towards her. Carudan had sent a carefully worded note in which she implied sympathy for Corinna's position and offered spiritual support. Corinna could not help feeling that wasn't much use to her at the moment. It was from Endaline that Corinna learned what was going on in the city, the rumours, the gossip. Apparently, posters had been put up around the place advertising a Grand Meeting which would be held in a week's time. Its venue was to be in the largest public place available, the athletic stadium. All women were urged to attend. Corinna supposed this would be when the Dominatrix would reveal part of her plan for the people. No doubt it would be done carefully and subtly so that the women would be wooed into accepting it. By clever indoctrination over the years, the Dominatrix had already caused the upper class of Silven Crescent to alienate men from their lives. Only the common, working people would have to be convinced. And of course, the rebels had been playing into Yani Gisbandrun's hands with their terrorist tactics; there was little sympathy for them for this reason alone, never mind the fact that they were mainly a liberation movement for men. Endaline said that, as an incentive, rewards would be given for women who 'made sure the new regulations were adhered to'.

'That means informing on neighbours and friends, I suppose,' Corinna said. Endaline sighed.

'Yes, I suppose it does.'

'Will the people fall for it? Will they be prepared to spy on their friends like that?'

'The rewards will be substantial,' Endaline replied drily. She and Corinna were still rather careful what they said to each other on the matter but, in this case, there was no need to say more. Below the hill, women were not that well off. They were kept down; skilfully. Loyalty to the Dominatrix, fired by her strength of will and personality, her promises for the future, blinded them to the dance they were being led by the woman. Soon, things would begin to happen; bad things. 'Goddess, let L'Belder come back soon!' Corinna prayed desperately.

One night, not long after Carmenya had left the house,

having stayed for dinner, somebody knocked softly on Corinna's parlour window. Corinna realised it must be someone who knew her well, who knew she always retired to the parlour for an hour or two before going to bed. There was only one person she knew that well. Opening the curtain a little, Corinna saw a robed figure with half-covered face standing with its nose pressed against the glass.

'Carudan?' Corinna whispered.

'Open up, quickly!' came the muffled reply. Cursing the screech of the lock, Corinna opened the windows. Carudan shot into the room and rushed to the door to the hall, locking it on the inside.

'What's going on?' Corinna asked. She closed the windows and drew the curtains against the dark. 'Are you in trouble?'

'How many of your household do you trust?' Carudan asked in a clipped voice.

'Why?'

'Corinna, just answer. We haven't much time.'

'Endaline, I suppose. The men. I'm not sure about Sheba, she's easily frightened and a great fan of the Dominatrix.'

'Well, she might not be soon, as I suppose we'll have to risk it. Get them here. All of them. Now!'

'What? They'll be in bed!'

'Then wake them up! Hurry! This is important.'

Corinna couldn't understand why Carudan had locked the door. She unlocked it and let herself out. 'Hurry up!' Carudan called behind her . 'I can't stay here long.'

Corinna roused a bewildered Endaline first. 'Get Sheba. Bring her to the parlour,' she said, shaking the woman. 'Be quick about it. It's important.' Endaline didn't waste time with words. Eyes still half closed, she was already reaching for her clothes. 'Where's the key to the men's rooms?' Corinna asked.

'There are two,' Endaline said, pulling a woollen over her head. 'Sheba has one and the other hangs on a hook behind the kitchen door.'

'Good. Be quick, Endaline. Carudan is waiting for us in the parlour.'

She saw a hundred questions in the woman's eyes. 'Carudan will explain,' she said.

The corridor to the kitchen was freezing cold. Corinna was barefoot, having kicked off her slippers in front of the parlour fire. 'Something is happening,' she thought. 'This is it, something is happening!' She felt excited, not frightened. She was prepared to fight, having thought about nothing else for days. Had L'Belder come back? Was that it? Was Carudan going to take her and her household to Denderberry, to join with the others? It had to be that! What else could it be? She yanked the key off its hook and scampered up the back stairs. The men's rooms were in a dark, lonely corridor at the top of the house. She didn't know which doors to try. There were about a dozen. Some were unlocked, revealing empty, moonlit rooms beyond. Some had locks that the key wouldn't fit. Her hand was shaking. In triumph, she would burst into these rooms and tell the men they were free. She stuck the key into yet another lock and it turned. Throwing open the door, she virtually fell into the room beyond. There was no curtain at the window, no furniture. She saw one of the younger men, sitting up, wide-eyed with shock, half-covered in blankets on the floor. 'Get up!' she said. He didn't move. 'Come along.' No response. Snorting she went and grabbed his arm to pull him from the blankets. He whimpered and shied away, hands to head. Corinna experienced a shock when she felt how thin his arm was. He was so young, so pitiful. He crouched, shivering on the wooden floor. Corinna found a pile of rags she presumed were garments. 'Get dressed!' she ordered. The man, who was really just a boy, only crouched nearer to the floor, hiding his head. Corinna started to feel angry. 'Look,' she shouted. 'You have to leave here! You have to get dressed! You're being taken to Denderberry! Do you understand?' She wasn't sure if that was true. Now the slave was rocking, moaning. He was terrified of her. Uttering an exasperated snort, Corinna ran from the room. She'd have to send Endaline up. They wouldn't take any notice of her. Sweating, even in the cold air, she went on to open the

244

other rooms. One of the other men was older, more coherent and less cowed. He was already out of bed when Corinna opened the door, having heard her shouting at the others.

'What's happening?' he asked.

'I don't know,' she answered. 'But someone from Denderberry has come and asked me to assemble my household in the parlour. Can you get the boys down there, quickly?'

'Yes,' he said and hurried past her. I should have spoken to that one before, Corinna thought, but it's too late now. Too late. She stepped out into the corridor and closed the door behind her. The man was going into one of the other rooms. She could see his long, pale hair in the moonlight. What life have they had? she wondered. If I had spoken to him before, he might have become a friend and I'd have had someone to talk to these past couple of weeks. I'd have learned things; it's too late. She broke into a run and went back downstairs.

Sheba and Endaline were already there. Sheba looked terrified, almost as speechless with terror as the boys had been. 'The men are coming,' Corinna said, and then realised that they probably did not know which room the parlour was. After all, they never had any need to come into this part of the house.

'What's happened?' Sheba asked, in a high, hysterical voice. Carudan was leaning against the mantlepiece. She'd thrown back her hood and Corinna could see that her handsome, patrician face was unnaturally pale, her expression strained. She shook her head.

'What I have to say is for all of you,' she said. Sheba uttered an unconvincing moan and Endaline took her arm protectively. There were several minutes' horrible silence, broken only by Carudan chewing her thumbnail. Then there was a welcome sound in the corridor.

'Ah,' Carudan said, in relief. The older man slave was ushering the other two into the room. He alone looked unafraid. Corinna shut the door behind him. 'Your name?' Carudan asked him.

'Gavron Histable.' He stood like a guardian in front of

245

the other two who could only blink through their hair.

'Gavron, there is a crisis. In essence, you are now free, but I would advise you and your fellows to stay with us for the moment. We have less time than I'd like, but, Corinna, I think drinks are in order. Let's calm our nerves. We shall be needing them later.' Carudan now seemed to have regained her composure, and her colour. As a contrast, Corinna was so keyed up she could barely pour the drinks. Endaline came to her assistance.

'I'll do this, madam. You sit down,' she said.

'Now, sit down, all of you,' Carudan said. 'I won't say this again, so listen carefully.' She accepted a glass and twisted its stem between her fingers. 'All of you under this roof are in danger.' This was punctuated by another feeble moan from Sheba. 'You have two options. The first is stay here and face whatever might happen, the second is for you to come with me to a safe house where at least you will be out of reach for the time being.'

'Out of whose reach?' Endaline asked.

'The Dominatrix,' Carudan answered.

'What's happened?' Corinna asked, above a predictable outburst from Sheba. 'Why are we in danger now?'

Carudan sighed. 'Word has come to us from one of our sources on Palace Hill that the Dominatrix means to arrest all those resident in this house as dissidents or possible dissidents. The men will be executed outright. You will be interrogated and imprisoned, Corinna. Your female staff will no doubt be accused because she will consider them loyal to you. . . ' She fixed Sheba with an accusing eye. Sheba responded immediately.

'I've done nothing!' she said angrily. 'I'm not leaving! I've done nothing. I told Carmenya I wanted to leave Mistress Trotgarden's employment weeks ago. That's my defence. How can I be in danger?'

'Don't be an imbecile, woman!' Carudan said coldly. 'The Dominatrix won't make distinctions, she can't afford to. You're nothing to her, no-one of importance. You are expendable, as you'll no doubt discover if you remain here.' Sheba bit off a cry, knuckle to teeth, shaking her head.

246

'When will this happen?' Corinna asked.

'Any time. That's why we have to be quick. Get ready to leave.'

'I'll pack your things, madam. Don't worry. You stay here,' Endaline said. 'You pour yourself another drink. Don't you worry.' Corinna was touched by her concern.

'Hurry up the rest of you!' Carudan said. 'Are all the doors to the house locked?'

'Yes, madam,' Endaline answered. 'I suggest we leave by the cellar route. An underground passage comes out near the back entrance to the garden. It is used to transport coal and supplies to the cellar.'

'Good idea!' Carudan said. 'Be quick.'

Corinna sank into a chair. 'No time for that!' Carudan said, now full of a sense of urgency again. 'You need a coat. Come on, they could be here, any time!'

'Why?' Corinna asked. 'Why has this happened now? What does she suspect me of?'

'Corinna, Corinna, it's not just your house. Last night, another friend of mine was raided. We couldn't make it to her in time. Now her house lies empty, windows open to the rain. Many other women are under threat, not just you. The Dominatrix fears the rebellion. You are from the marsh, you slighted her; that's reason enough. She fears spies everywhere. No doubt Carmenya has been trying to defend you, much as I loathe to say anything in her favour, but she's been unsuccessful.'

'Then why hasn't she warned me herself?'

'Probably because the Dominatrix has appointed her as the one to arrest you.'

'No! I won't believe it! She was here tonight, dined with me. . .'

'Face it, Corinna!' Carudan interjected harshly. 'Carmenya won't stand by you against the Dominatrix. You must face that!'

'How long will we be safe in Denderberry?'

Carudan shook her head. 'How can I say? The mangaks will come looking for you, but we have hiding places. Let's hope they're discreet enough.'

Endaline opened the door. 'I've thrown a few things into

247

a bag,' she said. 'Here's your thickest coat.'

Corinna stood up. 'What about my animals?'

'What have you got?'

'Only the felids. You've seen them.' Carudan sighed, realising argument was useless.

'Leash them, Endaline,' she said. They all went out into the hall. Sheba was standing, red faced and resentful by the corridor to the kitchen.

'I'll never forgive you for this,' she said to Corinna and then spat. Nobody said anything to her. Corinna could not blame her, really.

Everyone was ready. The felids were leashed and shivering, bags were packed, everybody wrapped in coats. The two younger men linked arms and shrank against the wall. 'To the cellar, then,' Carudan began cheerfully but was cut off by the sound they'd all be dreading: a pounding on the front door.

'Goddess!' Carudan hissed. There was a moment's stasis, before Corinna whispered hoarsely, 'Get them out of here, Carudan. I'll stall the mangaks.'

'Don't be stupid, they'll take you away. Come with us, now!'

'No! If they're in the garden, they'll see us come out of the cellar passage. That's not enough of a lead. Get going Carudan, don't argue! If you're worried I'll betray you; don't. I'll die first.' For an agonised second as the sound of pounding and shouting filled the hall, Carudan hesitated. Then she exhaled, long and deep.

'We love you,' she said. 'Prey Carmenya will help you in some way.'

'I'm not afraid,' Corinna answered. 'You told me I might have to die for this cause. I'm not afraid. Now hurry!' With a whisper of shuffling feet, Sheba led the way down the corridor. Now she seemed anxious to escape the soldiers. Gone was any idea of staying behind and pleading her case. Endaline lingered in the hall. She dropped her bags, and Corinna noticed that she'd surrendered the felids' leashes to somebody else. 'Go!' Corinna said.

'No,' Endaline shook her head. 'We'll have to put on a

performance here, madam. We have to keep them here for as long as possible. I'll go back upstairs. Take off your coat, let them in.'

'Endaline, are you mad?'

'No more than you, madam.'

Corinna managed a weak smile.

'Take off your coat,' Endaline repeated, picked up Corinna's pathetic bag of belongings, 'and make sure they all come in the house. We don't want anyone lingering in the garden, do we?' She winked and then ran lightly up the stairs. It had taken only seconds but it felt like minutes.

'Corinna Trotgarden!' boomed a voice outside the door. With trembling fingers, Corinna hung up her coat on the hall stand. She rubbed her hands together and opened the door. Carmenya was first over the threshold.

CHAPTER THIRTY-TWO

'I'M AFRAID I have to ask you to come with me to the Palace.' That was what she'd said, cool as you like, not a flicker. It was as if the past few months had never been. Corinna had gone cold.

'What is the meaning of this?' she'd said, stiffly, pompously. Carmenya had given her a knowing look, or had it been knowing? What kind of look had it been? I am a young angeldt of Palace Mount just disturbed late in the evening, Corinna thought. That is how I should behave. 'What do I have to go to the palace for? Can't it wait until tomorrow, Cara? It's so late.'

'I'm sorry, Corinna. I have my orders. The voice was flat. About half a dozen soldiers were clustered uncomfortably in the hall behind her. Corinna found that she had backed up against the parlour door. Anything to take their attention away from the corridor to the kitchen, although surely Carudan must be out of the garden by now. Corinna blinked several times, swallowed.

'Why now? Why didn't you take me earlier – when you were here before?'

'Corinna, please don't waste my time. I'm on duty now. These orders were received when I reported to my post this evening.' Were they really? Corinna wondered. Or had Carmenya eaten dinner with her knowing even then that she'd be back later to take her away?

'Very well, General. I'll get my coat. And some shoes. Would you wait a moment.'

'Of course.' When Corinna was a few steps up the stairs, Carmenya said, 'Oh, while you're up there, C'rinna, wake your women and have them bring the male slaves down,' will you?'

'What for?'

'Just do as I say. Make it easier for yourself by co-operating.' Corinna paused a moment.

'As you wish.'

She went straight to Endaline's room. 'They're in the hall,' she whispered. 'What do we do now?' Endaline pulled Corinna down next to her on the bed.

'We sit here and we wait,' she said.

'They'll know,' Corinna said, agonised. Endaline put an arm round her. Corinna could see her nose shining in the moonlight. She felt like laughing.

'If you mean they'll know we've sent the others away, I think they'll realise that anyway.'

'But how do we explain. . . '

'How we were warned? Simple. I'll say a note was pushed under the door and that I brought it to you in your parlour about half an hour ago. Naturally, I destroyed the note as soon as you'd read it. You've never seen me lie, Corinna, but I assure you, I'm very proficient at it. Otherwise, Rosanel wouldn't have had me work for Carmenya in the first place.'

'What?!'

'Hush. Trust me. We'll wait.' Endaline decided what they would say when Carmenya found them. Corinna memorised it. Then, they waited.

Of course, the first thing that Carmenya did was split them up. Corinna was escorted to the palace by three of the guards. Carmenya remained in the house with Endaline. Outside, Corinna found that the night was warmer than it had been of late. A cloudless sky, full of stars, stretched over the turrets and towers of the palace. This was the same sky that shone over Vangery. These stars witnessed everything. 'Shyya!' Corinna thought desperately. 'Shyya, hear me!'

'Move!' One of the guards pushed her roughly through the palace gate. Corinna remembered every other time she had passed under the arch; hurrying on her way to work, calling a greeting to the guards, with whom she'd become familiar. There were no friendly faces now. The gate-houses were in darkness. Different women policed the walls at night.

She was taken, not to some kind of dungeon as she'd feared, but an administrative office off one of the many courtyards. As they entered the building, Corinna noticed a young clerk still at work in one of the offices. The girl pushed back her hair and looked up as they passed her window. Corinna saw the brief expression of alarm that crossed the girl's face. Everyone was learning to be frightened in this city; everyone. Corinna heard the clerk's thoughts as if they were spoken aloud: 'Goddess, not again. Who is it this time? Could it ever be me?' In a world ruled by suspicion, people could be wrongly accused, whether through malice or ignorance, and in that world innocent people could get hurt, badly.

Carmenya did not come to question Corinna. Perhaps the Dominatrix had tested her loyalty by ordering her to arrest Corinna, and perhaps that had been enough. Another general waited in the room they marched her to, a stranger. This woman was heavily built, definitely man-like, with cropped greying hair and a square jaw marked on the left side by a deep, irregular scar. She was standing by a table, one foot up on a chair, leaning on her raised knee. A studied pose, Corinna thought.

'You are Corinna Trotgarden?' the General asked.

'I think you know that,' Corinna answered. The woman made no comment. She picked up a noteboard from the table and scanned it. One of the guards handed her some more papers, upon which, as they passed her face, Corinna recognised the scrawl of Carmenya's handwrit-ing. The General read the papers and shook her head, smiling.

'Why am I here?' Corinna asked. 'If I am accused of conspiracy, then let me defend myself.'

The General looked up. 'Sit down, Mistress Trotgarden. I hope this will not take long.' A guard pushed Corinna down into a seat. Corinna shrugged off the intruding hands angrily.

'That will be all,' the General said to the guards. Once they were alone, she sat down across the table. 'I am General Serilda Nathaniel. It is regrettable that we have to take this action, Mistress Trotgarden, but these are troubled times.' She cleared her throat, businesslike. 'Now, from the report it appears you cleared your household before my colleague General Oralien arrived. That seems premeditated, does it not?'

'If you've read the report, you'll see that we were warned,' Corinna answered.

'Who warned you, and why act upon it anyway? If you are innocent, Mistress Trotgarden, surely you had nothing to fear?'

'Forgive me for saying this, but the way things are at the moment, innocence is no guarantee of safety. I'm sure you know that, even if you won't admit it.'

'Who warned you?'

'I've no idea. My maid found the note. I read it and decided the best thing to do was send my staff away. They've done nothing. I've no wish to be responsible for their deaths.'

'Only the men would die. They don't matter. Or do you care about their fate?'

This was the moment Corinna had been dreading. Would she perjure herself now and deny her feelings? Would she say, no, I do not care? She had no way of knowing how she'd react until it was asked.

'I care about the fate of all living creatures,' she heard herself say, 'their sex, or even whether they are human or not, means nothing to me. I respect life. When I go to the temple of Parthenos, I remember this. It is supposed that we all must, but even a Goddess' word can be over-ruled by a strong leader, can't it!' Corinna found herself upon the floor, lights dancing across her vision. Her mouth was numb. She realised she had been struck. It had been so quick. She blinked, dazed. The General was standing over her; she kicked the fallen chair out of the way.

'Never speak that way in this palace,' she said coldly. 'You are here at the Dominatrix's pleasure. You could be killed anytime.'

Corinna pulled herself up by the table. Her nose was bleeding. She was so numb, she couldn't think.

'It is clear you are a dissident, Trotgarden. You don't even make an effort to hide it. Who are your contacts?'

'If I am a dissident, then it's because I always have been. I have no contacts. I don't know what you're talking about. I've only been here a few months.'

General Nathaniel righted the chair and pushed her down on it. Corinna was pinching her nose. She felt so hopeless, yet so angry at the same time. She didn't care about death because she had a feeling life could never be the same again for her anyway. Good times were over, no matter what. That was a fact.

'Why did the woman Endaline stay with you?' the general asked.

'I didn't want her to, but she insisted. Perhaps she thought I was over-reacting. Perhaps she thought the note was a hoax. I don't know.' Questions. Questions. More followed, the point of many of them was lost on Corinna. The business of her affair with Carmenya was never touched upon, however, although her friendship with Carudan was mentioned.

'I met her at the temple. We made friends. Is there something wrong in that?'

'She's a priestess. Not generally the sort of friend a young girl from the marsh would make when she arrived at court.'

'The girls at the court bored me. Does that satisfy you?'

'Hardly! In my opinion, whoever brought you here made a grave mistake. They have made you suffer, haven't they?' They both knew who that was, even though her name would never be mentioned. 'That's the trouble with lust, Corinna Trotgarden, it fuddles the senses, and can be very dangerous.'

Corinna was not blind to the veiled insult in those words. General Nathaniel thought she was Carmenya's concubine and was probably thinking that Carmenya would have been more sensible keeping her out on the marsh, where, although their liaisons would have had to be more sporadic, would at least have kept undesirable elements

254

out of Silven Crescent. Corinna had a feeling Carmenya was going to be in quite a lot of trouble herself over this. The one good thing, Corinna thought, was that because she was from the marsh, the people here considered her rather a bumpkin. She thought that General Nathaniel believed her story. How that story would hold up under torture, she could not bear to think about. Best to make it convincing now, so that would never arise. 'What will happen to me?' Corinna said. 'Can I go home? I never wanted to come here, General; I had no choice. Will I be allowed to go back to the marsh?'

'I'm afraid that's not for me to say,' Nathaniel answered. 'Are you sure you want to go back there?' Corinna realised that question was probably a test to see if Carmenya had told her any of the Dominatrix's plans.

'Yes,' she said. 'Of course I do. I was happy there. All I ever wanted to do was work on my mother's farm. I'm a boat-builder, a dank-trainer, not a courtier. I never will be.'

General Nathaniel sighed through her nose, sucking in her upper lip as she considered Corinna's words. She did not seem a woman who was terribly unfair. No doubt she felt she was wasting her time questioning this gauche angeldt who though misguided in her feelings was not politically active. Carudan's position had protected her. No further questioning in that direction had arisen, although Corinna herself could see a hundred loopholes in it that Nathaniel could have investigated. If Corinna had been born and bred in the city, her offence would be more serious. Her history was protecting her. Perhaps they would let her go. Perhaps.

'This matter is not ended,' Nathaniel said, putting her papers in order. 'You will have to remain our guest for a while, Mistress Trotgarden. I regret the inconvenience, but I'm sure you appreciate our position.' She smiled grimly and called for a guard. Corinna was led away.

They locked her in a cell further up the corridor, which was fairly comfortable, but lit by a stark light that Corinna doubted ever went off. She eyed the bucket in the corner with distaste. Everything was white and clean, rather like

255

Corinna imagined a hospital to be. There were even a couple of books for the prisoner to read, lying on a low table by the narrow bed. One was a paper-covered booklet of the Dominatrix's most passionate speeches, which Corinna threw onto the floor with a growl of disgust, the other a pious, wildly impractical religious tract, the Goddess's rede, carefully twisted so that all the Dominatrix's actions and decisions fitted within it. There was nothing like having one's nose rubbed into the dirt, Corinna thought. She sat on the bed, wondering if she was going to cry. Some part of her felt she should but her body and mind still felt numb. Occasionally anger would surface, but that was all. She was glad that Carmenya might suffer because of her. Of course, the General had had no way of knowing what Corinna was like before she brought her to the city. No doubt that decision was being bitterly regretted at present. Carmenya had never bothered to get to know Corinna at Vangery, even though she'd had many opportunities. Maybe, if she had, Corinna wouldn't be in Silven Crescent now, and then she would never have found out about the Dominatrix's plans until the mangaks came to the marsh to take the men away. 'Has it helped me knowing that?' Corinna thought. 'Has it helped my family in any way?' She stared down at her bloody hands where they rested on her red-spotted lap. Her nose had stopped bleeding back in the office. Perhaps she should clean her face and hands. Why bother? She went to the small white sink and bent to take a drink of water from the tap, rubbing her mouth with her hands. What next? She went to lie down on the bed, but could not sleep. What next? What next? What had happened to Endaline? Had Carudan got the others safely away? Now, Corinna felt cold. She pulled the white blanket over her body. 'Let them do what they like, let them do what they like, bitches, bitches, bitches. . .'

CHAPTER THIRTY-THREE

SHE WAS KEPT in that room for two and a half days, fed regularly, but otherwise left alone. On the second day, she began to read the propaganda because her nerves had become raw with boredom and suspense; a strange mixture. About lunchtime on the third day, she heard marching feet in the corridor outside. Her first thought was that Carmenya had come at last, but no, it was only an escort of three guards to take her somewhere else. They wouldn't tell her where.

Her clothes were still stained from her nosebleed. Her hair was in disarray. She felt dirty. At mid-day, of course, the palace was swarming with people, though none of them stopped to stare. Rather, there was an accentuation of downcast eyes, a hurrying of steps, the hot, frightened smell of 'could that be me?' Corinna kept her eyes just above the horizon. She did not want to catch sight of anyone she knew. The sweet fragrance of Spring was in the air; Corinna inhaled deeply. She caught a brief reminder of the marsh in that scent; the green smell of bursting seeds and pods and thrusting spears of reed. For the first time, she felt like weeping. 'Let L'Belder come back' she prayed, visualising the image of Parthenos. 'Let him save the people. Let him win, my Lady.' Corinna did not imagine for one moment that the Goddess could have any sympathy with the Dominatrix; not the *real* goddess. A deity would have to be above that petty kind of power. Could she hear her honest devotees? Could she witness their suffering without turning away, without doing anything? Then Corinna heard Carudan's voice in her head, as if she stood beside her. 'The Goddess is within you,' the voice said. 'Nowhere else. Don't look outside; you'll find nothing. She's within you, within all of us.' That meant the Dominatrix too, of course. This battle was a battle of goddesses, elemental soul against elemental soul. Looked at that way, the odds didn't seemed stacked so high against Corinna. Whoever she faced within the next few minutes, she would face at gut level; soul to soul. Position and power wouldn't come into it. In the sight of the Goddess, all were equal. And no matter what they did to her body, her soul was inviolate.

They took her deep into the palace's heart, through corridors and halls she had never seen before. Even in such dire circumstances, Corinna could not help but admire the beauty of the place. It was enormous, tasteful and symmetrical. The deeper they went, the more the women they passed seemed to reflect these qualities. Eventually, they marched down a high, sunlit corridor which came to an end at a pair of huge wooden doors. Of course she knew this place. Wasn't it the very heart of the palace? Didn't all passages lead to these rooms that faced her now? The first time she had come here the doors had been open and she hadn't noticed the carvings around them. Now they seemed horribly ominous: a cable of naked women, linked by flowing hair. Their eyes were blind, their stone mouths open. To Corinna, it looked as if they were crying out in fear. Beyond this door the great, bloated she-spider crouched and spun. She was being taken into the presence of the Dominatrix herself; why? She was a nothing, a nobody. What possible interest could the Dominatrix have in her other than to make sure she was no trouble? Was a personal interview necessary? Did she do this with every suspected dissident?

The doors swung open and one of the guards nodded at her curtly. Corinna stepped into the reception area beyond. As before a woman sat behind the desk. 'If you would go right into the Inner Salon,' she said to the guards, not looking once at Corinna. There was no question of being kept waiting this time. That too was ominous. Corinna was led along carpeted corridors that hushed the sound of feet. The guards said nothing to her. She wanted to collapse, blot everything out, but could only keep walking. They passed a servant woman who glanced nervously at Corinna's stained clothes and hurried on. It's as if I'm dead already, Corinna thought. I am a condemned woman. I will never see the marsh again, never see my mother, Meonel, Shyya. Self-pity filled her eyes with tears, which she fought back and scrubbed away with a damp hand. No time for that. She must be strong.

The Inner Salon. It was red, very red indeed; curtains, carpets, couches; everything. Red candles in redwood sticks, ornaments carved from the same warm wood. And in the middle of this bloody chamber, on a crimson foam of cushions and tassels, reclined the only pale object in evidence; the Dominatrix. She was dressed in white. Around her, three women obscured by scarlet robes knelt with lowered heads. Corinna stood just beyond the threshold and the door whispered shut behind her. She didn't know what to do or say. She was damned if she was going to bow or throw herself at this woman's feet.

'Come closer, Corinna Trotgarden, I want to look at you,' the Dominatrix said. Corinna paused before complying. The three women in scarlet never moved. Close up, the Dominatrix looked devoid of anger; her face was bland. Neither was there evidence of cruelty or obsession in her eyes. It was the face of an ordinary woman; a mother, a friend. Corinna was non-plussed. 'Sit down, girl,' the Dominatrix said, and indicated a low, red, plush-covered stool a couple of feet away. Corinna sat down.

'Well,' the Dominatrix said. 'I just had to see you for myself, girl. I wanted to see what Carmenya was causing all the fuss about. She doesn't think you're one of the dissidents; is she right?'

'I have my own opinions, madam, but they are only my own. I speak for nobody else.'

The Dominatrix nodded, tapping one finger against her lips. 'You are a friend of the priestess Carudan are you not?'

Corinna nodded. 'Yes, though perhaps 'friend' implies more than our relationship really is. I didn't fit in very well

259

at court and Carudan took pity on me. She used to take me out sometimes.'

'Mmm. I am suspicious of priestesses, young Trotgarden.' The Dominatrix stared at her owlishly. 'I can see that surprises you. Well, nothing surprises me. No-one can keep a secret from me, girl; I know everything. I know how you feel, how Carmenya feels; you can be sure of that.' Corinna felt this was just a bluff to put her on edge. If the Dominatrix knew exactly how she felt then why have anyone question her? 'The temple is a famished beast,' the Dominatrix continued, 'and its sisterhood would suck the country dry if they could. It's a battle of wills, I suppose. I am aware that some of them, and it's undoubtedly a small minority at present, have perverted the Goddess's word to suit themselves, and that's why I tend to be cautious about them. Such priestesses might *appear* to lend their support to the dissidents because then they could use them to overthrow the present government. If they succeeded, the rebels might find they were no longer quite so welcome in Silven Crescent as they thought they'd be. I never quite trust organised religion, because it is power-hungry. Can you see why I mistrust this Carudan's motives for befriending you now? It is known she often goes to Denderberry sector distributing money to the undesirables there. Has she ever said anything to you that may support my misgivings?'

'She feels sorry for the poor,' Corinna said earnestly, wrinkling her brow, 'but I never heard her say anything against the government. She's a dreamer, is Carudan.'

'And what are her dreams?'

'To contemplate the Goddess eighteen hours a day, I suppose.' Corinna was becoming wary now. She could so easily get Carudan into trouble. Even saying, 'she's interested in the history of religion' could be dangerous, because the history of religion meant religions other than the Dominatrix's.

'Those evenings in her company must have been more boring for you then than being with the young girls of the court you couldn't get on with,' the Dominatrix drawled, somewhat slyly. Corinna shrugged.

'We used to go to different eating-houses. I liked that. Carudan looks on me as yet another charity to give to, I'm sure, but I was grateful because it got me out of the house one night a week.'

The Dominatrix nodded. 'Yes. I'm sorry about all of this, my girl, but these are troubled times. We have to be careful. You probably think I'm being extremely over-cautious, even tyrannical, but I'm not. Our society is comparatively small. I don't want it torn apart by frictions that should have been left behind on the home world. Oh, I know that was all a long time ago, and as such, nothing to do with what's happening now, but I am afraid, Corinna.' She smiled and leaned closer. 'In the archives there are records of what man did to women in the past. Corinna, I could show them to you and it would appall you! We cannot risk that happening again. I know I shall be reviled for what I'm doing, that mud will be slung on my memory, my name cursed, but I also know that however harsh my actions seem, it is all for the good of Artemis. Men are my people too; I care for them too, but they have to be protected from themselves. Men like that L'Belder stir up the dark side of their sex, wake it up, make it want blood and power. They are dangerous, self-destructive creatures! Leaders? No, murderers, that's what they are! Men need controlling. If our methods seem harsh, contemplate the fact that extreme measures are needed to make changes. The hardest edges shall become smoothed with time. . . ' Corinna could not see any point in putting forward her opinion on this. She just stared the Dominatrix in the eye, feeling she must look like a stubborn, stupid dank. If the woman was so damn all-powerful couldn't she see that Corinna thought these words were bullshit? All the same, there was no denying Yani Gisbandrun believed what she was saying, and that, in spite of everything, there was an unbelievable feeling of gentleness about the woman. It was hard to imagine her condoning killing somehow.

'I hope I'm easing your mind,' the Dominatrix said. 'I hope I'm making you see why certain things are necessary. Am I?'

'You are good at explaining, madam,' Corinna said. 'I understand what you're trying to do.' Absurdly, that was satisfactory. The Dominatrix leaned back, breathless. Corinna decided to attempt another experiment. 'I suppose I find it all bewildering because I have never met anyone like you before. Where I come from no-one would care so much about everybody else,' she said, 'You must put so much of your energy into it.'

Yani Gisbandrun smiled. At this moment of extremity, Corinna was behaving as the Dominatrix would have liked her to during that first interview. 'There are prices to pay, my girl. My energy is not limitless. But, as I said, I'm prepared to pay the price, if it achieves justice in this world.'

'You humble me,' Corinna said in an uneven voice. It was an effort to continue, but the words came from her as if she was entranced. 'Even now you take the time to speak to me, a nobody, accused of a crime against you. I never thought you'd do something like that. You humble me.' The Dominatrix's face was now positively wreathed in smiles. Corinna could not believe it. Was she such a sucker for flattery? What unbelievable vanity. Corinna was inspired by renewed confidence. Surely, anybody could woo their way into Yani's presence and then pull out a knife. Rosanel could have done this. Perhaps the Sky-reachers hadn't been devious enough. Perhaps they should have kept their beliefs to themselves and then wheedled, flattered and cajoled their way into positions of power. Could that have been possible? Perhaps the Dominatrix was fooling her now. Perhaps a cold, calculating mind beneath the smiles was laughing at her, seeing through her, like the Dominatrix said she could. Corinna's confidence wavered. She was confused. What was going on?

'It pleases me that I'm helping to clear your mind,' Yani said, leaning back further into the cushions and throwing out a careless hand. 'But trust has to be earned, my girl. It is hard for me to say this, because I love every one of my subjects, but you must prove your devotion to me.'

'In what way, madam?'

The Dominatrix frowned. 'Well, I shall keep you here in my staff for a while. You can take the red for a while.' She pointed at the motionless girls that Corinna had forgotten were there. 'Then a time will come which shall be a time of testing for everybody. Being in red will give you opportunity for reflection. When the time comes I will give you a task and you will prove yourself to me. . . '

'I. . . I don't know what to say,' Corinna said. 'You honour me, madam.'

'No need for thanks, Corinna Trotgarden. I only want you to benefit. I am your servant as well as your queen.'

'But why me? Aren't there a thousand girls more deserving of this position?'

'Why you?' She laughed. 'Well, first because you need it more than the girls you call deserving and second, because I want to know what it is about you that has my hard-as-nails, most trusted general coming to me to plead on your behalf. I want to know your magic, Corinna. Carmenya thinks you are headstrong and unenlightened because of your youth and your upbringing. She obviously sees qualities in you that aren't apparent to the casual observer.' Here, she brought herself up sharply. 'Naturally, *I* can see those qualities, but I want to experience them myself. Corinna had a horrifying idea that the Dominatrix might be implying she wanted more than a working relationship with her. Her face must have reflected some of that thought.

'Obviously, I cannot know you as Carmenya does,' she said, with sorrowful expression. 'I deny myself upon that path, my dear. Sacrifices have to be made for someone to achieve my position. I am celibate. Loneliness is the price I pay for power. Suffering. . . ' She sighed. 'You have a new name now, Corinna. That is the last time you will be called by that name. I choose for you; Lunt. You are Lunt. It is not a pretty name like the old one, but then, none of my scarlet girls have pretty names. That is one of the prices you will have to pay. It's a small one, I'm sure you'll agree.' She sat up. 'Rudd, Gick, take Lunt to her new home. Prepare her, she is to be one of you.'

Two of the kneeling girls stood up, still with lowered

heads. A slow, cold, feeling of horror was creeping through Corinna's body. She felt she did not want to see the true nature of the girls in red. They held out their hands to her, to draw her to them, to lead her away. She saw their faces and could not help uttering a single, helpless cry. Scarred, they were scarred. Across both cheeks, deep lines puckered the flesh. They had no eyebrows, no eyelashes. Corinna backed away.

'Gick, show her the marks of honour,' the Dominatrix said silkily. One of the girls lifted her veil, threw it back. Her head was bald, tattooed, but that was not the worst thing. She had no ears either. Corinna screamed then; she couldn't help it.

'Take her with you,' the Dominatrix said, and the papery, cold hands were laid upon her arms.

CHAPTER THIRTY-FOUR

'CORINNA!' SHYYA WOKE up, her name upon his lips, the image of her face, still screaming, hanging before his eyes like a ghost. He could hear his own breath sobbing as if he'd been running hard. Breath mist obscured the after image of his dream.

'What is it?' Now Meonel was awake as well, his fingers digging into Shyya's shoulder. 'You shouted Corinna's name. What is it?'

'Corinna is no more,' he answered, not knowing where the words came from.

'She's dead?!' Meonel's cry was agonised. 'Shyya, is she dead?' Shyya swallowed hard. His throat was prickly and dry. He crawled from the sleeping bag, fumbling for the water bottle. 'Shyya, answer me! Is she dead?'

'What's all the noise?' This was a sleepy mumble from L'Belder who was always hard to wake.

'Shyya's had a dream. About Corinna. I think she's dead,' Meonel said. Now L'Belder was fully awake.

'What was the dream, Shyya? What happened in it? Tell us!'

Shyya was still drinking. He wiped his mouth.

'Wait a moment!' he said, gasping.

'Way anyone else in the dream? Was it real?' L'Belder seemed panicked. Meonel presumed he was thinking about the Garmelding woman he often talked about.

'I did not say Corinna was dead,' Shyya said. 'Something bad has happened, but I don't think she's dead.'

'You said she was no more,' Meonel said. 'What did you mean?'

'I don't know. The words just came into my head. I can't

remember the dream now. If you two hadn't asked the questions you wouldn't have made it fade away.'

Tempers were becoming frayed within the little party. They'd been travelling for two weeks now. From Vangery the forests seemed so near, just a couple of days' ride away. That was because nobody realised how tall were the trees of Ire and Penitence. Now the sky to the east was virtually obscured by them. The danks travelled swiftly over the marsh with their big, splayed feet, but it had still taken this long to get within ten miles of the forest. The nearest was Ire. Already the ground was drier as the marsh receded. In this area the forest was not floating at all; the ground sloped uphill. Plants and animals that none of the men had seen before began to make appearances. There was a particular species of bright green bird that made a complete nuisance of itself by trying to pluck hairs from the travellers' heads. A couple of nights previously a huge, aggressive insect had chewed determinedly into L'Belder's hand as he slept. Only Dannel's well stocked package of medicinal herbs had staved off a serious infection developing. As the land dried out, the air became more humid. They realised that to attempt this journey later in the year would probably have been impossible; undergrowth would make the forest impassable. It caused a few moments of light-heartedness when Shyya actually discovered a strong, mature stand of sheek weed. Meonel plucked a few heads to dry and take back for Dannel, presuming they ever did go back. He also noticed many other plants that might be good for cultivation. They would have to be tested for toxins of course, but he thought that the idea of 'we have what we need, why take more' was a ridiculous one. The marsh sustained the people more than adequately but it seemed a waste not to go for variety and try new crops. It was incredible to think that the marsh families never came to investigate the forests. Simply because the cities said no, they obeyed. What a small world we've been living in, he thought. This planet is vast, and we exist on just a little part of it. Anything could exist beyond the marsh; anything.

'A pity your wife wouldn't let us use the skipper,' L'Belder had said. Meonel agreed. Again, if they'd known how long the journey was going to take, she probably would have done. How stupid, how disorganised of us not to know, Meonel thought.

Now the massive trunks of the forest of Ire were close. Another half day's swift travelling and they'd be pushing through the outer scrub. What would they find?

Shyya felt disorientated for most of the day after his dream about Corinna. As they drew nearer to Ire, he recognised the superstitious fear that kept the marsh dwellers away from it. In this mood, he seemed more sensitive to the silent, overwhelming power of the trees, the intense life contained within them. He felt that once the dark of the forest closed over them, they would never see clear sunlight again. Yet it was the kind of fear that excited him, made him want to dare its shadows. How many people had paused at the edge of this place and not gone in? How many had stood a moment and then plunged forward? Were they still inside? The danks had become nervous, too. They honked at shadows and tried to walk sideways, so they could keep one eye on the marsh they were leaving. The marsh was their natural habitat; they did not think it was a good idea to step off it. Perhaps they knew something the men didn't.

At sundown, a camp was set up next to a tumble of rocks which formed a barrier around the forest. Shyya filled all the water bottles, concerned that whatever pools they might find within the trees might not be so good to drink. The danks grazed dispiritedly, starting at every sound that came from the trees. Even here on the outskirts the trunks were unbelievably thick. It would have taken twenty men with outstretched arms to surround one. Hundreds of feet up foliage formed a dense blanket, but nearer to the ground smaller trees and shrubs and lichens grew in a tangle that would take time to penetrate. They had knives and machetes with them (Dannel's idea) but even using these, the forest would be difficult to negotiate. Could

267

anyone live in there? Shyya thought the forest was hostile. It fascinated him, yet he was dreading going into it.

Next morning, Meonel and Shyya stayed in the tent to pack their belongings while L'Belder went outside to build a fire. They had decided to cook a large meal before venturing into the trees. A shout from L'Belder had them hurrying outside. 'What is it?' Meonel asked. L'Belder, wild-eyed, half frightened, half elated, pointed a shaking finger at the forest.

'I saw someone,' he said.

'Saw someone? Who? What were they like?' Meonel asked, squinting. He could see no sign of life.

'Just a figure,' L'Belder said, shaking his head. 'It was watching me, I'm sure. It went into the forest.'

'Have we found what we're looking for, do you think?'

L'Belder threw up his hands, uttered a sound that may have been joyous.

'Perhaps we have, Meonel. Perhaps we have.'

Whatever it was L'Belder had seen, it made no further appearance. They fought with the foliage for three days, having to hack out a place to erect the tent every night. The light was bad, always twilight. It seemed they frightened away any animals or birds. The silence was terrifying. Strange vines threatened to trip the danks; they had to dismount and lead the animals. Fleshy flowers grew directly from tree-trunks and in their luminous depths lurked livid pads dotted with the shrivelled forms of partially digested insects. Horrible fungus that resembled humped, deformed dwarves huddled round pools, the water skinned with pond lichen, but like no pond lichen any of them had ever seen. It seemed to pulsate with a life of its own. Once, a line of large moth-like insects flew in formation above the men's heads. They uttered a flute-like song but paid no attention to the travellers. At night, lichen spurs burrowed into the sleepers' skin through the ground sheet of the tent, causing itchy, running sores. Only L'Belder's conviction kept them going. Both Meonel and Shyya were beginning to doubt whether anybody, Greylids or not, would exist in this forest. 'If they are as wise and all-seeing as the legends imply,' Meonel commented to Shyya, 'they certainly wouldn't make a home here, that's for sure!'

L'Belder flogged their drooping spirits, reminding them of the figure he had seen. 'They must be watching us,' he said. Meonel and Shyya exchanged a glance. Shyya shrugged. He was unsure. The woods harboured something, that was obvious, but he doubted whether whatever it was would benefit L'Belder or his cause. The night after they'd seen the moths, L'Belder would not come into the tent to sleep. Meonel and Shyya sat up together, exhausted but unable to sleep themselves, listening to his restless pacing. 'Is he mad, do you think?' Meonel asked.

'Perhaps not a question we should ask,' Shyya answered. 'Remember we are the ones following him.'

Meonel pulled a face. 'He seems fanatical. The so-called "appearance" has only fired his zeal.'

'He believes because he has to believe,' Shyya said. 'He has no other hope.'

'This place may kill us. What on earth are we doing tagging along?'

'Perhaps because we want to believe as well. Because we want L'Belder to prove something to us? Oh, I don't know. I know I'm tired and I feel sick and I dream of Vangery. But we can't go back, can we, Meonel?'

Meonel was still for a moment. That question had changed things considerably. He realised it was the first time Shyya had ever asked his opinion. It was the first time that Shyya had ever turned to him for confirmation or reassurance.

'No, I don't think we can,' he said. They fell silent, still listening to the sounds outside.

'You've changed,' Shyya said at last. 'This journey has done you good. You haven't been unbearable once, well, not as much as usual anyway.'

'How could anybody not change?' Meonel asked. 'It's hardly what we're used to, is it?'

'Are you sorry you came or glad?'

'Neither. I wish it wasn't necessary, that's all.'

'Is the future of Artemis in our hands, do you think?'

'I don't know. We seem so small.'

269

'Are you afraid?'

'Are you?'

'It's a feeling, but I don't know what it is. I hope Corinna's alright.'

'Yes.' It made Meonel uncomfortable thinking about Corinna and her hundred possible fates. 'You know, it's strange but I never feel bored now,' he said. 'It's like dying and being reborn. The life before this journey is a dream. We have always been travelling. I can't envisage an end to it.'

'Maybe there is no end.'

'There is. It's near. I can feel it.'

'Meonel?'

'Yes?'

'You just contradicted yourself.'

They both laughed.

'We'd better try to sleep,' Meonel said. 'Let L'Belder do the worrying for tonight.'

By dawn, L'Belder had still not come into the tent. Meonel woke up first. The light was murky, as usual, the silence outside tense as if filled with listening ears. Leaving Shyya to sleep, he crawled from under the canvas, brushing twigs and lichen from his crumpled clothes. L'Belder hadn't built a fire yet. Meonel thought he must have fallen asleep outside. He sauntered round the tent. There was no sign of life, other than the four danks who looked at him warily with lowered heads. He called, 'Elvon!' and his words didn't even echo. Nobody answered. 'Shit!' he said, under his breath and ducked back inside the tent. 'Shyya, wake up, L'Belder's gone!' Shyya pushed his hair from his eyes; he looked fearful. A mirror, Meonel realised, of his own expression.

'Are the danks still here?' Shyya asked.

'Yes. Elvon's too.'

'What's happened to him?'

'I don't know,' Meonel answered. 'Let's strike camp. Let's get out of here.'

'In which direction? Onwards or back?'

'What do you think?'

270

'We said last night we couldn't go back. . . '

'I don't know, Shyya. What can we do? I don't know.'

'Are we going to look for him?'

'You think we'd find him in this jungle?'

'There may be signs, broken branches, signs of a struggle.'

'We don't know that he was. . . taken. He may have just wandered off and got lost.'

'In that case, we should at least try to find him.'

Meonel sighed. He knew Shyya was right, and yet he was too tired to muster any enthusiasm for a search. The act of continuing this journey had become almost an obsession; pointless, but impossible to give up. It was like searching for death, for release. Neither he nor Shyya could envisage a happy ending to it. Silently, they took down the tent and packed up their belongings. Shyya prepared a small, uncooked meal. To the left of the clearing they had occupied was a stagnant pool sunk into the moss. Beyond it was a path of sorts through the trees. Perhaps L'Belder had gone, or been taken, that way. Skirting the pool, Meonel and Shyya led their animals onto the path. It hadn't been formed by human or animal feet, that was clear, for viridian moss grew lush and thick upon it. The briars and shrubs of the earlier part of their journey seemed to be thinning out now; the trees were different, the light somewhat brighter. Every object was blanketed with the same brilliant moss; stones, trees, even the path they followed. Birds with shrill, scornful voices now sang in the high branches; their plumage, as green as their surroundings, almost rendering them invisible. There was no sign of L'Belder. Meonel felt that sooner or later, he and Shyya were going to have to make a decision about this. Should they continue the search for the Greylids? Could they get their point across as well as L'Belder? How long should the search be continued? When should they give up? These were questions that Elvon L'Belder could no longer answer for them. He realised that he and Shyya had taken the man's disappearance very calmly, almost as if they'd expected it. Perhaps it was just that exhaustion had dulled their senses.

271

Round about mid-day, they stopped to eat. There seemed little to say. Though the forest had become more benign, more soothing to behold, both of them felt tired and listless; the slightest movement was too great an effort. Even speech was one of these movements. Groaning, Meonel stretched and stood up to leave. Shyya mumbled. 'I don't want to go on.'

'What? You want to go back?'

'No. I just don't want to go on. Bear with me, Meonel. I have to think.'

Shyya had gone very pale. Meonel sat down again on the moss beside him.

'What is it?'

'Wait!' Shyya sat cross-legged, straightened his spine. 'Don't disturb me. I need to meditate.'

Sighing, Meonel slumped down again. He lay back on the moss, staring up through the softly waving branches far above. 'Rest,' he thought, 'rest. There is no point in continuing. We must rest. Then. . . ' Even before the rest of that thought came to him, he'd slipped into sleep.

The moss was narcotic; Shyya knew this. It lulled them, it brought them dreams, as it released its gossamer spores into the air. Shyya breathed them in; deeply. He was not surprised to find that one of the effects of the moss spores was clear sight. Within only a few minutes, he found out that L'Belder had not gone from them forever. Meonel and Shyya had only to sit and wait for him to return. They waited for an hour.

L'Belder had been so overwhelmed when the pale, ghost-like shapes drifted out from the trees towards him, that he'd forgotten completely about his companions. They had appeared about an hour before dawn, drawing substance from the grey light hanging between the trees. L'Belder had just stared, blinking, at them for several minutes. He could not be sure whether he was hallucinating or not. Their bodies were concealed by tattered, moss-stained robes, even to their faces. Then one of them had extended a thin, pale arm and beckoned. Surely these were the people he had sought? Yet L'Belder could not move. He knew that if he did not respond to the summons, he had wasted his journey. But still he was afraid. The figures began to recede and a single bird called a waking note above his head. The undergrowth around him rustled and the figures retreated even as he watched. L'Belder stood up. 'Wait,' he said, and stumbled forward. The figures seemed to shimmer, deceiving visions betwen the matted trunks and hanging lichens. 'Wait!' He slipped into the pool, putting one hand into the sucking mud. Fingers closed around his arm. He was surrounded and they lifted him.

The Greylids carried him deep into the forest, to the place where the moss was king, and they told him with their minds that here the hidden stones of the Lord of Rocks had been consumed and destroyed by the greater strength of the Moss King. Both the Moss King and the Lord of Rocks were aspects of their own deity, whose name they would not speak. L'Belder decided they could not possibly be human. Not just because they could speak with their minds, but because of the way their clothes hung upon their bodies. He had a feeling something completely alien was concealed beneath, yet they did not feel hostile. He tried to tell them why he was there but they knew, and silenced him. 'Where are you taking me?' he asked and they replied as one; a huge, swelling wave in his mind.

'To Vez'n'kizri.' The words were a torrent of emotion that pierced him like a spear of light. He caught fleeting visions of a string of half-formed images Vez'n'kizri; sanctuary. The place where the Moss King held back the Lord of Rocks. When he reached that place, he would learn, and half of his questions would be answered.

CHAPTER THIRTY-FIVE

IN THE BEGINNING was the disease and its name was Wanderers' Sickness. Artemis had a different name then, pointless now to recall it, for that time had gone. The Wanderils, those infected by the disease, were the special children of the One God of that planet. He was a lesser-known deity in astral terms, not particularly all-powerful, and for the most part, unrevered. The people of old Artemis had turned their backs on him; he was a god without a following, but for his children. The population of Artemis did not know how the disease was contracted. All they saw was the result – the wanderers. They saw the malformations of limb and face and shuddered. These unfortunates were barred from entering the towns and cities, because people feared infection, but in the open country they were sometimes tolerated or even consulted in matters of divination or healing. That was another manifestation of the disease; the sick could heal. A paradox.

The people did not know that Wanderers' Sickness could not be contracted through the sufferers themselves. They did not know about the One God, exiled and brooding, who emanated a call that few could hear. Those to whom the call became an unbearable summoning, stumbled blindly to its source, becoming in their ultimate contact with divinity irreversibly altered; the One God's unique disciples. He bided his time, waiting in his dark fortress temple among the rocks, north of the marsh, far north. One day he would punish the godless population of Artemis, and the stilted cities of Thog'granah would fall into the reeds and rot, but not yet. He was patient; time meant nothing to him. As for Wanderers' Sickness itself, it was a state of being more than a disease. The god distributed his power generously among his children and the people of Artemis were cautious in vain; it was not infectious. How could a privilege be infectious? No, the condition meant a change of form, sleek power, the ability to bend and shape at will. What the common people saw as disabilities were refinements of form. What use does a creature who doesn't need to ingest food or talk or breathe have for a mouth? None. Those whose mental powers exceed the imaginations of humanity have no need for arms, those whose minds can travel at will over the world and are strong enough to bend and shape matter without the use of limbs have no need for legs. The people of Old Artemis never raised their heads from the ground often enough to see the winged ones, beautiful as birth and death, soaring high above the marshes towards the mountains. So the disease remained a misunderstood condition. It was foolish of the people to drive the Wanderils away, foolish of them not to question. They deserved their fate. That time is unchronicled, or at least so Elvon L'Belder was told, their ideas and thoughts pulsing directly into his mind without the use of words. The people he had encountered in the woods were all that remained of the Wanderils, indeed the whole indigenous population of Artemis. They hid themselves well. No scouting party had ever discovered their existence and they had sought to keep themselves apart from the human settlements. Naturally, refugees had gravitated towards them for the pull of the calling was still strong even after millenia, and these people had swollen the ranks a little for the Wanderils would never refuse someone in need. L'Belder was encouraged by this. They had implied they understood his need; would they help him? Their power obviously far exceeded even his wildest fantasies. They were so much more than he could ever have imagined. Also, even though it was left unspoken, it seemed these people had once overthrown and destroyed an entire culture. Could they do that again? It had happened many thousands of years ago. Perhaps whatever warlike qualities

275

their god had instilled within them had withered. They did not seem like warriors, but then again, the power of the mind far exceeded the power of the flesh. L'Belder had a wondrous vision of Silven Crescent destroyed by magical fire, the Dominatrix twisting and squealing in a torrent of hot flame. It delighted him. He asked to speak with the Wanderils' leader; they replied that they had no leader. They had no need for hierarchies; no one led them. 'Have you no elders?' L'Belder said. 'I need advice.'

'That will be given to you,' was the reply.

The Moss Halls of Vez'n'kizri, appearing from between the trees, silenced any further questions on L'Belder's lips. Here were spore-furred buildings hung with ancient lianas, tasselled with lichen and hairy ropes of webby moss. Lean figures glided soundlessly among the green pillars; a swaying walk swathed by robes. L'Belder saw no children. His guides deposited him below the steps of a soaring, crumbling temple, whose flaking columns were held upright only by the clinging embrace of the moss-vines that covered it. L'Belder sat down on the green-cushioned steps, shivering with delayed shock. Vez'n'kizri loomed around him, ancient, silent, watchful. He drew up his knees, resting his chin upon them. Shapes glided at the edge of his vision, but he was not approached. After a while, feeling a little more composed, he stood up and found that one of the Greylids immediately appeared at his side. Perhaps they had come out of the temple behind him, their footsteps muffled by the thick moss.

'I need to talk to someone,' L'Belder said. The Greylid observed him through a fold in its all-encompassing robes. L'Belder wondered whether it had understood him. 'I am Elvon L'Belder,' he began and held out his hand. The Greylid made no move to take it.

'You creatures need your names,' it said. If a felid could talk, it would have a voice like that; purring, but with the suggestion of a growl. 'For your comfort, you may address me as Ee-kha-ha, which is an approximation of my essential resonance.' The name was hardly more than a sigh. 'Follow,' it said, and turned away, in a whirl of moss-stained, tattered cloth. L'Belder was compelled to follow

276

it. He was led through narrow streets where he felt as if he walked on carpet, through overhanging buildings whose windows were filmed with yellow powder. Eventually they came to a high, damp wall that had water running down its weathered bricks and hosted brightly-coloured slimes. Ee-kha-ha paused in a gateway, although the gate had long gone, doubtlessly rotted by the constant flow. L'Belder looked up. The wall disappeared into a thick growth of shiny leaves; it was impossible to see where the water came from. Ee-kha-ha waited for him to catch up before going through the gateway. L'Belder followed the creature down a wide flight of steps that was quite treacherous underfoot, and into a roofless pit of black rock where water gleamed at the bottom. L'Belder's eyes had begun to ache from all the green. He was grateful for the gloom. At the foot of the steps, he could see the water bubbling and steaming; a natural spa. Here, ancient flags, warm beneath the feet, were laid out around the pool. Stone benches stood in niches carved in the rock. Brightly coloured birds danced in the warm steam. At the rim of the pool the Greylid turned to face L'Belder. 'Tell me what you want of us,' it said, lisping the words as if unused to human language.

'Your help,' L'Belder replied. Was the creature speaking aloud to make him feel at ease? How did it know his language anyway? From refugees the creatures had taken in?

'We understand your position,' Ee-kha-ha said, 'but cannot see how we can alleviate it.'

'You have such power!'

'And you do not understand. The small people will always behave as the insects. Out there you run in their mazes and must obey the maze law. If you wish to remain here, of course you may, but the knowledge of Vez'n'kizri is not for the small people.'

'Have you thought that the Dominatrix may one day become a threat to you too? Don't you value your privacy? The woman is a maniac! She wouldn't leave you alone if she knew about you!'

Ee-kha-ha laughed; at least L'Belder presumed the odd,

277

gutteral sound to be a laugh. 'She, and any of her people, are nothing. They are brief like insects and they buzz loudly, but they are nothing. The fringes you call Ire and Penitence can defend us more than adequately and even if they didn't, well. . . ' Ee-kha-ha made an elegant gesture. 'It is no problem, I assure you. Forget your war, Elvon L'Belder; it means nothing. In a thousand years no-one will even remember it. Live your life, experience the pain if you want to go back; everything is relevant. Life is learning. Your lessons are hard, but perhaps beneficial.'

'Then you will not help us?'

'We will not involve ourselves in the ways of insects, Elvon L'Belder.'

'Every world needs insects. Aren't they part of the chain of life? And could it not be said that in a way you are involving yourselves because you won't get involved?' he was improvising wildly. To him, his words were largely nonsense, but the Greylid still paused to consider them.

'An interesting concept,' it said. 'Perhaps you are right. You have invaded us and will leave your leaping thoughts behind you when you go. There are other such thoughts in Vez'n'kizri, left by other hectic minds. They do not seem to fade in the same way as other vibrations. We have tried to learn from them – we waste nothing – but the lessons are very brief and teach us merely what to avoid.'

'I need your help, Ee-kha-ha. I really do. There is no other way for me.' He realised that it was probably futile to try and appeal to some kind of compassion in the creature for he had no certainty Ee-kha-ha possessed such traits. 'I want your power,' he said, ignoring his instinct's plea for caution. 'Show me what you are, Ee-kha-ha. I'm not afraid.'

The Greylid seemed to ripple within its robes; a gesture reminiscent of a shrug. L'Belder could not see its face properly. He could not tell what he was looking at. Perhaps he had offended it. Perhaps the Greylids never revealed themselves, even to each other.

'You wish to understand us, at least our physical aspect,' Ee-kha-ha said with no particular tone to its voice. 'If you wish it, then let it be so.' There was no time for L'Belder

278

to change his mind and for a split second, the fragment of a second before the concealing robes vanished like smoke, L'Belder's courage wavered. It was too late; the Greylid was uncovered before him: the tempting, locked door was opened, the darkest vault of shadows investigated. Unknown, untasted sensations waited inside.

L'Belder fell back. It wasn't horror, or fear, or revulsion, or awe or admiration. It was none of those; just a mind-numbing sense of incomprehension. The Greylid seemed to hang in the air before him, at first shining like an angel, then concrete and lustreless as old bone. Some rational part of his mind accepted that what he was looking at possessed a bizarre beauty, far beyond the imagining of men, but it was beauty contained in a skeletal form, where every bone could be seen through the skin; even its colour. Ee-kha-ha did not vacillate or shimmer, but it seemed to L'Belder as if his own awareness of the creature did. Between seconds, the Greylid seemed nearly mechanical, then bio-mechanical, then absurdly plant-like; an ancient, gnarled and twisting broken branch. Almost as if a parody of humanity, the creature was adorned with heavy male genitals between the legs, yet when it raised its arms, what looked like female orifices were revealed in each armpit. Surely a mockery? L'Belder was frozen still, his mouth open, his body inclining away from what stood before him. The Greylid turned its back on him. 'I am. . . ' it said. 'You have seen. Now you must decide. You can be part of this or return to your own lands; it is your choice, but it must be made quickly.'

L'Belder was crouched on the ground. He hid his face in his hands and would not look up. But he had to ask. He had to be sure. 'Show me your power. I want to see its extent.'

Again Ee-kha-ha made the laughing sound. 'What you consider is folly beyond credibility, but if you wish it, let it be so. Look at me!' L'Belder lifted his head and it felt as if his eyes were sucked straight from their sockets. Some part of his essence slam-banged between the Greylid's eyes, deep into the creature's brain, where every alien concept scraped his nerves like rabid claws. L'Belder could not scream and he could not close his eyes to the visions. They were a tumult, a thousand thousand years spilling like coloured jewels before his mind's eye, a whirlwind of energy, a beating, a caress. He could not breathe, the colours stole the air from him. Just as the agony of asphyxiation became almost too great, the Greylid spat L'Belder out of its mind. He lay writhing and gasping on the warm stones.

'You have seen,' the Greylid said and sat down upon one of the benches to wait for his recovery. It must be supposed that it already knew L'Belder's answer to its question.

CHAPTER THIRTY-SIX

STILL WAITING, SOME distance from Vez'n'kizri, Meonel and Shyya were shocked when they saw L'Belder stumbling towards them through the greenery. He looked drawn, frightened, exultant, crazy. Shyya had had some intimation of this, but the reality was still disturbing. Two of the Greylids had brought him back to them. Now he ranted of wild plans that they could not understand, primarily because all of L'Belder's words were running together. 'Come to Vez'n'kizri!' he implored, taking their hands in his own, which were trembling. Meonel regarded the silent, robed forms of the Greylids. Their effect upon L'Belder had been traumatic; he wasn't sure he wanted to share that. He looked to Shyya for reassurance.

'I don't sense harm,' Shyya said. 'I think we should go.' There was no need to repeat the 'no going back' part now. This was the end. Sighing, Meonel gathered up the reins of the danks and they followed L'Belder back the way he had come.

A single-storied dwelling, garlanded in moss-vine, was provided for their comfort on the outskirts of the settlement. Inside, in the larger of the two rooms, they found a pitcher of water, cooking pots and fresh food laid out waiting to be cooked. The furnishings were minimal but the place was clean. It did not feel as if anyone lived there on a regular basis. Shyya and Meonel were unsure of what was going to happen next. They did not seem to be expected to *do* anything. Once shown into the dwelling, they were left alone. It appeared that the Greylids had not exactly offered direct help to L'Belder, but he wasn't being particularly lucid about it. Despite this, he still seemed

281

fervent about his cause, if not more so than before. Meonel was wary of this frantic enthusiasm. Shyya was intrigued. Between them, in the green, underwater light of the kitchen, they managed to boil up a pot of water and make some tea. L'Belder sat at a bleached wooden table and tried to relate everything that had happened to him.

'So what are you going to do?' Meonel asked. 'Are you going to stay here and join them?' He was not really surprised that L'Belder hadn't found a solution to his problems. He considered that L'Belder should take up Ee-kha-ha's offer and remain here. What good would it do for him to return to Silven Crescent now? He'd been pondering the fate of himself and Shyya, and had decided the best thing they could do was leave the forest further north and keep heading that way. He was thinking long-term and it scared him to think of growing old with Shyya, hiding from other people until one of them died. If Shyya died first then Meonel would kill himself too. It was not a happy train of thought.

'Meonel, I have greater plans than that,' L'Belder said, the unhealthy fire still glowing in his eyes.

'And what are they?' Shyya asked tentatively.

'Obvious, my friend! I shall allow these people to 'infect' me, as they put it, but instead of remaining here in idle tranquility, doing nothing, I shall take this power back to civilisation. I will use it! It's so simple, really. The Greylids believe the Dominatrix cannot harm them and I expect they are right, but I could not live with myself if I took the change and did nothing. I must go back, but not as a man.'

'You are mad!' Meonel exclaimed. 'Even if you were successful, what then? Would these people have you back? I doubt it! And would you be happy living among humanity being *like that?*' He waved an arm at the door, pulling a disgusted face.

'The mutation takes many forms,' L'Belder said stiffly. 'Each one of these people is different.'

'And can you choose what form it will take?'

'I don't know.'

Meonel was going to speak again but Shyya interrupted. 'It's your choice, Elvon. I can see what you're trying to do.

282

It may work. As long as you understand the risk. . . '

'I do,' L'Belder answered grimly. 'Now that you two are safe, I shall seek the one named Ee-kha-ha again. I shall ask to be infected. No thinking. No waiting. I've done enough of that. I don't want to change my mind and, if I think about it, I might. This is the only chance our people have. If I have to sacrifice myself, then it's a small price to pay for saving so many.'

'You also want the power, don't you?' Shyya said quietly. 'If that's not the first reason you'll become infected, it's certainly the second.'

L'Belder nodded. He did not speak. Once the tea had all been consumed, Shyya and Meonel watched him walk out of the door.

They sat together in the green twilight as the day faded. Eventually they boiled some of the vegetables and ate them. There seemed little to say. Meonel was wrapped up in black thoughts of the future; Shyya felt tired and dispirited. What was L'Belder doing now? Meonel felt helpless against the man's madness. How long could they stay here? No-one was going to come and impart great wisdom to them, that was clear. There were no real answers in Vez'n'kizri. It was already dark when someone came to knock on their door. They looked at each other. Meonel got up to answer it. A shrouded Greylid stood on the threshold. 'You have been kept waiting,' it said. 'Our apologies. You must want to bathe and refresh yourselves.'

'What's going on?' Meonel asked. 'Where is our companion?' The Greylid inclined its head.

'No need for you to worry. Which one of you would like to come with me?'

'Where?'

'As I said; to refresh yourself.'

Shyya and Meonel shared an uneasy glance. Then Shyya shrugged.

'I'll go,' he said.

Meonel was left alone, staring at his hands clasped on the table. Why were they being separated? Was this ominous? Could Shyya be in danger? Or had they just become too suspicious? It did not feel as if the Greylids wished to harm them, far from it. But they were eerie and inhuman; Meonel did not feel comfortable. The minutes passed. Outside, all was silent. Meonel experienced a kind of dread that he was really all alone in this vast, sleeping ruin. He went to boil more water on the stove and his every movement seemed enlarged, the sounds he made amplified and shrill. When he heard approaching footsteps outside, he had to fight an urge to creep and crouch and hide. No need; it was Shyya returning. Meonel was so relieved he almost hugged Shyya to him. 'You've been so long,' he said, trying not to sound anxious.

'Not really,' Shyya replied. 'By the Goddess, Meonel, I feel marvellous. I don't know what they put in their water around here but it's a real tonic.'

'Where did they take you?' Meonel asked suspiciously.

'To some kind of spa. It's virtually underground. They'll come for you soon.'

'I'm not sure I want to go.' Meonel eyed Shyya's scrubbed, glowing appearance with apprehension. Sorcery! he thought, but did not have the courage to refuse when a different Greylid came to escort him to the spa five minutes later. The streets of Vez'n'kizri were virtually deserted. Meonel felt he was slinking along like a smoom. Had this once been a city? Hard to tell, now everything was so plastered with moss and lichen. He liked its weird beauty though. The Greylid led him to the same pit where Ee-kha-ha had shown himself to L'Belder. Roughly-spun towels, a comforting sign of normality, were left across a stone bench for him to use. Globes of light cast a wan glow over the gently shifting pool. He was left alone. Lying in the warm, spuming water, Meonel gazed up through the steam. Dannel would like this place. If only the people of Vangery could come and live here in secrecy together. Not with the Greylids though. He wished they could have it to themselves. Here, it would not matter what the Dominatrix did in the cities or on the marsh. It felt safe and concealed, and, Meonel felt, capable of protecting itself from invaders should the need arise. As Shyya had told him, the water was indeed invigorating. Meonel felt his tiredness slip away into the softly moving liquid. His spirits began to lift as if each emotion in his heart was untangling itself from an ugly ball. Soon he felt he would be able to view things objectively and answers would come to him. Soon, if he stayed in Vez'n'kizri long enough. He sat on the mossy lip of the pool and towelled himself dry. Good humour had returned. He would have to discuss the future with Shyya now. They had plans to make. A lot of the blackness, the fog, was dissipating. There was still hope. While they lived, there was still hope of finding peace and happiness.

Just as he stood up to leave, wrapping one of the enormous towels provided around his hips, he noticed his silent guide had returned, standing in the shadow of an overhanging curtain of evergreens. It stepped forward and bowed. 'Are you refreshed, Meonel Trotgarden?'

'Thank you. Yes. Tremendously.' He wrapped another towel around his shoulders.

'Good, then please accept this gift with our compliments.' The Greylid handed him a glass vial.

'Well, thank you, but what is it?'

'Scented oil,' the creature said. It threw back its hood and Meonel saw the face of a lovely, yet mature woman. However, in the light of what L'Belder had told him, he could not be sure if what faced him was truly female.

'Perfume? Thank you,' he said and uncorked the vial. The overpowering scent nearly knocked him over.

'To be used with caution,' the Greylid said. 'It is very refined.' It smiled kindly and gestured towards the steps. 'Return to your lodgings and do not fear tomorrow. Your path is hard, Meonel Trotgarden, but not unpleasant. When the time comes, go and take your wife's daughter from the Maze. You will know peace in your lifetime.' Then it ran swiftly up the steps without looking back. Meonel looked at the vial. What an odd gift, he thought.

It took him some time to find their cottage again, even though Vez'n'kizri glowed with a strange light of its own at night. He did not mind. Never, in all his life, had he felt so safe. Not even at Vangery, with all the shutters closed against the winter. Gone was his apprehension of only an hour previously. The spa had stripped that from him.

Now, he belonged. Vez'n'kizri sheltered him; the outside world could not intrude here. He wandered along the still avenues where old dwellings leaned and brooded. He was sure most of them were unoccupied, but neither were they desolate. The place was a history book, each building a chapter that could be opened and read. Meonel felt as if he were just looking at the illustrations, soothing to the eye. And what were the Greylids? Perhaps the language that told the tales. Had L'Belder persuaded these people to change him yet? Meonel shook his head because the thought made him uncomfortable. He wondered what craziness would drive a man to accept such a mutation. It held no attraction for Meonel at all. Still, he had to smile, what would the Dominatrix think if L'Belder should burst into her palace armed with such alien power? He would like to see that, but preferably from a distance.

When he eventually returned to the cottage, he found Shyya in the back room. Lamps had been lit, filling every corner with a golden glow. Shyya was sitting on a thin, blanket-strewn mattress on the floor, brushing his hair. He was staring into one of the lamps as if dazed. 'Still feel good?' Meonel asked, unsure. Shyya nodded.

'Yes. Comfortably tired, but yes.'

'They gave me this,' Meonel said, holding out the vial. Shyya smiled and there was a hint of craziness in it. 'Are you sure you're alright?' Meonel asked.

'Yes. Like I said, just tired.'

'Then get some sleep. We can talk tomorrow.'

'Yes.' Shyya crept between the blankets before removing his towel which he fastidiously folded and placed on the floor beside the bed. Before quickly glancing away, Meonel could see Shyya's naked back still marked with the sores and scratches of their journey.

'I've been told to fetch Corinna,' Meonel said, picking up the hairbrush. Shyya had closed his eyes.

'Something like that was said to me also,' he said sleepily. 'What's going to happen?'

Shyya opened his eyes, but didn't speak. Meonel stared back for a few moments wondering what was wrong with the boy. Then he felt a prickle of fear because soon he recognised the silent words within the eyes. You are going to come to me, they said. Shyya had been sitting here alone waiting for him. What had he been thinking about? L'Belder was no longer with them, Vangery was far behind. Lost longings surfaced once again in a pool that had become calm. The journey was over. Meonel looked at Shyya and felt cornered. He wasn't sure he' could provide what Shyya needed from him. He wasn't sure he was that strong. 'I'm not sure I can,' Meonel said aloud. He sat down on the mattress, put his head in his hands, and groaned. This is what I want. This is not what I want. What do I want? Step over this line and everything will change, a nagging voice in his head shrilled carpingly. It sounded like Dannel in a bad mood. Already he was aroused, conscious of Shyya lying naked behind him, Shyya whom he'd desired for so long. But wasn't part of desiring Shyya the fact that he was unattainable? The voice said, Look at you, Meonel, you are a disgrace. You are becoming part of the animal that you despise. Look at you. He still held the glass vial in his hands. Almost unconsciously, he removed the cork and tipped some of its contents into his hand. The room filled with an eye-watering scent. Meonel wiped the liquid on his leg where it tingled and glowed, seeping into the scars of recent insect bites and grazes, making the flesh grow hot.

'Why are you afraid, Meonel?' he heard Shyya ask him. 'I speak to your soul, not your body. Bodies don't matter. Our souls love. What we are, who we are, is immaterial. Can't you see that?'

'Then why do bodies lust, if love is so spiritual?' he asked bitterly.

'For some it is merely gratification. I've known that. So have you, but sometimes, if we are lucky, it is merely one soul trying to reach into another. Our physical forms separate us so cruelly, shrouding our spirits, making us clay. We make love to try and overcome that. It doesn't always work, but sometimes. . . '

'Will you answer every objection I throw at you in this way?'

Shyya was silent, but even without looking at him,

Meonel could feel his smile. He stood up and threw off the towels. A mirror caught his reflection and cast it back unashamedly. Shyya spoke of spiritual communion, grace and melding, but there was hunger too. The animal could not be denied completely. Meonel climbed into the bed. He lay in the golden light, feeling as if he was still floating in the spa. Heady perfume coiled around the room like smoke. Some moments later, he felt Shyya's hand creep into his own. These hands had touched him many times, but this was different. Why should it feel so different? 'Are we committing ourselves, Shyya, are we?' His voice sounded loud, as if it carried all the way to Vangery.

'We only have each other; of that we can be sure.' Shyya's voice, by contrast, was a silky whisper. Perfume voice, the heavy scent. Meonel closed his eyes; his head was swimming. Shyya swirled around him like water, the essence of Shyya, the scent of Shyya. Shyya's hands upon his face, Shyya's lips upon his own. Meonel felt as if he was disintegrating into a million shining particles, particles wholly controlled and moulded by Shyya. The perfume of the Greylids has many uses. Most of them were discovered that night. One of them was the induction of euphoria and the rest followed naturally.

CHAPTER THIRTY-SEVEN

THERE'D BEEN LITTLE pain since the first day; Corinna supposed she was lucky because of that. She shared a room with another girl, Engo, but there was little conversation between them. The room was several storeys up, overlooking an inner courtyard of mossy stone. It was a cold room, a coldness that had very little to do with temperature. There was a shelf for books that was empty. No hairbrushes of course. No mirrors. The beds were narrow, unshareable. In the wardrobe six red robes hung close together at one end. Corinna wasn't allowed to wear one at first. At night, Engo whimpered in her sleep. Like Corinna, few of her mutilations were evident to the casual observer.

From the moment she had been dragged away from the presence of the monster Yani Gisbandrun, Corinna had been protected by a kind of numbness which descended like a grey fog. It filtered all that happened to her so that her mind could remain detached. The first humiliation was the removal of all of her body hair. Admittedly, it had been done carefully, no torture-chamber punishment this. Clippers, scissors, razors, tweezers. They'd even plucked her eyebrows and lashes clean away. At the end of it, she wasn't even scratched, but it left Corinna feeling cold and scored. Someone spoke about how often this depilation would have to be undergone. Corinna wasn't really listening. Afterwards, she couldn't remember what had been said.

The following day, there had been a full-blown ritual, during which she had received the facial scars of honour.

The words of the ritual had been beautifully poetic, even moving. Corinna had felt dead; she felt nothing as they drew the knives across her skin. Because being in red was regarded as an elevated position, those that suffered it were treated with reverence. Potent anaesthetics were administered before any of the 'honours' were bestowed. The Dominatrix was not barbaric with her girls; nor did she attend any of the ceremonies.

Two more days passed. Corinna lay on her narrow bed with itching face. Twice a day someone came to rub something into the scars, not to make them heal faster, but to ensure that they stayed livid forever. It did not hurt, no, but it itched naggingly. Engo rocked on her bed, muttering. Corinna could not communicate with her, neither did she want to. On the morning of the third day, they would not let her eat breakfast. This was generally brought in at dawn by the servants who attended the girls in red. That day, only Engo was given a tray which she hummed over as usual, eating like a scared cat. Corinna stared at the servant. 'Where's mine?' she asked. The servant shook her head. They never spoke. Corinna sighed. She was so full of anger and frustration, it had become hard and unfeeling. Her whole body was rigid with it; fury had crystallised. Half an hour later, a woman dressed in white like a nurse with a beaming smile and a large bosom came and injected Corinna in the leg. 'Today's the day,' the woman said with a grin.

'What are you doing to me now?' Corinna asked. 'What is this? What are you doing to me?'

'Now, now, pet, don't get worked up. I've given you a little something to make you feel happy. Just relax.' The woman was inhuman.

'What are you doing to me?' Corinna screamed, nudged out of her apathy for the first time in days. Her breathing had become sobbing. Engo began to rock and sing tunelessly on her bed. The nurse shook her head.

'Now, now, missy! You're upsetting your friend here!' she said waving a finger.

'Fuck her!' Corinna shouted. 'She's not my friend. Fuck all of you!' The disturbance attracted other women in white. The outcome of it was Corinna found herself waking up in a room that was not her bedroom. She felt dizzy, unsure of what had happened. Have I dreamed? she wondered. No, that would be too easy. This room was high up in a tower. Corinna could tell because of the way the wind was speaking outside. All the windows were of stained glass. Other than that, the room was very plain. She was lying on a cold, hard table in the centre of the room, covered by a thin sheet. She sensed movement behind her head but felt too groggy to turn and see what it was. Whispered voices, footsteps beyond the closed door and that most terrible sound of all; the subdued laughter of free people sharing a joke. Two women in white appeared around the corner of her vision. They smiled tightly at her as they tied her to the table. She was spreadeagled, wrists and ankles secured to short metal rods attached to each corner. 'Lie still,' one of them said, as she wriggled. Corinna let her cold, naked head fall back on the unresisting surface. This is it, she thought. Will it be my ears, my nose, my hands? What will it be? She wished she could cry or even just feel a little sorry for herself, but the hardness that had become her inner self would have no truck with that kind of thing. She had a feeling her inner self was laughing, saying, 'Fools! Do all you want to this flesh, you can't touch me. You'll never touch me!' This was true, of course, but Corinna's conscious mind still cared about her body. It was like being the host for two entities, one weak, one strong. Her face began to itch unbearably. How long were they going to keep her waiting like this? They were cruel, evil. 'Don't be stupid,' the inner self said. 'You know that already. Why be surprised, why hope for different treatment? You let them win that way.' All the women in white had filed from the room. She was alone, covered by a thin sheet, shivering, terrified and uncomfortable.

The drug she'd been given must have made her doze again, for Corinna's next experience was of waking up once more. The light in the room hadn't changed. She hadn't been unconscious that long. At the foot of the table stood a girl in red, the upper part of her face concealed

291

by a drooping hood. Corinna raised her head an inch or so and a voice said inside her, 'This is the dark, this is the dark. Look at it. The dark face.'

'I am named Last Light,' the red girl said. With a sudden gesture that made Corinna jump, this friend whipped the sheet from Corinna's body. She stood there, hunched like a red carrion bird, with the sheet in her raised hand. Even though the hood hid her eyes, Corinna could tell that she was gazing, quite unashamedly, between Corinna's spread-eagled legs. Last Light licked her lips with a dead, white tongue. 'What is about to happen to you will remain with you until the last of your days,' she said in a flat voice. 'It must be made memorable; pleasurable as well as painful. Experience this fully, Lunt. Then you shall be given the red.' A small, tight smile was working its way round Last Light's face. She threw back her hood and her head, like the others, was shaved. It wasn't a pretty face. 'I must look like that,' Corinna thought and called out, in a last, despairing moan, 'Oh Goddess, Oh Goddess,'; a cry that tapered away to an animal sound. What the monster called Last Light did to her was an obscenity. It involved teeth and fingers and hard, cold instruments. The obscenity was that Corinna had no control over how her body reacted. Last Light was clever. Corinna fought it, but the rising tide of enjoyment could not be denied. As an orgasm filled her body with sensation, she had a vision of the cave on the marsh. Last Light's high-pitched giggling brought her back. An obscenity. Last Light said to her. 'That's it; that is your last time. Last Light, last time. Remember it, Lunt. It's all you'll have to comfort you from now on.' She laughed, wiping her mouth, rearranging her hood. Corinna banged her head against the table, but she could feel nothing. It didn't hurt. She watched Last Light steel herself to leave as if part of her mind wasn't functioning correctly. There was a crazy jerk, a pause for just too long. Eyes unfocussed, Last Light swayed from the room. Corinna lay numb upon the table. Her ankles and wrists were tingling; she felt wet and used up. She felt like vomiting.

Ten minutes later, the women in white filed back into the room. Now they wore membranous gloves and stiff aprons. Corinna swore under her breath, a long, low tirade which they ignored. They sponged her down and adjusted the straps around her limbs. Something that felt like wadding was stuffed carefully into her vagina until she felt unnaturally stretched. More sexual torture? 'Let them do what they like,' the inner self said and turned its face away. They injected some drug into her veins, that acted almost immediately and made her feel physically numb from the waist down and mentally numb from the neck up. Some thought was ticking away that would not form itself into a shape that Corinna could understand. Her brain was reeling. She knew something; she knew nothing. There was a clink of metal. Corinna closed her eyes; she felt nothing. The women talked amongst themselves as they worked; a soft murmuring that made no sense, its volume fluctuating like the sound of water. It took so little time. Corinna was aware of the women straightening up, smiling at each other in a congratulatory way. Corinna remembered saying, 'Is it my ears?' although she knew it wasn't. The women did not answer. They lifted her gently and placed her on a stretcher. Then they removed their gloves which were slightly bloody. A trolley was wheeled away, rattling. Corinna drifted into a semi-conscious state. When she opened her eyes again, she was back in her room. She could hear birds calling out to each other beyond the window. Nothing itched, nothing hurt. She could sleep.

For the rest of that day, and most of the one following, she was hardly aware of who or where she was. Women in white came to attend to her needs which she could remember nothing about. By the evening, after an afternoon of deep slumber, she had come to her senses. It was then that she discovered the nature of her mutilation. She would never enjoy the pleasures of love-making again. They'd taken away all the parts that responded to arousal. She'd been effectively gelded. Now, she was like Shyya. No, not like Shyya. Lying on her bed in the mellow, evening sunlight, she laughed aloud. It was

293

the laugh of the inner self who had escaped violation. Engo lay on her bed and moaned as Corinna laughed. Engo's inner self had not survived whatever torment Yani Gisbandrun had decided must be inflicted on her. Now she was too crazy even to end it all. As she laughed, Corinna wondered whether she too would ever lose the strength to keep the darkness at bay. In years to come would she be rocking madly in a mental vortex as another girl lay here and laughed?

Now, Corinna was entitled to wear the red robe officially. She found that her duties were minimal. The girl called Rudd came to talk to her the morning after she'd recovered from the anaesthetic. She was business-like and contained, which Corinna found reassuring in a strange way. 'You'll need time to adjust,' Rudd said, without sentiment. 'Try to overcome feelings of bitterness because they are self-destructive. You'll find life isn't as bad as you'd think here. Everything has its benefits.'

Whether it was a precaution against possible attack, Corinna didn't know, but no girl in red attended the Dominatrix, until she'd been in the palace for at least six weeks. Perhaps, in that time, the girls accepted their situation and were less inclined to seek revenge. Yani didn't demand much of them anyway, just their presence, a silent testament of loyalty at her feet. Duties were widely spaced because of a rota system. Those in Red were waited on by a sizeable staff that never wanted to look them in the eye. Each one of the red girls was a tragedy, each a different story of mutilation and degradation; missing fingers and toes, missing features, missing breasts and some, like Corinna, whose scars could not be seen. They never talked about it, never comforted each other. Left alone, they spent their time, not in meditation or other pious pursuits, but in getting completely catatonic through liberal helpings of narcotics and alcohol. Corinna saw no reason not to emulate that behaviour at first, but after a week actually became bored with it. She took care to behave just like all the others in front of outsiders so as not to attract attention to herself. When she discovered a rarely used room full of clean, white reed-paper, paints and charcoals she felt as if she had saved her life. Its walls were lined with bookcases, on which she found old novels, some of which were romances where men were heroes. Clearly, this room had not been looked at too closely for many years. Corinna took to spending most of her time there. No-one would ever look for her behind the little door at the end of the corridor. She locked it from the inside and drew violent pictures of the Dominatrix being destroyed in various ways. After a week, she got bored by that too, and began to read the books. She wondered what she'd do once she'd devoured them all. One of the books was full of photographs of the marsh. Smiling families stood before their farms; it looked old and faded. Soon, this may not exist, Corinna thought and decided to paint pictures from the photographs. The paintings could stay in this room, no-one would ever see them, they'd be safe. Perhaps one day, in a hundred years, someone would come across them by accident and would read the tales within them. Perhaps. Corinna was not a good painter, but she had plenty of time and plenty of paper. In the mornings, she read. Then it was into the common-room for lunch. In the afternoons, she painted. Of course, it was difficult not to think while she painted. Only reading could take her mind off what had happened. At first, the thoughts hurt, because they were of Vangery. After a while, they became a comfort. Deep within her a small flame breathed the words, 'Wait, wait, get your strength back, get your bearings, wait.' Clearly, inner self did not believe in the permanence of her situation. She had been astounded by the depth of her inner strength. She could not understand why she was still so sane, when all the other girls in red seemed crazy. The mutilations did not hurt so she forced herself to think they did not matter. Hair could grow back. The scars did not interfere with any part of her but her vanity. And there was more to life than love-making. Being dead between the legs didn't mean she couldn't stand once more on the marsh and bask in the unbelievable light of this planet's beauty and strangeness. They'd have to clip away at her mind to affect that, and she knew now, with a strange certainty, that they couldn't. Something inside her told her to wait, and it was a great comfort.

Corinna had cringed and shrunk against the wall, the first time she'd seen Last Light again. This was unnecessary, because Last Light didn't even recognise her. It soon became clear to Corinna that Last Light was a kind of figurehead to Those in Red. She was treated differently. Corinna couldn't understand why. Perhaps they looked upon her as an insane oracle; perhaps they viewed her madness as strength, unassailability. There was more than one way of being free. What kind of suffering Last Light had been through to become the way she was didn't bear thinking about. The human mind is very resilient after all; it takes a lot to shatter it completely. Of course, there was always the possibility that Last Light had been deranged from birth. Corinna had as little to do with her as possible. One or two of the other girls didn't seem quite so strange or hopeless and Corinna formed nodding acquaintanceship with them. She had been surprised by the fact that none of the girls in red appeared to be angry about what they had become, neither did they exhibit any hatred towards the Dominatrix. There was no way of knowing what went on inside their heads of course; it may have been a survival tactic. There were quite a few who blamed themselves for their fates and who carried their scars with a kind of revolting piety. Corinna had no sympathy for them. When she was on her own in her little, dark room, she fantasised about how the girls in red could rise up and tear Yani Gisbandrun limb from limb. These were graphic fantasies. Corinna would dearly have loved to rip flesh from the Dominatrix. She didn't want to kill her; that would be too kind. She also wondered whether she was alone in having these kind of dreams. It was difficult to tell. Apathy held sway in the rooms of the Red. Of course, there had to be benefits, and there were. Everything was in plentiful supply; foods, drugs, perfumes, wines, trinkets, games. Every evening, entertainers arrived in the lounge and danced or performed plays. The girls would sit around only half paying attention and get mindlessly drunk. There was a grim, unsentimental kind of camaraderie among the girls in red. When they were off duty, they could do as they pleased as long as they didn't leave their own quarters. And even that wasn't as bad as it sounded because they had hundreds of rooms at their disposal and two very large gardens, with pools and shady trees and tame iridescent ditch-cranes to patrol the grass. The rota meant that duties were fairly divided, and didn't come around too often. Corinna wondered a couple of times how many of the others had been cut up in the same way she had. It was impossible to tell. Those in Red were not sensuous in a physical sense. They had their dreams, and in the dreams they was no place for scarred faces or missing limbs or organs. Special friendships were not discouraged, probably because they never arose.

Corinna had been in the palace for about five weeks when her turn for duty came up. She wondered how she'd feel when she had to lay eyes on the hated Gisbandrun woman again, and took the precaution of ingesting an euphoric drug before starting work. With lowered head, she shuffled into the Dominatrix's morning salon and took a place at her feet. Yani Gisbandrun did not even look at her. She knelt on the floor for two hours while the Dominatrix conducted an audience with some women from another city. It passed quickly because of the drug and she did not even feel the pins and needles in her legs. Over the following two weeks, she had three more duties of similar length. It was just about bearable as long as she wasn't sober. By clearing her mind, she could avoid angry, livid thoughts about throwing herself on the Dominatrix in a lust of rage. Such action would be suicide; she knew that. 'Wait, wait,' her inner voice said. 'Makes no waves. Be invisible. Wait.'

One morning, Corinna was walking past the noticeboard where the rotas were pinned, just as Last Light had finished putting up the duties for the next week. 'You're Lunt, aren't you?' Last Light said, squinting. Corinna nodded and stared at the notice-board. 'Thought so.

There you go, Lunt; you have a privilege. Fill your pockets if you get the chance.'

'With what?' Corinna asked, squinting at the rota. 'What is this?'

'Evening shift.'

'Evening? I haven't done an evening before.'

'Course you haven't. New, aren't you? It's the old girl's one indulgence. You'll see. Also, there'll be plenty of Eema's Itch around. Later on, nobody'll notice if you pocket a bunch of it.'

'Eema's Itch?'

Last Light rolled her eyes; a gesture that seemed to go on for some minutes. 'Yes. Potent weed; the best. Yani keeps it for herself because someone has to go beyond the boundaries to harvest it. It's special and forbidden for the likes of us. Reds on evening duty have an arrangement. It's called helping your sisters. Bring us some back.'

'O.k.'

'O.k.' Last Light parodied Corinna's response, grinning. 'Keep your eyes open,' she said and swayed away. Last Light always swayed, mainly because she was never sober. She seemed to have no real recollection of who Corinna was or what she'd once done to her. All in a day's work for Last Light.

CHAPTER THIRTY-EIGHT

L'BELDER WALKED A dark, damp path. It was deep beneath the ground, silent as a grave and just as fragrant. He felt that he was out of his body; he could not remember what had happened to him. He just *was*. Then he was floating in a pool of stars and his flesh had become translucent; lit from the inside. He had the creature named Ee-kha-ha in his arms and could feel the bones flexing beneath his hands. 'Touch our God,' Ee-kha-ha said, and its head was flung back. Its neck split and a red light issued forth like blood.

Stone. Mountain. Darkness. L'Belder flew without wings around the giant, stone face of a carved deity that brooded in a lightless, cavernous chamber underneath the earth. The blind eyes of the statue were open, the mouth frozen in the centre of a word. L'Belder flew in through the mouth and found himself in another stone chamber. Here, vague light came from a row of windows on his left side. The windows were paned with coloured glass and disappeared into the distance until they were just specks of light. L'Belder walked to the first window and his footsteps echoed around the chamber until it sounded as if many feet were making them. He looked behind him and saw only a breathing blackness. Sound came from the window. He looked. The picture in the glass was of Rosanel. He could see her sitting in her parlour, staring into the fire. A half-empty bottle of ebony port stood on the floor by her feet. She held a glass to her lips, not drinking, just staring. He put out his hand to touch the glass and the picture faded until it was just meaningless

299

blotches of colour. He gazed at it for a moment and then passed on. In the next window he found a picture of Vangery. It was seen from a distance, hugged by a morning mist, but he could still make out the large form of Dannel looking through her window at the marsh. She looked forlorn, hopelessly watching for the return of her family. He passed to the next window and here was a moving picture of Meonel and Shyya making love on a carpet of moss in Vez'n'kizri. L'Belder had to smile at that. He felt proudly responsible for it. Some, at least, had found happiness. The next twenty windows gave him images from his past, both sad and joyful. He walked past them slowly, nodding to himself. Yes, this is right, and this, and this. Then he came to a window larger than the others. It glowed with an aching light that made his head roar with blood. He did not want to look within it, no, and made to hurry by, but it was beyond his control to do that. The window drew him forward. He saw a grey stone room, high up in a tower, filled with narrow, slanting beams of light. He saw a naked girl spread-eagled on a table. Even without her hair, he could tell it was Corinna. He did not want to see any more because a richness the colour and texture of blood was beginning to seep through the glass from the top to the bottom. He wanted to turn away, but could not move. His eyes were fixed upon it. The scene was witnessed through a film of red, but he saw it all. In the end he was trying to smash the coloured glass with his hands, but all he was smashing was smooth stone. The windows had gone. Corinna. Could he feel proud responsibility for that?

'Give me the power!' he screamed at the darkness. 'Give it to me!' He wanted Silven Crescent destroyed; it was more than just the people. The city was foul. It must rot, burn, drown! He fell to his knees, knuckles pressed against his eyes, weeping. He knew Corinna, but she was only one. How many more were there? He put his hands upon the stone floor and saw a crack appear within it by his knees. The crack was as narrow as a hair. As he watched, it stretched itself and became longer. His hands hugged his face; he stared at the floor. A weird, commanding pull made him stoop lower. There was no light coming from the crack. What was it? The pull became stronger, more insistent. L'Belder tried to turn away, stand up. The power. . . With a sickening, sucking sound, his body began to liquify, was drawn towards the crack in the floor, obeying an irresistible call. He struggled, feeling himself, the essence of his being, slipping away, and a blinding flash suffused his vision. He experienced acceleration, descent, tumbling, rushing. Down through the crack, the infinitesimal crack. Change form, change form. Pearly, sentient light swirled around him, cushioning his fall. Now he was floating in a ring of Greylids, insubstantial matter, and all their hands were reaching out for him, eyes burning. They moulded him into a new shape, feeding him strength. He hung before them, naked, shining, like a drawn sword. One by one, because he was now their brother, the Greylids, revealed their mutations to him, pulling aside their robes, standing tall and flickering like candle-flames; glorious, terrifying, hideous, beautiful. A voice said, 'You will become an arrow. You will achieve your desire. You will become an arrow of light that shall fly to the city of women.' L'Belder had taken the changing. He was no longer human, but transformed; a Greylid, Wanderil, native Artemesian, whatever. There was no longer any need for names. But even as he changed, the fire within him still burned. He was given the choice, he could turn away from it forever if he wished, but the memory of the largest window stayed with him. He turned towards Silven Crescent, attentuated, glowing, strong. The changing had taken many weeks. Shyya and Meonel had left Vez'n'kizri some time ago and were nearly at the city. They did not know what had become of their friend Elvon L'Belder.

Meanwhile, in Silven Crescent, Rosanel Garmelding waited for news and, in the palace, in the small, dark room, Corinna painted pictures of the marsh and waited for the time of her release. Everything was poised, everything was moving into place. A conjunction of events was approaching. It was approaching fast.

CHAPTER THIRTY-NINE

THOSE IN RED were revered. Other women bowed as they passed. It was a position as privileged as it was lonely as it was barren. Corinna had learned the taste of the hot, dry longing that had no name. Outside, sketches of life carried on, but the people had become unreal. The house Carmenya had bought for Corinna might well have its windows open to the rain; Carudan and Rosanel might still confer in smoky, midnight rooms rancid with the sweat of fear, but to Corinna this meant nothing. She didn't feel angry; there was no word for what she felt. She would just wait.

That night, the last Corinna ever spent in the palace, began as usual with the late afternoon meal. Corinna surveyed the sumptuous delicacies, took a small portion, ate it alone. She sat in a corner of the lounge, looking out of the window. Behind her, Last Light's voice sounded like a long blade slicing the air of the room. A few people were laughing, sitting round her feet, lapping up her insanities like pearls of wisdom. Corinna drew up her knees. There were no mirrors in the Rooms of the Red, although Engo, in a rare moment of lucidity, had remarked that the facial scarring did possess a beauty all of its own. Corinna didn't want to see. For one wistful moment, she thought, 'I want my hair back.' Strange that she should think that. She did not yearn for her family, her freedom or indeed the ability to enjoy sex; what she yearned for was her heavy hair. In the back of her mind was the faint, repressed hope that someone was going to get her out of this. She didn't, even in her blackest hours, ever think being in Red would last forever. There was no feeling of permanence about it. She would not let herself think this was a delusion. Nothing feels permanent any more, she told her inner self. The inner self abstained from comment. It hadn't made up its mind yet. Corinna had not seen Carmenya since the night of her arrest. She'd not seen, or had word about, Endaline either. She presumed Carudan had got the rest of the people away because the Dominatrix would have wanted her to know if they hadn't. Also, she believed she would be dead now if any concrete evidence had been found to link her with the dissidents. Sometimes she allowed herself the luxury of thinking. 'They will succeed; L'Belder will come back,' but not very often. Each day dawned like the one before it; no changes. Carmenya must know what had happened to her and had done nothing. She'd been abandoned by her friends and her lover. She was too dangerous to know; a sentiment shared by both sides. Corinna didn't want them to see her. Rescue was a dream. She was ashamed of what had happened to her. If Carmenya should come into the Dominatrix's presence when Corinna was there, she would hide.

Corinna looked down from the high tower into the garden. The suns were sinking, making the palace walls look beautiful, kind, untainted. Corinna thought about leaping from the window, but it was brief. Then she thought that because of the drugs and the wine nobody would try to stop her if she just walked out of here. At night, there were guards on the gates and the walls. If she tried to escape the chances were she'd get shot, but wasn't it worth the risk? 'Why haven't I thought of this before?' she wondered. 'It's so obvious. I'll just walk out of here. If I'm killed, then that's Fate. If I'm meant to escape, I will. I'll just walk out of here. After tonight.' The only real chains about the ankles of Those in Red, were the ones of despair, depression, self-disgust, lethargy – and the dependence on the luxuries that were provided for their use. She already knew that many of them felt they deserved their scars and their imprisonment. Because she had made herself inconspicuous, she was sure no-one would miss her for quite some time. What Last Light gave

Corinna a call to remind her it was nearly time for her evening duty, Corinna was thinking, 'I'm going to leave here. I'm not coming back. They will have to kill me. I'm going to leave.' She nodded at Last Light, uncurling from her place by the window, putting down her plate, arranging her robes.

'Take the back doorway at the end of the south corridor,' Last Light said, jerking her head in the direction of the Dominatrix's apartments. 'It will be in the inner room. Gick will be with you. Don't forget the Itch.'

'I won't.'

'Get going then.'

That night, Corinna had her plans changed for her.

The inner room had no windows. It was warm and the light was dim. As usual, the Dominatrix was holding court over a group of sycophants, opining upon the subjects dear to her heart. Her cronies sat on the floor gazing up at her with adoration. As she saw the woman, Corinna experienced the usual lurch of hatred, which she took care to smother quickly. Why make herself feel bad? The force of her hatred was wasted on Yani Gisbandrun. She took her place beside the cushions, kneeling on the floor, so that those going off duty could leave. 'We are invisible,' she thought and looked across at Gick, who was one of the few girls in red she had any liking for. Gick grimaced and smiled, before modestly lowering her eyes. Yani Gisbandrun clapped her hands and serving girls came into the room, bringing trays of wine. 'Drink, drink!' the Dominatrix cried. Her followers were happy to comply with that command. Even Gick and Corinna were offered a glass, but Corinna's throat was closed. She could not drink it.

By late evening, after having listened to Yani holding forth for the entire time, most of the women were beginning to make their excuses and leave, so that only Yani's closest friends remained. Most of the ones departing looked as if they'd make straight for the nearest sink to throw up. The air stank of stale wine. Corinna had kept her head down. Was this the Dominatrix's one indulgence then, getting drunk? Her voice was slurred now, losing its

304

habitual mellow tone and becoming much louder and coarser. Some of what she said didn't make sense at all. Now, as Last Light had predicted, servants brought out the Eema's Itch and the Dominatrix burst the pods of powder herself. A dish of hot charcoal had been placed in the centre of the room. The Dominatrix demanded it be brought over to her. She took a silver spoon and placed some of the coals in the wide bowl of a tall pipe standing on the floor. A generous pinch of Eema's Itch was sprinkled over the coals. Yani took the stem of the pipe and inhaled. Her cronies cheered drunkenly. Yani affected a comical, dazed expression and passed the pipe to the woman on her left. Very soon, everyone was intoxicated by the smoke, all giggling uncontrollably and rolling around the floor. Corinna was astounded to see mature, dignified women of the court honking like danks and making utter fools of themselves. Expensive gowns were dishevelled and spotted with wine, beginning to drop from shoulders that were usually held rigidly erect. Corinna had a headache. She felt slightly nauseous and uncomfortable. Her stomach had begun to hurt. Would it be noticed if she crept out now? Just as she was considering such action, the Dominatrix bawled out, 'Now!' which prompted another burst of cheering from her friends. 'Now, we shall be entertained!' The cheering was augmented by a ragged clapping of hands.

'Yes!' the women howled. 'Yes! Yes!' The Dominatrix sat up on her cushions. Her face was red and damp, her white robe splashed with wine. She barked an order and the doors to the room were thrown open, accompanied by an absurd blast of trumpets. Corinna's jaw dropped in amazement. About half a dozen young men somersaulted into the room, followed by a skipping band of musicians of both sexes. Lovely creatures they were, slim and lithe, scantily clad in silk and feathers. All the women cheered and clapped some more. Dancers? Corinna looked across and caught Gick's eye. Gick gave an imperceptible shrug, but there was no mistaking the scorn in that gesture.

'Show us what you can do,' the Dominatrix said, and her cronies echoed,

'Yes, yes, show us what you can do!' They all laughed.

The men began to dance; swaying, chanting, bending to the music. It was clever and indeed beautiful to watch, but Corinna was still astounded. What were men doing in the palace? It soon became clear. The women threw them their jewels, followed shortly afterwards by various items of clothing. Pausing elegantly in their movements, some of the men picked the garments up, wrapping themselves in robes, cavorting comically in a parody of refined dignity. The women cheered through the thick smoke of Eema's Itch. Now the dance took on a more sensuous aspect. Corinna looked away. She desperately wanted to leave. Would she be noticed sneaking out? Surely not. The Dominatrix and her friends were far too engrossed in the dancers to pay any attention to a mere girl in red. She began to stand up. A hand shot out and gripped her wrist. 'No!' It was Gick's. Corinna could see the girl's eyes flaming with a weird, intense light beneath her hood.

'Let me go,' Corinna hissed back. 'I feel sick. I have to leave. No-one will notice.' Gick shook her head.

'Doesn't matter. Don't be squeamish, Lunt. You must see this. You must.'

'I've seen enough.'

'You've seen nothing.'

'Gick, let me go.'

'Shut up; just watch. It will open your eyes.'

The Dominatrix hadn't noticed this exchange. She was lying back in her cushions once more, a collapsed bundle of inelegant limbs, one hand straying inside the neck of her robe. Gick pulled a face. 'She's a monster,' Corinna whispered.

'It can't last for ever,' Gick answered and gave Corinna a brief, tight smile. It became clear in that moment why Gick had been honoured with the Red. Like Corinna, she was a dissident, but not involved enough to deserve execution. Like Corinna, she kept quiet about it.

'Gick,' Corinna began, meaning to use this rare moment of intimacy to ask some searching questions, but Gick cut her short.

'Don't say anything,' she said abruptly.

306

'O.k., we wait,' Corinna said and squeezed the hand that was still gripping her wrist.

Gick nodded. 'Yes. Now watch. It's important that you see.'

Now five of the men were caressing the prostrate body of the sixth. The watching women were leaning forward, baying and cat-calling.

'I can't see why. . .' Corinna began but again Gick cut her short.

'Watch. Look at her!'

Corinna glanced at the Dominatrix. She was clearly aroused by the scene before her. Was she going to participate? Was the statement about celibacy a lie?

'Ella over there is a new servant,' Gick said, jerking her head at a young, bemused girl who had backed cautiously against the far wall. 'This will be her treat, Lunt. This is the nature of our beloved leader.'

The men were a writhing heap of limbs by now and the Dominatrix was unashamedly rubbing herself into a similar frenzy, legs splayed wide upon the cushions. She paused, as if picking up some stray thought from Corinna or Gick and then frowned. She called out a name and one of the men looked up. What must he think of her? Corinna wondered. The queen of Silven Crescent was lying like a whore on soiled cushions, her hand still working even as she issued orders. The dancer inclined his head as Yani nodded slightly in the direction of the servant girl. What followed made Corinna sicker than anything she'd yet experienced. The dancers dragged the girl into the middle of the room and soon her pathetic cries rose as an accompaniment to the Dominatrix's pleasured moans. Like crazy women, the Dominatrix's cronies threw themselves into the melee, stripping off the remains of their robes, exposing pale flesh that crawled and spread over the heap of bodies. There was nothing remotely sensual about it, Corinna was sure. It was blasphemy, as much a defilement of the sacrament of love as changing the words of a solemn ritual to an obscene parody. For the first and perhaps only time, Corinna was glad that the ability to enjoy such things had been taken

307

from her. It was revolting. The whole set up was lie. The Dominatrix was a lie, her words were lies. This woman who proclaimed that men oppressed women was now lying watching an innocent girl being raped by six men and several women, whilst pleasuring herself in the process. Loved all her people did she? 'When can we go?' Corinna asked. 'Will we be expected to. . . take part in that?'

'No.' Gick shook her head. 'Don't think some of us haven't though, but it was purely by choice. Those in Red are honoured; they are never conscripted into stuff like that. But that doesn't mean that some aren't into it. I've seen boys murdered, girls cut to ribbons, children raped, oh, all manner of atrocities committed in this room. Tonight is nothing. Why do you think the place is red?' She laughed cynically.

'Gick, why don't you leave here?' The question hung in the air against the appalling backdrop that was a scene from hell. Gick narrowed her eyes.

'I have nothing to go back to,' she said.

Corinna looked away. 'I'm sorry. I shouldn't have asked. Look, I don't care if it's allowed or not, I'm going back now. Are you coming?' She began to stand up. Gick nodded.

'Might as well. We won't be needed here again tonight, will we?'

Corinna looked across at the Dominatrix and for a brief second met the addled gaze of the red eyes. There was no hint of recognition.

'Come on then,' Gick said, putting a hand on Corinna's arm.

'O.k. Let's. . . '

'. . . go.'

And then Corinna was on the floor, her words whipped away from her. She choked, unable to breathe as if a gigantic fist had punched her in the stomach. After a moment she could look up. What had happened? Gick was trying to get up nearby, her backside pushed in the air, her head exposed to reveal the pathetic remains of her ears. She was coughing. All the others in the room were looking around themselves confused. 'Was that an earth-

308

quake?' someone asked. The licentious activities were forgotten. Women were reaching for their clothes. Even the servant girl Ella had silenced her sobbing. Something had happened. 'What the hell was that?' Corinna hissed. Gick shook her head. The air in the room had become strange, somehow thick and difficult to inhale. Corinna thought it was like a nightmare. Maybe, in a moment, she would wake up in Carmenya's house, on the marsh, anywhere. Anywhere but here. Was any of this real? Was it? No, impossible. Things like this don't happen. I'm dreaming. I'm dreaming. There was a sudden stasis. Corinna could not move. Then the Dominatrix broke the spell by lurching clumsily to her feet, tripping over the cushions, arms waving.

'Get out!' she shrieked. 'Get out!' The room erupted into activity, voices started up again, half-clothed bodies tumbled and struggled, blindly colliding in panic. Yani was afraid, and because she said she feared nothing, that terror in her voice was the worst thing her cronies could imagine. Corinna reached for Gick's hand. She felt blind. Her hood had also fallen back; it seemed like her naked head was burning. 'Out,' Gick repeated, struggling, pushing Corinna backwards. 'Get. . . get out!'

'What's happening?'

'Don't know!'

'I can't see. I can't move. Oh Goddess!'

Gick remained absurdly calm. 'I have your hand. Follow me. Quickly.' Corinna felt the pull and stumbled forward. Surely they must be near the door? Chaos reigned in the room behind them. She could hear shouting, the pounding of hands upon wood. Goddess! The doors were barred to them! The doors were barred! 'Gick!' she screamed, but again the cry was blown back into her lungs by a great, invisible fist. An impossible crescendo of bursting glass threw them to the floor. Gick screamed; a sound echoed by many other voices. Every window in the room, every mirror, every goblet shattered to admit a searing wind that swept curtains, cushions and lighter objects high into the air. Corinna curled her arms around her head. She could hear the Dominatrix shouting. And then there was the

Voice. This Voice became the room, the air itself.

'On your face, Yani!' It was a vibration that set Corinna's teeth on edge and prickled her skin. Gick was trying to crawl towards her, edging through broken glass and torn fabric. 'Yani! Yani!' The Dominatrix was making a confused sound, trying to remain in control. Corinna could hear a commotion outside the room, shouting, running feet. What was happening? She tried to rise and the wind seemed to blow long hair back from her face; an illusion. Her sight had cleared, but what she saw nearly made her hide her face again. The room was wrecked, people crawled round the floor, some lay motionless. In the centre of the room something that could only be termed an apparition hung two feet in the air. It was the form of a man, angelic, shining, whose glow caused spinning sparks to fly from each shard of broken glass. 'Goddess,' Corinna breathed. 'What *is* that?' Gick had stumbled to her side and was now hanging on to her arm. The figure spun, causing another hot blast of wind to blow everything into the air. Corinna narrowed her eyes and the features of the apparition became clearer to her. She couldn't believe it. Though transformed beyond all that was possible in her world, Corinna recognised the face of a man she'd known as Elvon L'Belder. He'd come back. He really had. But *what was he*? L'Belder raised a hand towards the Dominatrix. She put up both of hers in a gesture of protection. The Voice said,

'Try me!' and then the doors to the room were bursting, not inwards, not outwards, but just bursting, splinters of wood shooting out like bullets. A group of confused flamists spilled into the room, brandishing weapons, their leader shouting incoherent orders. 'Try me.'

The Dominatrix mustered some kind of composure and screamed, 'Kill it!' The flamists surged forward. Was Carmenya with them? Was she? Corinna could not see. The figure of L'Belder laughed and spun lazily in the air. There was an abrupt flash and then the group of flamists were no more. The room stank of burning meat. Corinna couldn't believe it. She let the hysterical laughter in her chest burst out. Gick leaned against her shoulder, one

310

cheek bleeding heavily. Her laughter was weaker. Corinna
could feel her shaking.

'Freedom,' Corinna said. 'Freedom! Freedom!' She was
still saying it even as the new creature that had once been
Elvon L'Belder poured out the full might of his power
against the woman who crouched in the cushions.

It should have ended then. It should have been the final
scene in Yani Gisbandrun's perverted life; but it wasn't.
However much she'd been scorned, the Dominatrix still
had power of her own. Power and courage. Even in her
fear she could construct a shield. L'Belder's weird fire just
flowed around her. He howled and shimmered and
writhed. The Dominatrix grinned. She raised a hand,
made words of war become real and retaliated. L'Belder
took the full force straight in the chest. His glow
diminished. He sank into the smoking carnage of the
Dominatrix's elite guard. Now she lunged towards him,
confident of victory, totally unprepared for the burst of
frightening radiance that splashed out from the prone
figure of L'Belder. The Dominatrix growled, knocked
backwards. There was a sound of more people
approaching outside. Corinna and Gick had reached the
back door to the room, hardly aware of how they'd
managed it. 'I must leave,' Corinna thought, 'Get out while
I can. Oh, Elvon!' At that moment, he turned his golden
face towards her. She saw the pity in his eyes, but not just
that; admiration and respect were there too. He did not
speak aloud but Corinna heard him all the same. 'Go to
the marsh,' he said. 'Meonel will be waiting for you on the
old road that leads from the city. Go home. Gather your
people and whoever will follow you. Get away!'

'Elvon!' she said aloud. Gick was trying to pull her
through the door. 'Elvon.'

'Leave here! Now!' he told her.

'You must win!' she wailed. 'You must.' The glowing
figure closed its eyes. There was so little time. On the
cushions, Yani Gisbandrun would be mustering her
strengths.

'Rosanel,' L'Belder said. 'Take her with you.'

311

And then a squealing rose of light bloomed in the room. Whoever was responsible for it, Corinna could not see. Mindlessly, she fell into the corridor beyond, Gick almost dragging her along the floor. They were running even before they could think about it. Ghostly, flashing light glanced off the walls, coming from behind them. There were sounds outside the palace, strange sounds, like a host of angels singing their way to battle. They ran past the passage that led to the Rooms of the Red, panting, never pausing. The only thing they could understand was the animal instinct to escape, to reach the open air. Without exchanging a single word they galloped down corridors, down stairs, always down, down, down. Then they had burst out into a courtyard at the bottom of a tower, pausing for a moment, blinking in sunlight. What had happened to the night? No, it wasn't sunlight, just radiance. Silven Crescent shone like the moon, every brick, every tile, shining with its own refulgence. 'What is this?' Gick said at last. Corinna didn't answer. Women were rushing around, looking up, disorientated.

'We must get to Denderberry,' Corinna said.

'Why?'

'I have people there. I have to get them out of the city.'

'You know what's going on, don't you!'

Corinna smiled at her. 'Yes, I do. Come on!'

What a sorry sight they were: two bald-headed women, bleeding from the face and arms, running in tattered robes through chaotic streets where insanity held sway. The palace hill was in turmoil. Mysterious fires had started, blocking the path of women who were sensible enough to run down town. Corinna saw houses spontaneously burst into purple fires. She saw women run blazing from the ruins. Everywhere, streets were obstructed or impassable. She began to feel afraid. Gick thought she knew what she was doing; if only she did! They ran past the turning that led to Lavinia Drive. Corinna would not look down it. Soon afterwards they came across three confused danks, still wearing carriage harness, who had broken free and were wandering helplessly through the streets. Between them, she and Gick managed to calm two of them enough to mount and drive them in the direction of Denderberry. Corinna closed her ears to the terrible cries coming from inside the houses. They kept heading down, along roads Corinna had never travelled before, but always down.

Behind them, Palace Mount burned and suffered. The wind blew haunted cries ahead of them, cries that dissipated in the maze of Denderberry. L'Belder had come back and the rebellion had risen and burst. He'd done it alone. Flames tongued towards the stars. Skyreachers, Corinna thought, how bizarrely apt.

CHAPTER FORTY

SOME MILES OUT from Silven Crescent, at the place where the roads began and the marsh started to firm up, Meonel and Shyya watched the Palace Hill go up in flames. Shyya's first comment was, 'By the Goddess, he did it!' Meonel was not so convinced.

'Let's get going,' he said. 'Corinna's still in there.'

They still had no idea what was going to happen after all this. Should they go back to Vangery or head somewhere else? It was difficult to make decisions when the future was so vague anyway. During their stay in Vez'n'kizri the mysterious Greylids had remained virtually out of sight. Occasionally, sacks of vegetables and the odd small, gutted animal carcase would be left on the steps of the cottage. Meonel and Shyya were clearly regarded as guests, yet their hosts appeared to desire no contact with them. One night, however, a knock came upon the cottage door just after sundown and they found one of the Greylids standing there asking for permission to enter. Meonel offered it a cup of tea, which it accepted graciously. He recognised it as the female-looking Greylid who'd given him the scented oil on their first night in the place. It sat down at the table and warmed its hands on the cup that Meonel offered it. 'Tomorrow you must leave,' it said.

'Have we outstayed our welcome?' Shyya said. He had enjoyed the quietude of Vez'n'kizri so much he was reluctant to turn his back on it. The Greylid shook its head.

'No, under normal circumstances you would be able to remain here for as long as you wished, but in view of

314

certain events, we feel it best that you begin your journey to the women's city as soon as possible.'

'Why?' Meonel asked sharply. The Greylid looked up at him mildly.

'Your stepdaughter will need you and it is your friend's wish that you should go. Doesn't he have family there?'

'Which friend? You mean L'Belder?'

It nodded. 'Yes. Just be sure you don't *go back*. Go forward; there's more to be learned that way.'

'We will never *go back*,' Meonel said. 'You needn't worry about that.'

'And stay away from the insects.'

'We'll try.'

'You can come back to us later, if you wish.' The creature looked at them searchingly as it spoke. They both knew that the invitation was extended to no-one else but them, no-one from Vangery, no-one from Silven Crescent. They saw in the Greylid's eyes the knowledge that if they should accept and return to Vez'n'kizri to become transformed like L'Belder, they could expect to live for a thousand thousand years and Shyya would no longer be unwhole. It was an offer to be considered seriously. Meonel looked at Shyya and Shyya shrugged and then shook his head. They would have been safe perhaps, but they would no longer have been human.

'We'll think about your offer,' Meonel said and the Greylid inclined its head and stood up.

'You were welcome here,' it said. 'Provisions will be supplied for your needs and a guide will take you to the edge of the old road to the city. Goodnight.'

After the Greylid had gone, Meonel said, 'Do you think we should come back?'

'Alone?' Shyya had replied. 'What about Dannel and Corinna and the people of Vangery? What about L'Belder's precious Rosanel? Aren't we now responsible towards them, in a way?'

Meonel sighed. 'You're right. Goddess knows what will happen.'

'What will happen is that we'll get our people off the marsh – northwards. Let L'Belder stay and fight if he wants to. I don't think that's the best way.'

The Greylids led them from the forest and directed them onto the wide, slabbed road. They rode south. They kept on riding south until they saw the glow in the sky and knew that Elvon L'Belder was in the process of achieving his dream. Corinna was in there; time was short. At their command the swift but ungainly danks flew along the old road towards the city.

Denderberry was hysterical. People were running around, screaming, not in terror like on the Hill, but in excitement and craziness. Because the rebel groups had become so scattered and disorganised, nobody knew who was responsible for the fire, each supposing one of the others had finally taken radical action. Now people were being urged onto the streets, urged towards the richer quarters of the city, with firepower in their hands and vengeance in their hearts. The dissidents had exposed themselves, no longer afraid of discovery, sure of victory. There was almost a festival air in Denderberry that night.

It took a while for Corinna and Gick to find Rosanel's house, mainly because Corinna only had a vague idea where it was. Several times they had to ask the way. To get an answer Corinna would say. 'The rebellion is here. L'Belder is back and is firing the Hill. We have news for Milady Garmelding; where is she?' Most of the answers were garbled. Some sent them in the wrong direction.

'They don't know what we are,' Gick said.

'It's a good job they don't!' Corinna answered. She realised that their appearance must be quite frightening. Looking at Gick she saw the soot-smeared shaved head with its pathetic stubs of gristle for ears, her scarred and bloody face, her torn clothes. She realised that she must look very similar.

'We're free, aren't we?' Gick said. 'No matter what, we're free now. Do you think this is all going to turn out alright?'

'Who cares!' Corinna replied. 'As you said, we're out of it. Let's get right out of it. Ah, I recognise this street.'

Gick had never been to the house before, even though

she was vaguely known to its owner. She told Corinna all that seemed such a long time ago. Once, she'd been a young courtier who'd been infatuated by a glamorous lady of higher rank named Rosanel Garmelding. She'd been in awe of Rosanel and had eagerly adopted the same unpopular beliefs as her heroine. Eventually, this had become evident to the Dominatrix; but Gick had had no real contact with the dissidents. She was just another casualty like Corinna. Unimportant, but there to take the punishment. 'What is your real name?' Corinna had asked her, but Gick had only shrugged.

'It doesn't matter any more. That was before. I'm Gick now. Maybe I'll change it again, maybe I won't. It's not important.'

It was important to Corinna. She never wanted to be called Lunt again.

Rosanel's manservant Collin opened the door to them. He stared blankly and enquired their business, looking over their shoulders occasionally at the riot in the streets. Corinna had to admire his cool.

'I am Corinna Trotgarden,' she said. 'A friend of the priestess Carudan. Is Milady Garmelding at home? I have news for her.' The name obviously rang a bell with him. He frowned, unable to put Corinna's face to the name. 'I've been here before,' she said and squeezed past him into the hall. Gick followed.

'Nice place,' she said.

'I'm afraid Milady Garmelding is not at home,' Collin announced, as if she'd just popped out to her hairdresser.

'Then send somebody to find her!' Corinna ordered. 'This is important. I have news which Milady has been waiting for. You'd better hurry. I can't wait for ever and I think she'll be greatly displeased if she misses me.'

Collin considered her words, before blinking in a stately manner and inclining his head. 'In that case, if you would be so good as to wait in the library, I'll have someone fetch Milady immediately,' he said, rather frostily.

Corinna led the way into the library and threw herself down on the sofa, followed by a more cautious Gick. 'She's

317

probably out there crying for glory, with a raised sword of liberty in her hands,' Corinna said. Gick glanced up sharply at the sarcasm.

'Are we safe here?' she asked.

'I won't feel safe until the city is behind me,' Corinna answered. 'Oh, to feel clean and rested once more!' She smiled. 'Don't worry Gick. I'm sure this won't take long.'

'What won't?'

'Persuasion.'

'What kind. . . ?'

'The kind that makes a dreamer wake up, I suppose. I expect a certain amount of resistance.'

'Oh,' said Gick, dubiously.

After only a few minutes, the doors to the library were thrown open and Rosanel herself came hurrying into the room. Gick, who had been chattering inanely to pass the time, shut her mouth quickly with an audible click. Rosanel walked slowly towards them, her face unable to repress what she felt.

'*Corinna?*' The tone, utter horror mingled with pity felt, to Corinna, like a knife cutting into her gut. Rosanel, of course, was the first person who'd seen her, other than L'Belder, and he wasn't quite the same as he used to be either.

'Don't stare,' Corinna said.

'I'm sorry. . . I. . . '

'Please don't say anything. I'm alright. I have news for you.'

Rosanel sat down on the edge of a chair. Despite evidence of concern for Corinna on her face, she looked radiant.

'Yes?' she said.

'L'Belder's back.'

'Elvon?'

'Who else.'

Rosanel jumped to her feet and virtually danced round the room, smiling but wringing her hands. 'I knew it! I knew he'd come back! Ah, what a night! What a night!' She actually leapt into the air with ecstatic euphoria. 'Where is he? Have you seen him? Does he know what's happening here?'

Corinna sighed, contemptuous of Rosanel's display. 'I expect so, Milady. He was responsible for it.'

Rosanel uttered a delighted scream. 'Wonderful!'.

Corinna almost felt sorry about tarnishing her joy. 'At the moment, he's in the palace wreaking havoc,' she said. 'but when we left, the Dominatrix was putting up a pretty good fight. We have to leave Silven Crescent, Milady. L'Belder wants you to come with me.'

Rosanel stopped dead in mid-prance. 'Where? Why? What's Elvon going to do?'

'My step-father is waiting for us on the marsh. I don't know where we'll go yet. And I have no idea what L'Belder will do. He told us to get out. I think we should trust his judgement.'

'And leave my people?! Don't be absurd, Corinna. If we have to fight, I have to be with them.'

'If L'Belder can't cope with this on his own, I don't think any of us will be able to do anything. He's changed, Milady. He must have found his Greylids. I don't think he's even human anymore.'

Rosanel digested this impossible remark with scepticism. 'I can't just leave,' she said, looking quickly round the room. Corinna was able to divine her thoughts; this house was her home. There was no proof harm would come to it; she couldn't just leave. Corinna considered that Rosanel was really quite ignorant of the true barbarity of what she was up against and that losing a home could be the least of her worries if she stayed. Corinna stood up. At least she'd done what L'Belder asked. She couldn't force Rosanel to follow her.

'We have to get going, Milady,' she said. 'A chance to clean up and a change of clothes would be appreciated.' She lifted the hem of her torn, red robe with scorn. Rosanel was looking at her speculatively, assessing the changes that were more than just external.

'Are you turning your back on the rebellion, Corinna?' she asked in a clear, confident voice. 'Look at you! Look what they did to you! How can you run away without making them pay? What about all the ones that didn't get away? You know there's no real haven on the marsh. Stay and fight! Stay with us!'

'I'm not running, Milady, not in the way you think. There's nothing left for us here. We have to start anew.'

Rosanel threw up her hands. 'And that's easier than staying to fight? Where can we go? What about all the others? I can't just walk out on them.'

'We'll take as many as we can, obviously. . . '

Rosanel narrowed her eyes, listening for a moment to the havoc in the street outside. 'You don't care anymore do you?' she said. 'They've broken you! Why, you haven't even asked for Carudan and the people from your house she brought here!'

'How are they?' Corinna asked without feeling. She couldn't care about anybody at the moment, wanting only to put the city behind her.

'They're fine,' Rosanel answered tightly. 'Carudan is worried about you, Corinna. We knew you weren't dead. Word came to us from the palace about what happened.'

'Really! You ask me to care and yet you knew about me and did nothing?' Corinna rubbed a weary hand across a brow that ached with frowning.

'There was nothing we could do. Security. . . '

'I don't want to hear it! I want to be clean and away from here. Don't ask any more of me.'

'We appreciate what you did. . . ' Rosanel looked uncertain. She was unused to people losing their fire or lust for revenge. She also believed Corinna would be safer in Denderberry than anywhere else. Not like L'Belder. L'Belder hadn't been safe anywhere. Rosanel did not have a really objective view of what was happening. 'I'll see to what you want,' she said. 'Wait here.'

Corinna sank back in the cushions and closed her eyes. She thought, I don't feel the same. I feel flamist. I feel hard and uncaring and strong. I want the marsh.

'You upset her,' Gick said, her first words since Rosanel had joined them. Corinna opened her eyes and looked at the door.

'Gick, *I'm* upset! I want to be utterly maudlin and see my home once more, just in case it changes, or disappears.

I want to go home. What are you going to do?'

Gick sighed. 'I have no home; not now. The palace was all I knew. I was brought up there. I suppose I'll stay with Milady Garmelding, if she'll have me.'

'You don't have to. If you want, you can come with me. Taste freedom, Gick. Leave these fools to their pretend games that end up being real and hurting people. They haven't seen the worst yet, I'm sure. I wonder if L'Belder has killed her yet. I wonder if she's killed him. Are they still fighting, do you think?'

'I don't know. I have no idea. Perhaps we should have brought some of the other Reds out.'

'They'll find their own way out if they want to.'

'Mmm. I'd do anything for some of that Eema's Itch now, wouldn't you?'

'No. I'd like my hair back and my face and my sex. Other than that, the city can keep all its luxuries.'

Some minutes later, relaxing in a hot bath upstairs, Corinna watched steam rise around her, watched dirt and blood lift from her skin and float away. She felt her head. It had been shaved again two days before but was already felting over with new growth. How long would it take to grow back? She was still numb inside from the shock of what had happened to her and what she had seen; the true nature of Yani Gisbandrun. Yet despite the turmoil surrounding her and this house, the only thing that felt real at this moment was the homing instinct; and that was very strong indeed. She gazed down at her body reflecting on the fact that she'd lost a lot of weight; pounds she could ill afford to lose. Her mind took her back to the marsh, to the time with L'Belder in the cave. She let it dwell there for a while; it didn't hurt to think of that anymore.

She heard somebody knocking at the door downstairs, a hollow, ominous sound. Who is that? Who is that? 'I'm too jumpy,' Corinna thought but still climbed out of the bath and wrapped herself in a towel. 'It could be news,' she thought. 'It must be.' Leaving the forlorn pile of rags that were her red robes on the bathroom floor, she padded out onto the landing. This bathroom was too far from the front door for her to hear anything further. Any visitor would probably have been shown into the library by now. Shivering, she padded to the room that Rosanel had provided for her use. In it, new clothes, laid out neatly on the bed, were ready to put on. Corinna dressed herself. It felt odd to be wearing trousers, more so because they didn't fit her too well, bunched up at the waist, loose across the backside. Now is the time when the lady sits down to brush out her wet hair, she thought, glancing dismally into the mirror above the dressing-table. She sat on the stool and leaned towards the glass. Even my expression looks different. . . The frown between her eyes looked as if it had decided to become permanent, the skin beneath her lower lids was dark and puffy. The scars on her cheeks seemed to pull her expression into one of eternal bitterness. For a moment, she thought of love and it seemed just a word, nothing more. There were scars, on the inside and on the outside, that had destroyed her innocence; and what is the ability to love but a form of innocence? This was doubly tragic because there were still people in the world from whom she would have liked comfort, for whom she still had some kind of feelings, but she could not stomach the thought of them touching her now. Perhaps she thought, the only person I could ever feel close to now is poor Gick, another casualty like myself. She found this a depressing idea. Not that she disliked Gick, but just that the thrill of being able to attract someone like L'Belder or Carmenya had gone. At the sound of her door opening, she glanced up into the mirror and saw Rosanel standing there. Corinna sensed her discomfort immediately; first at what she had seen – a young, mutilated girl staring sorrowfully into a mirror – and second, because of what she had to say. 'You'd better come downstairs, Corinna,' she said.

'That name is ridiculous now,' Corinna thought. 'It's a pretty name; it's ridiculous.'

'Why?'

'Carmenya is here. . . '

An unexpected arrow of emotion had Corinna on her feet immediately. Not joy certainly, or hope, or fear. It was

322

anger. 'Carmenya, here? What for? To take me back?'

Rosanel shook her head. 'I . . . I don't think so. I don't know. She's alone.'

'How did she know I was here?'

Again Rosanel shook her head. 'No idea. I don't like it. She won't go until she's seen you, Corinna. You've got to get rid of her.'

Yes, get rid of her, Corinna thought darkly. She smiled. Bitch, you did this! You let this happen! Bitch!

Carmenya was leaning edgily on the mantelpiece in the library, watched solemnly by Gick, who was still dressed in her tattered red robe. She nursed a glass full of mulled wine. Corinna could smell the sharp tang of spices as soon as she entered the room. She was glad she'd cleaned herself up before this confrontation. She had considered wrapping a scarf around her head, but had brutally decided against it. Let the bitch see! As she looked at Carmenya, her first thought was, 'She's as beautiful as I remember her,' but it was like facing a stranger. It was facing an old lover when the flame of love has not been completely extinguished and many hurts still linger unresolved. Gick, shrinking back into the sofa and trying to look defiant, appeared gawky and boyish in comparison. 'Never,' Corinna thought with an irrepressible shudder, 'never. I am alone now and I'll always be that way.'

She noticed with a surprising satisfaction the way Carmenya's face changed when she saw her; the smothered horror of the person who accidentally lets their gaze linger a second too long on the cripple in the street, the quick glance away. Perhaps Corinna's first words should have been, 'Yes, look at me. You could have prevented this. Take a good look.' Instead, she said, 'What do you want?'

Carmenya was studying the fire. 'Technically speaking, you are now under arrest,' she said. The word 'audacity' – a restrained one – was drumming through Corinna's brain even as she leapt forward. Before her outstretched fingers, curved into claws, could make contact with Carmenya's face, Rosanel had pulled her back. Corinna could hear Rosanel's breath in her ear, a slight rasp of panic. Carmenya's eyes were wide, her face white.

'I said, technically speaking, C'rinna; that's the reason I'm here. I didn't mean that I intend to uphold that reason.'

'Then what do you want? How did you know I was here? Who told you?'

It was obviously still painful for Carmenya to look Corinna in the eye. She put both hands on the black slate mantle and turned her back on the room.

'After. . . what happened in the palace, I looked for you,' she said, with difficulty. 'Some of your colleagues told me you were on duty tonight and I feared the worst. Then I heard that you were seen running out of the palace with another girl. I checked your house; it was empty. And then, I somehow knew you'd come here. Your friend, the priestess Curadan, has been watched recently and has been seen coming here often. You weren't with her, I checked, so where else was there for you to go? All dissidents are fleeing to Denderberry. This is the rebel headquarters, isn't it? One of them.' At that point, she turned and directed a piercing, soldier's glance in Rosanel's direction.

'Don't talk rot,' Rosanel said. 'You have no proof of that. Just because I'm humane doesn't mean I command everybody else. Didn't I come back to court as you suggested?'

'That is irrelevant. Neither does it explain satisfactorily why Corinna is here. Don't waste time bandying words with me, Milady. I know what you are.'

'And I know what you are,' Rosanel replied, coolly, folding her arms. She caught Corinna's eye and in that moment, Corinna knew that Rosanel did not intend for General Carmenya to leave this house alive. 'Answer Corinna's question; why are you here, if not to try and take her back to the palace?'

'So, you are the one giving orders now, are you, Rosanel?' Carmenya sauntered over to the sofa and sat down next to an extremely discomforted Gick. She removed a cigarette case from her pocket and lit a long,

324

black cheroot, tapping it on the enamelled lid as she talked. From outside, faint but distinctive sounds of conflict approached the house with mounting clamour.

'This is my house, General,' Rosanel said. 'This city has gone crazy. No-one is safe anymore.'

'You certainly are not, Milady.' Carmenya laughed lightly and lit the cheroot. 'As for your question, I'm here to tell you that your hero has failed you.' She let these words sink in. 'Did you really think a mere man could defeat the Dominatrix? Are you all mad?'

'Defeated?' Rosanel said, dully. 'Is. . . is he dead?'

Carmenya shrugged. 'If he isn't, he will be. If you've any sense, you'll pack up your household and leave. . . now.'

'Leave. . . ?' Rosanel looked dazed.

'Yes, leave!' Carmenya leaned forward. 'You stupid bitch. I despise you! If it wasn't for the fact that Corinna was here, I'd have let the Dominatrix send in her military and slaughter the lot of you. That may still happen. I don't know how long you've got. The only reason you've had this much time is because everything's gone crazy, as you put it. You've outlived your usefulness, Milady. No longer a bait for L'Belder. The rebellion is effectively squashed. Don't stand there gawping like a child; get your people together! I want to talk to Corinna.'

'I want to know what's going on first,' Rosanel insisted, mustering her strength. 'What's happened to Elvon?'

Carmenya stood up. 'I wish I could answer you; I can't. My orders aren't coming directly from the inner chamber now. That's all I know.'

'Then you can't really be sure that L'Belder is defeated, can you?' Corinna said. 'You didn't see him, General. If you had, you wouldn't refer to him as a "mere man", or think that Gisbandrun could finish him off so easily. He's found some power somewhere, and I'm sure it's far more than even your Dominatrix can cope with.' There was a silence while Carmenya squirmed with discomfort. Corinna could see her struggling to find an answer.

'No matter what happens to Yani, her organisation will live on,' Carmenya said at last. 'One man cannot change things, *whatever he is*, and he certainly won't find sympathy

325

with the people after destroying their homes, will he? Nobody really wants this so-called rebellion, Rosanel. You are a pathetic minority. It's a pity you and your friends didn't realise that. You can't win, you never could have. Just get out while there's still time.' At the suggestion, however slight, that Elvon L'Belder might still be alive, Rosanel had changed her mind about staying to fight. This was not as strange as it seemed. If she was dead, she'd never see him again. Clearly, as he'd suspected, L'Belder himself meant far more to Rosanel Garmelding than any political principle.

'Will he come after us, do you think?' she said to Corinna.

'You didn't see him,' Corinna answered. 'I'm not sure you'd want him to.'

'Appearances don't matter,' Rosanel said acidly, not understanding the nature of his change. Carmenya raised a surprised eyebrow and looked sharply at Corinna, wondering whether she'd taken that remark personally. Corinna was smiling in a feral, carnivorous way. Carmenya realised, at last, that this girl was now a stranger to her.

'I'll get everyone together,' Rosanel said, her murderous intentions towards the General abandoned. 'Come with me, Gick.'

'What is the truth?' Corinna asked, once she and Carmenya were alone.

'We don't know what's happening; that's the truth. The palace is sealed. Even going near it gives you a headache. There's strange light shooting out all over the place. I don't know what the hell's going on. All the generals have gathered lower down the hill; we're running things from there. Any moment, we'll be moving in on Denderberry to scour it of rebels. That's something we understand and can do something about! Corinna, you have to get out.'

'And go where exactly?' Carmenya looked at her sharply. 'I mean, the marsh isn't even safe, is it? Where do I go? Where do any of us go?'

'Corinna, this planet is vast. We know only a tiny part of it.'

326

'Exactly. Nobody knows what's beyond the marsh in detail, do they? It could be as fatal as remaining here.'

'Possibly, but it's the only chance you've got. Look, I know how badly I let you down. . . '

'Shut up!' Corinna interrupted. 'That's pathetic and you know it. Let me down? Are you joking? Carmenya you *condemned* me to torture, humiliation and slavery. And for what? You and your fellow flamists are living a lie. I've seen what goes on in the inner chamber. I know. The Dominatrix is a raving lunatic. She gets high on watching slave boys rape girls and each other. She gets high on mutilating people. She's sick and mad and she's in charge of the human population of an entire planet. She has to go, Carmenya. I don't care if the generals carry on the man-hate thing after her; nothing can be worse than she is. The sickness has to go. If I'd had anything about me, I'd have given my life to see her dead myself. She's a fake and you all worship her. . .'

'Be quiet!' Carmenya stood up. 'I don't worship anybody! You don't have to say these things to me!'

'Anything for a quiet life, was that it? Even to the extent of betraying the girl who you'd slept with and professed to love?'

'Maybe. I don't pretend to be perfect, Corinna. My job is my life. I've had to make sacrifices to protect my position. . . '

'Haven't you just!'

'I was wrong to bring you here. I know that. But I'm trying to make amends by helping you get out. Can't you see the risk I'm taking coming here? I could be branded a conspirator. It's known the dissidents have eyes and ears in the palace. Everyone is a suspect. What would it look like if I was found here?'

'Oh, don't worry. I appreciate what you're doing,' Corinna said coldly. 'You're trying to make amends? Forget it! But you were right about one thing. I have to leave – now. I'm going back to the people I love, the men I love. I have to get them off the marsh.' She stood up and made to follow Rosanel. She thought there was nothing more to say.

'Corinna,' Carmenya said behind her. 'I'm sorry. What else can I say? I didn't want to lose you. . . '

Corinna wheeled around angrily. 'Didn't you? Well, if you're telling the truth, why don't you really try to make amends and come with me. Let's have a real love story ending to this, shall we? Why don't you stick by me, or what's left of me?'

Carmenya lowered her eyes and took a troubled draw off the stub of her cheroot.

'Fine!' Corinna said. She went out of the room. She slammed the door.

They took danks, carts, and loaded them up with all that they could carry. Even as they left Rosanel's yard behind the house, they could hear the tramp of soldier's feet and see people running by, blind with terror. 'Hurry,' Corinna said.

'We have to find Carudan,' Rosanel replied angrily.

'No, we can't. There's no time! Come on!' Corinna had to haul Rosanel physically up the road. They were accompanied by Rosanel's household. Gick and the remains of Corinna's staff from Lavinia Drive. Corinna had been surprised by the warmth of Sheba's welcome to her. There'd been a few tears shed for Endaline of whom there'd been no news at all.

'You were right, Mistress Trotgarden', Sheba said. 'Your bravery is remarkable, your courage. . . '

'Alright, alright,' Corinna said hurriedly, 'Remember Endaline too was brave and courageous and she is probably still having to be.'

'If she's lucky,' Sheba added.

They kept to the smaller alleys, Corinna and her erstwhile man-slave, Gavron, pushing the largest cart, while everyone else did their best to calm the hysterical danks who had almost been overcome by the stink of death and terror. Rosanel still ranted about Carudan, and although Corinna sympathised, it was obvious that the army would soon make short work of Denderberry in their lust to weed out the dissidents. Carudan at least had the protection of the temple, and she was no fool. Corinna did not share Rosanel's panic about the priestess.

The last few yards' dash from the shelter of a dark alley to one of the lesser south gates of the city was a time of extreme tension. The danks were honking and dancing around, their sense of direction confused. The heavy cart got one of its wheels stuck in a hole in the cobbles. Everyone kept looking backwards, looking sideways, dreading the arrival of soldiers. Corinna was surprised that the road beyond the gates looked so empty. Why weren't others making the same decision to leave? Why hadn't the flamists thought that the Skyreachers would try to escape Silven Crescent and blocked all the exit roads? 'Well, that is not my worry,' she thought, putting her shoulder to the cart. No doubt the flamists knew that the rebels, confident of victory, were stupid enough to stay and fight.

'We need skippers,' Rosanel said. 'Speed will be essential.'

'I agree,' Corinna replied drily, 'Where do you suggest we get them from? Shall we go back and ask Carmenya if we can borrow a couple of hers.'

'Corinna, I am the last member of one of the oldest and most affluent families in Silven Crescent. I have my own skippers, thank you. They are moored about a mile beyond the city.'

'Well, let's get to them,' Corinna said. She wished she could control the irritation that Rosanel inspired in her now. It helped nobody when they were bickering, least of all herself.

They reached the moorings and the Garmelding skippers without further obstruction or delay. Behind them, Silven Crescent bloomed into the sky; a bloody flower whose cataclysmic unfolding was punctuated by the firework crack of explosions on Palace Mount. Rosanel and Collin checked the fuel of the craft and made a hasty inspection of the mechanisms. Corinna counted heads and started loading the fractious danks onboard. She kept looking north along the old road, anxious because there was no sign of Meonel and Shyya. L'Belder had said they'd be here; she couldn't leave without them. Where were they?

'Come on, Corinna, we're ready,' Rosanel said.

'My stepfather isn't here yet.'

Rosanel made an angry sound. 'You were the one pressing for haste!'

'You go on, then. Leave me a dank and I'll follow later.'

Corinna was still staring up the road, trying not to betray that she was so concerned about Meonel's absence. Her shaved head looked boyish and defenceless and she had a black air of loneliness about her that made her look small even though she was trying to appear hard and strong. Rosanel relented.

'No, we'll wait for you. If Elvon said they'll be here, they will, I'm sure. A few minutes won't make that much difference.'

'That's not necessary, Rosanel. Start the craft. I'll ride north up the road for a while. I'll find you. Follow the main waterway toward Stilt Vista. I'll not be long.'

'I don't think we should split up.'

'It's alright.' Corinna turned round and smiled at her. 'Look, I'd rather meet them alone, anyway. Understand?'

Rosanel looked at her for a moment. 'Yes. Take the dank. But you must let us wait for you at Stilt Vista. I insist.'

'Yes, yes. Just get going!' Corinna softened her waspishness with a grin and Rosanel smiled back. Collin started the first motor, before leaping onto the next skipper and showing Gavron how to operate it. The craft bobbed in the low water, beginning to rise as their vanes became erect. Rosanel was sitting pale and dishevelled in the stern with Gick and Sheba and the other women of her house beside her. 'We'll see you soon,' she said. Corinna led a prancing dank onto the road.

'Yes,' she said. 'Good luck.'

She watched as the skippers dipped and swayed, veering round to face north. Everyone waved at her as the craft leapt forward throwing up two great plumes of spray. After they'd gone, Corinna paused for a moment before mounting the dank. The creature pressed its nose against her shoulder and she put up her hand to reassure it. Dawn was coming to the marsh, silver-grey dawn. She closed her eyes and listened to the waking chant of insects, birds and amphibians, the whisper of the dawn wind through the rushes and reeds, the gurgle of mud-pools, the hiss of water fur ejecting air. Tears formed behind her closed lids, squeezed between her stubby lashes and grew cool on her checks, running into the scars. 'Vangery,' she said, 'Vangery.' She had not wept for a long time and it felt like a great release, a great bursting, like Spring throwing itself up through the marsh. 'I'm going home,' she told the dank, before hurling herself against its hard neck, sobbing out the agony and hurt of the past few months. This would be the last time she shed tears because of it.

After a few minutes, she straightened up, wiped her nose on her sleeve and climbed onto the dank's back. The old road was red and gold with dawn light. She started along it at a brisk trot. Then, darker against a bank of plaisels to the right, she saw two other riders approaching, walking their animals as if they'd ridden through the night. Early sunlight was reflected off a familiar head of pale hair; Meonel, with Shyya behind him. She raised her hand and shrieked, 'Hello! Hello!' They couldn't see her properly at this distance. She could kick her dank into a gallop and they would not see her clearly until she was really close. She saw them increase their speed likewise, arms waving, their cries of relief and greeting thin through the dawn air. This was the welcome; this was real. They could not see her face. Not yet. Until they did, the occasion could be joyous.

CHAPTER FORTY-ONE

THERE WAS SMOKE in the southern sky. All day, people on the marsh had been aware of a strange, acrid smell in the air; now this. One of Dannel's people had come to her office to tell her. When she reached the edge of Vangery Isle everyone was there already, looking south. By evening Yaschel Tendaughter had come over in person. 'This bodes ill, I can feel it,' she said, accepting with enthusiasm the glass of wine that Dannel offered her. 'Dannel, I'm afraid. What's going on? It looks as if the city burns!'

'We couldn't see that from here,' Dannel said.

'Exactly!' Yaschel replied. 'At least, not a normal conflagration. I can smell death and there's a definite threat inside it. I'm sending Sander and a couple of men south tomorrow to find out what's happening.'

'I wouldn't do that, or at least, if you do, make sure they are very, very careful and definitely unseen,' Dannel said.

Yaschel narrowed her eyes, looking at the furtive expression on Dannel's face. 'You know something, don't you?'

'I know there's trouble, certainly, if not the form. I know that for some time Silven Crescent has been an unknown threat to us. Yaschel, I share your fears. I fear that the time of the marsh families is approaching an end.'

'You can't be serious!' Yaschel's round eyes betrayed that she knew Dannel was.

'I can't tell you everything, Yaschel, but I think the families should band together at this time and keep alert.'

'All the more reason for someone to go and see what's going on then,' Yaschel decided. 'Dannel, I need to know more.'

'Of course you do, but I don't want to be the one to tell you. I don't think you'll like what I say. It may go against your beliefs.' There was a look on Yaschel's face, deepening with every moment, which portrayed a realisation of something terrible and momentous. Dannel had never spoken in this way to her before; it was uncharacteristic and thus, very disturbing.

'Tell me what you know,' Yaschel said.

Three days later, Sander and members of several other marsh families nearby went south to scout for information. Everyone kept their eyes on the horizon. Lookouts were posted, beacons built, ready to be lit should an alert need to be given. On the morning of the fifth day, Dannel went down to the shore. There was a slight mist over the marsh. She could hear the chitter of waking wervels and the gaunt, feathered plumes of marsh grasses swayed like wraiths from the water. Far away came the mournful lament of a single ditch-crane. Dannel was alone. She looked back at the house fondly, fearfully. She felt as if she wouldn't be able to do that for much longer. What was going to happen? She shivered, half blinded by sudden tears, and stared once more out over the tussocks. In the distance a red glow took form; a beacon fire. Dannel stared at it in disbelief. Was this the end? Was this what they had feared would happen? Names tumbled through her head; Corinna, Meonel, Shyya, L'Belder. Her belly felt weak. Then, through the thick, morning air, came the low, haunting boom of the sentinel's horn. It was the signal that meant news was coming. Not attack, just news. The news was coming towards her. Flares bloomed closer and closer as other horns took up the throbbing note. An avenue of flame, trumpets belling through the pearly mist. In this way were the fugitives from Silven Crescent welcomed to the marsh. In this way did Meonel, Corinna and Shyya return to Vangery.

There was a meeting that very morning. Families from close by, Tendaughters, Angwells, Shavesocks, Guardwells and several others, took their places round the table in the

Frontwater Salon of Vangery. The matriarchs gathered, the power of the marsh, and the air was full of change. Dannel could only look on in shocked silence as this new, flamist-looking female, scarred and brutal, who had once been the dreaming child Corinna, stood at the head of the table and declaimed in a loud voice what was happening in Silven Crescent. 'It is my belief,' she said, 'that the majority of you will be unmolested by the city, but because the outcome of L'Belder's attack is so vague I cannot speak in truth as to whether your menfolk are safe or not. The decision, therefore, is yours. You have three options: remaining here to fight, remaining here to comply with whatever they ask of you, or coming with us to the north. We can spread word as we travel. If other families wish to join us, so be it. I cannot guarantee that we'll ever find a safe haven that is far enough from the cities, but even if we don't succeed, at least we'll live and die in freedom, existing as we wish to exist, living our own laws. It will be known that Rosanel and I have fled to the marsh and, if L'Belder does not succeed, the mangaks will soon follow, you can be sure of that. Therefore, there is little time. I propose that those of you who wish to join us assemble here at daybreak. Pass the word to whoever you can. We shall be leaving tomorrow. Others may follow us later. Thank you for your time.' She left the room, followed by Gick. A numb silence followed her speech, but gradually, the marsh women came to life. Meonel and Rosanel were there to answer what questions they could. People wanted to know about the Greylids, they wanted to know about the true nature of the Dominatrix, the true nature of L'Belder. Rosanel had a tight, exhausted cast to her face, but she answered patiently. Dannel couldn't speak. All she could see were the scars on Corinna's face, Corinna's vulnerable, boyish, shaved head, the lines between her eyes and from nose to mouth. It was as if her daughter was dead. How could anyone. . . ? Carmenya! 'My fault,' Dannel thought. 'I sent her away. It was my fault.'

Of course, Corinna had waved this suggestion away for Dannel had voiced it as soon as she'd set foot back on Vangery soil. 'We haven't time for that kind of indulgence,

mother,' she said. 'Reserve your energy for travelling and
building a new life. Recriminations are worthless. What is
happening now is the important thing; get on with it.'

Dannel's worst fears had become reality. She had let one
of her family out alone on the marsh and they had
suffered horribly because she hadn't been there to take
care of them.

In the dawn, skippers and long boats and dank chains
and rafts clustered around the shores of Vangery Isle.
People milled on the lawns and the landings, churning the
new grass to mud. The house itself had been hurriedly
cleared of necessities; now it looked ransacked, forlorn,
violated. Unsmiling but determined marsh-dwellers
sought out the daughter of Dannel Trotgarden. Most of
them needed to see for themselves what the city had done
to her. The role of leader had automatically fallen upon
her because she could clearly be seen to be a martyr to the
cause. Rosanel had fine words but she'd only been
romancing on the sidelines; Corinna had been at the
centre, in the frontline, and the marsh people looked to
her for guidance because they sensed the strength within
her. She had been to the mouth of hell and had come back
sane to warn others away.

Bolivia's reaction had been a surprise. Both Dannel and
Corinna had expected her to want to remain behind in
Vangery, seeing as she'd always professed her devotion to
the Dominatrix, but she'd told them she had no intention
of doing so. There had been a strained conversation
between her and Corinna in which Bolivia tried to convey
feelings of sympathy and admiration for her sister. 'We
don't really know each other do we?' she said.

Corinna had felt awkward with this sudden openness in
Bolivia. 'I don't think I know myself,' she said gruffly.

'I wanted to go there you know, to the city. I was going
to write to you and. . . ' She paused and sighed, perhaps
perceiving Corinna's embarrassment and understanding
that any closeness between them would take time to evolve.
She sighed and turned around in the room; Frontwater
Salon, denuded and cold. 'Well, this was to be my

heritage,' she said, lifting her arms and grinning without warmth. 'All mine, one day. How I dreamed of that.'

'Bolivia, you don't *have* to come with us. I'll understand, we'll all understand. . .'

Bolivia cut her short. 'No. No, C'rin. It's over. Over and gone. I admit that I agreed with a lot of the things the mangaks upheld, but my family comes first. You're surprised? Let me speak my mind and say, if you want a reason, look in the damn mirror!'

Corinna smiled at that. It was a Bolivia remark that was familiar and therefore comfortable.

'Don't you think it makes me look kind of distinguished?' She pulled a sneering face. Bolivia tentatively pushed her shoulder.

'Distinguished? It'd turn milk! Come on, little sister, I believe we have work to do. Let's get on with it.'

Corinna had held out her arms and they'd clasped each other's hands briefly.

'Thanks for your kind words, sister dear!' She laughed. 'I couldn't have let you stay behind here really, you know. Who the hell would have kept the men under control during the journey?'

Down in the kitchens, Gabriel packed away his lovingly polished pots and pans, glancing round his domain for the last time. He tried to keep the spirits of the other staff high by making his usual jokes and acid quips, but his heart wasn't in it. He could only think of the misery of the journey; no warmth, damp and hard work.

Meanwhile, Dannel went through the books in her office, deciding which of them she could not live without. So much would have to stay behind. She was filled with a shifting ache, comprising relief because her family had come back, a faint wistfulness because Meonel and Shyya were in love which she felt would keep Shyya away from her, and deep, heartfelt sadness because she was leaving her beloved home. She was not afraid. If a hundred mangaks leapt onto Vangery soil at this moment she would run out to fight them, even if death was inevitable. Carmenya had taken Corinna away from her for good. The person who'd come back to Vangery was not the girl

336

who had left it last year. Carmenya had let her die. She'd done nothing. She'd let her die.

Of the other families nearby, only three had elected not to join the Trotgardens. As if linked by some kind of telepathy, the others hardly questioned Corinna's word; they simply believed, and in their believing they packed away their belongings, locked their doors, (putting keys above the lintels, just in case) and turned their boats towards Vangery. By mid-day, the place seemed like a market; the atmosphere began to lighten as the feeling of doom dissipated with the grey, morning mist and a spirit of adventure came with the suns. It was planned the party would leave at mid-day, giving anyone who wanted to join them enough time to reach Vangery Isle. Stragglers would just have to follow them as best they could. Corinna was down at the boat-shed with her brother Orblin supervising the packing of equipment, harshly ordering some things unloaded as being unnecessary. Ever since she'd returned, Orblin had clung to her side, putting on a brave face and trying to show that he was man enough to shoulder some of her responsibility. Shyya was with them. It had been harder for Corinna to face Shyya than anybody else because she'd feared his appreciation of her beauty would turn to pity in his eyes once he'd seen her scars. She'd dreaded meeting him for that reason, even though some part of her hoped it wouldn't make any difference, but the expression had been there, just as she'd anticipated. In addition to the change in her, it was clear Shyya himself had changed because of Meonel. It was obvious to Corinna almost from the first moment she'd met them on the old road that now they were a pair. It had hurt to witness it. She envied them their closeness. After an initial stunned silence, Meonel had quickly said, 'Corinna, whatever has happened to you? Have you been fighting?'
'Yes I have, of sorts,' she'd replied.
'Such impressive scars, my dear! I'm sure there's a good yarn behind them!' Dear old Meonel. While others expressed pity or looked away, he made a point of mentioning it. It was the best way. 'Can't say I think much

of the fashion in hairstyles the city has nowadays either,'
he continued. 'What on earth made you do it, Corinna? It
looks awful!'

She'd laughed and said, 'I love you Meonel. I'm glad to
see you,' and he'd smiled in return and said, 'Let's go
home.'

Corinna had wondered whether she could confide in
Shyya about her more private injuries. He alone could
empathise with what she felt, she thought. But it was
different for men. She knew that. At the moment, Shyya
had eyes only for Meonel. She didn't want to broach the
subject, so she kept her mutilation a secret. Let them think
it was just facial scars. She saw no reason why she should
ever have to tell anybody. Shyya was happy, Meonel was
happy; they were different. She looked up and caught
Shyya staring at her. 'Are you alright?' he said and
touched her arm. She smiled.

'Yes. I'm fine. Just tired.'

'Corinna?'

'Just tired – honestly. Pass me that twine would you.' She
braced herself and made an effort to shrug off the weight
of sadness. There was work to do; she had no time for self-
pity.

Someone called her name. She looked up. 'Yes? What is
it?' Shyya took her arm again, cocking his head to one side.

'Listen,' he said.

She thought, 'All I can hear is my heart. That's all.' Beat.
Beat. No. . .

'No!' she said, and then they were both running towards
the landing. Other voices were calling out to her and the
voices shouted.

'Skippers! Skippers!' Yes, yes, that was the thrum, the
appalling beat that she feared was her own heart.
Skippers!

'They're coming fast, C'rin. They're coming bloody
fast!' Shyya said under his breath.

'I know that. I know that. Oh Goddess!'

'People from the marsh, do you think? Someone coming
to join us?'

She dragged a hand over her head, a gesture retained

338

from when she'd still had hair.

'No, Shyya, no. Too many of them. Too fast. Only city people have skippers that travel that fast.'

'Where were the flares? For the Goddess's sake, why didn't anyone *warn us*?'

'Don't be a fool! The way from the city is deserted now.'

'We should have left people! Why didn't we?'

'Too late for that! Get these people in order!'

She ran down the bank, jumping from raft to raft until she reached the clear water. She hunkered down on the stern and leaned forward squinting. There was no doubt about it; the skippers skimming towards Vangery were the sleek craft of Silven Crescent. Behind her, she was aware of the marsh people panicking, shouting to each other, calling for weapons. The last fight? Maybe. Maybe. Then Rosanel was beside her, holding guns.

'How many?' she asked. Corinna took one of the weapons from her, wondering if there was any point.

'Hard to tell. Not many. Half a dozen maybe.'

'Is that all? Goddess! They must have one hell of a weapon to come with so few. That's bad news.' The craft were approaching so fast, it was now possible to see the figures standing on the nearest prow. Corinna's heart sank to her stomach.

'Shit!' she said.

'What?'

'Look. Look! Can't you see? Can't you see who that is?'

There was no doubt about it. The woman standing defiantly in the prow of the first craft, with her long, red hair whipping back was General Carmenya Oralien.

'Oh no!' Rosanel cried inadequately.

'She let us escape!' Corinna shouted. 'The fucking bitch let us escape and let us herd everyone together here. No-one could have done a better job. Goddess, Ros, she's going to wipe out all the marsh people who are against the city in one fell swoop!'

'She can try!' Rosanel answered fiercely, but without much hope.

'Well, this is it,' Corinna said wearily. She took one glance back at the bank and then raised the long-barrelled gun to her chin. 'Strike first,' she thought. 'If I am to die then that bitch goes first!' How she could have scored a direct hit with her eyes closed is anybody's guess.

'Wait!' Rosanel's hand came down on the barrel of the gun and it clanged on the edge of the raft. 'Wait, C'rin, look!'

The skippers were close now. Anyone could see that it wasn't soldiers on the deck behind Carmenya. It was children, women and children huddled together. Corinna dropped the gun. Rosanel had stood up and was waving her arms at the people on the landing and the other rafts who had all equipped themselves with firearms. 'Wait!' she was crying, 'Wait! There's kids on board!' And they waited. They waited until the skippers furrowed into the soft earth of Vangery bank and they heard what Carmenya had to say.

On the half dozen craft were all those people that Carmenya could gather together in the small amount of time left to her in the city. But it was not just Carmenya. Rosanel gave an almost hysterical whoop! and was splashing through the shallows to embrace a grimed, tatter-coated woman who had started to disembark. It was Carudan. Hanging onto the priestess's arm, Rosanel dragged her over to where Corinna was waiting. 'Surprised to see me, kid!' Carudan asked and then threw herself into Corinna's arms.

'Glad to see you! Glad! Glad!' Corinna replied through tears, and they were tears of happiness. Carmenya stood back with folded arms and watched the reunions, the refugees welcomed by the people of the marsh. She'd brought about thirty people with her including children. Corinna was surprised to notice three other flamists in the party, erstwhile soldiers of the Dominatrix's palace. They had blank, weary faces and dusty, torn uniforms. Eventually, Corinna could put it off no longer. She found herself knee deep in water facing Carmenya where she still stood in the prow of the leading skipper. 'You see, I came,' Carmenya said, but it was without arrogance; almost reluctantly said.

'Why?' Corinna asked.

Carmenya shrugged. 'I would like to say it's because I think you are right, but it's not; not exactly. When I left you at the Garmelding house, I saw a screaming woman watching her son being butchered in the street. I saw women hung from street lamps just because they were screaming. I was afraid. I wanted to turn my back. I must have lost my head a little, because there was no escape you see. It was everywhere. There was a single face I recognised in that hell; the priestess. Your friend Carudan was running around Denderberry like a headless bird. I told her you and Rosanel had gone and she said, "let's follow". It seemed like the best thing to do. The city was breaking up, the madness just beginning. I felt helpless, powerless, yet distanced. I couldn't join in, so I had to leave. Carudan grabbed my arm and we just ran. The people we have with us are all we could grab on our way from the spot where I found her to the city gates. Perhaps more will follow. I hope so.'

'And L'Belder. What of him?'

Carmenya shrugged again, sighed. 'He's lost, he's won. I don't know. Perhaps he was just a catalyst. . . ' She smiled, rather unconvincingly. 'We must leave,' she said. 'Hysteria travels fast. Those who escape will fuel that hysteria. We must leave.'

'Yes.' Corinna held out her hand which Carmenya stared at blankly. Corinna dropped her arm. 'Let's get these people organised then,' she said. She turned for a moment to look at the house, gazing above the heads of all those people waiting for her words. She had believed that Vangery was really part of her, that the people she loved were really part of her. Corinna sighed. She would survive. She would go on. There were other islands waiting.

CHAPTER FORTY-TWO

THE HOUSE OF Dannel Trotgarden is empty now. Smoke curls from a single fire upon the beach, soon to be extinguished. Already the marsh mist has crept through doors and windows to fill the house, smothering the furniture left behind, the discarded clothes. In Bolivia's room a picture of the Dominatrix lies on its face, evidence of a single, purposeful act, a single denial. Of the travellers, there is no sign; they are long gone. Ditch cranes stalk the muddied banks of the isle, picking at rubbish. Night falls on Vangery Isle and the wilderness creeps in.

Of L'Belder nobody ever heard a word again. When the next morning dawned the chaos which had gripped the city had spent itself. It was said the Dominatrix was found dead in her room, but there was no sign of Elvon L'Belder. Perhaps she had destroyed him before her own destruction, perhaps he had left Silven Crescent to rejoin the Greylids in the forest of Ire and Penitence. Although he had not won in the way he'd hoped, L'Belder's last attempt at control left many positive results. A new government was formed by the generals. True, it was matriarchal and still upheld many of the Yani Gisbandrun's beliefs, but there were no more girls in red and the idea of imprisoning all men on Artemis was abandoned as being inhumane. A moderate voice had come to Silven Crescent. However, it was still looked upon as perversion if a woman formed an intimate relationship with a man. The Dominatrix's dream of nationwide artificial insemination did come about to a degree, but through choice. In years to

342

come men and women would live together, work together, but in friendship not in love. The marshes were eventually declared a female province as Yani had planned, but the men that lived there were removed to the cities for alternative employment, in the foundries and factories, not to be interned in prison camps. This plan was initiated because it was felt the marsh women had an unhealthy relationship with men, that was to be discouraged as unwholesome. All those families who were strongly against this move had either left the marsh with the Trotgardens or followed them later. Many of those that did follow went in different directions to the main group. Some met up with it eventually, while others simply found new ground for themselves in the north. In the city, it was debated whether people should actually be allowed to leave the country governed by Silven Crescent. Wouldn't such people eventually become a threat? The temple spoke out then, pointing out that the people who'd left were pioneers who had shunned oppression and conquest. Was it likely they would one day abandon their principles, turn to the south and seek to steal Silven Crescent's land away? No, not really. Let them go, the temple said, and pray that one day, we shall be reunited with them as sisters and not oppressors.

Artemis turned in the heavens, a jewel among planets, whose face was moving slowly towards the other worlds once more.

343

AN EXTRACT FROM
THE JOURNAL OF
CORINNA TROTGARDEN

ON THIS LONG journey north, at night, Rosanel Garmelding lies awake in her tent and thinks of Elvon L'Belder. I think she realises now that she will never see him again, no matter how her dreams have sustained her in the past. A new life is waiting before her now, waiting for all of us. Whether L'Belder lived or died really does not matter any more because his spirit, his ideals, will live forever in the hearts of those who remember him and, in the future, his dreams will become our reality. Goodbye Elvon. Sleep well, for we think of you. We are you; we are free. You have won. Time will pass. These past months will recede in our memories, drift further and further away, become a speck, and the universe will turn, dreaming and dreaming. We believe we are important, that we shall be remembered, that the burning caused by our conflicts and tears will be eternal, that our struggles are unique and must be won, now, because there will be no other chance. This is not so. We are still specks, and the turning continues whether we are aware of it or not. Other souls will rise, as we did, and believe they hold in their hands, in their minds, the knowledge, the truth, that must be given to all. We may be specks that gleam brightly, but only for a time. Dream well, Elvon, the law you followed will live as long as the universe itself, and even in the face of ultimate repression and cruelty, there will always be those who will see its light and follow its path behind you.

Oh, I nearly forgot: today we left the marsh.